The
Dividing Season

For Helen, my comrade-of-the keyboard!

Karen Casey Fitzjerrell

A Novel by
Karen Casey Fitzjerrell

WKMA Publishing

Copyright © 2012 Karen Casey Fitzjerrell

Inquiries should be addressed to:
WKMA Publishing
infowkma@gmail.com
or
kcfitzjerrell@gmail.com

First Edition 2012

Library of Congress Control Number
2011944742

Fitzjerrell, Karen Casey
the dividing season / Karen Casey Fitzjerrell
p. cm.
ISBN 978-0-9847768-9-4

Permission to quote part of Buck Ramsey's poem, Anthem, from
the book GRASS (published 2005) received from Texas Tech
University Press.

Printed in the United States of America
McNaughton & Gunn, Inc., Saline, MI

For
Bill and Carol Metz
who helped me escape

And in the morning I was riding
Out through the breaks of that long plain,
And leather creaking in the quieting
Would sound with trot and trot again.
I lived in time with horse hoof falling;
I listened well and heard the calling
The earth, my mother, bade to me,
Though I would still ride wild and free.

Buck Ramsey, *Anthem*

The Dividing Season

PART I

On a blustery and cold March morning in 1910 Nell Miggins took a jar of India ink from the desk drawer, wrapped it in a neckerchief and slipped out the kitchen door with it hidden in a pocket of her dead father's old riding coat. She saddled her horse, Jingles and rode to the highest point on Carrageen Ranch - a benched hill strewn with wagon-sized boulders. There, in early morning sunlight, she dismounted and climbed to the eastern face of a towering rock wall.

Nell pulled the jar of ink from her pocket, uncorked it, and poured some into the palm of one hand then set the jar aside so she could rub her hands together. Then she turned and pressed her ink saturated palms to the gritty surface of the rock. More than anything in the world, Nell wanted to be like the ink and have the rock soak her up as proof that she had existed, loved this place, her ranch, like a mother loves her child. After a long moment she withdrew her hands and stepped back to watch sunlight glint on the dark wet images of her hands.

When she returned to the ranch house, the sky had grown wispy and dark in the northeast where the road from town followed the Guadalupe River westward. Between the cloud bank and ranch house, a dusty brown funnel billowed from behind the knob of a low hill. It was Grady Monroe, friend and lawyer, driving his new Maxwell automobile at breakneck speed over the rutted road. Nell knew this because the day before she had sent Thomas, the last cowhand her father hired before he died, into town to tell Grady she needed to consult with him.

She tethered Jingles to a gate post and tried to wipe the ink off her hands with a neckerchief. Across the way Thomas pushed through the bunkhouse screen door and shuffled to the shade of live oaks where he hammered a stake in the ground for a game of horseshoes. The syncopated pinging of hammer against metal mingled with clucking hens, the whinny of horses behind the barn and a breeze soughing through the trees. When Grady passed through Carrageen's gate a half-mile away, Nell walked around to the front porch and clasped her hands in a tight knot at her waist, bracing herself for the painful weight of what she was about to do.

"Dammit, girl," Grady boomed when he pulled up to the fence surrounding the yard. "I still can't see why you want to live way out here at the very end of the earth." He climbed down from the big Maxwell, removed his hat and slapped at his legs with it as if he had ridden a horse and needed to dust his clothes.

"Lupe," Nell called through the screen door. "Mr. Monroe is here. We'll have our coffee on the porch." She turned back to Grady. "Maybe I'm too close to the edge of the earth and am about to fall off." She motioned to one of the rocking chairs on the wide porch. He sat, but she remained standing.

"Just what do you mean by that, Missy?" Grady had known her family so long he looked upon her as he would one of his own daughters.

"I've decided to put the ranch up for sale. I've written my cousin, Hester, in case she wants to buy me out. A courtesy, you understand. I doubt she will want it."

"What in tarnation has brought this on all of a sudden? Good God in heaven, I can just hear your Pa now lettin' out a roar from his grave yonder." Grady waved his hat toward a grove of live oak trees that circled the family cemetery.

"You just said you don't know why I live out here. Now you question my decision to leave?"

"Hell, you could have Pablo and Lupe run this ranch and you could live in town. In your Sunday House. Go to teas, join the Ladies Aid Society and—"

"I'm not getting any younger, Grady. I've missed any chance of marrying or having a conventional life. You know full well all I've ever known is this ranch. And all I know of the world comes from a few trips here and there to different cattle companies across Texas with Daddy when I was little. Now I'm thinking there may be things I want to see or do..." Nell let her voice trail off when Grady's gaze dropped away. She read his mind: she had spent so much of her life isolated on this ranch that some said she was odd, favoring the company of her dead daddy's old cowpoke partners, or riding the range looking for strays with Pablo, the Mexican her father had always treated like family.

When Lupe appeared in the doorway with coffee, Nell was grateful for the interruption.

Grady heaped three spoons of sugar in his coffee. "Are you sure you've thought this thing through? What will you do? Where will you go?" He narrowed his gaze. His bushy eyebrows knotted together over his big red nose. "And what about the Sunday House in Wishing? Will you keep it?"

"I don't know. It seems to me that if I can get a reasonable sum for this ranch, I can do just about anything I want as long as I do it before I'm too old to enjoy it."

"Go on now. You talk like you're an old maid."

Nell pulled a long stretch of air into her lungs, looked out over the cattle pens and corrals and past them to the wide valley between her beloved hills. "Will you be prepared to draw up the necessary legal papers?" She returned her cup to a small table between the rockers.

"Sure thing. But give yourself a little more time, will you? Let this all sit for a while."

"I've thought about nothing else for a long time."

"Well, tell you what. Make a list of all your assets here. Livestock, out buildings, equipment and such that you want included when you sell. I'll go over the records I've got and next time you're in Wishing come see me. We'll get this thing moving. That is, if you still hold to the notion."

Nell walked Grady to his automobile where he paused to push his hat down on his head. "Ever wonder why town is named Wishing?"

Nell thought for a moment. "I guess not."

"Because pioneers who first came to these parts were always hankering – or Wishing – for something else, somewhere else. Human nature, I suppose."

Nell watched Grady climb back into his big black automobile and bounce and sputter back to the main road. Beyond him, near the horizon, rain was falling in silver streaks and seemed to be moving toward Carrageen Ranch.

Now that her plan had been set into motion, the realization that one decision generated a need for many more hung over her like a heavy cloak. She felt hollow, like she was about to cave in or fold over, damned with the burden of operating the ranch against impossible odds. Drought, bad beef prices, Mexicans warring on this side of the border. And damned with guilt for selling out.

Often in years past she'd sought serenity in the sweeping wide open range to overcome her suffocating loneliness. She had ridden wild and stayed out for a week at a time and wondered after doing so how she could ever want for more when she had this land to call home. Nell had always felt she and the land, bequeathed to her by her father and to him by his father, completed each other somehow. But time had changed everything. She found it harder and harder to hold Carrageen Ranch together and she was tired. Plain tired.

Her gaze traveled over the folds of land where hills and valleys touched and trees reached for the sky. Cattle in the distance appeared as great humps with twitching tails. Her world was this vision and it whispered to her now on wind blowing down from rolling thunderheads.

***

TINKER WEBB'S WAGON topped a hill heading out of Bandera County. From there, he followed a road that lead north. Old man Taylor near Indian Springs had asked him to swing by to help put a new roof on his barn. After that, Tinker planned to travel west and stop at the little town of Wishing to see if there was any work there before crossing the Guadalupe River and turning back north. His dog, Jack, sat on the wagon seat next to him. Jack was a puzzling patchwork of canine breeding. His ears stood in sharp peaks above a slack-hung jaw, and his eyes rolled continuously as if he could fall asleep at any minute.

The wagon had been an old army freight wagon before Tinker bought it in Fort Davis. He'd built a cabinet with a fold-down door on the back, like a chuck wagon, including cubby holes and drawers where he stored his tools. Old timers still thought of Tinker as a windmiller, when the truth of the matter was he repaired few windmills these days. Folks could order them from a catalog at the general store and put them together themselves. But it mattered little to Tinker how people thought of him, windmiller or prairie hobo. He just appreciated the feel of his wagon swaying down ill-marked roads, bumping over rocks and splashing through creeks.

"Well, I'll be damned," he said out loud. Jack tweaked his ears without opening his eyes. "Today is my birthday. Forty-ninth, if I figured it right."

When he thought further on the subject of time and age, Tinker realized it had been a lifetime since he left home. His father had given up raising cattle because of barbed wire and bad beef prices. He'd said the best thing to do was to try raising cotton. Tinker couldn't imagine himself a cotton farmer. His life up to that point had been one of boots and spurs, roundups and cattle trails. Because he and his father were at such odds on the matter it seemed best to try college. Since Tinker had a leaning toward building things, studying architecture seemed a natural place to start.

And just look where it had led him. He shook his head in private disgust. High society and financial success with a prestigious architectural firm, first in the Northeast, then later in Galveston. Trips to London, Paris...distinguished vainglory. Through it all, he never got over leaving his home and harbored a dream to return to it someday to stay put.

To Tinker's way of thinking, Galveston would always be a city of sickness. Steamers belching white smoke from their stacks, tracked endless circles around the globe bringing to Texas shores all the things needed to make life easy and pretty. Warehouses lined up like so many toy blocks, filled to overflowing with goods traded for money to line the pockets of men like himself. The smell of salty Gulf waters and fish and hemp. The sound of endless south winds in oleander branches, gulls crying out like old women. All of it reminded him of yellow fever and pain and a constant longing to reverse time.

He had left Galveston, still a young man, carrying a burden of regret and deep heartache he felt would stay with him the rest of his life. And so far it had. But he accepted the melancholy shadow like he would a bad relative, and settled on becoming a sojourner.

As if there had been a blueprint for his life somewhere, he struck up a conversation with a Mr. Guntenheimer in a livery stable in Seguin, Texas. Mr. Guntenheimer had been in the process of repairing a gun hammer when the two of them met. Tinker learned the kindly old German traveled from town to town building and repairing windmills. The work evolved to include blacksmithing and gunsmithing.

"Have you ever designed a windmill?" Tinker asked.

"Nah, to be sure is all I can do to keep up repairing dem tings."

"Why don't you hire help?"

Mr. Gunteheimer had pushed his tiny glasses down his nose to peer at Tinker. "Dem young ones all want to cowboy and hoot and holla' all de time." He pushed his glasses back up his nose and humped over his work. "Besides," he added, "they don't like high places. And me? I'm gettin' too old already."

"I'll work for no pay if you'll teach me what you know."

After serving two years as Mr Guntenheimer's apprentice, Tinker bought him out. He missed the old man's companionship, but with the passing months and years, a kind of calm settled on him. He learned to listen to the cicada-chattering, owl-hooting melodies of Texas nights as if it were conversation.

Then Jack appeared at the edge of Tinker's campfire glow a couple of years later. The dog was all hide and bone and sores. Tinker fed him, and when he realized the dog intended to keep following the wagon, he bathed him and gave him a name. Tinker felt foolish thinking it, but now their two wandering, wounded souls had become kindred in spirit. Late afternoon of his forty-ninth birthday, fourteen years after meeting Mr. Guntenheimer, Tinker Webb crossed Indian Spring Creek and reached to give his dog a pat.

A series of popping noises broke the quiet. Jack ruffed and looked at Tinker. Tinker listened. Three, maybe four more pops. Gunfire. Could be Mr. Taylor target practicing or sighting a gun. But he thought not and snapped the reins. His wagon lurched down into a shady little valley and a while later rounded a bend. About a half mile out a column of smoke rose skyward. To the west of the smoke a band of horsemen with about five head of cattle in front of them were running hell bent over a hill.

At the Taylor place, Tinker found Mr. Taylor sprawled out behind his well house. He was all shot up and his throat had been cut. Tinker lifted the man's head and attempted to give what comfort he could.

Taylor gasped. "The brothers..."

Tinker didn't have a clue what he was trying to say. "Your family?" He glanced at the house that had all but burned to the ground.

"In the house." Taylor coughed blood and grabbed at the front of Tinker's shirt. "Garza brothers done killed us all, Webb."

***

PABLO RODE ALONG in the wagon with Nell when she went to Wishing to talk with Grady about the details of selling the ranch. Afterward she stopped by the post office where she found a letter from Hester. She read it over coffee in the lobby of Wishing's only hotel while Pablo loaded supplies at the general store.

April 21, 1910   San Antonio, Texas
Dear Cousin Nell,

Your letter has me so melancholy I can hardly function. I cannot comprehend the thought that you would sell Carrageen Ranch.

Please do not do anything until we talk. John, who is sometimes short on patience, has been thoughtful enough to say that he would take charge of the household and children for a week in order that I may travel to Milcom County to visit you. He will leave tomorrow for another week with the Rangers on sortie looking for bandits who have crossed the border. The situation has gotten much worse west of here. Three of Mr. Garwood's men were shot just days ago while riding herd. One of the men died.

As soon as John returns, I will leave for Wishing. My train will arrive in the afternoon, May 12.

Hester

Nell put Hester's letter back in the envelope and wondered how long it would take to convince her that no one horrible thing made her decide to sell. Nell and Hester had been like sisters growing up. Their fathers were brothers. However, because Hester's father found ranching far too much work for so little profit, he sold his inheritance to Samuel, Nell's dad, when they were small children.

A burst of shouts and activity filled the street outside the hotel window where Nell sat reading mail. Apparently a train had arrived in Wishing and since it was the end of the line, all travelers disembarked and either stayed in the hotel or continued travel by horse or wagon.

Three men entered the lobby. One, who seemed to be in charge, wore a dark brown suit with a fancy brocade vest. His prominent square jaw was clean shaven and when he turned to lift his bag, a shaft of bright sunlight from the open double doors shone directly on his face. Pock marks, probably from some childhood sickness, dotted his jaw line.

Nell had heard her father say often that without the railroad and hotel, Wishing would have dried up with the drought long ago like dozens of other little cow towns across Texas. But the hotel and railroad were bittersweet blessings for him. She recalled the marching band and street dances the day the big black engine actually chugged its way over iron rails that stretched across the prairie. She was about twelve years old, her mother, Hilda long dead.

Her father had seemed wistful that day and when she asked why he tried to explain. "Change happens all the time, Nell. Mostly we don't notice. It just happens real slow whether we want it or not. But this here big iron horse of a thing..." He had paused then and squeezed her hand. "...this is change we can see. When you look that a'way down those rails you know you're connected with San Antonio and when you turn and look that a'way? Well, you know before long those rails will connect you with El Paso." He shrugged and mopped his face with his neckerchief. "Seems like barbed wire cut us off from the land and now the railroad is gonna connect us to the cities."

"Miss Miggins?" Willie, the hotel waiter interrupted her thoughts, but before she could respond, shouts drew her attention to the open doors.

"What's happening?"

"It's them motor cars. They sure stir up the wagon teams round here. The army sent 'em with some foot soldiers to hunt Mexican bandits, I reckon. There's talk of revolution in Mexico, you know. More coffee?"

Nell moved to the door without answering. Willie followed. "I reckon some of them boys is just tenderfeet looking for a way west." He stood on tiptoe to see over Nell's shoulder. "And would you just look at them automobiles. Why, there is sure to be trouble from all the ruckus."

A column of soldiers marched down the middle of the street four abreast behind two puttering motorcars. Horses tied to hitching posts rolled their eyes and stirred nervously, kicking up dust. At the opposite end of the street horses squealed like a pigs.

Nell turned in time to see Pablo struggling to restrain her wagon team. The horses broke away from him, reared and ran with bulging eyes directly into the path of the automobiles. Nell bolted out of the hotel as the wagon hurled by. Dust flew into her face, blinding and choking her. She ducked her chin, gasped for clean air.

She heard a guttural, angry shout. "Get outta my way, you flea infested Mex-can."

Nell blinked to clear her eyes. A man climbed down from one of the cars. He had greasy colorless hair to his shoulders. It stuck out every which way from under a mashed cavalry hat. He stood at least six and a half feet tall and, Nell would guess later, weighed over three hundred pounds. She was still gasping for a clean breath of air when he raised a riding quirt over Pablo's hunched shoulders.

"I said git outta my way, you sorry *sister*." The quirt came whooshing down over Pablo's back. Nell lunged for the big man, grabbed his arm and felt her feet leave the ground as he swung upward for another lash. She lost her grip and was pitched against a water trough. A woman screamed from somewhere across the street.

Nell grabbed a wood bucket sitting beside the trough and slung it across the man's broad hulking back.

"What the hell? I'll string—" He swung around to face her. Nell's hat had been knocked off by her efforts and was swinging from a leather strip tied around her neck. She raised the bucket over her head and threw it with all her might. It hit the man's right foot with a loud crack.

He leaped with a howl of pain and rolled to the ground clutching his foot. A roar of laughter from the gathered crowd turned his ugly opaque skin bright crimson before he managed to stand and limp off into an alley. The seat of his britches twitched from right to left, to right, like big empty flour sacks over his flat backside as he went.

***

SKIN HARRIS SLUMPED in the shade between the livery stable and dry goods store to pull off his boot. He just couldn't figure how or why he always got things so messed up. It was his daddy who named him Skin on account of his ugly milky looking skin. Maybe that put him on a bad path. Nah. And anyways, he couldn't do anything about it. Deep in his heart, Skin always believed his keen sense of smell would save him. Why, he could smell rain two counties away, and sometimes even a town long before he could see it on the horizon. But so far his keen nose hadn't help change him from sinner to saint.

He tried to squeeze his swollen foot back into his boot but it hurt too bad, so he pushed up and limped through the back streets to the edge of town, humming softly to himself as he went.

Maybe folks here 'bouts would forget the little fiasco in the middle of the street. Anyways, he hoped them army boys had camp set up. He could sure use a bite to eat.

***

NELL HADN'T REALIZED until she turned to help Pablo to his feet that a crowd had gathered to watch the commotion. She caught a glimpse of the man with the pocked face standing in the doorway of the hotel. His mouth pulled to one side in a half grin as he tipped his hat to her.

She wheeled around and rushed down the street with Pablo to find the wagon and scattered supplies.

"Stop at the Sunday House," Nell said as they climbed onto the wagon seat. "I need to take a look at your back. It's bleeding."

He gave the reins a pop. "It is all right. We have wasted enough time already."

Nell was five years old when Pablo was born and each had been an only child since their mothers died when they were small. Nell couldn't remember a time when a bond hadn't existed between them. As *hermano* and *hermana*, brother and sister, they grew up sharing a childhood completely unrestricted by social structure.

When Pablo married and brought Lupe to the ranch to live, Nell's father, Samuel hosted a wedding fiesta under a grove of live oak trees not far from the house. Lupe's family came in carts from across the border toting children and baskets of beans, tomatoes, peppers and corn. Table after table was laden with food and tequila was served generously.

She delighted in the music of the Mexicans, loud brassy horns and big guitars and she loved dancing with her father and Pablo's cousins. The songs, when she was able to follow the words, were of bad luck and drunk roosters and about happy people with hearty passions and deep longings. Others were about dying lovers and wild vaqueros.

The thought of a border between Texas and Mexico or, a division of any kind – between families, cultures, countries – had never occurred to any of them.

Later that evening, when Nell and Pablo reached the ranch, she sent Pablo to the house while she unhitched the wagon team. When she finished and made her way under dark skies to the house she found Lupe and Pablo at the kitchen table.

"Mother of God, what happened?" Lupe poured Mercurochrome into a small dish.

Pablo sat leaning over the long table with his bloody shirt draped over his legs. Each time Lupe wiped at the long angry blisters on his back, he sucked in a tight breath of air. "The horses spooked and ran into the path of motorcars, made a man angry. Nell, she hit him when he hit me."

"Ah, Nell, why do you do this?" Lupe was appalled.

"The man said I have fleas." Pablo answered for her. "And Nell? She looked like a she-cat. Not a word, just bust his foot with a bucket and then she walked away, just like that."

Nell held the dish of Mercurochrome for Lupe. "Who was that man anyway, Pablo? I've never seen him before, have I?"

"I think he must be with the army somehow. A scout maybe. I hear talk at the dry good store. The army men don't know this country and don't know where to find bandits. A scout, he is, maybe."

After Lupe dressed Pablo's wounds Nell washed up and left them to coo over each other. She loved watching them live their lives and build on their love day after day. It seemed so natural and warm and right. Their little boy, Juan had been asleep when she and Pablo returned from Wishing. He was a four-year-old replica of Pablo, with dark liquid eyes that danced with enchantment over everything his young life encountered.

Nell slipped into uneasy, troubled sleep that night while images of border bandits and army troops marched across her mind. The face of the strange square-jawed man at the hotel also appeared in her dreams as the moonless night passed over the ranch and turned into a gray morning glow. But her first thought on waking was of the dirty man she had encountered in Wishing and his awful white skin.

***

HENRY BURLESON CLIMBED into bed glad for the stroke of luck he and Scottie had in finding this hotel in the middle of nowhere. Wishing was a metropolis compared to some of the places he'd seen between Chicago and here.

It had rattled him to admit to Scottie chances were slim they'd find evidence that priests traveling this region with Spanish explorers in the sixteenth or seventeenth century had brought along Mayan peasants. Still, if he could raise enough interest in the possibility, he'd be able to convince the directors of the Studies of the Americas at the University of Chicago to finance an archaeological expedition to the Yucatán. And since that was his main goal, it was worth a try.

Scottie had argued the subject. "You, more than anyone, are aware of how little survived the burning of the Mayan cities by the Spanish. With the peasant uprisings taking place in Mexico and along the border lately, I doubt the board of directors will approve a preliminary study there."

In the end Scottie – Professor Lawrence Scott, the leading authority on archaeological sciences in the United States – had given Henry his full support. Henry never doubted he would. He'd been one of Scottie's best students with a natural aptitude for the details of hieroglyphic transcriptions and now enjoyed a prestigious position on the university staff as well. And Henry had every intention of being known world-wide for his discoveries in Mayan antiquities before his fiftieth birthday.

The hotel bed creaked when Henry turned onto his side anxious to get some sleep. But voices in the street below annoyed him. He got out of bed and looked out. The big man who had tangled with the Mexican and woman earlier that day was talking to some soldiers.

"Hey, Skin, need bigger boots, do you?" A young soldier snickered and slapped the big man on his back. Two other soldiers who were looking on laughed like kids. The man they called Skin growled something Henry couldn't hear, then all of them threw back their heads howling with laughter. One pushed a bottle of whiskey into the face of another.

Skin jerked his head west. "Once't we leave for them mountains yonder, we'll just see who's laughin' at who. You sisters got no notion what's ahead when it comes to lookin' for them bandits." He walked his tired looking horse off into the darkness.

Discussions with Scottie about the dangers of roaming the Rio Grande region looking for archaeological evidence while bandits played cat and mouse with U.S. authorities were sometimes heated. Newspaper reports gave grim details about ranchers being terrorized and killed. The expedition had been offered a military escort, but he turned it down, reasoning that the extra attention brought on by having soldiers along would only add to the danger. Bandits would appreciate the notoriety if they could wipe out an army troop along with a couple of professors. If what he had just seen from his window was any indication of the quality of military protection, then he felt even better about the decision to travel unprotected.

Henry smirked. Their little excursion would do better to have the lady with the bucket escort them. Henry, Scottie, and Jim Hargrove, a student at the university in Chicago brought along as an assistant, had just come downstairs to eat when they saw the lady run into the street toward a line of army troops. Scottie was flabbergasted at what he'd seen and Jim roared with the crowd. They'd never seen a woman act so forcibly. But, for all her bravado, Henry would have sworn he saw her hands trembling when she reached to help the Mexican to his feet.

***

LOUD RAPS ON the door jerked Henry from his jumbled sleep. He opened it a few inches and saw Jim Hargrove's grinning face.

"Morning, Mr. Burleson, sir. I'm waking you, six o'clock. Just like you said."

"Is Scottie up yet?"

"Said he'd meet us in fifteen minutes." Jim's big hat made his ears stick out.

"You go on ahead then. I'll be right down."

Scottie was sitting at a table with Jim when Henry joined them in a corner of the lobby where meals were served. Over coffee, biscuits the size of a man's fist, steak that ran pink in the middle, and enough eggs for an army, Scottie briefed Henry on the last minute arrangements.

"I managed to hire a man to help with camp duties. Bob. Didn't give me a last name." Scottie was wearing a white linen coat with a red silk kerchief around his neck and a white Panama hat.

Henry looked away. The garb was sure to draw bandit attention.

"Bob said he would arrange to have our horses and supply wagon ready. And a pack mule if we think we'll need it."

"The wagon ought to do," Henry said. "We can camp on the river bank and branch out our search on horseback from there." He turned to Jim who was stuffing biscuits in his mouth. "Jim?"

"Yessir." Jim swallowed but his cheeks still bulged. "Me and Bob got all our supplies packed. Extra shovels and the trowels you wanted."

An hour later they met Bob at the edge of town. A large tattered sombrero framed his black grinning face. White fuzzy hair fringed his jaw and stuck out from under the sombrero like cotton. Henry guessed him to be at least eighty years old, but he couldn't see that he would gain anything by complaining to Scottie. He didn't want to waste time trying to locate a new supply boss at this late stage. Besides, Bob did have fresh horses and was ready to ride as he'd told Scottie he would be.

Henry led the way west out of Wishing. His plan was to veer southwest after crossing Devil's River. When they hit the Pecos River he'd follow it south until he found a place suitable to cross and keep going southwest until they came to the canyons along the Rio Grande. Two, maybe three days ride.

The road leading out of town dwindled to nothing more than a trail by noon. The country was wide and dry. White billowing clouds puffed up out of their flat bottoms into a sky that, to Henry, looked bleached.

Scottie tied his mount to the wagon and joined Bob on the seat. The two had a deep conversation going about Buffalo Soldiers.

Bob grinned his way through tale after tale about his soldiering days at Fort Davis.

"I's with the 10th Reg'ment of the Cavalry, don't you know. There was this Cap'n Nolan fella thought hisself was really sompin. Back in '77, August it was, he taken off to look for Injuns on that there Staked Plain. Ooo-wee, yessir, a bad place it was. Still is. First thing you know, Cap'n Nolan got lost out there and we's sent out to go find 'em. Four of 'em died before we got to 'em. Poor boys. Them what lived had lips dried out and rolled back. It was that hot. They's near three days without water in that heat. It was bad, lem'me tell you."

***

HENRY WAS UP at daylight the next day to scout a passage suitable for the wagon. An hour later he found a sloped trail down into a long canyon and farther downstream, a sand bar reaching almost all the way across the Pecos River. Beyond it, low on the horizon, he could see the amethyst-colored mountains of Mexico. It took most of the morning to get the wagon down to the canyon floor, and since all four men were exhausted, Henry suggested they stop to eat and siesta.

"I have no argument with that idea." Scottie sank beneath a stubby tree.

Crossing the Pecos was harder than Henry anticipated. The place he decided on, while not wide, was so deep and the current so strong that the wagon floated twenty yards downstream and busted a wheel on a submerged boulder before they could get it landed on dry ground.

"How long will it take you to fix it?" Henry asked Bob.

"I reckon it'll be 'bout dark."

Henry wheeled around, shook his head and slapped at his leg with his reins, then turned back. "Get started. We'll camp here. I'm going to ride on up ahead, scout a good trail. I don't want any more problems."

The next day Henry led the way to a towering canyon along the Rio Grande River and had Bob set up camp on a sand bar. From there he and Scottie made short trips up and down the river looking for anything resembling the descriptions an anthropologist associate had given them about the discovery of a pictograph that appeared hundreds, not thousands of years old. It was the depiction of a slope-faced individual very similar to those unearthed at various archeological sites in Mexico. Jim stayed in camp with Bob most of the time logging the few bits of pottery and arrowheads they found.

On the third day Scottie yelled down a ravine to Henry. When Henry caught up to him, Scottie pointed to the bottom side of an overhanging rock. He'd found an Indian painting of an antelope. They searched feverishly up and down the same ravine for more but found nothing. Still, Henry was relieved to find anything that gave a little encouragement. He flagged the ravine to make it easier to find the next day.

Dusk fell like a black curtain over camp. Jim seemed pensive, in deep thought. "Mr. Burleson, do you think we'll see bandits?"

Henry rolled over in his bedroll. "I doubt it."

"Humph." Bob folded his arms across his chest as he gazed into the fire.

"What does that mean?" Scottie asked.

"They's watching us. Make no mistake about it. They just ain't decided what we's worth to 'em yet."

Henry shot a questioning glance in Scottie's direction. Scottie shrugged.

That night thunder rolled in the distance, echoed down the river canyon. A short time later rain began to fall in torrents.

Sometime before dawn Bob shook Henry awake. "We best be movin' to higher ground. That river is comin' up fast."

They worked until daylight maneuvering the wagon to higher ground. Then all four men had to sit on damp bedrolls holding their horses' leads until mid-morning when the rain finally eased up.

Bob handed out soggy, cold biscuits and pieces of jerky. Henry seethed with lidded anger over the delay and inconvenience.

At first light the next day, he started barking orders. Bob was to stay in camp and keep an eye on things while Jim helped scout the area where Henry and Scottie found the painting two days earlier. As Henry expected, the marker he left had been blown away in the storm, but despite losing the reference point, they were able to locate the overhanging rock without much doubling back. He bent low to make drawings of the painted antelope

Jim roamed around the north edge of the rock outcropping and climbed to the top. A short time later, he let out a bloody scream.

Henry grabbed his gun. Scottie ducked.

Jim shouted, "You better come look, Mr. Burleson. I think it's one of those paintings."

"Damn." Henry growled when he realized Jim had yelled out of excitement, not danger. He and Scottie climbed up the steep rocky slope to join him.

Scottie leaned forward with his hands on his knees. "Well I'll be damned." Another crude, barely visible pictograph of a man's head in profile gleamed in the bright sunlight.

"Is that supposed to be a Mayan?" Jim asked.

Henry slipped his hat off. "There is no doubt about it." Blood flooded his face. One step closer to a major discovery, to his dream of fame.

"Scottie, get my notebooks. I want to copy as much of this as I can make out from this vantage point then do the same from that ledge farther up. I want to be sure to capture every detail. Jim, you scout on up the ravine. See if you can find anything else."

"We covered that area pretty good yesterday," Scottie said.

"I have a hunch. Look at that water running from around this boulder. The flooding last night might have washed things around a bit."

In no time Jim called out a second time, his voice was muffled by echoes. When Henry caught up to the boy, he pointed to a narrow crevice in the canyon wall. "You're not going to believe what's in there."

Henry had to duck his head in order to walk into the opening. Scottie followed, but Jim stayed behind.

In the deep shade of the crevice, Henry squeezed his eyes, wondered if what he was looking at could be human bones. Surely not. "Got a match, Scottie?"

Scottie withdrew a small box from his vest pocket but dropped it while fumbling to find room to squat in the tight space. Henry grabbed the box and struck a match across the rocks three times before it lit. In the flickering light, gray-green bones of a skeleton lay calcified in a grotesque, twisted pose.

Scottie clasped Henry's shoulder. "Look there." He pointed among the bones.

Henry lifted the gummy rotted folds of what apparently had been a leather-bound book. The shape of a cross tooled into the leather was visible only when Henry held it at an angle to the match glow.

"Damn!" Henry flipped the burnt match to the ground and sucked his scorched finger. He struck another and leaned closer. Among the flattened rib bones he found a trinket the length of his first finger. A carved jade figurine of a man with the same sloped profile as the rock painting. The feet were turned in and up and the arms slashed with deep slanted lines.

Henry's gut whirled like a Kansas tornado. Unbelievable. He'd done it – a major discovery.

***

"MY FIRST IMPRESSION is that the pictograph is about two hundred years old. And the person who painted it was not very skilled," Henry said, riding back to camp late that same day.

"Meaning?" Scottie asked.

Henry loved it when Scottie took that role.

"Maybe the scribe was new to the art." Henry shook his head, amazed by the possibilities. "When we return tomorrow with a lantern and the means to remove the skeleton, I'll be able to make a better assessment."

"Mr. Burleson, look." Jim pointed in the direction of their camp. Buzzards circled high up in the thermals. Dozens of them. But Henry never guessed what they would find. Bob was laid out spread eagle on a dry sand bar, naked except for his socks. His body had been cut open from his throat to his privates and he had been strangled with his own intestines.

"Dear God." Scottie turned to warn Jim but was too late. The boy turned white and slid from his horse to vomit.

Bob hadn't been dead all that long, Henry decided, or the buzzards would have started on him. "We better get him buried. Whoever did this may still be around."

Scottie scanned the canyon walls. "Bandits?"

"Has to be."

They wrapped Bob in his bedroll and buried him on the sandy river bank. Scottie wanted to bury him above the canyon wall but it was too rocky.

When they stepped back from the rock-piled grave, a gun blast boomed across the canyon. Henry glimpsed a Mexican sombrero against the darkening sky and yelled to the others to take cover. He fumbled around in the wagon, found a Colt and tossed it to Jim, who crawled under the wagon and began to shoot at shadows.

Henry gave Scottie Bob's shotgun and kept the rifle for himself. The echoing noise from the gun battle was deafening, as if they faced a whole army. Aiming was hopeless in the dark shadows. By nightfall the gun battle had gradually died down.

Scottie stood to stretch. "My legs are killing me."

"Get down, damn you, Scottie. We're in it deep here and I need all the help I can get."

"Are we going to get killed, Mr. Burleson?"

"I'm sure as hell not planning on it, Jim."

Scottie dug around under the wagon sheet. "Maybe Bob left us a cold biscuit or two. We'd feel better with a little nourishment."

"Get down!" Henry warned through gritted teeth.

Two shots popped off from halfway up the opposite canyon wall. One ricocheted off a boulder above Scottie. The other hit him in the hollow of his shoulder.

"Mr. Scott! Oh no!" Jim grabbed Scottie as he slumped down. A big red splotch spread across his chest.

Henry helped Jim lean Scottie against the wagon wheel. He pressed the wound to check the flow of blood. "Looks like the bullet went through. You've got a hell of a hole on your back, Scottie."

Scottie grimaced. "Sorry about this."

"One hell of a mess." Henry scooped his hat off and rubbed his face.

A pebble dropped from overhead, bounced off his shoulder. He wheeled around but before he could get his rifle into position to fire, Skin Harris held up his gun and a bloody knife to show he was not there to harm anyone. "Looks like you sisters could use a little help. Put your fire-power away. I done took care of them Mex-cans."

***

RAIN FELL ALL night making a steady drumming noise on the roof. In Nell's mind the sound filled the corners of the big empty ranch house. She listened, let it hold her in a trance. And then at dawn she put on her robe, descended the wide stairway, and went out the front door. Her bare feet made soft platting sounds on the cool surface of the wood floors as she went. The sound sent echoes of her childhood trailing across her mind.

From the porch she studied the low hills in the east. Pablo appeared silently, handed her a cup of coffee, then leaned against the porch railing. For as long as either of them could remember, the business of operating Carrageen Ranch had begun in precisely the same way every day, with hot coffee on the porch at dawn.

Nell tightened her robe against the dampness. "Hester's train arrives this afternoon. If this rain lets up, I'd like to take the wagon to meet her and bring back a barrel of dip."

Pablo nodded.

"If it doesn't let up," she continued, "we should take the buggy. You know how Hester is."

Pablo grinned, flashing the black hole where his eye tooth had been. Not long after Samuel hired Thomas Babb to help with spring roundup, the cowhands heard about a Negro cowboy who would slip from his horse onto a steer's shoulders then wrestle it to the ground. Thomas dared Pablo to try it. Pablo took the dare and landed face down on the rocky ground on his first try. He was lucky he hadn't done worse than lose a tooth and bust his lips. He was still spitting blood when they rode up to the barn late in the day.

Samuel had yelled red-faced with anger. "You boys are hankering to kill yourselves and I'll not have it." He docked their pay for wasting time, but everyone knew after all was said and done, Samuel wouldn't hold it against them.

The sky in the east grew brighter. The distant rain looked like silver threads falling in slanted lines. Pablo reached for Nell's cup. "More?"

"I'll get it. I have letters to write before we leave for town. As soon as this rain eases, you and Thomas need to clean the dipping chute, get everything ready."

Later that morning the rain played out and left a lazy haze over the pasture land. Nell and Pablo left the ranch in the wagon for the day trip to Wishing and back.

In town Pablo went to pick up supplies while Nell waited for Hester at the train depot. Hester's dark blonde curls in a window caught Nell's eye as the train chugged up to the platform. They hugged each other with big grins, then Hester stepped back while holding onto Nell's shoulders. "Look at you," she said. "Tanned as a cowgirl in a dime novel."

Hester's broad smile exposed straight, prominent teeth set in a narrow jaw. She was taller than Nell and fine-boned. Her eyes trailed down to the tops of Nell's muddy boots.

"And you, Hester, fresh and pretty." Nell couldn't help but notice Hester's dress of navy blue gabardine. It overlapped across her flat bosom and was edged with a delicate gold braid the same color as her hair. "I'm glad you're here."

Pablo drove up in time to help a porter with Hester's trunk.

"Pablo." Hester acknowledged him then dabbed at her nose with the lace handkerchief. She had never held back her negative opinion of Pablo and "his like." Especially when it came to having responsibility for any part of ranch business.

Nell drove the wagon with Hester on the seat beside her. Pablo rode on top of the supplies and Hester's trunks in the wagon box.

"Wishing will always be a dusty little trading post to me." Hester waved her handkerchief at bales of cotton. "Why, my goodness. Just look at all that cotton. I had no idea cotton could be grown here. Maybe you should try that instead of raising cattle."

"Not a good idea," Nell said.

"Why not?"

"Labor costs. Almost impossible to make a profit."

"You always knew as much as any man about such things," Hester said watching the streets of Wishing tick by. "Oh, do drive by the Sunday House. I have so many memories of the place."

Nell reined the team to a stop in front of the Sunday House their grandfather had built for overnight use when he traveled to town to conduct business. It was hard to collect mail, pick up supplies and do his banking in a day's time so he'd stay there overnight and head to the ranch next morning. Their grandmother first coined the name Sunday House because they stopped there every Sunday after church services to eat a basket lunch and take naps before the long return trip home.

"Oh Nell, I'm glad you've kept it all these years," Hester whispered. "Let's go in."

The Sunday House was nothing more than a large room, about fourteen feet square, dim and musty. A sink with town water stood in one corner and the opposite corner was enclosed to hide a commode. Two beds with a small chest between them lined one wall. Samuel had told Nell many stories of "sowing wild-boy oats" within the Sunday House walls, everything from big money cattle buying to shifty poker games.

Hester sat on one of beds. "Do you come here much?"

"I sometimes make it to a church service." Nell shrugged. "But I don't have any more in common with town ladies now than I did when you still lived here. They're so tedious."

"Do you remember the first time we stayed here alone?" Hester trailed her finger across the dusty chest of drawers.

"You mean the first time *I* stayed here alone, don't you?" Nell made no attempt to hide her sarcasm. When she was eighteen and Hester just turned twenty, they received permission from their fathers to attend the Cattleman's Ball and stay overnight at the Sunday House afterward.

Hester's dance card had been filled before the first tune finished. Clyde Mitchell, a bank clerk from Dallas, approached Nell with a stiff little bow and asked if she'd put him down on her dance card for the next waltz. She dropped her card two times before she managed to pencil Clyde's name on it. He eyed her blank card. "And maybe a couple of polkas, too." Nell remembered thinking Clyde's pale "banker's skin" and sweet green eyes made him seem altogether different from any of the young men she'd known.

Hester danced mostly with John Woodvine, who was to graduate from law school that same spring and wedding bells were all but ringing. He was one of the youngest members of the Texas Rangers and could hold Hester and Nell in morbid trances telling his bloody tales of Indian raids and bandit hangings. Nell often thought he got a kind of evil enjoyment out of repeating the gory details in which he always emerged a hero.

Half way through that evening Hester had grabbed Nell's arm. "John and I are going for a walk. You go on to the Sunday House and I'll meet you there later."

Before Nell could express trepidation, Hester was gone.

Clyde walked Nell to the Sunday House around midnight and when he tried to kiss her, she ducked her face away. He mumbled an apology then quickly disappeared down the dark street.

She had been so mortally embarrassed and tongue-tied that she couldn't explain she hadn't intended to turn him away. It was just that she'd never been kissed.

Hester returned to the Sunday House at dawn, tousle-headed and wrinkled and said almost nothing for days.

"Nell...?" Nell jumped, startled from having her thoughts yanked back to the present.

Hester pushed up from the bed. "I was just asking, whatever happened to that Clyde Mitchell boy you met the night of the Cattleman's Ball?"

At the window Nell moved the thin curtain back. A shaft of sunlight beamed in a shallow angle to the floor. "I heard not long ago that he died of some strange weak blood disease. Left a wife and half a dozen children behind."

When Nell turned, her eyes met Hester's gaze across the shaft of light. She wanted to scream at the irony of their lives.

They climbed back into the wagon and continued through town past the baseball diamond where their fathers had played on teams of ranchers and farmers after church services. Their mothers had packed picnic lunches and jars of tea on those occasions. And in the evening after church, baseball games and picnics, they went to concerts at the gazebo if Wishing was lucky enough to have musicians tour through town. Children played games of tag and hide and seek while grownups lounged on the lawns around the ballpark. Back then, when twilight came, fireflies led them on giggling excursions down the paths along the creek and around the gazebo.

Nell thought just now, with Hester on the wagon seat next to her, that she could still hear their parents calling out, beckoning them to gather for the journey home.

Pablo tapped her shoulder when they reached the edge of town. "Stop here. There is more talk in town about a gang of outlaws from Mexico." He handed each woman a gun but Hester refused hers.

Nell took the gun from Pablo and handed it to her. "I don't think anyone is giving you a choice."

Pablo loaded a rifle for himself and returned to his perch on top of Hester's trunks.

"John would not approve of my being in a situation requiring a gun," Hester said. "Did I write you about his work with the army? He may be appointed to lead a battalion to Castolon and help establish a fort on the Rio Grande."

When they arrived at the ranch, Billy was propped against the railing beside the porch steps dozing. A soft light from the glass panels on either side of the front door cast him in a long shadow.

"You know," Hester said as they came to a halt. "I can't remember a time when old Billy wasn't dawdling around here. He must be...how old?"

Nell looped the wagon reins over a hook. "I don't think even he knows."

The old man's head bobbed to his chest before he woke with a jerk. "Who is it?"

"We are back," Pablo said.

"Any troubles? I got to worrying when it got late. Told Lupe I'd stand guard till y'all—"

Nell touched his shoulder as she moved by him. "Thank you, Billy."

Hester followed Nell into the house and stood in the great hall for a moment then circled it, studying the walls, floors, and stairway. Beyond a set of double doors to the left, on the massive dining table, Lupe had left a tray of cold sliced beef, flour tortillas, and a bowl of stewed pears sweetened with honey. Pablo hefted Hester's trunks up the stairway while Nell and Hester ate.

"I don't blame you for wanting to get away from here," Hester said. "This house is like Wishing. Sort of gone to seed, but I still don't think you should sell it." She paused to take a bite then swallowed quickly. "Oh. John found a marvelous cook, a Negro who used to work for Allie McDunigan. You remember meeting her don't you? The judge's wife? Anyway, Frannie, that's the cook's name, is wonderful."

"You must be exhausted." Nell hoped she didn't sound impatient. She was tired and wanted the long day to end. "I suggest we get right to bed and start catching each other up on family matters early tomorrow when you're rested."

Pablo stepped from the kitchen at the end of the hall as they were leaving the dining room. "Is there anything more?"

Nell shook her head. "*Buenos noches.*" They exchanged smiles and a lingering gaze before she turned to climb the stairs behind Hester. Halfway up, she stopped abruptly. "Oh, wait, Pablo. Did you ask around town for someone to take a look at that windmill? You know the one? Last time I was out that way the tank was almost dry."

"*Sí*, I remembered. Mr. Parker, at the livery, says he will send the windmiller here, to Carrageen, when he comes to Wishing."

***

PABLO WATCHED UNTIL Nell and Hester reached the top of the stairs. A grin moved across his mouth. Later, sitting on the edge of the bed where Lupe waited for him, he said, "They are the same as when we were all children."

"What do you mean, Pablo?"

"Hester, she talks always. And going up the stairs she is jerky, and slow. Such fine clothes, you know? Then Nell with that straight back, so smooth and sure, but..." He let his boot drop to the floor and laid back with a tired sigh. "Nell is like a brown chi-chi bird. I don't notice it until Hester, the shiny parrot comes."

Lupe laughed quietly to herself. "But chi-chi birds are like the fire mountain that goes without notice until it turns inside out."

"This is so." Pablo turned to his side. "Still, they are both full of sadness, I think."

***

BY MID-MORNING Nell grew restless waiting for Hester to wake. Balancing a tray of coffee, toast and honey, she tapped on the door to Hester's room. A sea of ruffle and fluff billowed in the middle of the bed. Hester raised her head and smiled without opening her eyes. "M-m-m. You treat me like a queen."

"And try to tell me you don't expect it? I thought you might like to take a picnic basket to Weaver's Draw today."

"Fine, but first," Hester slid from the bed, flung open a trunk, dug around and found three large boxes that she handed to Nell, "These are for you."

"You...shouldn't."

"But I did."

Nell opened the largest box first. It contained a pale green silk dress with a lace jabot scooping the front bodice. Flat pearl buttons trailed down the back and the hem flared with dozens of gored insets. "It's beautiful." Nell bit down on her bottom lip to hide her excitement.

"Of course, I think it's much too plain." Hester tossed her curly head back and sipped her coffee. "But I'd rather get you something you'll actually wear."

"When will I ever have an occasion to wear this?" Nell had begun to take off her clothes.

"I'm hoping to talk you into traveling. Maybe to Europe."

"Europe? There's too much political trouble there now."

"Well, then New York, Chicago, or west to California. You need to get away for a while. This ranch has been your life's blood. But I can see you're tired and, well, lonesome."

Hester helped Nell into the dress then turned her like a child to button the tiny buttons down her back. Hester turned her again to face the dresser mirror. "Now look at you."

Nell couldn't believe how odd it was to see herself in such feminine clothes. Hester flung open a second box and withdrew a wide brimmed jacquard hat with a silk gardenia fastened to the band. The last box yielded ivory colored shoes that buttoned on the side instead of having laces. "From Italy!" Hester beamed and kissed Nell's cheek.

"Actually, I'd already thought about traveling." Nell touched the soft leather shoes then turned her back to Hester so she could unbutton the dress. When she stepped out of it she returned Hester's kiss to the cheek. "Thank you. It's all wonderful. I'll meet you outside. I need to have Lupe pack a picnic basket."

Back downstairs Nell noticed a heaviness about Lupe. It happened often lately and this morning she looked especially pale and tired. Juan was playing with wood blocks on the floor at her feet. "Lupe, I'd like to take Juan with us on the picnic. What better time to have children along than on a picnic?" She watched Juan's face light up as he waited for his mother's reply.

Lupe turned from the sink and nodded. Juan raced to Nell and hugged her legs.

"Lupe, rest while we're gone. There'll be little time for it once we start roundup." Nell took Juan's hand and walked to the corral to tell Pablo to hitch the dun horse to the buggy.

A while later Hester appeared at the back gate wearing a white gauzy cotton dress and white gloves. Pablo circled the buggy out of the barn and they climbed in and drove out across the pasture in bright sunshine. "Would you just look," Nell said. "Wildflowers cover the range like a bright quilt. Yellow, red, orange and blue."

Hester fanned imaginary lint from her dress and peered out to her left. "All this emptiness can be stagnating."

"Or soothing." Nell ignored the insult.

The buggy bounced and bobbed along the rough road through rocky passages and live oak groves. Nell found a grassy patch under some pecan trees at Weaver's Draw where they spread a quilt and ate the basket lunch Lupe had prepared. Hester stretched out on the quilt. A dry breeze fanned the grass and made whispering sounds in the trees. Juan's chubby legs carried him up and down the banks of the rocky draw that trickled water from the recent rain.

Nell pulled a reed of grass. "Tell me about my nephew and nieces."

Hester drew a lazy breath. "They are the light of me. You know that. Marshall wants to go to law school, and the girls keep me busy as always. Nan is still the quiet one. Agnes is just Agnes, everywhere at once."

Nell stood and tightened the hairpins in the braid knotted at the nape of her neck. She walked to the creek bank where Juan squatted to stuff pebbles in his pockets. "Can I help you, *amigo*?" He grinned, handed her a fistful.

Later they rode west of Weaver's Draw to what used to be Hester's father's ranch, Hester's childhood home. Nell drew up the reins at the gate.

Hester side-glanced her. "Why are you stopping?"

"Look how rutted the road is. Someone's been here since the rain." Nell continued at a slower pace.

The house was not much more than crumbling rock walls. It had been considered lavish when Hester's family lived there. A cedar porch post had been knocked askew, probably by a cow trying to scratch, and the overhang drooped almost to the ground. Nell often felt guilty that the house had been abandoned after so much life had been lived in it. Discarded, old and unusable.

She took the rifle from under the seat and told Hester to stay put until she had a look around. She circled the house, went in the back door and emerged out the front.

"Someone's been here, no doubt about it," Nell called out. "Warm ashes in the fireplace and a pile of wood in the middle of the floor." She looked around the overgrown yard then walked to the leaning barn. When she returned to the buggy she told Hester it was safe to look around if she wanted to.

"No, I want to go. I've seen enough."

"But—"

"I can't bear to be here. Let's go."

On the return trip to Carrageen, Juan fell asleep with his head in Nell's lap. Hester was quiet, something Nell found almost as unbearable as her chattering. She scanned Hester's rock hard profile. "I think drifters spent a night or two in the house but I can't be sure. Could've been that band of outlaws Pablo heard about in town."

"That's all John talks about. Bandits and outlaws. The children and I are squeezed between his law practice and the Rangers."

Nell couldn't remember Hester ever saying anything about John's activities that wasn't boastful and had no idea how to reply.

The Carrageen sign was swinging in a strong southwest breeze when the buggy passed under it late that day. In the distance, the ranch house was visible in glimpses as the road leading to it rolled up and down with the swells and valleys of the range. It looked like a decaying castle on a dome of land with the prairie grasslands sloping down and away in every direction.

The next few days of Hester's visit, Nell occupied herself with preparations for spring roundup. Everything seemed complicated by the fact that she planned to sell most of her stock, the first step in liquidating her assets. She'd sent Pablo and Thomas to Kerrville to hire three or four men to help with roundup chores, but they were able to find only one. Nell shook her head dismayed. In times past, men lined up out under the live oaks waiting for Samuel to sign them on to trail his herd to Kansas and then later to the railhead in Fort Worth.

"Humph," Billy said when the hired hand showed up. "That fellar walks like a gall-dern goose. And how you reckon he can rope with all them missing fingers?"

Goose – Billy's name for the man stuck – told her he was a drover for a ranching outfit in Wharton County before the rancher sold out to a large investment company back East.

For the most part, Hester read ladies' magazines during the long days. The last evening of her visit Nell asked her to play the piano. "The thing sits quiet all year, and I've always loved hearing you play."

Nell drifted out to the porch where Pablo and Lupe joined her to listen while Juan played with his pebbles in the fading light. When the second quarter moon reached the top of the hackberry tree, Pablo scooped Juan into his arms and Lupe followed them to their foreman's quarters behind the main house.

"*Buenos noches*," Nell called softly to them. She wondered where life would lead her as she watched stars rotate slowly overhead, dragging the night across her porch.

She rose and went into the house and sat next to Hester on the piano bench. "I learned to ride and rope and you learned to play Schubert and Chopin. What a pair we make."

***

NELL NODDED AT Billy who sat whittling at the barn door. His skin hung like worn out burlap around his face and neck. It gave him the weathered look of an old hound.

He returned her nod. "Right nice day to get started."

"Where are the others?"

Billy poked the air over his shoulder with his thumb. "Arguing over which mounts to use. Told 'em no matter, they all give saddle sores."

Billy followed Nell through the barn and out to the corral where Pablo was trying to convince Goose that Heller was the best choice for a brush popping horse. Thomas watched the arguing from the top rail of the corral.

"She's fearless," Pablo said. "Tough hide for getting whipped by low brush. She will keep you upright."

Goose scratched his chest and studied Heller's bony stance. "Maybe I don't want to go where she's tough enough to take me."

Nell approached the group. "Billy, see to it Goose has heavy chaps." She looked Goose in the eye and pointed to the horse in question. "That horse is your mount." She turned to Thomas. "Saddle Jingles for me and take your pick of the rest. Pablo, take Goose and Billy up the east-west ravine to Weaver's Draw, work the cattle east. Billy, you ride back down the ravine. Keep strays to the north of it. Thomas and I will start north and work south."

When Thomas shoved off the rail his legs collapsed underneath him like damp laundry. In his struggle to recover, he rolled over fresh horse dump. "Ah h-h-hell." He reddened, holding the shoulder of his shirt away from his body.

Goose chuckled. "Ain't you got bones, boy?"

The shadow of the live oak tree at the barn door had shortened a foot by the time roundup started. Nell and Thomas headed northwest toward the river. Pablo led Goose and Billy up the ravine that more or less divided Carrageen into north and south halves.

"Y'all didn't say nothing 'bout having a lady boss when we's talkin' roundup back in Kerrville," Goose bounced up and down with Heller's rough gait.

"Don't see it matters none," Billy said. "Miss Nell's been bossing roundup long enough to know how, I reckon."

At Weaver's Draw Billy found a little shade where he could whittle and wait a spell before heading back to turn strays trying to cross the ravine. Pablo and Goose fanned out and spotted the first group of cattle in thick grass.

Pablo remembered the great drought when he and Nell were too young to know how serious such things were. Samuel Miggins had to sell most of his cattle for next to nothing just to keep from watching them die of thirst and hunger. Great storms of static wind had blown dust swirls around the dry creek beds as if teasing the animals. His own father and other vaqueros stared at campfire flames, awestruck by the magnitude of Mother Nature's fickleness and wondered what would happen to them and their way of life if rain didn't come soon.

The thought struck Pablo just now that the drought had marked the end of an era. An uncertainty hovered in the air over Carrageen and though Nell never talked about it, he'd bet she felt it as well. She had relentlessly fought to hang onto her father's worn out dreams. Forming new plans to save the ranch seemed ridiculous given the problems she faced. Sure, things were turning for the better, like today with so many strong calves and the price for beef up, but change wasn't happening fast enough to do her much good.

Still, Pablo wished he could lighten Nell's uneasiness, see her free-spirited as she had once been before the drought and Samuel's death. She was like one of those strange blooming bushes whose flowers bloom a more faded color each year until they have no color at all.

Looking back over his shoulder, Pablo watched Goose head for a thicket of mesquite and brush. He would have to be mindful of Goose's whereabouts in case he got into trouble. Pablo worked in a crisscross pattern. Each time he came near the thicket he could hear breaking branches and thrashing in the brush. Goose let out a yell every now and then and a cow or two would come lumbering out of the brush. Pablo circled and worked them in with the rest.

Goose reached the end of the brush line ahead of Pablo and pulled Heller up to a halt. He hooked his right leg over the saddle horn to examine a hole in his chaps.

Billy came over a rise working three strays. He waved at Goose slumped in his saddle. Heller had her weight cocked over on one hip, lumps and bloody cuts up and down her legs. "Nary have I seen a more bedraggled pair," Billy said.

Goose shoved his hat back on his head and reached for his canteen with his missing-finger hand.

"Reckon how you lost them fingers?"

"Well sir, they's pinched off against my saddle horn where I had the end of my rope tied. I's ropin' me a real mean critter and grabbed a-holt my saddle horn to keep from fallin' off my mount when I throwed." Goose held up his hand and studied it. The last three fingers looked as if they had been chopped off at a clean, measured angle. "That old cow jerked just right and..." He looked back at Billy. "I's ridin' trail with a outfit outta Live Oak County some years back when it happ'ned."

They turned at the sound of hooves and watched Pablo herd a large number of cattle their way. Goose and Billy helped him turned them into a slow mill then gave rein to their horses while they drank from their canteens and ate cornbread and bacon from a cloth bag Lupe had prepared for each of them that morning.

The cool air was dry and dusty, for summer was a month away yet. Each man, Pablo, Billy, Goose, studied the hills in the distance and fell into a quiet trance of private thought as they chewed and sipped from canteens. Each had a history on horseback, living and working under blue expanses by day and silver-dusted blackness by night. A history of following the seasons without restraint and each, within their own mind, in their own words, marveled at their blessedness.

***

NELL AND THOMAS swung by the northwest tank to see if any cattle grazed on bermuda grass that grew in the moist soil around it. The windmill adjacent the tank stood like a frozen relic with blades, some of them broken or missing, straining in the breeze. Water hadn't been pumped into the tank for at least a month. What little bit there was looked like chocolate mud. Samuel swore this tank and windmill had kept the ranch going time and time again during long dry spells.

A terrible thump and screech noise vibrated the ground near the base of the windmill.

Nell called out to Thomas. "See if there's any oil left in the can up on the platform."

Thomas walked his horse over to the windmill, dismounted and stood leaning back with his neck craned skyward. Nell watched him with amusement. He lowered his chin to his chest for a moment before starting up the windmill.

She recalled the day thirty years ago when Ramirez, Pablo's father and Samuel, her father had stood in that same place, at the high end of the rincon. She and Pablo watched and listened to their fathers envision a water tank. Ramirez told Samuel, "I build it for you *Señor*."

"A dam?" Samuel had asked incredulously. "I can't afford to have the materials shipped out this far."

"No need. I make live lime as in Mexico."

So Ramirez had begun, and each day for six weeks Nell and Pablo, twelve and eight years old, followed him on their ponies. He used a Fresno pulled by a team of horses to dig an enormous hole, "as big as as room," Nell had shouted to Pablo as they clopped along. Ramirez recruited help from idle cowboys, had them haul wood to fill the pit. He layered the wood with rock gathered from Weaver's

Draw, bounced back and forth from pit to draw in his wagon day after day. He worked as if in a methodical daze. Nell marveled at his patience, felt she and Pablo were invisible to him.

After layering wood and rock in his hole until it reached ground level, he poured kerosene over his labors and set it all on fire. For another week he continued to add rock and wood to his burning pit. At night Nell sat at her upstairs window, watching as low clouds reflected the fire's orange radiance. That the endeavors of such a small, quiet man could be seen so many miles away amazed her. She imagined Ramirez perched on a rock staring at his flames as if spellbound, his face a magnified sphere glowing in the dark Texas night.

Nell and Pablo spent afternoons in the top of a tall cottonwood tree next to the rincon watching cowboys haul rocks and sand from the draw to be mixed with the resulting lime from the pit. The cowboys grumbled, complained that they'd rather shoe horses or mend fences, not dig a well. But Ramirez ignored their complaints and continued to give instructions in his hushed, gentle way. Over time a dam took shape across the rincon, an accomplishment Nell thought equal to the pyramids of Egypt she read about in a big book in her daddy's office.

Then a windmiller came with a wagon load of lumber to build a windmill tower. The enormous cypress bladed wheel eeked and screeched in a breeze until the gears were oiled and worn to a settled whur-r-rum, whur-r-rum. Nell asked if she could climb up to the big platform. Samuel had told her, "No! Never! Much too dangerous."

But she had climbed to the platform anyway. Often. Not even Pablo knew she did it. Something magical compelled her to go up there, to look down on the land to see as a bird sees, or God.

The windmill beckoned her back time and time again to watch cloud shadows spill over Carrageen like ink. It had always seemed odd that when the shadows passed over her, like gray veiled secrets, she felt changed. Even more odd was that no one ever seemed to notice.

Thomas called down from the tower. "Miss Nell, this here ladder has some mighty loose rungs."

"Never mind it." She motioned him down.

"From the sound of that racket, the problem ain't at the top anyways. It's them pipes down in the ground." He wiped his sweaty face on the arm of his shirt.

They mounted and rode toward the Guadalupe River. At a bluff on the south bank they separated to work cattle to an imagined line between them.

An edginess buzzed Nell's head like a bug around candle flame. She could give up and sell the ranch. But she was certain the memories would never leave her be.

***

TWO DAYS LATER, outside the barn in the dim light of dawn, Carrageen's outfit prepared for the last day of roundup. Pablo drew a line in the dry dirt while the others watched. "We ride west to this ridge. Goose, you go south to the road, work the cattle north."

"Is there any fencing?" Goose asked.

"Just mesquite and very rocky. We meet here." Pablo drew an X in the dirt and circled it.

Goose looked pained. "Mesquite, you say?"

"Stay away from the bluff along here."

"Why's that?"

"No cattle there, my friend. Too many big cats."

"Mountain lions?"

The back door to the ranch house opened and a shaft of yellow light blinked across the yard at the men gathered around Pablo. Lupe stood in the doorway handing Nell cloth bags. Nell crossed the yard, greeted the men with a silent nod and gave each a bag. Billy led Jingles through the barn door and handed her the reins.

After the first day of roundup Pablo had suggested Billy stay behind to keep an eye on the holding pens. He had three motives for the suggestion. One: It was the best way he could think of to let Billy take it easy and yet save his pride. The old man would never refuse to ride no matter how hard it was on his brittle old body. Two: Lupe, tired as she was lately, could use an extra pair of hands around the place. And three: The Mexican bandit situation bothered him. They'd all be safer with Billy there to help watch for trouble.

A mile west of the corral the group separated. Nell and Thomas rode south while Pablo and Goose continued west.

Pablo spurred his horse into a high lope, anxious to get the work of the southern half of the ranch behind him.

At noon Goose circled the cattle, whistling and calling as he went, while Pablo ate in his saddle and watched for Speckles in the herd. Speckles was the longhorn bull Samuel had purchased from a rancher on the Gulf Coast years ago. The bull had been in a steady decline for some time now, and Pablo hoped he wasn't a heap of bleached bones lying among the rocks somewhere.

Later in the day, Pablo met up with Nell as she worked her bunch of strays toward Thomas. "Any sign of Speckles?" she called.

"None," he yelled back.

Nell waved her arm in a wide arch signaling an area she wanted checked. Pablo walked his horse around huge boulders and down into shallow canyons and gullies in the direction Nell had pointed.

The two met up at the end of the ridge. Nell sighed. "Let's give it up for now."

"*Sí*. Maybe tomorrow Speckles, he will show up at the holding pens looking for his cows."

"I hope so. I don't know which I'd dread most, another day in the saddle or giving up and not knowing if Speckles is dead."

Pablo studied her face, surprised that she begrudged the thought of being in the saddle for another day.

"It's knowing this will be the last roundup," Nell said. "And knowing how proud Daddy would have been. Makes it hard."

"Why not ride the bluff back? Maybe we will find him yet." Pablo knew Nell had talked to Grady about selling the ranch. It was all he could do to keep from begging her to reconsider. As far as he was concerned it was a half-cocked notion so he tried to change the subject any time it came up.

Nell turned Jingles and rode the ridge line while Pablo headed into the ravine that paralleled it. After a short time, Pablo pulled his horse to a halt to listen, thinking he'd heard something. He motioned to Nell that he would make a loop down behind a wall of tumbled boulders.

Midway he paused, tried to remember if she was wearing her holstered pistol. Would he ever feel comfortable allowing her to remember on her own to arm herself when she was out on the range like this? She had faced many dangers with him and her father and still continually had to be reminded to wear a holstered gun.

He heard the sound again, a cow blowing and bawling, and so hoarse he hardly recognized it was a cow. He finally spied the cow nervously pacing off a half circle around a deep gully. Then he heard the weak nasal cry of a calf from the gully itself and kneed his horse to get a closer look. Beyond a rock ledge he could see the calf, about a week old, in a pit formed by tumbled boulders. Apparently it had slipped and fallen while trying to keep up with its mother. It was lying on its side, weak and barely able to answer the cow's pleas.

The cow pawed the ground and tried to charge when Pablo attempted to dismount. He slapped at her with his hat and gave a fierce yell. She fled in a gallop with her full bag slapping her legs as she went. About fifteen yards away, she turned and stared at him, blinking and bawling.

Nell caught up to Pablo as he was lowering himself into the pit by a rope he had looped on his saddle horn. "Pour little one needs mama, eh?" He cooed down to the starving animal.

Nell dismounted. "Is it hurt?"

"Hungry is all, I think." Pablo made a loop in the end of his rope before letting it hang free then examined the calf.

"He's surely Speckles'," Nell called down. "Look at his markings."

Pablo gently stroked the calf, cooing in Spanish, and scratched its flaky head. The calf was too weak to protest. "Let's get some milk for you, eh, little one?" Pablo lifted the calf to his hip then hooked the toe of his boot in the loop at the end of his dangling rope. He squinted up at Nell and nodded.

She led the horse slowly away from the pit, hoisting Pablo and the calf up. He used his free foot to kick away from the rock facing. At the top, Nell rushed to grab the back of his belt and helped him over the edge. He unhooked his boot from the rope and laughed when the calf's struggles knocked both of them off their feet.

Suddenly his horse reared and took off scrambling over the rocks. Nell's horse did the same thing on the opposite side of the pit. Before either of them could get to their feet a scream pierced the air. The sound vibrated up and down the ravine with chilling clarity.

"Mother of God!" Pablo struggled with the calf still clutched under his arm. He clamped his hand over the calf's muzzle. A mountain lion crouched on a rock ledge at eye level less than horseshoe-throwing distance away.

"My gun, slowly," Pablo whispered.

Nell reached to ease Pablo's gun free of the holster.

The big cat hissed at the cow and gave Nell such a scare she jerked and dropped the gun. It bounced once then slid into the pit.

"*Carajo!*" Pablo swore through gritted teeth. "Your gun?"

"In my saddle bag."

"*Ay-e-e, carajo!*"

The mountain lion crouched lower, glared at them. The cow trumpeted an agonized plea but continued to stay well away. They were trapped by the pit on one side and a steep rocky slope on the other. Nell squeezed Pablo's arms, leading him to inch backward up the slope. "Pablo?"

"Mother of God." He shook his head slowly.

"Pablo, you have to let it go."

"How many times, *hermana*, have I said..."

"Put – the calf – down." Nell's voice cracked with fear.

Pablo shook his head no. He struggled to think of another solution.

The mountain lion licked its slimy mouth, grinned into a pant, then slowly stood and lowered its head.

"Now!" Nell gasped.

Pablo slipped the calf to the ground and scrambled backward up the steep slope. Nell grabbed his shirt collar, half guiding, half pulling him up behind her as she clawed over the rocks. Blind horror drove them to endure pain in their ankles and knees as they slipped and righted themselves in one motion over and over again until they reached the top of the ridge.

When they looked back, the mountain lion had the calf's neck in its great jaws. The calf twitched pathetically, whined low and breathy as its life flickered away. Then the big cat dragged the lifeless form over rocks to a flat area where it turned, laid the calf down and stared back at them. It stood blinking and panting triumphantly for long minutes before locking its jaws on the calf's neck again to drag it out of sight.

Pablo jerked his hat from his head and threw it to the ground. "How many times do I say, wear the holster and gun?" He flushed with rage.

Nell sat down hard on the rocks and buried her face in her hands. Pablo stormed off, muttering in Spanish while the cow's hoarse cries echoed up and down the ravine.

***

IT TOOK PABLO half an hour to catch up to Jingles and another half-hour to find his own horse. Nell said nothing to him when he brought Jingles to her. She mounted and rode off due north as fast as the terrain would allow.

While it seemed to him that much had changed over the years, why, he wondered, couldn't Nell change and remember to carry a gun?

It was a fool thing she was doing, to sell the ranch. She told him she was tired. But he had asked Lupe once, "Why wouldn't Nell keep the ranch to return to from wherever it was she planned to go?" True, he understood her practical need for cash, and he agreed she needed a break from the pressure of trying to keep the ranch savable. But surely she could do a little traveling with the profits from this year's cattle sale or sell off smaller pieces of her land.

The thing he could never bring himself to discuss with Lupe was their future after the ranch was sold. With all the trouble in Mexico, he wouldn't think of returning to their families there. He supposed the United States Army would not have him since he was Mexican. And when he looked at Goose and Billy he knew that the way of life they had chosen was slow death by poverty, romantic though it seemed to a man like Goose to roam the country from Texas to Nebraska. Goose and Billy had no wife and child and could well afford to ignore the fact that their time had passed.

Nell, he thought, is in the same river with the rest of them, treading as hard as she can, hoping to find a handhold. The struggle she inherited was felt by everyone. Ah, but hadn't they enjoyed the good times as well?

Strong. That was Nell and she expected it of others. Today, hadn't she been the first to say that the calf would have to be let go to save them? A decision made harder for her, no doubt, because she could have saved the calf if she'd had her gun. He heard what people said about her behind her back. Even Hester thought Nell was pitiful and lonely, spending her days with the likes of him. Hester said it with her eyes, mostly, when Nell couldn't see.

Billy met up with Pablo at the corral. "Must a' been a hell of a ride, son. Nell looked 'bout as tuckered as you."

Pablo turned his horse loose with the rest of the remuda and hung his gear on a hook in the barn. He ambled across the way, passing Thomas and Goose who were hollering and splashing like kids in the water trough. In the foreman's house, Lupe had several kettles of hot water on the stove for his bath. She stood by with a towel and soap while he poured the water in the tub.

He pulled his shirt off over his head. "How long is it that Nell is back?"

"Not long. There was trouble?"

Pablo stepped into the tub, waved the question away. Lupe rubbed his neck and back with a sudsy cloth. The scars from the stranger's quirt were still angry and red.

At twilight Nell came out of the house to join everyone gathered around a table Billy had fashioned from sawhorses and some old planks he found in the barn. Lupe had cooked an enormous pot of beans and baked four loaves of bread while Billy watched over a slab of beef cooking on an open pit. Pablo occupied Juan on his lap while Lupe set plates around the table.

"Forgive me." Nell said as she walked over to where Pablo sat. She stood so close to him and spoke so low that only he could hear. "I should have had my gun holstered on my hip. I put us both in danger and—"

"I should have reminded you. I should have had you stand guard, *hermana*."

***

SKIN WATCHED MIST rise up from the Rio Grande and hummed "Jeanne With the Light Brown Hair" quietly to himself while waiting for the professors to wake up. His mind went back to wondering where his life had taken a bad turn.

The more he thought about it, the more he thought it was the day his keen nose led him to find out about Uncle Jeb and his mama. Uncle Jeb, his daddy's brother, lived with them on a little dirt farm in the hills of northern Alabama. He was about thirteen when he, his two brothers and Lamar, his daddy, cut out to hunt coons. Lamar stayed behind in camp on the east side of Dryer Hill saying he wanted to have a snort or two and keep the fire a goin'.

In his mind, just now, Skin could see Lamar sitting by that fire like it happened yesterday. He hadn't been surprised to find Lamar passed out cold when he got back to camp with the one coon he'd managed to shoot.

Skin spread his blanket, all full of holes, it was, beside Lamar and fell asleep waiting for his brothers. Next morning, just like always happened, the smell of the sun coming up over the hills woke him. His brothers and daddy were heaped in a pile and he could tell his brothers had drunk themselves senseless and passed out same as Lamar. Skin figured they'd be a long time sleeping it off, so he struck out for home alone, hoping his mama would have coffee going and if he was lucky, maybe even a piece of bacon.

Coming over the crest of the last hill home, and peering down into the holler at their shabby little house with the scraggly garden out back, he could see a wisp of smoke trailing from the chimney, which meant his mama was up. He'd shot two rabbits about half way home and tied their hind legs to his belt loop with string. He could feel the last of their life's warmth through the thin cloth of his pants as he made his way down the hill. Skin had thought his mama was going to be real proud to have them to cook for supper.

He knew even then, when he was just a kid, how hard his mama's life was. He had overheard her talking to a neighbor lady one time. "It wouldn't have mattered if Lamar had a job or not, Junior was on the way so we married quick-like. I figured I didn't have time to think it over none."

And another time he saw his mama crying while she looked at a little piece of broken mirror. When he asked her why she was crying, she took to shaking her head and cried all the harder. He'd thought at the time that he would like nothing better in the world than to fix whatever it was made his mama cry.

Before reaching the porch with his dead coon and rabbits that morning, he heard a banging noise out behind the hen house. Thinking it was a possum, he'd eased his coon to the ground, but left the rabbits tied to his belt loop. He slipped up to the hackberry tree, dropped a plug in his gun and listened. Whatever was making the banging noise was a sight bigger than a possum, that was for sure. Inching forward again, with the rabbits swinging and tapping his leg, he hid behind the cistern and leaned out to get a better look.

It was his Uncle Jeb with his pants down around his knees bouncing his white ass up and down against his mama. She was leaning on the hen house pulling Uncle Jeb's face to her throat and kind of gurgling soft-like.

Skin recalled how he'd torn out running for the hills, didn't stop till he got all the way to Simpson Creek where he fell on his knees to splash cool water on his face. When he straightened, the little rabbits were staring up at him with dead eyes, blood a-dripping from their gaping mouths. He used his skinning knife to cut the rabbits free, then watched them float away down the creek.

Not long after that he just up and left. Maybe he should've stayed. Shot Uncle Jeb or took his mama away from there. Brought her here to Texas. Hell, he was just a kid then and all that was so long ago he doubted any of 'em were still alive.

***

HENRY PROPPED HIMSELF up onto his elbow, and strained to pull his brain out of a confused, exhausted sleep. Skin Harris sat across a camp fire humming, of all things.

"I smelled it," Skin said.

"Smelled what?" Henry sat up. Everything hurt, his shoulders, neck, everything.

"The sun." Skin blew on a stack of twigs to coax a smoky flame under the coffee pot. "I got a nose like a bloodhound."

Henry reached over to touch Scottie's chest.

"He's still alive," Skin said. "Lost a lot of blood though. Best get him to some doctoring quick as we can."

Scottie stirred, flickered his eyes open and then closed them again without focusing on anything.

Jim rolled over and sat up. His face was swollen and red splotched. Skin handed him a cup of coffee. Jim shook his head.

"Best take it, son. You look like you could use a little hair on your chest 'bout now." Skin shot Henry a side-glanced grin.

Henry wiped his forehead with a neckerchief then held it over his nose. Damn, if the big barrel-chested fellow claims he can smell so good, why in the hell can't he smell himself? The odor reminded Henry of rotted animal hide in a lab at the university.

The man looked familiar but... "We're grateful for your help, Mister...what did you say your name was?"

"Harris. Skin Harris, scout for the United States Army, at your service."

Henry choked on his coffee. So much had happened and so fast that he failed to connect this smelly buffoon with the one in the street back in Wishing. How could he have missed it?

"Ah, well, thank you, Mr. Harris."

"Call me Skin."

"Mind if I ask what you're doing in this remote area?"

"Ever'where out here is remote case you haven't noticed. Let's just say I'm doing my job."

"Scouting for the army? Can you arrange an escort—?"

"We'd best get a move on." Skin stood, scratched his crotch. "Don't reckon your friend there is gonna last too much longer iffen we tarry." Skin threw the dredges of his coffee on the fire. Henry did the same, glad the big smelly man was willing to take charge.

They layered blankets on the bed of the wagon then Skin lifted Scottie up to Henry and Jim. They left the camping gear behind, taking only Henry's notes, drawings and maps he'd made of the pictograph site. Henry hoped that by traveling light, they could travel faster. Scottie's condition was very fragile.

Henry wrapped the jade trinket in his neckerchief and tucked it inside his shirt. He was as scared as he had ever been. But the figurine was so great a find that surely nothing could get in his way now. Scottie would recover, Henry was sure, and would be there to help him contend with university hierarchy when the time came to fund an expedition to Mexico.

Skin drove the wagon while Jim stayed in the wagon bed with Scottie. Henry rode mounted, carrying the lead for two horses. They would need them if they were attacked again.

They pushed ahead all day and into the night, pausing only long enough to rotate positions. At midnight, with the full moon turning the flats and cacti silver, Skin called to Jim who was driving and told him to get some sleep. Henry tied his mount to the wagon and joined him.

By dawn Skin's chin lolled atop his big thick neck. He twitched awake in time to keep from falling off the wagon seat. He squinted at the horizon. "Hey, mister! Wake up! There!" He stood and pointed. "I knowed I saw a house out this a'way. See yonder?"

Henry was so drained of strength that he no longer felt whole but he managed to follow the direction of Skin's pointed finger out to a green bulge of land half way to the horizon. Skin slapped at the team of horses. The wagon lurched, waking Jim who pulled to his knees to look over Skin's shoulder.

They crossed a road that Henry assumed was the same one they'd taken from Wishing, but he couldn't recall seeing a house. But then he'd been so intent on his expedition that he hadn't been aware of much else. This venture, he hoped, would give him the fame he wanted. There simply had been too much on his mind to notice anything else.

They approached a stand of trees that opened up to vistas of green rolling range land that sloped behind and to either side of a large house. Henry had to lean out to see around Skin's stinking bulk.

Skin suddenly reined the team to a slow trot.

"What the hell are you doing?" Henry craned his neck further to see around Skin. Two horsemen were riding full speed toward them. In the distance behind them, Henry made out a few men standing around a barn. Then he heard a popping sound and saw a puff of smoke come from the lead horseman. Rifle shots.

"Horse shit." Skin reined in the team. They were less than a quarter mile from the house with the horsemen bearing down on them. Another pop and puff of smoke.

"Looks like they're firing overhead. That's good isn't it?" Henry asked.

"I figure they think we could be trouble. They's just being careful is all. Lettin' us know they're armed. Don't do nothing to spook nobody."

The lead rider slowed to a trot and called out, "Sorry to be inhospitable but I need to know your business before you come any closer. Been lots of outlaw trouble lately."

Henry was taken aback. The rider was a woman.

"Ma'am, we got us a hurt man here," Skin yelled.

The woman slowed her horse to a walk then stopped, and lowered her gun slightly. Her eyes, partially hidden in the shadow of her hat brim, narrowed, her face hardened. "I'm afraid you've come begging at the wrong gate, you big worthless bag of buffalo bile." She fired at the ground a few feet from the team of horses.

Skin yanked on the reins when the animals tried to bolt. He managed to turn them in a tight circle. Henry and Jim ducked over Scottie to keep him from bouncing when the wagon lurched.

"Now there's no count for that, Miss," Skin said. "We just need some food and water. Medicine if you got any. Then we'll giddy-up and be on our way to Wishing..." His voice cracked and faded to a whisper. "Well I'll be a son of a bit—"

"What in the Almighty is wrong now?" Henry said trying to free himself of Scottie's blanket. When he got to his feet behind Skin, he was looking down the barrel of the woman's rifle. He recognized her immediately as the same woman who had fought Skin in the street back in Wishing. Henry raised his hands to show neutrality. "He's right," he said quickly. "I'm Henry Burleson, professor of archaeology at the University of Chicago. My colleagues and I were attacked by outlaw bandits when this, ah...ah," Henry motioned to Skin, "gentleman rescued us."

He felt foolish with his hands in the air like a criminal. He was sure he must look like Skin's counterpart, not having shaved or washed for days. He cautiously lowered his hands glancing quickly at the man with her – the Mexican she had helped that day in town. He was holding a rifle against his shoulder and had it aimed at his head. A stretch of silence.

"M-my colleague here has been shot." Henry indicated the bed of the wagon. The woman kneed her horse, moved closer, but, like the Mexican, kept her rifle pointed at them. Henry pulled the blanket back from Scottie's bleeding shoulder. She exchanged a lengthy gaze with the Mexican. Henry couldn't read what passed between them.

She looked back at him. "Throw out all your guns, "Professor...?"

"Henry Burleson."

"Mr. Burleson, you ride on the wagon seat with your hands up."

Skin threw his gun and holster to the ground while Henry and Jim dug around the blankets for the others. Henry climbed onto the seat next to Skin.

"Take it real slow," she told Skin then rode behind the wagon with her rifle tucked under her arm. At the gate she told Skin to stop and wait.

She walked her horse over to the barn and pointed back at them as she talked to the men there. Henry wondered how, out of all this wide-open country, how had they managed to end up here with that woman and Skin Harris facing each other down?

"Mr. Burleson, what's going on?" Jim whispered.

"Maybe our esteemed scout here can answer that question."

Skin snapped his head around to face Henry. "What are you talking about?"

"I'm talking about you and that woman in the middle of the street back in Wishing."

Jim's eyes bulged. "Hey, now I remember! Yeah, she nearly broke your foot. We watched from the walkway in front of the hotel."

The woman galloped back to the wagon. "Pablo Ramirez here is my ranch foreman." She nodded toward the Mexican. "He'll retrieve your guns and return them when you leave. It's unfortunate, Professor Burleson, that you keep such company." She cut her eyes over at Skin. "I'm afraid I have to insist this man camp outside the gate."

"I didn't exactly have time to be choosy about my traveling companion, Miss."

"My name is Nell Miggins and this is my home, Carrageen Ranch. But all this can wait until later. We need to see to your friend." She turned back to Skin. "Pablo will show you where to camp."

"Yes, ma'am." Skin deflated like a big hot air balloon in descent. He climbed down from the wagon, untethered his horse and followed the Mexican on foot.

At the house Miss Miggins called orders to an elderly man. Before Henry could climb down from the wagon, Scottie was being carried inside by two cowboys. A young Mexican woman with a long braid down her back tugged at his sleeve and motioned that he and Jim should follow her. She pointed to the end of a big hall, speaking hurriedly with a heavy Mexican accent.

"Lupe has food for you," Miss Miggins called down from the stairwell where she had led the men carrying Scottie. Henry couldn't believe she was dressed head to toe in men's clothes.

"You go on ahead," he told Jim, then climbed the stairs two at a time. From the landing he could see into all the rooms upstairs. They carried Scottie into a room with a big double bed in the center, bunk beds along one wall and a single bed along the third wall. After the men lowered Scottie onto the double bed, Miss Miggins withdrew scissors from a basket and began to cut away his blood-soaked shirt. "Thomas, bring me warm water. Make sure Lupe has plenty on the stove." One of the men left the room.

"Goose, see if Pablo needs help." She pushed Scottie over to his side to look at the exit wound on his back.

"Take his boots off," she ordered without looking up.

Since no one else was left in the room, Henry assumed she was talking to him. "Is there a doctor who can see to him?"

"It'll take a while to get word to town. Meantime, we better see what we can do ourselves." She looked up at him. Her features were plain but their particular arrangement was striking, wide spaced eyes and a deep nave on her full upper lip.

"His boots, Mr. Burleson." She resumed cutting away Scottie's shirt. "You say this man is your colleague?"

"And friend. We were attempting to find evidence that Spanish explorers had Mayan captives with them while roaming up and down the Rio Grande." Henry let Scottie's boot fall to the floor then struggled with the other one.

"Treasure hunting?" She paused with the scissors in mid-air.

"Hardly."

Thomas burst through the door with a pitcher of water in one hand and a full bucket in the other. "Miss Miggins, Lupe, she's not doing too good. She's gone white as a ghost in the kitchen."

"You see to heating water then and send her home." When he wheeled around for the door she added, "And tell Billy I need him." She gently pressed Scottie's ribs. "Looks like the bullet splintered a rib. I'm not sure about his lung." She spoke to herself more than to him. As she washed Scottie's grimy neck and chest, Henry felt ill at ease, like he shouldn't be watching. She washed his shoulders, arms, and throat, pausing now and then to rinse the cloth in clean water. With a dry cloth she patted his entire upper body, then to Henry's utter puzzlement, pressed her lips to Scottie's eyelids. When she drew back a little, Scottie flickered his eyes and called out for Priscilla.

Miss Miggins whispered "yes" then pressed her lips to his temple. Henry was feeling uncomfortable as hell with the familiarity this peculiar woman displayed but was too intrigued to say anything or turn away. She seemed almost otherworldly in the soft patterned light that filtered through the lace panel covering the window.

When she turned her face to him, he blurted out. "What are you doing?"

"Lips sense heat better than fingers. And fever is better felt on the eyelids and temples than on the forehead. Who's Priscilla?"

Henry got lost in her intrigue. "What?"

"Are you all right?"

"Uh, yes." He slumped into a chair beside the bed. "His wife. She died a while back."

"He has a fever, an infection." She rummaged in the basket again and pulled out a blue stone. She scraped it with the tip of the scissors over a small porcelain bowl then mixed the resulting powder with some sort of oil.

"This is copper sulfate for the infection. It's all I can do until the doctor comes." She motioned to Henry to roll Scottie to his side then smoothed the medicine over and into the wound on his back. She leaned so close Henry could see brown flecks in her green eyes. She glanced up and spilled some of the blue salve on the bed clothes. Henry had a feeling he was the first person, and a stranger no less, in her home for a long time. And perhaps the first man to look at her closely in many years.

The old man he'd seen outside earlier shuffled into the room. Miss Miggins introduced him as Billy and explained to him what she'd done for Scottie. Billy seemed to have had quite a bit of experience with bullet wounds from the way he probed and pushed on Scottie's ribs. He told her that she had done all she could for Scottie.

Miss Miggins wiped her hands on a clean cloth. "I want you and Thomas to ride to town and tell Doctor Copeland we need him as soon as he can get out here."

"What about the cattle, Missy? Don't you need Thomas here?"

She shook her head, shrugged, and let her arms flop to her sides. "I don't think we can risk anyone riding that far alone. You see what's happened to this man. Lupe isn't well. Pablo needs to see to her and Juan. That leaves me and Goose." She continued to shake her head. "The best thing to do is have Goose keep the cattle quiet until things settle down."

"We've imposed on you at a bad time, haven't we?" Henry leaned back in the chair. He felt faint.

"As the Mexicans say, Mr. Burleson, *no hay remedio*. There is no other way." She'd said it in a kind way but Henry sensed she found their situation as troubling as he did.

Thomas banged his way up the stairs with more hot water. Miss Miggins met him at the landing where Henry overheard her tell him to fill the bath tub. Then she fetched clean towels from a large oak cupboard in the hall. She hurried into one of the other rooms, returning with an armful of men's clothes. Henry was aware of her hurrying back and forth but was not able to keep track of her intentions. His peripheral vision was shrinking. He felt fuzzy headed, exhausted.

***

LONG EVENING SHADOWS stretched across the garden outside the kitchen window where Nell stood washing dishes. The sun, low in the west, turned everything in her view the color of tiger lilies. Incredible how a day could change so quick. Two strange men sleeping in her house, one on the verge of death.

She watched Thomas lead the boy named Jim from the tank house below the windmill to the bunkhouse where he would sleep with the cowhands. She had a feeling the arrangement appealed to Jim who looked more like a lost child than young man.

Billy and Thomas had returned from Wishing to report that Doctor Copeland wouldn't start out for the ranch until the next day. He was keeping watch over the preacher's daughter who had appendicitis and if he had to operate, he'd be even longer. Nell felt there wasn't much more to be done for Professor Scott anyway. His recovery would depend on his fortitude. Unfortunately he seemed, along with Mr. Burleson, to be short on fortitude. "Greeners." She heard Billy describe them. "Probably couldn't cut a lame steer from a tree."

Jim explained a few details of their attack to Thomas. Seeing the Buffalo Soldier with his throat slashed, horribly murdered, would have been difficult for hardened men, but for these three it had been enough to send them into shock.

Skin Harris told Pablo he had come upon them just in time. But could such a man be trusted to tell the truth? Nell felt bad, now when she thought about it, that she had Pablo escort him to a campsite away from the ranch. She should have been more sensitive to Pablo's position and had Goose do it.

When Nell finished getting the kitchen in order she dried her hands and walked through the dark hall to the porch. The flame of sunset had died away leaving the house blanketed and dark. She dropped into one of the rocking chairs and thought, suddenly, of her father.

"You gonna be all right, Missy?" Billy asked from the bottom porch step.

Nell was startled. "Billy? I didn't see you."

"Goose is watching the cattle and them boys is sleeping like babies."

"Will you have Thomas relieve Goose in a few hours?"

"You bet."

"Better get some rest yourself then."

Billy pushed himself up and gimped his way across the yard, disappearing into the blue darkness. Nell could hear Goose in the distance intermittently whistling to the cattle then blowing a sweet melody on his harmonica. "Thank the Lord," she whispered out loud. "At least the cattle are settled and quiet."

Fatigue paralyzed her body but her mind whirled with worry. How was she to carry on with the job of getting the cattle sorted, ear-notched, branded and sold with a strange man dying in her house? How could she ask Pablo to leave Lupe, who seemed so ill, to help with the cattle? And what was she to do about the other professor, Henry Burleson?

Life had played a trick on her. Nell was sure of it. Who would have dreamed she would see the man with the pocked face ever again? The same man who, along with his companions had checked into the hotel the day she sat reading Hester's letter. At one time in her life she would have been pleased to meet a fascinating, educated man like Henry Burleson. She blushed with private embarrassment now, remembering that she let the bowl of salve go all askew when she looked up and realized he was so close and staring.

And what a jarring thought that the three men, from Chicago of all places, should be rescued by none other than filthy Skin Harris, and that all four men were here unannounced.

Nell left the porch, made her way up the dim stairway to her room where she lit a lamp and washed in its meager light before sitting down to write Hester. In the letter she told of her plans to trail the cattle to Wishing where they'd be shipped to Fort Worth by rail. She would sell all but a few to use for brood stock, in case a buyer interested in the ranch requested it.

If all her plans held, she would travel to the Seasider Hotel at Tres Palacios on the Gulf Coast. She'd read about the hotel in an Austin newspaper. The advertisement said the hotel had the longest gallery in the United States. A grand pavilion built over the water drew vacationers and investors from all over the country. Since the train to the coast went directly through San Antonio, Nell wrote, she would stop for a short visit with Hester and her family on her way.

Nell added some details about repairing the ranch house and windmill in preparation for putting the ranch up for sale. But she didn't mention the four strangers who had descended on her that day. Hester could be so tiring and would only hound her to death for taking strange men into her house.

She sealed the letter and propped it against a vase. Then she wrote the Seasider Hotel and enclosed a check on deposit for a room with a view of the bay and pavilion. When Dr. Copeland came out she would ask him to mail them for her and then pray that all her troubles would be cleared away in time for her travels.

Robed, barefoot, and carrying an oil lamp, she moved across the upstairs hall to the room where the professors slept. Their room was hot with the heavy dampness of perspiring bodies. She held the lamp over Mr. Scott. His fever raged. She opened a window and washed his face with cool water, but he writhed with pain when she tried to bathe his wounds. She repacked them with fresh salve and continued to bathe his face and neck. He turned to her, rolled his eyes against burning lids, and called for Priscilla again.

She washed her hands and walked over to Mr. Burleson sleeping in the bed along the far wall. She watched his ribs expand and contract. Light from the lamp turned his skin gold except for the shadowed pockmarks on his angled jaw. It made him appear rugged. A false image? An archaeologist? Somehow he seemed to belong somewhere in Egypt or Africa paying respectful visits to dead kings or pharaohs in the sand dunes along the Nile. Not Texas.

She reached a hand to his face. Just as her fingers brushed his brow, Mr. Scott groaned and thrashed fitfully across the room. She jerked back, relieved that Mr. Burleson hadn't awakened. She rushed to quiet Mr. Scott with a cloth to his forehead. He seemed quieter with her close so she went to her room across the hall to get her grandmother's diary to read while sitting with the professors. She had found the diary along with a pair of lace gloves the week of Hester's visit, when they'd climbed up into the attic to see what needed to be cleared away before the ranch was sold.

When she entered her room, fire light outside the window caught her attention. At first she thought it was a brush fire then remembered Skin Harris was camping beyond the gate. Stepping closer to the window, she could swear shadowy figures moved back and forth in the fire light. She turned from the window and grabbed the diary off her bedside table, admonishing herself for inventing problems.

Back across the hall, she pulled a chair close to the lamplight and read her grandmother's words that had been inked a full generation before she was born. Her grandmother had started the journal as a young bride, deeply in love with her husband and enchanted by the wilds of Texas where he'd brought her to live.

***

SKIN WATCHED THE ranch house and countryside fade in the dimming twilight. The house looked yellow, then red, and then blue, like a magic fairy tale house. He reckoned it would be right fancy to live in a house. An honest-to-god home with people who knew you and where you came from and what your worries were. Someday, he thought. Someday.

It had been a mighty long time since he left his mama. Even though he was full growed now, and then some, he just wanted to be like everybody else. He poked the fire, watched smoke curl.

He hummed "Bringing In the Sheaves," a hymn the old preacher's wife near Birmingham had taught him that time he nearly died of starvation. Fact was, the woman – mean as a snake she was – had given him one helluva gift in teaching him to sing. Got him through some hard times. Like now, singing low and soft took his fear and loneliness away. Other times when he pushed the notes up from the soles of his feet, it gave him courage and strength. Yessirree. Singing put sound to what was in his heart.

Night eased up on the big house. One by one lamps were lit and moved from room to room. Even the bunkhouse windows had a glow in them.

Then one by one the lights went out, making the house look like it was closing its eyes. When black night surrounded him, Skin untethered his horse and rode northwest. He figured it wouldn't do him no harm to do a little scratching around. Sooner or later, God willing, Ol' Skin Harris was gonna get a little more out of life than lonely campfires and lice.

He made his way slow, singing hushed and whispery. "Let Your light shine bright tonight, Oh Lord, and in the dawning." He gave his horse ample time to find good footing in the darkness, surveyed the sky and made a note of the position of the stars. He wanted to be sure he made it back to camp before daylight.

***

TINKER CROSSED THE bridge into Wishing and found the sheriff leaning against a post in front of the jail house. When he told the sheriff what had happened at the Taylor place he removed his hat and shook his head. "Good family. An awful shame. Taylor has kin east of here. I'll let them know."

Tinker couldn't think of more to say. Though he knew "an awful shame" wasn't enough. A whole family wiped out for hate and a few cows.

The sheriff put his hat back on. "Just so you know to keep a keen eye, I'm hearing stories about the Garza boys. Half brothers, Cornelio and Antonio. Connie, the oldest wears a huge sombrero.

Saddle has enough stolen silver on it to fund this town's budget for a
year. Andy is just as ruthless, even though he looks like a momma's
boy."

Tinker thanked the sheriff for the warning and headed to the
livery stable where Mr. Parker handed him a list of inquiries. "The
Miggins ranch foreman was in town not long ago asking about you."

Tinker glanced over the list. A couple of jobs right here in
town. "I don't remember stopping at the Miggins place before. Any
idea what kind of work they have for me?"

"Not sure. Used to be a dozen hands worked the place, but I
hear tell the Miggins woman is ready to sell out. Come to think of it
Pablo, her foreman, said something about a windmill."

Tinker tipped his hat to Parker and walked next door to
check in at the hotel. He ordered a hot bath, the one luxury he'd
missed when he left his old life behind in Galveston. Not that he
begrudged a slow, quiet soak in a creek. Fact was, when he first
struck out on his own, the solitude of the hills and savannas was
eerie as hell when he stripped off his sweaty clothes, as if he had
been doubly exposed. One kind of exposure from being naked and
another from being alone.

Eventually he had mastered the language of the land, a
language of vision and touch and sound. Like seeing wind knead
prairie grass, feeling it on his face, hearing the ground crunch under
wagon wheels, and coyotes calling at night. Given the choice he
preferred that kind of "talk" over the endless empty chatter of
people.

He used to wake up in the middle of the night, thinking he'd
heard the earth's heartbeat and for some reason, the thought helped
him come to terms with his implacable aloneness.

He leaned back in the tub of hot water. None of that meant
he liked being alone. He just happened to have a good grip on it.

He dressed in his best boiled city shirt and trousers and went
downstairs to get a bite to eat. Evening closed in on the little town as
he ate and watched the street from a window. From behind the
swinging doors of the saloon across the way he heard an out of tune

piano. Soldiers from a camp on the outskirts of town drifted in and out, no doubt looking for a game or two on corn husk mattresses with painted ladies and maybe a whiskey for the road back to camp. Most of them seemed like boys, about the age his own son would have been. William Owen Webb, dead for so long now.

Tinker pushed his chair back with a loud scrape, picked up his plate, and walked out a side door and across the alley to the livery. He found Jack on the wagon seat patiently waiting for his return. He gave the dog his scraps and rubbed his ears. "You stay put, boy. I'm sleeping in a bed tonight."

But nighttime brought earsplitting revelry from the saloon and in the end proved too much for him. Tinker got out of bed to pace. Damn town anyway. Been in open spaces too long, getting set in his ways. Maybe a drink would — to hell with it.

He jerked on his pants, tucked in his shirt, and smoothed down his hair that still showed some dark brown through the silver. Inside the smoky saloon he ordered a whiskey and leaned against the bar to watch a game of dominoes. Six men slumped around a gaming table, but only four were playing. The other two, wearing army uniforms, were passed out cold with their heads plopped forward on the table. The piano in the corner suffered under the talents of a large woman with a dyed ostrich feather in her hair. While she banged away, soldiers sang different versions of a bawdy song. Whores hung on their necks, laughing and poking.

Another young woman with hair the color of a rooster's comb, sauntered over to Tinker. "Can I interest you in a game of poker, Mister?"

"Just stopped in for a drink."

"Can't get nobody interested in poker." She leaned on the bar next to him. "Just that sissy domino game." She looped her arm around his neck. "Maybe I can interest you in a game upstairs?"

Tinker finished off the shot of whiskey, motioned for another before looking down at her. The whites of her eyes were yellow. "Like I said, just a drink."

He figured his passions were as strong as any man's but there was something about the smell of whiskey and cigars on a woman he just couldn't overlook. This was one time he wished the hell he could. When she moved away, he pulled a chair up to a sleeping domino player and anted up.

The large woman at the piano started singing about a cowboy getting shot in the streets of Laredo. A fool thing to do when most of your customers were soldiers headed for the border. The mood in the saloon turned somber after that and since the domino game was down to three uninterested players, Tinker figured he better get some sleep. On his way out of the saloon, he tipped his hat to the woman who had offered to entertain him upstairs. She sighed and watched him cross the street and enter the hotel.

***

HENRY FELT A sucking sensation on his brain. Something pulled on him, wanted him to leave the warm depths into which he'd sunk. It needled at the holes of his ears, trying to work him loose. A roar came from a long way off and the sound grew nearer, like the sound of a train coming. He heard voices within the roar. Women's voices. They were close, in the same room. The roar growing louder and louder. Finally, unable to stand the noise any longer he opened his eyes. The noise stopped immediately. He looked around the room.

Nell Miggins was standing over Scottie, talking to the Mexican woman. They moved about in soft light. Was it morning or evening? Henry couldn't tell. He closed his eyes again to think and then remembered. In the night, that woman, Nell Miggins, stood over him. He remembered smelling lavender. The same as when she leaned over Scottie to wash his wounds. She had appeared as a dream last night, moving soundlessly around the room, occasionally speaking to Scottie in that enigmatic alto voice. He opened his eyes again and remembered everything. A bath, clean clothes, food, collapsing into bed.

"How is he?" Henry asked the Miggins woman. The hoarse crackle of his own voice sounded odd.

Miss Miggins looked up. "Better, I think." The corners of her mouth tilted slightly. She moved around to the end of his bed. "Are you able to dress and eat downstairs or should I have Lupe bring food up to you?"

"I'm fine."

"Very well. I hope these will be sufficient." She motioned to a chair piled with clothes. "Yours will be washed today. We'll be downstairs if you need anything."

Henry sat up. "I can't remember. Is a doctor coming?"

"It may be afternoon before he gets here. Meantime, Lupe will try to persuade Mr. Scott to drink some honey water. Maybe you can help. He seems to be coming around."

Henry startled, jerked on the blanket covering his bed. "My clothes! I had a — "

She held up her hand to stop his panic and opened a small wooden box on the table beside his bed. "This fell out of the cloth you had inside your shirt."

Relief flooded Henry when she handed him the jade figurine. Miss Miggins and the Mexican woman she called Lupe left the room without another word.

By the time he dressed and made his way downstairs, the sun was high and hot. Lupe served his breakfast in a large dining room. She looked more relaxed, spoke English a little more clearly.

The house echoed with emptiness. Henry wondered where everyone had gone but didn't ask. After eating he walked across the hall to the parlor. An antiquated piano graced one corner of the large room. The furniture and rugs were clean but worn. Windows stretched from ceiling to floor with heavy velvet drapes pulled back so that sunshine flooded the room. Henry brushed at the faded fabric and experienced the same sense of mystery he had every time he held pieces of Mayan antiquity.

Outside the window, he saw Nell with a ledger of some kind in her hand. Pablo and the man she called Goose moved among the penned cattle on horseback. Billy and Thomas were rolling barrels into the barn. Even Jim seemed to be in on all the activity carrying buckets of some milky looking liquid.

"*Señor?*" Henry turned. Lupe was standing in the doorway with a tray. A little boy held the hem of her skirt in his tight fist. His gaze was unnerving.

"Would you like to help with your *amigo?*"

"Of course." He followed Lupe up the stairs. She was small with smooth skin the color of rich honey. Henry watched her hips sway under the sack-like peasant dress she wore, while a single long black braid tapped her backside with each stair step.

Scottie was very pale. Henry held the cup Lupe had handed him to Scottie's lips. "Here, old boy, you must drink something." Scottie rolled his glassy eyes open. He sipped and choked. Henry tried again, eventually getting a few swallows of the warm liquid down his throat. Henry told Lupe she could go, that he would stay with his friend.

Late that afternoon, dozing in the bedside chair, he heard voices on the stairway. Miss Miggins knocked once then entered the room with a cherub faced, bald-headed man. After introducing the man as Dr. Copeland, she excused herself and left. The doctor dug a pair of spectacles out of his bag, placed them on his nose and drew a deep, wheezy breath. He smelled like camphor.

"I'd say you came to the right place at the right time," the doctor said. "Not too many here 'bouts have the knowledge to see to your friend in such an efficient manner. Yes sir, Tita is the choice in many a pinch." He glanced at Henry over his glasses.

"Tita?"

"Miss Miggins. A nickname. Her daddy always called her that."

"Where is he?"

"Why, gone to the great beyond. Pushing up daises. Or, more likely, prickly pear cactus."

"Isn't there a man running this place?"

"No. Only Nell." The doctor pressed on Scottie's ribs.

"She's never married?"

The doctor shook his head. "Kind of sad really." He removed his glasses. "Chance just passed her by somehow."

Nell met Henry and Dr. Copeland as they came down the stairs. She invited them into the parlor where Lupe served coffee.

"Your friend is a lucky man," Copeland said. "The bullet not only missed the lung but exited his body. If I had to operate to remove a bullet, he more than likely wouldn't make it. Lost too much blood."

Nell passed coffee to Henry. "What about infection?"

"You already have that under control. But I'll leave you some poultices that may be a little better than what you're using."

"When can we return to Chicago?"

"I wouldn't try to move him for at least four or five days, seven or eight would be ideal." Dr. Copeland looked at Nell as if he needed her approval.

"Four or five days!" Henry couldn't keep the shock out of his voice. "But my work—" He stopped himself, not wanting to seem callous about Scottie's condition.

Nell sat forward. "Mr. Burleson, please don't be concerned about your welcome here."

"I don't understand. If his fever gets better, can't he be moved, at least to Wishing? I could use the telegraph there to notify the university of our circumstances."

"I took the liberty of having Billy report the raid on your camp to the sheriff," Nell said. "The sheriff contacted authorities in Austin who sent a message to your university by telegraph."

"You've been put out so much already." Henry stood and pushed his hands deep into his pockets as if to keep them still. "I feel we owe you our lives. I don't want to impose further."

"No imposition. Let's just do what we can for Mr. Scott."

When Doctor Copeland stood, Nell walked him to the hall where Henry overheard her ask him to mail some letters when he returned to town.

The doctor's voice echoed in the big central hall. "Grady tells me you plan to sell your spread, Nell. I assume it's no secret. Folks are going to be real disappointed."

"It was a hard decision."

"I wish you luck. Though I can't imagine this part of Texas without you."

"Sometimes I can't either."

"Here is the salve for Mr. Scott. And for you, I suggest rest. You look dreadful."

"As a matter of fact, one of those letters contains plans for a pleasure trip to the coast. I've never done anything like that, you know?"

"Good for you, Tita. Oh, by the by, I had a look at Lupe. She's fine, just fine. By September I expect she'll be delivering another baby, yessir."

"A baby!"

"You didn't know?"

"I've been so preoccupied with Hester's visit, the cattle and then the professors that, no, I'm ashamed to say, I didn't."

Their voices faded as they moved out to the porch. Henry crossed the hall to the stairs and seeing Lupe through the door to the kitchen, asked if she would tell Miss Miggins he would sit with Mr. Scott the rest of the afternoon.

Upstairs he paced. There had to be a way he could return to Chicago. Think, he told himself, think. He couldn't remain here for days with no contact with the university.

He paused at the window and leaned on the sill. Cattle were being moved, regrouped and sorted. How could anyone keep track of so many moving animals? For that matter, how could anyone tell one from another?

Henry felt a sour mood fester and grow. He had never been able to accept being trapped in a situation for any reason. He was sorry for Scottie, but— four or five days?

At twilight Pablo came into the room and asked Henry to dinner downstairs, but he was confused when Pablo led him out of the house toward a stand of trees.

"I hope you are comfortable with our informal way." Miss Miggins said when he approached a long table set up under the trees.

"Your hospitality is above reproach."

She was wearing a white blouse buttoned to her throat and a long skirt, a stark contrast to the trousers she'd worn since his arrival. Jim and Thomas, looking for all the world like life long friends, walked up from behind the barn.

Jim brightened when he saw Henry. "Mr. Burleson, is it true what Miss Miggins says, that Professor Scott is going to be all right?"

"Thanks to her kindness and expertise, yes." Henry flashed his best smile at her. She indicated a place for him to sit.

Over potatoes, cornbread, and beef steak, talk centered on cattle rustling stories. Old Billy seemed to think himself the expert storyteller, reminding Henry of Bob the Buffalo Soldier.

Billy stuffed his mouth with potatoes, swallowed hard. "When we's in town looking for the doc, all the talk was about the Garza brothers. Sheriff said the windmiller come up to the Taylor place in time to see a bunch of bandits high-tailing it back towards the border. Rustled a bunch of cattle to sell to Poncho Villa's army is what the sheriff thinks."

"The Taylors?" Nell seemed shocked, dismayed.

" 'Fraid so." Billy's face dropped. "Windmiller said they kilt the whole family. Sheriff said everybody ought to be on the lookout."

A silence traveled around the table.

Nell cleared her throat. "Mr. Burleson, you —"

"Henry, please. I insist."

She looked away and began again. "Henry, you said you and Mr. Scott are archaeologists studying the Maya?"

"That's right."

"I tend to associate archaeologists with Egypt or Africa.

Henry noticed tiny sun lines edging her eyes and a wisp of hair cupping her ear. "Have you read much about the Yucatán Peninsula or the Maya?"

"Almost nothing. My limited knowledge comes from an encyclopedia in my daddy's library. A great deal of mystery surrounds them. Is that right? Speculation about what happened to make them leave their great cities, to disappear?"

"You know more than the average citizen." Henry was impressed. "Little is known about them because their hieroglyphs, for the most part, remain un-deciphered. That is my particular field, Miss Miggins. Hieroglyphs."

"Nell. I insist." She smiled.

The next day, Henry woke to slamming doors, yelling and yelps. Lupe came into the room just as Henry pulled on his trousers. "What's going on?"

"Speckles, he came here in the night and all the cows go with him." Her little boy climbed on the end of Scottie's bed. Scottie watched him with blank eyes.

"Speckles?" Henry asked.

"*El toro*, the bull."

Henry looked out the window. Men were running here and there collecting rope, saddles, chaps. He saw Nell run into the barn, her long hair hanging loose down her back.

"Scottie, I'm going to go see if I can help down there. This lady will get you anything you need." Henry gave Lupe a questioning glance.

"*Sí*, is good," she said.

At the corral, Henry stopped Jim who explained a very old bull showed up during the night and enticed the cattle to lean hard enough on the rails to knock them down. The herd had followed him to parts unknown.

Henry placed his hands on his hips. "How do you suppose anyone knows that the bull was here during the night?"

"Nell overheard his question as she rode out of the barn. "By his hoof prints. He's done it many times."

"Oh. Lupe is with Scottie. Can I help?"

She turned in the saddle. "Billy, give Henry your mount. Lupe may need help with Mr. Scott." Then to Henry, "It could be hard riding."

"I need to get out of the sickroom."

When all the riders were assembled, Nell turned to Pablo with a nod. He said, "Three groups, two each." He indicated Henry with Nell, Thomas with Jim and Goose with himself. "Best to try tracking first since the ground is still with dew. Maybe we will get lucky."

Pablo led the way westward. A chilled dampness pressed against Henry's skin as he loped behind the others. They rode up and over a knoll of land, a river to his right, mist floating above it like a long snaking cloud. The horizon in the west was still dark.

They rode, increasing the distance between the three groups, in a fan pattern. Nell never took her eyes off the horizon. The others, riding to their right, were visible only in glimpses as they rode over the gently rolling land. Around mid-morning someone yelled from the left and a little behind them. Nell and Henry were confused since no one had ridden that direction. Before long a horseman leading an animal came into view. Pablo and Goose met up with Henry and Nell and convinced Nell they should go see who it was. Jim joined them and asked Henry if he thought it was bandits. But Nell answered for him. "I don't think there's much danger. Most aren't bold enough to ride out in the open like that."

The horseman turned out to be none other than Skin Harris. He had Speckles roped by his great span of horns.

Pablo grinned wide and looked back at Nell. "Fool thing to do."

Skin told them he had roped Speckles during the night when the bull trailed his harem of cows near his camp. He had been trying to drag the bull back to the corral ever since.

"I figured you'd have a easier time rounding up all them cows if you had a holt of him, beings how they like following him so much," Skin said. "He's gentle as a pup iffen I sing to him. Ol' boy likes opera. All his cows are off over thataway."

"You've saved us a lot of trouble," Nell said. Henry watched glances pass between Pablo, Nell and Skin.

"*Gracias*," Pablo said after a bit.

"Well, I reckon it's the least I could do after actin' like such a jackass 'fore this. Guess I's feeling full of myself back in town, getting to be a army scout and all." He slipped his hat off and smoothed the brim between his fingers.

Pablo interrupted the uncomfortable quiet that followed. "I suggest we free Speckles since many of us are here to haze the herd back."

Nell turned to Skin. "If you help us there will be a meal waiting for you at the ranch."

Skin stared at her as if he hadn't heard. His eyes narrowed then relaxed.

"Is something wrong?"

"Ah, hell. I mean, much obliged, ma'am. I...I...," he lost his tongue altogether and ended up shaking his head in silence.

Henry wondered if she hadn't made a terrible mistake. Thomas and Jim were already covering their noses with their neckerchiefs. Henry decided to position himself upwind of Skin Harris from then on.

While Pablo and Goose worked to free Speckles of Skin's rope, Nell said, "Once we find the rest of the herd, Thomas and Jim will ride point, Goose and Skin, drag. Pablo, one side, Henry and me on the other."

Henry found the work grueling. At times the dust was unbearable. If it wasn't blinding him, it was choking him. He saw Nell only occasionally since she rode a little behind him. Her flat brimmed slouch hat was pushed down low on her head and when she spurred her horse after a stray she seemed joined to it like a centaur. Her hair was still flowing free down her back.

She noticed him watching her and rode up to his side. "Are you worried about Mr. Scott?"

"No, no. I'm just watching the way all of you move the cattle. It's amazing."

"I'm sure I'd find archaeology equally amazing. Come with me, I want to show you something." She skirted the herd and waved a signal to Pablo who gestured something back. Nell halted and strapped a gun around her waist. "A precaution. We had a close call with a mountain lion recently."

He followed her into some pretty rugged looking country. When she slowed her horse to a walk at a dry creek bed she turned and tracked down the middle.

"Mind if I ask where we're going?" Henry called out.

"When we were children, Pablo and I roamed every square mile of this ranch. I'm taking you to one of our secret places. No one else knows about it." She paused to glance at him. "Since you're an archaeologist, you may find it interesting."

At a sharp turn of the creek bed, Nell dismounted and tied her horse to a low hanging branch. He did the same. They continued on foot until it seemed they were walking in a shallow canyon.

"There." She pointed up at a jagged rocky ridge.

Henry shaded his eyes with his hand but the sun still blinded him. He took his hat off and used it to shade his face. Nell had already climbed the rocks in front of him, unaffected by the heat and rough riding. She stopped, turned to look down at him. He wished to hell he could define what made her seem so reserved and self-contained one minute and a natural part of her surroundings next. The way she was now. The way she was the first time he saw her in the street in front of the hotel.

"See it?"

Henry followed her gaze. Above her were four faded stick figures painted on an overhanging rock shelf.

"I think this one is supposed to be a deer and this one…" Nell leaned back to see better. "What do you think?"

Henry chuckled as he climbed up beside her. "I can't believe this. And look here. A hand with a missing finger."

"Pablo and I always wondered about that. Did the painting fade or was it painted that way?"

"I believe it was painted that way. I recall reading somewhere that Lipan Indian women amputated their fingers."

"Whatever on earth for?"

"A way of mourning their dead husbands."

"Oh. And how did the men mourn their wives?"

Henry felt tricked, though the question was a logical one. "I have no idea." He sat next to her, leaned back to study the pictographs better. "These could be as old as a thousand years. You know that, don't you?"

She shrugged. "I haven't thought about time much. Until recently anyway."

Henry glanced over at her. The same wisp of hair that cupped her ear the night before now clung to the skin of her damp neck. Her head was thrown back, exposing her throat, white and close. He clamped his jaw teeth and drew a slow breath to steady the quivering in his gut.

***

NELL HAD SECOND thoughts as she carried a tray of food upstairs. She had offered to bring their evening meal to Scottie's room so he wouldn't have to eat alone. Henry agreed it was a good idea. But now she wondered if he hadn't merely been humoring her. At the landing she waited for Henry, who followed with a second tray.

Once they were in the bedroom, Henry rolled an extra pillow behind Scottie's shoulders. The two men fell into casual conversation about Scottie's wounds, the trip back to Chicago, the skeleton they'd found before being attacked. Henry also told Scottie about the pictographs Nell had shown him.

A babble of voices outside the window distracted Nell – Lupe chattering loudly in her native language. Rarely had Nell heard Lupe raise her voice. She tried to appear interested in the conversation between Henry and Scottie, but hearing Billy's wheezy laugh tweaked her curiosity even more.

She leaned to the window and looked down. Lupe was circling the table under the trees where everyone sat eating. She had her hand over her nose. Goose, Thomas and Jim were staring at her open-mouthed as if she had gone mad. Billy was laughing so hard he flushed bright red and Pablo's shoulders quivered as he tried to hide his snickering from his wife. Skin sat scooping food into his mouth, oblivious to anything around him.

Henry joined Nell at the window. "What's going on?"

"I'm not sure."

Lupe untied her apron and used it to swat at Skin. Goose, who sat next to him, jumped up, grabbed his plate, and backed off to give her room.

Skin raised his elbow against her blows, a confused look on his face. "Would somebody please tell me what this woman is saying."

Thomas jerked his head back in laughter, but Jim still hadn't grasped what Lupe was so upset about. She took another swat at Skin and turned to Pablo, who was doubled over, unable to hide his mirth any longer. She swatted at him a time or two, then grabbed Juan and took off toward her house.

"It's Skin," Nell explained to Henry. "Lupe is trying to get him to leave the table because he smells."

Between snorts of laughter Billy tried to tell Skin that Lupe found him offensive.

"Why, all ya'll can just keep your blamed fine ways," Skin responded. "I happen to be a working man." He stood and hitched his britches up over his big belly. "Iffen it's all the same to ya, I'll be taking first watch with them cows." He ambled off hump-shouldered toward the corral.

"He really is pitiful." Nell placed her empty plate on one of the trays.

"I'm afraid I agree with Lupe," Henry said. "I can't get beyond the smell, which is why I was so grateful you offered to bring our food here. But I'm confused about his employment. Is he really an army scout?"

"It's not all that uncommon for drifters to fall in with army troops heading west for the border. Skin probably saw it as an adventure and claimed to be part of the army for prestige."

That night Nell found sleep impossible. A terrible longing for something undefined gnawed at her, made her restless. She was vital to no one but liable for the well being of everyone and it was strangling her.

She wrapped a shawl around her shoulders, tiptoed downstairs and out to the porch. It was near midnight, a new moon hung low in the southwest, barely shining enough light for her to make her way without a lamp.

She recalled reading her grandmother's words, that she too walked in the late night. "It is my catharsis," she had written, "to walk and let all my worries melt away in the night air." The diary was like a messenger to Nell. The telling of life long ago, an attempt to give reason for Nell herself, her life this night, here on the porch.

But Nell's spirits were too low to try to make sense of her life. If her daddy was still alive, he would tell her to hush sniffling and complaining. But what would he have thought of Henry Burleson? A man educated and polished, admiral traits to be sure, but alien to ranch life.

She set the rocker into motion and hugged her knees to her body. In the darkness somewhere near the barn a man started singing a familiar tune. As she listened closer, it became apparent that the tune was an old hymn her mother used to sing while hoeing her vegetable garden.

Nell walked to the far end of the porch and looked toward the holding pens. Skin sat on the top rail of the corral, a black silhouette against a slate sky. His rich, mellow baritone voice made the night tremble and warm ever so slightly. Nell was astonished. She should have guessed he had a redeeming quality. Ramirez, Pablo's father, said once that God gave everyone a glimmer of hope. Some more than others, but never less than a glimmer. Skin's intoxicating, velvety voice made her feel hopeful for the first time in a long while.

***

NELL SAT AT the kitchen table with Pablo, leather folders and ledgers of various sizes scattered in front of them. "I'll need the cattle sorted into three groups," she said. "Select fifty of the best yearlings. Twenty-five should be ear-marked, over-bit on both ears. The other twenty-five should be ear-marked left ear only and branded. The rest of the herd are to be branded only."

Nell had never used ear-marking as a way to keep track of her cattle, but this year, since she needed three groups, it seemed the easiest way to keep track. The small v shaped cut on the ear was common years ago, before barbed wire made it easier to keep cattle separated. It made identification and counting more accurate, especially if a cow hadn't been branded deep enough to scar.

Pablo rubbed his chin. "How will we get the herd to town with so few of us?"

"I've worried about that. I suppose the best way is to make two drives, half the herd each time. It will be more work and take a couple of weeks longer dragging it out like that." She studied Pablo's face as he reached for his coffee. "What do you think about hiring Skin?"

Pablo shrugged.

"Do you think he can do the work?"

"*Sí,* yes."

"It's his character that bothers me, Pablo. His shady side."

"Is just his way, I think." Pablo glanced over at Lupe who was taking biscuits from the oven. It was obvious Lupe avoided his gaze.

"Pablo, I'm asking if it would bother you to have him around any longer than necessary. The man did try to beat you."

"Is okay, I think. He was only boasting."

Nell wasn't sure Pablo should be so accepting, but she had few options for help with the herd at this point. As she gathered her cattle records, a banshee cry came from the direction of the bunkhouse. She snapped around to look out the window. Lupe looked quickly over her shoulder at Pablo.

The door to the bunkhouse burst open, hit the outside wall and bounced shut again. Another deep-throated, booming yell rolled across the dusty yard. Nell was surprised the windows didn't rattle. The door blasted open a second time and Skin stepped outside into the bright sunlight, naked as a baby except for a bed sheet swaddled around his middle. His greasy, matted hair stuck out from his head in stiff peaks.

"Where the hell are my britches?" His eyes shifted back and forth across the way. "And my boots?"

Nell, reached for the door, realized that Pablo and Lupe had not moved. "Well?" She looked from one to the other.

Pablo held his coffee cup in front of his mouth but it didn't hide the mirth in his eyes.

Nell transferred the questioning look to Lupe.

"I had Thomas bring the clothes to tank house...so I can wash."

"I think I'm beginning to understand." Nell looked out the window again.

Thomas and Jim sauntered out of the bunkhouse behind Skin, their hats pushed back on their heads, obviously enjoying Skin's predicament. Skin turned on them like a big roaring bear but he couldn't attack for tripping his bed sheet. His milky white skin mottled with rage when he stepped on a corner of the sheet trailing between his legs. He spun around, and crossed the yard to the kitchen door.

Lupe grabbed her broom and positioned herself on the back stoop, ready to swing.

Startled by Lupe's behavior, Nell turned to Pablo. "Do something."

Pablo stepped onto the back stoop behind Lupe who had resumed the verbal blasting she started the night before. She had never been able to speak English when flustered, which in this case, was probably a blessing. Skin matched Lupe's determination with the volume of his wrath. Billy sidled out of the bunkhouse to watch with Thomas and Jim. Everyone seemed entertained by the confrontation except Lupe and Skin.

Lupe took a few swats at Skin with her broom. Finally, Pablo moved in to quiet her.

Billy eased up beside Skin. "Son, stifle yourself now and let me explain."

"Of all the conniving—"

"Now just hold on." Billy tried again. "Lupe is just sayin' she's in the mood to do a little laundering and she's invitin' ya to have a little soak in the horse trough whilst you wait for her to get it done. That's all."

"I'll make crow bait outta all you sisters iffen you don't give me my britches."

Billy stood humped and bowlegged, hands on his hips. "Like I always say, it don't make sense to poke at a rattlesnake. Just do what the little lady wants and you'll get your clothes back."

Skin paced back and forth, stopping in front of Billy every now and then as if he had something to say.

"Go on now," Billy said. "And I'll have some cow juice and hen fruit ready when you're done. It'll all be over before you know it."

Nell thought later that Billy had been a little too optimistic in his assessment of Skin's bath. Lupe had her broom and suds flying most of the morning. She insisted Skin needed a year's worth of scrubbing in one day. While she fought with him at the horse trough, the others were busy sorting cattle. Nearly half the herd still needed to be run through the dipping vat.

By noon Lupe, having spent her energy on her Skin-washing crusade, wilted into a pale heap at the back door. When Nell left the corral to tell her to go home, she noticed Henry and Scottie watching from the upstairs window. She waved and smiled, glad Scottie felt well enough to sit in a chair.

Henry caught up to Nell in the kitchen as she prepared a tray of cold sliced beef, boiled eggs, bread and honey.

"Is your life always so entertaining?" Henry asked. "I've been watching the bath episode."

"Actually, my life was quite dull until your friend arrived."

"As I said then, I didn't have time to be particular." They exchanged smiles.

"Lupe has gone home. I need to see to the noon meal for the cow hands."

"I'll carry this up." Henry took the tray. "Scottie will want to nap after he eats, so don't worry about us."

Later that afternoon Henry joined the others in the barn and offered to help with whatever it was they were doing. "I've been sitting up in that room trying to imagine what was taking place in here...water splashing and all the noise."

Pablo and the newly clean Skin were moving cattle single file through a maze of chutes that led into the barn. There, Henry saw a long, narrow cement trough or vat in the ground. It was filled with some kind of milky liquid.

"What's that smell?"

"Insecticide for lice and ticks," Nell said.

The cattle had little time to balk before plunging from the chute into the smelly liquid. Thomas and Jim stood on either side of the vat prodding the cattle to swim the ten or twelve feet across to a ramp leading to a separate holding pen outside where Billy made sure the confused cattle didn't try to double back.

Nell explained that the cattle would again be run through a maze of chutes so that, one by one, Billy and Pablo could cut notches in their ears. "Normally, the jobs are done simultaneously, but we're short handed."

"I'll help."

"It would take four more men to do both jobs at once, but thank you for offering." Nell handed the ledger to Thomas and told him to take over counting. Henry followed her out of the barn. She asked, "Do you think Scottie will feel well enough to eat on the porch if we help him down the stairs?"

"I'll ask him. It would be good for him to move about and build his strength." Henry hurried to follow Nell out of the barn. "Look, I must leave no later than day after tomorrow. There's been too much delay already."

Nell startled at the harsh way he barked the words.

"Sorry. Guess I'm feeling a little cooped up." He opened the gate leading to the side yard. Nell passed through the gate and paused in the shade of a hackberry tree.

"Scottie understands. He's worked with me every step of the way on this project and is as anxious as I am to get back to Chicago." He looked at the horizon. A breeze blew his brown hair away from his forehead, exposing deep, hairless indentions above each temple. He was wearing a city shirt and suspenders.

Nell studied the hard angle of his jaw. "Your work must be very important to you."

"As important as this ranch is to you. From bits of overheard conversation, I understand that you're going to sell it."

"That's right."

"Do you mind if I ask why? I mean, you seem so rooted here."

"That's difficult to answer in simple terms. It's just time, I suppose. Making a go of it gets harder every year. Most of the good cowhands are in bad shape like Goose and Billy. The others, the younger men, are joining the army to fight revolutionaries crossing the Rio Grande. I look for Thomas to leave after this spring."

"I feel I've known you longer than a few days. It's strange."

"My daddy always said crisis creates kinship."

"Your father must have been a very proud man." His gaze held her eyes for a beat then moved to her mouth. A warm sensation fluttered under Nell's breast bone. She realized Henry found it hard to think beyond his work and that, most likely, genuine caring was difficult for him.

Nell trusted her skills to some extent when it came to judging character, as in the case with Skin. So the fact that she was unsure about Henry bothered her. She could only guess that somewhere deep in her mind she harbored a school girl attraction for him and it was impairing her judgment. Maybe he was toying with her. Trying to make a fool of her for being an old maid. Certainly a man of such bearing would not find her attractive.

Nell quickly turned and headed for the kitchen door. "I need to see to supper."

Henry hurried to step in front of her. "Am I so bad looking?"

She ducked her chin, laughed self-consciously.

"That's what I find most intriguing about you."

Nell shrugged, hadn't a clue what he was talking about.

"Your laugh, your voice. It's out of place here."

"What?" Nell wondered if that was another way of saying she was plain, as Hester had said so often.

Henry ran his fingers through his hair. "I've chosen the wrong words."

"I have work to do." She stepped around him.

"It's a compliment." Henry followed her. "Your voice is melodious, out of place here in this sparse and distant place. To me, you are a mystery, a paradox."

Nell stopped, turned and pointed her chin directly at his face. "And that is what I find intriguing about you."

"What?'

"Your way with words."

"But I meant you are..."

At the back stoop, Nell paused to pick up a bucket of smelly gruel. "My daddy also said to always beware of oily-tongued devils." She held the bucket out to him.

He looked at it with disgust. "What am I suppose to do with that?"

"You asked if you could help. Well, go slop the hogs." Nell let the screen door slam behind her.

Two days later Skin carried Scottie down the stairs and carefully placed him on the buggy seat.

"Miss Miggins," Scottie said, "I will always remember you with tremendous gratitude. Thank you for saving my life."

Nell handed him a basket of bread and jam for the long trip back to Chicago. "You're welcome, Mr. Scott. But remember you are not out of the woods yet. Be careful not to over do."

"I may surprise you one of these days and return to have you show me those pictographs we talked about."

"It would be a pleasure, that is, if I still own them."

"Ma'am." Jim tapped her shoulder. "I could stay and help you get those cattle to town."

"I think it may be best for you to see your parents first. They'll be worried about you. Besides, if I sell this ranch right away, you'd be out of a job."

Jim pushed his big hat down to his ears and climbed into the buggy.

Henry took Nell's elbow and led her a short distance away from the others. "I wish you well. I am sorry I gave you the wrong impression the other day."

She tried to interrupt when he paused.

"No, let me finish. I realize now that it, your voice I mean, and you fit this country perfectly. Forgive me if I embarrassed you."

"That's not necessary." Nell tried to wave away his words, but his eyes held hers. She was more confused than ever and could say no more so she simply nodded like a mute.

He placed his hat on his head then and took her hand in his. "I truly hope, Nell Miggins, that we'll meet again." He climbed into the buggy and gave her a last glance before Pablo snapped the reins.

Nell watched until they passed through the gate and moved down the road. She imagined Henry Burleson turning to see if she was still there, knowing that if he did, she would have blended into the landscape as if it had swallowed her whole.

A dry wind tugged at the unruly hair at her temples. "Skin," she called over her shoulder to where he stood next to Billy on the porch.

"Yes'm."

"Come into the house. I want to talk to you."

***

TINKER DROVE HIS wagon through the Carrageen Ranch gate and made a mental note of the loose hinges. A south wind blew clouds into white wisps overhead and the gamma grass waved a like a shallow sea. He pulled his wagon to a stop in front of the barn where he assumed most of his work would take place. Jack fidgeted excitedly when an old man with a leathery face sauntered out of the barn. "Hidy." The man nodded.

"Tinker Webb, windmiller."

"Right. I'm Billy. Come with me." Billy led him through the front door of the main house where a woman met them in the hall. Her hands were clasped tight at her waist, her face sober, a kind of sad strength about her eyes.

"This here's the windmiller, Tinker Webb," Billy said.

"Thank you for coming out."

"I understand your husband has some work for me."

"I own and manage this ranch myself." She motioned to him to follow her then called out over her shoulder. "Billy, find Pablo. Have him join us."

Tinker remembered Mr. Parker saying something about a woman selling the place, but he assumed she had a husband. He followed her into a small room at the end of the hall. Two walls were lined with shelves stuffed to overflowing with books and ledgers. A third wall supported a white stone fireplace that needed mortar repair. The rock below the mantel was stained with soot. The fourth wall, divided by ceiling to floor windows, had a large mahogany desk facing away from it.

Nell Miggins stepped behind the desk. "Is it true you do carpenter work as well as repair windmills?"

"Repairman would be a better name for me than windmiller. I'll take a look at any work you need done. If I can't fix it or build it myself, I'll arrange and supervise contract work."

"I see."

Tinker turned at the sound of footsteps in the doorway. A youngish Mexican man greeted him with a handshake and introduced himself as Pablo Rameriz. Tinker glimpsed the woman trading a communicating glance with Pablo but pretended not to notice.

She handed Tinker a list. "I would like an estimate of these repairs. Pablo will escort you around and explain our needs in more detail. I plan to sell Carrageen Ranch. That's why I need everything in good working condition. The most important task, one I'd like you to start right away, is a windmill that supplies water to the north tank. The ranch isn't worth salt without it."

Her gaze dropped for a moment before she continued. "I think you should know I won't be able to pay you until my herd is sold. And, since I'm having trouble finding hands, I'm not sure when that will be. Of course, I will understand if you find it necessary to postpone the repairs until then."

"I don't think that'll be a problem, Miss Miggins." Tinker glanced over the list she'd handed him. "In fact, if you can supply a mount, I'll help trail your herd."

Pablo stepped forward. "Ah, I did not tell you. I saw Newton Campbell in town and he is having trouble moving his herd also. He said if we help him, he will loan his vaqueros for the same work with Carrageen's herd."

"That may be our best solution. That way Mr. Webb can start on the windmill while the rest of you help Mr. Campbell." She turned to back to the Tinker. "Newton Campbell is a rancher south of here."

"Skin should stay here." Pablo said. "Remember Mr. Taylor?"

"Oh, yes. Mr. Webb, we heard you were the one to discover trouble at the Taylor place?"

Tinker smoothed his hat brim. "I got there in time to see outlaws, or bandits, can't be sure, ride off with some of Taylor's herd. The house burned to the ground, the whole family with it."

Nell moved around the desk. "A couple of archeologists sought help from us not long ago. They'd been attacked while researching the Pecos and Rio Grande region. Their wagon boss was horribly murdered."

She moved to the window with one hand on her hip and the other on her throat. "Pablo, explain our situation to Newton. Take the others, help him and if he feels he needs another hand, then come back for Skin. Otherwise, I think I would feel better with Skin and Billy here. She turned from the window. They both nodded.

Tinker spent the rest of the afternoon following Pablo around the house and barns. The Mexican spoke of the ranch with uncommon pride. Tinker was impressed with the house, the old-world carpentry methods used to build it, though it wasn't elaborate or lavish by any means. And, while it hadn't been neglected exactly, things seemed to have been patched rather than repaired.

Tinker used a knife to poke at the mortar between chimney rocks. "I'll have to do some of the work from the attic to repair this chimney."

"It is tight up there."

"You work here long?"

"*Sí*, all my life. And my father before me."

"How about Miss Miggins?"

"Three generations her family has been here." Pablo leaned on the gate to the hen house. He set his jaw, stared at the ground, then squinted at the sky.

"What will you do when the ranch sells?"

Pablo folded his arms across his narrow chest. "Maybe the new owner will hire me, but I think not. Cattle business is bad. No one wants this life anymore."

"Is that why she's selling out?"

"Lupe, my wife, she says Nell is worn out by loneliness, not work. Nell loves this land. This I know." He kicked at the dry ground with the toe of his boot. "You can stay in the bunkhouse if you like. Use the tank house for washing up."

The tank house, in the shadow of a cypress windmill derrick, was actually a stone-walled room built around the bottom half of a cistern tower. The cistern gravity fed water into the tank house, main house, and foreman's house.

Glancing inside, Tinker saw a big wash tub with a ringer in one corner, shelves of soap and powders above it. High on the opposite wall was a faucet, apparently used by cowboys for washing up in wintertime. "A pretty fancy design for a water system."

"*Señor* Miggins, Nell's father, he say water is the key to raising cattle in Texas. Carrageen had three springs but one is gone, dried up. The others, they are slow. The windmill north of here feeds water into a tank my father built. It saved cattle many times."

"If it's all the same to you, I prefer to camp my wagon. Seems simpler that way, especially if the windmill is off a ways."

"Is okay, but too late to start for the windmill now. I leave first light to help Mr. Campbell so Miss Miggins, Nell, she will take you there tomorrow."

Back at the barn, Tinker found Jack patiently withstanding the affections of Pablo's little boy who alternately tried to kiss him and ride him like a horse. Billy sat nearby whittling. They gave him directions to a campsite on a bluff between the ranch and the windmill. Nell Miggins would pick him up on her way out in the morning. He shook Pablo's hand again and tipped his hat to Billy.

After making camp, Tinker eased back on his bedroll and propped his head on his folded arm to watch the sky. Darkness was a growing thing to him, the way it started at the horizon in the east and eased up over head leaving twinkling stars scattered everywhere.

Jack sat at attention at Tinker's shoulder. "At ease, boy." Tinker gave the dog a pat. His mind scanned the work ahead here at Carrageen. He hoped the windmill proved as interesting as the time-worn old house. Before long the steady, lone song of a Chuck-wills-widow lulled him into a dreamy fog in which he tried to imagine what it must be like for a woman to run a place like this alone.

Next morning, sipping the last of his coffee, he watched Nell Miggins ride up from the house. Jack yelped and ran around in a tight little circle when she came to a halt. She had on pants and a heavy duck cloth shirt, and was leading a saddled horse.

"Morning," she called. "Sorry I'm late. Pablo had hard time getting things in order before leaving."

Tinker mounted and followed her northwest with Jack loping close behind. Since she rode slightly ahead, he couldn't help but notice how she fit the motion of her loping horse. Probably learned to ride before she talked.

A few miles out she turned in the saddle to catch his eye then thumbed over her shoulder.

The windmill was massive, like a sentry towering above a stand of cottonwoods. When they pulled to a halt at the tank, he could do little more than remove his hat and shake his head in amazement. "It's half again as tall as the county courthouse." Several blades hung loose and the big gears were rusted.

"What do you think?" she asked.

Tinker dismounted, checked the cross beams of the derrick while she explained all she remembered about its operation and repairs over the years.

"How long have you noticed that noise?"

"A couple of weeks."

"Looks to me like the fellow who built this derrick started with a Dutch style windmill in mind, then for some reason switched. I've never seen anything like this." She grinned and turn away. "What's funny?"

"This place – the windmill – symbolizes so much, and well, I'm glad someone else finds it interesting."

"It's interesting. I'll give you that much." He swatted at his leg with his hat. "Pablo called your place Carrageen. A strange name for a ranch."

"My grandfather's doing. He came here from Ireland. The first time he saw these hills was in the late fall and he couldn't get over the beauty. Said the hills were the color of Carrageen, a violet moss that grows in Ireland."

Tinker put his hat back on and started up the ladder, careful of the missing and loose rungs. A brace bar gave way when he tested it and ricocheted down the tower in loud plunks before hitting the ground. After looking things over from the top, he climbed down and sat with Nell in the shade of a cottonwood.

"You can fix it, can't you?"

"To tell you the truth, it would probably be less trouble and expense to start from scratch and build a new one." He picked a blade of grass worked it between his fingers. "You could order one from the general store in town. I've seen them. Not bad for the money. Your cowboys could put it together when they're finished with the cattle. Or I can do it."

"And this one?"

"Tear it down, I guess. You could use the lumber for fence rails." She drooped like a willow tree in driving rain. She had taken her hat off and he could see the clear green of her eyes flecked brown like the prairie. A blame fine woman, she was, he could just tell.

But oh glory, what was he to do now? Just when the depleted little lady was showing some shine he went and messed it up. "Course, with some lumber, cypress maybe, from the mill over in Comfort for new blades, a little oiling, and a whole lot of muscle, I think I can get this old relic churning again. Just depends on which way you want it."

She stood but kept her head lowered for a time before looking back up at the windmill.

"Miss Miggins, have you ever climbed up to the top?"

She snapped around to face him. "Why do you ask?"

"I have a hunch you have." She didn't answer. "Come on, I'll give you a hand."

"You must be insane!" She jerked away from him.

"Maybe, but so's half the world. I'm just thinking that if you climb up there, it'll help you make up your mind what to do."

He fetched a rope from the pommel of her saddle then climbed the derrick and tied it to the big gear post below the blades. He threw the loose end down to her. "Tie it around your waist."

She stared at the end of the rope.

"Go on, I'll keep you hitched up from here. No way you can fall."

He watched her struggle with indecision. "Is it more unlady-like to climb the derrick with me than alone?"

"You don't know that I've ever climbed up there."

Tinker looked around. "The countryside looks greener from up here. Over in the south looks like a cloud bank. Might rain."

She watched the end of the rope.

"Yeah." He squinted east. "And which way did you say Mexico was?"

She bit her bottom lip, grabbed the end of the rope, tied it around her waist with a jerk. "Check your knot." Her voice was shaky.

"I'll not let you fall, Nell Miggins." When she looked up their eyes locked and Tinker felt a jolt. A sudden feeling that something had come into focus, or slipped into place. An odd sort of comfort or ease he'd not felt for a long time.

Nell climbed, straining now and then to reach over the missing rungs. He pulled the rope tight as she ascended then extended his hand to her when she reached the top. They sat with their legs dangling from the platform forty feet above the ground.

Buzzards circled above a rocky drop not far away. Clouds drifted sluggishly overhead. The tops of the cottonwoods churned so the land look as if it breathed with its own inexplicable rhythm.

The quiet between Tinker Webb and Nell Miggins stretched.

Jack, sitting on the far side of the dam, whimpered then let out a sharp yelp.

"Hush yourself, dog," Tinker called down.

Nell was sitting close enough for him to see the shiny edge of held back tears in her eyes. "My cousin's ranch is not far from here," she said. "At one time there was some lumber stored in a barn there. Do you think it would still be good enough to use?"

He wanted to know what it was that caused her such anguish, but instead asked, "Why don't we go find out?"

***

NELL'S HEART FLUTTERED race-horse fast during the ride to Hester's old home ranch. As far as she knew no one had ever suspected she climbed the windmill tower. Yet the windmiller guessed it almost immediately and beguiled her into exposing something of her secret-self. Maybe she should be wary of him.

Seeing the land from up there one more time before leaving it had been like a balm. Many afternoons, and recently nights, she'd longed to climb the tower but was too fearful of its rickety condition. Nell decided she would always have a kind of affinity for Mr. Webb, for he evidently shared her sense of awe and grandeur for the windmill, had the same respect for the order of things viewed from high up.

Now, more than ever, she wanted the windmill repaired though it seemed a silly, childish dream. It might take a long time to sell the ranch and she'd be glad to have the tower to climb.

When they approached the cut off to the old barn, Nell noticed fresh hoof prints on the dusty trail. When she slowed to study them, Mr. Webb asked if she was looking for anything in particular.

"Last time I was out this way someone had been here. These tracks look new." She pulled her rifle from its scabbard, handed it to him, then drew a pistol from a pommel bag.

They found nothing amiss at the house. Jack led the way to the barn with his nose glued to the ground. At the barn door Mr. Webb pointed to the deep half circle scrape in the dirt. "Looks to me like this door has been opened quite a bit lately."

Nell nodded, not at all easy about the whole situation.

They found fresh footprints inside the barn as well, but nothing else unusual. Jack hurried about sniffing in all the corners, which helped assure them that no one was hiding in the shadows.

The barn leaned precariously and smelled of mouse droppings and soured hay. Nell pointed to a stack of lumber layered across two stall walls.

Tinker moved a few planks around. "It's in fine shape. Some of it cypress. I may need to buy more later, but this'll do fine to start."

He rolled his sleeves up exposing thick, tanned arms and when he reached to sort the lumber, his shirt stretched tight across his broad back. His close-cropped hair was the color of old silver. And when he glanced at her, she was sure his dark eyes twinkled. The look of him made her smile.

Mr. Webb's hands were like mesquite roots. Callused palms, thick scarred fingers. He climbed to the top of one of the stall walls, where he leaned against a post as he sifted through piles of old lumber. He held out a board. "Can you set this one aside?" he asked without looking at her.

"How did you come to be a windmiller?"

"I ran into an old fellow in Seguin years ago who was traveling around repairing windmills." Tinker paused, handed her another plank. "I was looking for work and knew quite a bit about windmills. Worked as the old man's apprentice for a couple of years." He strained to move a long, heavy board. "Then bought him out when he retired."

"How was it you knew so much about windmills?"

He stopped to rest a minute, drew a big lung of air. "I'd read a lot about them in architect school, a sort of hobby, I guess you'd say."

"You're an architect? Why on earth are you repairing windmills?"

"It's a long story, and I'm short on daylight."

Something in the way he closed the subject and turned back to his task sharpened Nell's curiosity, but she instinctively knew not to ask more questions.

They agreed the best course for the work ahead was for him to move his camp to the windmill site. She would send Skin out the next day with a wagon to haul the lumber from the old barn to the windmill. Then Skin would stay at Tinker's windmill camp to help with the repairs.

***

A FEW DAYS after Skin left the ranch house to help Mr. Webb, Billy knocked on the kitchen door. When Lupe opened it he was sitting on the stoop slumped and out of breath. "Tell Miss Nell I got a cow down and can't get her up."

"Billy?" Nell had overheard from the hall.

"That old cow'll be fine if I can get her to stand," he said. "She dropped her calf last night and now she don't want to get up, is all."

"I'll change my—"

"You ain't got enough muscle either." He pulled himself up to stand bowlegged on the stoop. "Maybe I could ride out and fetch Skin. Brute he is, he could pick that cow up like she was a kitten."

"I'll go get him. You better rest up."

What would she have done all these years without Billy? He and Pablo were all she had left of the old life and the guilt she harbored over leaving them behind when the ranch was sold made her heart ache.

While Nell changed into trousers, Lupe packed a box basket of food and filled a jar with fresh milk. Billy had Jingles saddled by the time she came back down the stairs.

Because the basket of food was bulky and bounced around too much, Nell had to ride at a slow pace. Spring had settled in at Carrageen Ranch. The air had a grassy, damp earth smell to it. To the north, hills pushed up, dark blue and shimmering in the dewy morning light.

She reined to a halt and scanned the horizon for a long moment then walked Jingles in a slow circle. East of Carrageen, the Guadalupe River made a wide sweep south toward the town of Comfort. Not far from there Confederate soldiers had attacked a group of German settlers sympathetic to the Union cause nearly forty years ago. Many of the nineteen killed had been old friends of her grandfather's.

From there the river outlined Carrageen's northern boundary and was the best place to cross when trailing a herd to Fort Worth. West, the hills eventually flattened, turned craggy and hostile, and the land there was full of myths about lost cities of gold, outlaws and even a beautiful *señorita* ghost who lived in caves along the Rio Grande.

Hundreds of miles of brush country stretched south all the way to the murky Gulf of Mexico where Texas rivers deposited silt skimmed from rich uplands. Nell wondered who would know of this moment when she and all the rest were gone. A strong wind could sweep any trace of her away and it would be as if nothing had ever existed without her there to remember.

She dismounted, raised her right arm and pointed at the horizon, circling again, memorizing, permanently etching Carrageen's history and the vision of it on her brain.

Jingles snorted and bobbed his head. Nell swung back up into the saddle, turned toward the windmill and gave the horse rein.

Skin was sawing a plank when she rode up to the windmill camp around mid-morning. Tinker worked atop a ladder propped against the derrick. He didn't see her until she called out over the noise of Skin's saw. "Can you spare Skin? Billy needs him."

"Anything wrong?" Tinker climbed down.

"He needs an extra strong back with a downed cow. I can stay and help here if you like."

"That'd be fine. I need someone to watch my plumb line and guide the mule."

Nell told Skin that Billy needed him at the barn and to stay there until she returned. He nodded and left quietly. His attitude bewildered her. When she had asked him to ride out to help load the lumber, he seemed dismayed and about to refuse. She wondered at the time if he was reluctant to work on a windmill, preferring cattle work instead, not an unusual sentiment among men who fancied themselves cowhands.

In their conversation the day Henry Burleson left, Skin's explanation of employment with the army had been a little muddled. Nell came to the conclusion that he had been tagging along with the troops, helping trail horses or hauling equipment in exchange for a hot meal, all without being officially hired or enlisted. His solemn eyes reminded her of a lost child. Since the week of his arrival, when Lupe forced him to bathe, he'd delighted everyone by washing on a regular basis and even let Billy trim his thin colorless hair. He now kept it tied with a length of rawhide at the nape of his neck.

Standing across the desk from her that day he crumpled his hat nervously while his sickly opal colored skin glistened. He told her he had been foreman at a sawmill in Mississippi before coming to Texas to become a Ranger, but he found the requirements too strict. In light of his discomfort she didn't ask exactly what he meant by "too strict." In the end, Nell decided it wasn't that important to know everything about his past.

"Skin," she had said, "I need to hire extra hands to trail cattle, mend fences, and keep night watch."

"Why, I'm your man, Miss Miggins." He had replied without hesitation.

"I realize you're willing to work and work hard. My concern is that I need help I can trust and I must say I haven't been as forgiving of your behavior the first time I saw you as Pablo." He sank into the chair in front of her desk. She had thought he was going to cry.

"I surely would like a chance to redeem myself to ya, Miss Miggins. 'Let us lie down in our shame, and let our dishonor cover us.' Jeremiah, third chapter, ma'am."

Nell was shocked he could quote the Bible. "So yours was a religious family?"

"Not exactly, no."

She had ended the confusing conversation that day assuring Skin that as long as he was respectful to everyone and did an honest job, he could work for her until she sold the ranch.

Now, as Nell watched Skin head back to the barn to help Billy, she felt that whatever the truth was concerning his past, he wanted to put it behind him, but his secrets continued to eat at him. Much the same way her memories continued to haunt her. How could she fault him for that?

She placed the basket of food on a small fold down table under the tarp canopy of Mr. Webb's camp. In a glance she noticed that everything was orderly. Every conceivable necessity for camp comfort was stored in cubby holes and drawers in the side of the wagon like a tidy kitchen cupboard. Two barrels with unusual hinged double lids caught her eye. Mr. Webb lifted the top portion to make a chair back. He bowed ceremoniously, holding the barrel chair and indicated she should sit. Nell, feeling blessedly at ease, smiled.

Mr. Webb pulled a tablet out of his barrel chair and drew a sketch of a windmill to help explain his plan for the repairs. First and foremost, the derrick needed to be secured before work on the blades could begin. This phase of the work, he said, was pretty simple. He would hoist the boards using a pulley and mule, replace some outer braces and cross braces. When the tower and platform were secure and the ladder repaired, he would replace the damaged blades with new ones.

"In the long run," he said, "it'll pay to use cypress for the blades. I'll secure them with green rawhide."

"I don't understand."

"Right here, I'll slip the blade in a notch then wrap it with soaked rawhide. As the rawhide dries it'll shrink and tighten. I guarantee it'll hold till Pablo's little boy is a granddaddy. But I still think I'll need more lumber."

"You and Pablo can bring it from town on the return trip after we trail the cattle to the Wishing."

For the next several hours they worked methodically. Tinker tied one board at a time to a rope strung through a large pulley positioned at the top of the tower. Nell tied her end of the rope to a saddled mule then led the mule away from the tower, lifting the board. On the derrick Tinker swung the board into place and nailed it. Several times Nell caught her breath as he teetered and strained to nail the boards while holding onto the ladder rungs or lateral braces. At one point he had trouble with a particular board and let go entirely so both hands were free to nail.

"Mr. Webb, wait. I can…" But he couldn't hear her. She tied the mule to the nearest tree and ran to climb the tower.

Tinker groaned when the board slipped before he had it nailed through. He didn't see her until she was more than half way up the ladder. From there she stepped onto a lateral brace and maneuvered close to the swinging board.

"What the hell?" Tinker looked down to see the mule tied to a tree. "I'm not sure about this."

Nell leaned over the cross brace, grabbed the board and positioned it. "Nail it before I lose my nerve or change my mind."

He grinned finally and thumped his hat in a mock salute.

With her working the tower next to him, the repairs to the cross braces went much faster and by late afternoon they were half way up the tower. But she was getting tired from the constant climb up and down the tower. A gust of wind blew her hat off and she grabbed for it without thinking. For one horrible moment the ground seemed to move and circle.

The windmiller quickly locked his thick hand around her arm. "That's it. Time to call it a day."

"No, it's all right."

He ignored her. "Besides, rain is coming."

She turned, saw the dark rain clouds he'd seen over her shoulder. Just then another gust of wind, stronger than the first, blew across the tree tops. The old tower shuddered. Mr. Webb, one level down from her now, was having a hard time freeing the rope from the pulley. It was thrashing about wildly in the wind.

She managed to climb up two more lateral braces to reach the pulley, but he called up saying not to fuss with it. "Just tie it to the beam you're on to keep it from tangling." Nell was able to grasp the rope after several attempts and tied it off as he suggested. She was just below the platform now, with one arm looped over a beam for security. She looked south and watched the tree tops thrash and twist in the wind. A low rumble of thunder rolled over the hills. The wind rose to a roar.

"Miss Miggins climb down! Miss Miggins, are you loco?"

"Ye-e-s!" She gurgled with laughter.

He shook his head in resignation and climbed up to stand on the lateral beam next to her. They clung to a cross brace with their faces to the wind grinning like children fulfilling a dare. "This reminds me of a widow's walk on top of houses in Galveston," he said.

"A what?"

"A covered platform on top of a house where a woman can stand and watch for the sails of her husband's ship."

"I wish I knew what I'm watching for."

"I've a feeling you'll find out one day, if you're patient. A preacher once told me that forbearance and steadfastness makes the spirit grow strong."

Patient indeed, Nell thought. She had waited her life away. She studied his craggy profile, the deep sun lines around his mouth and eyes. His face somehow conveyed tender harmonies and deep values. She'd bet a man like the windmiller had no use for pettiness.

When rain began to pellet them, they climbed down and waited under the wagon canopy with Jack until the first burst of rain eased. Then Mr. Webb loaned her his slicker to wear back to the ranch house.

Nell rode into the barn around dusk where Billy greeted her with a worried look. He explained he'd been teaching Skin to add and subtract his numbers. But what he dreaded was multiplication and long division. Nell assured Billy he didn't have to teach Skin anything if he didn't want to. The old man replied with a grunt.

Billy and Skin ate in the kitchen with Lupe and Nell and afterward Skin sprawled on the floor with Juan while Lupe embroidered a nightgown for her unborn baby. Nell stared at her grandmother's diary, tried to read but couldn't make her mind stay put. The lamp flame flickered in a draft caused by the awful wind and storm outside. She worried about Mr. Webb and his dog.

Lupe drew a threaded needle up from the white cloth in her hands. She seemed over the worst of her baby sickness, even had a radiant look about her now. Nell imagined faith in the future grew in Lupe's womb, placed there by the love she and Pablo had for one another. The baby would make them come full circle like the cycle of the seasons and the orbit of the planets. Pablo, Lupe, Juan, baby. Spring, Summer, Fall, Winter. Earth, Sun, Moon, Stars.

Juan stood, rubbed his eyes and climbed onto Lupe's lap. She was the most beautiful woman Nell knew. Clear, black eyes set wide in a round face, a smile full of straight teeth, a deep sloped forehead, and all of it glowing with the light of an unborn child.

Nell listened to her own thoughts and wondered if she was envious and thought not. But she did wish her time of hope had not passed.

Lupe glanced up and Nell smiled at her before trying once again to focus her mind on the diary.

"No rain now for almost a month. Indians stopped for water and frightened me to death until Paul came out of the barn to talk with them. I am only now learning to distinguish between the different tribes. I have heard many horrible stories about Comanches but the Indians today were Lipan. At least that was Paul's thought. They were an assembly of sad droopy souls, perhaps a dozen in all, mostly women, children and two old men. A woman among them looked to be dying. Paul thought it best not to interfere. We gave them water and cornbread and they left as quietly as they came, but the spirit of them haunts me still.

Tonight I will pray for rain and thank God for my beloved husband Paul. He divides my sorrows so that they are only half as painful and doubles my joys that they are twice cherished."

Nell thought her grandparents must have been like Lupe and Pablo. Each a magnifier of good in the other. The diary was her ballast during this time of uncertainty, though it paled in comparison to the stability her grandparents or Pablo and Lupe found in each other.

Nell's eyes moved to Skin as he pulled himself up from the floor. "I reckon I'll sleep in the barn. Them horses might get skittish in this here storm."

"Oh, I don't know, Skin. Sounds to me like it's dying down a little."

"No, ma'am. I take a deep breath and smell fish. This here weather's coming from the Gulf of Mexico. Liable to go on all night." He pushed his hat down and slammed the door hard against the wind as he went out.

She was sorry for him, pitiful and alone without so much as a diary to give him direction.

***

AROUND MIDNIGHT THE sky opened up with brilliant flashes of white lightning and torrents of rain. Jack whimpered like a kid, insisting he sleep across Tinker's legs for security. Before long, Tinker had to stand and stomp blood back into his numb feet.

A streak of lightning lit the sky daylight-bright and he thought for a second he glimpsed a rider in the outer reaches of the flash. Who'd be fool enough to ride on such a night? Maybe it was a boulder or tree shaped like a horse and rider. But then, could be one of Miss Miggins' men coming to look for him. Could be trouble somewhere.

The tarp canopy flapped in a high wind. He strained to see movement in the wet darkness, listened to the rain, allowed his thoughts to drift back to a time when Sarah was alive. Nights like this they would lie skin against skin in each other's arms, let the night engulf them in a cocoon of soft sound and clean smelling air. They had savored an exchange of physical love that in daylight and public made them shine like diamonds in the company of ordinary people. Tinker thought, had things been different, might be that their passions would have cooled by now.

Another bolt of lightning lit the sky and this time Tinker was sure he saw a lone rider. A bandit? Probably not. They moved around in packs like wolves. Curious. A shame that whoever it was didn't have sense enough to take shelter somewhere.

Never mind it anyway. Right now his back ached and his galldarned, flea-bitten dog had taken over the only dry spot in the bedroll.

***

NELL WAS ABOUT to send Skin back out to help Mr. Webb with the windmill when Pablo, Thomas and Goose galloped through the main gate and raced up the road, hats and mud flying.

They passed the house with a whoop and a "hidy" at her standing on the porch and then rode straight into the barn where their voices echoed back across the yard. Thomas doubled back out and circled his excited horse. "Miss Miggins, Mr. Campbell told us to come to his barn on Friday for a shindig. Said we all should plan on it. You, Skin, everybody."

Pablo joined Nell on the porch. "That is so."

"He must have gotten a good price for his cows."

"He did not say. But I think so."

"As soon as you've had time to see Lupe, I'd like you and the others to ride out to help Mr. Webb."

"*Sí*, and will he go to Mr. Campbell's barn dance?"

"I have no idea, but do invite him."

By noon Friday, having run out of lumber for the windmill repairs, the three returned to the ranch sounding like a room full of fussy children. Thomas worried because he couldn't dance. He explained his first attempt to Goose. "One little gal slapped me silly for stepping on her toes. And if that wasn't enough, some brute, whose daughter I asked to dance, drug me outside and boxed my ears good. Said she'd been spoken for already."

Goose chuckled. "Hell, you cain't walk straight. How is it you're ever gonna dance without gettin' your feet tangled?"

Nell had to give Goose credit on that point. That Thomas was still alive was a miracle in itself. His sloped shoulders and stumbling gait had given them all reason to gasp at one time or another. He always looked as if he could topple over at any moment.

Thomas was unaffected by Goose's judgement. "I'll learn. Way I see it, if you can play a harmonica with a messed up hand the way you do, I can learn to dance."

"*Ay-e-e.*" Pablo winked at Goose. "And would that little *Señorita* Louise Campbell have something to do with your determination, my friend?"

"Good Lord, son." Billy joined in. "You better watch out for yourself."

"Why's that?" Thomas asked.

"Well you might say that gal sticks to a cowpuncher like a tick on a hound dawg."

Lupe broke up the conversation to shepherd them to the tank house where she replenished the supply of soap and towels. From there the sound of boisterous belly laughter and the smell of pomade wafted across the way to Nell potting pepper plants on the front porch. She glanced up in time to see Mr. Webb roll up beside the barn in his wagon. He reined in his team, listened to the commotion for a minute, then looked over at her and shook his head. She shrugged. They smiled. He climbed down and approached the porch.

"I trust Pablo told you about the barn dance?"

Tinker nodded. "I'm thinking I ought to go along to keep those boys in line."

"Then you'd best hurry. There may not be any soap left when your turn in the tank house comes up."

"Soap? From the sound of it, those boys won't have skin left when they get through." Tinker shifted his weight. "If it's all the same to you I'll move my camp back to the bluff for the time being. That way I'll be a little closer to the cattle operations, if you still need me to help trail the herd."

She wiped her hands. "I do need the help and you can camp anywhere."

After Mr. Webb left the porch for his turn in the tank house, Nell made her way upstairs to begin her own preparations. For a time she'd thought better of going to the barn dance. On one hand she knew she would enjoy the antics and music, the fellowship and old friends, but on the other hand she knew she would feel awkward and out of place, always the oddball old maid. But when she imagined herself explaining that she would just as soon stay at the ranch alone, it became clear that the easiest, least embarrassing thing to do was go.

If she had to endure going to the dance, maybe she could make preparing for it a little entertaining. She remembered reading in one of Hester's Ladies' Standard Magazines that a fast way to curl hair was to twist a dozen or so ringlets and tie each with a strip of cloth.

The task proved more simply read than done, but she managed, leaving her head tied and bound while she bathed and searched for something to wear. While rummaging for earrings in a dresser drawer in the room across the hall, she found some lip rouge Hester left behind. She thought about smearing a little on her lips but a glance in the mirror startled her so bad she dropped the rouge. The bits of rag sticking out from all over her head made her look, for all the world, like a mad Medusa.

In a fit of giggles, she dabbed her mouth with the red goo then tried to wipe it off only to realize that a little of the color remained. Maybe a little on her cheeks would, as Hester claimed, give her a youthful blush. The thought made her snicker even more. Youthful blush indeed.

Convinced that she was well on her way to insanity, Nell feverishly tried to rub her face clean and before long was as red as a sunburned sow.

She jerked the tied strips of cloth from her hair and brushed it smooth. Without any more foolishness she stepped into the dress

Hester had given her and struggled with the dozens of buttons down the back.

Downstairs in the kitchen she spread a cloth over the basket of small cakes she and Lupe made earlier in the day. She heard heavy footsteps in the hall, assumed it was Thomas, but when she looked up, it was the windmiller standing in the doorway staring at her. "Uh, Pablo has everybody loaded and ready."

When he stepped forward to lift the basket off the table, Nell moved passed him and headed for the front door. The clippity sound of her footsteps - the pretty shoes Hester had given her - echoed in the big hallway, felt odd to her ears, so different from the thud of her boots.

Tinker rushed to catch up with her. "Miss Miggins." She half turned. "You look mighty nice."

Nell searched for something to say.

He reached around her for the doorknob. "Mighty nice," he said again before swinging the door open.

Outside, the Carrageen outfit, sitting stiff and crisp in the wagon hushed their playful bantering to watch her descend the steps. Nell's gaze went straight to Lupe. The validation of her smile just then stemmed from a reality that no other person present understood. Lupe was her confidante without words, sharing truths about things women never speak of but understand fully. They had uncommon lives, she and Lupe, yet the messages, one to the other, were commonplace and maybe, just maybe, they bore strengths neither of them could comprehend.

Lupe had the abiding respect of them all. In the shadow of that fact and Lupe's approving smile, Nell relaxed.

Newton Campbell's squeeze box could be heard long before his barn came into view. Mimmie Campbell called out to Nell when the Carrageen wagon drove into the barnyard. "Lordy, Lordy. If only your Pa could see you now."

"Mimmie, have you met Mr. Tinker Webb, the windmiller?"

"Don't recall if I have. You're mighty welcome here, Mr. Webb. Enjoy yourself, hear?" Mimmie pumped his arm up and down then turned to the others. "Everybody! Get down outta the wagon and come on in. The boys have their fiddles all warmed up."

Nell busied herself with the other ladies laying out food. Sissy Spencer sliced a big ham while Coreen McCann carried in a pot of boiled and buttered potatoes.

"There's enough food here for Coxey's army," Nell said. Platters of cakes, cookies and pies covered a second table on the other side of the barn.

Coreen let out a cackle. "I reckon it won't last long."

Sissy took the lid off her pot of beans. "Hear tell, word of this here brouhaha spread all the way north to Fredericksburg and south to Medina."

Nell glimpsed Thomas nervously approaching Louise, Newton and Mimmie's daughter. The girl was neither pretty nor homely, but so nearsighted she peered at her world with a permanent squint. If Newton was wise, Nell thought, he would encourage Thomas. Louise could do a lot worse.

Goose puffed on his harmonica with the small group of musicians assembled in the far corner of the barn, while Skin and Billy surveyed the food tables. A little later Billy, reminding Nell of an aged guardian angel, asked her to dance. She understood it was his way of making sure she wasn't a wallflower.

A few tunes later, Mr. Webb asked her to dance. She scanned his face, the outside corners of his eyes where tiny lines waited to fold with joy, his mouth ready to grin, and then took his offered arm.

"M-Mr. Webb?" Oh, good Lord, Nell thought.

"Yes?"

"What...?" She placed her hand on his shoulder.

He wrapped an arm around her waist. She felt engulfed.

"You want to ask me something?"

"Ah, you said you were an architect in Galveston."

"That's right."

She concentrated on her feet. "Is Galveston your home town then?"

"No, I was born on my father's homestead in San Saba County."

"I see. Do you have family there?" Nell wondered if he was married. He wore no ring, but that was not uncommon for a man who worked with tools.

"Just the homestead. My father sold his herd back in the seventies and tried farming. Cotton mostly. My work makes it easy to loop through the county often enough to keep an eye on the place."

"You've no interest in cattle?" She thought she bumped his boot toe.

"I do. Few years back I bought some Hereford stock hoping to increase on-the-hoof weight of some range cattle left over from my dad's day."

"What about your wife? Where does she live?" When Nell glanced up, the lines around his eyes unfolded and drooped. He adjusted his arm around her waist and all but lifted her as he whirled her around. He kept his gaze over her head, guiding her in and out of the other dancers.

"I don't have a wife."

When the music stopped he walked her to a table where Mimmie Campbell fidgeted with the arrangement of food. A quick sidelong glance at his sober face confirmed for Nell that she had overstepped an invisible boundary with her meddling questions, like the day they sorted lumber in Hester's barn.

"Y'all having fun?" Mimmie asked.

"Just the lady I was looking for." Tinker took Mimmie's hand. "Care to dance this lively polka, ma'am?" Mimmie threw her large head back and roared. Tinker winked at Nell as he led Mimmie away.

Skin astonished Nell by shyly asking her to dance. He was such a big man she worried that he might crush her in the exuberance of the polka. But, true to his puzzling character, he steered her through the vigorous dance as sure footed as a big graceful cat. Later she saw him jouncing little Juan on his shoulders while Pablo and Lupe danced in a quiet corner.

When the musicians took a break to eat, Newton Campbell joined Nell at the table where she sat with most of her crew. "My cattle brought a better price than I had anticipated," he said. "But I gotta tell you I'm down on my hands and knees holding this ranch together."

"You've heard I plan to sell my place?"

"Yeah. Boy, I hate to see it, gal. But don't nobody know better than I do what a hard time it is for you."

Nell bit the inside of her mouth. She had no idea it would be this hard to talk to her father's long time friend and neighbor about selling the ranch.

"Have you heard about 'em drilling for oil in east Texas?" Newton asked.

"I read a little about it in the newspaper."

"By dern, I just might give it a try. Won't be long, I'll not have anything left to lose. You catch my meaning?"

Nell nodded.

"Mimmie says you're going on a trip."

"That's right. As soon as I see my cattle loaded for Fort Worth."

"I'll send my boys over to your place first thing to help trail your herd."

"Thank you, Newton. For everything."

"You just take good care of yourself, hear?" Newton moved toward the musician's corner where they wound up playing a rowdy jig. The music and hollering drowned out all conversation. A group of cowboys from a ranch near Medina burst through the door just as the music reached a peak. They ran to the boards jigging and waving their hats. Nell could hear Mimmie's roaring laughter over the noise of feet stomping and hand clapping. One of the cowboys looked as old as Billy. His face turned crimson from the exertion and excitement. When the music came to a thunderous halt, everyone in the barn let out a yell.

Mr. Webb scooted across the bench to where Newton had been sitting next to Nell and waited until the noise died down before speaking. "I'll make you a deal," he said as she gathered plates and forks on the table in front of them. "I'll carry these dishes to the washtub if you'll dance the next waltz with me."

"There are more than enough ladies here to divide that chore but..." Nell smiled, thinking the carefree mood of the Medina cowboys had infected him along with everyone else.

"But what?"

"I'll dance the next waltz with you if you tell me whether or not Tinker is your real name."

"It's a deal." He smiled and walked off to get a tub. When he came back he said, "No, it's not."

"So what is your real name?"

"That's not part of the deal."

"At least tell me how you came to be called Tinker." She put a stack of plates in the tub he held.

"A school teacher started it. She gave me an old clock to take apart then try to put it back together. She said I was good at tinkering and dubbed me Tinker from then on."

"So, Mr. Webb, why—?"

Tinker set the tub down with a thud and reached for her wrist. "Call me Tinker, now that you know the history of my name, and dance with me."

"But, this is a schottische. I agreed to a waltz."

"It'll do."

There was a peculiar difference between standing a sociable distance from Tinker Webb and dancing with him. While Nell had not necessarily perceived him as a large man, he seemed substantial when she danced with him. That's the best way she could put it to herself. His chin nearly touched her forehead and she could smell the man-smell of him, of leather and outdoors, of boiled shirts and lye soap. She felt alien, as if another woman danced in the soft leather shoes that made the clippity sounds in the hall back home.

When the music stopped, she quickly stepped back to the task of clearing the tables. She felt flushed and fluttery. Something she ate, probably. Tinker carried the tub outside where she helped a group of ladies wash dishes and he drifted over to join in a conversation between Billy and Newton.

That night Tinker drove the wagon on the return trip to Carrageen so Pablo could ride in the back with Lupe. Juan's sleepy head lolled on the cushion of Skin's enormous belly. Thomas had lagged behind, slow to leave Louise, and for a while Nell thought he might want to stay and take his chances on getting a ride home later. But Tinker agreed to stop the wagon in front of the Campbell's house to give Thomas time to walk Louise to her door and tell her good night properly. Which, Nell assumed, meant give her a good night kiss.

They waited in the wagon for Thomas who was all but invisible in a dim shaft of light cast from a window of the Campbell house. Before long, he came bounding down the porch steps with his hands jammed in his pockets, a big white-teeth grin visible in the star shine. At the gate, instead of opening it and walking through, he executed a bad one-handed vault over it and landed, like a two hundred pound sack of potatoes, flat on his back on the other side. Everyone in the wagon except Goose looked away.

"I didn't count on you making it through the night without bumping the ground with your tail least oncet," Goose said.

Thomas pulled himself up, climbed on the wagon, and watched the Campbell's house diminish with the distance.

As always, when things were quiet, Skin sang. His tunes were usually soulful, his voice so sincere, it made Nell nostalgic and melancholy. She thought of her father and how, years ago, he stomped the jigs and twirled the ladies. A feeling of loss settled on Nell when she realized she could not bring his face to mind. But she remembered clearly the sound of his voice calling out her name and the feel of it vibrating in his chest while she, a small girl, sat on his lap listening to him read the newspaper out loud to her mother Hilda.

Thoughts of her mother conjured feelings of deep sadness and disappointment. How lonely they must have been, a woman without the genteel life she felt was due her and a man with no one to share his exuberance for ranching life. That they loved each other deeply was never a question in Nell's mind. She'd seen the tender glints in her father's eyes when he watched Hilda. And Hilda admired his quick mind and his courage. They were different poles attracted to one another, but completely incompatible.

Tinker turned the wagon off the main road and passed through Carrageen's gate. The moon hung low in the southeast casting an alien, phosphorescent light across the backs of wispy clouds. She shivered.

"Are you cold?" Tinker asked.

"No. I'm all right."

At the barn, everyone crawled sleepily from the wagon while Pablo and Thomas unhitched the team. Tinker said his good nights, made his way out of the barn and headed toward his camp.

Nell called out to him.

He stopped and turned.

"It's so late, why not stay in the bunkhouse? There's plenty of room."

"Sometimes I think I've slept outdoors so long that I prefer it."

"Before the bandit raids got troublesome, I'd camp out on the range sometimes, too. It cleared my head. At least that's what I told myself." She gave him a parting nod and turned to leave but stopped short. "Oh, I keep forgetting the slicker you loaned me. It's in the house."

He walked that way with her. "Nell, the other night, in the rain storm, I thought I saw someone moving around in the dark. Didn't think too much of it at the time. But remember the tracks we saw at the old barn? I'm figuring you might have a problem."

"Oh?"

"I checked the next morning and found fresh tracks from that rocky draw right up to the barn."

"I've suspected drifters have been using it. In fact, some of that bunch at the barn dance tonight could be planning to stop there before heading back to Medina."

"Nell, only trouble moves on a stormy night like that."

"I-I understand. I'll send Pablo out to look around tomorrow, but more than that, I don't know what else can be done."

"I thought you should know. Maybe have the boys watch for signs. I overheard you tell Newton you still plan to sell your place. I kind of thought you might have a change of mind if your cattle bring a good price."

"There's so much more involved than money."

"Like what?"

Nell sat on a porch step and drew up her knees. Tinker's face was barely visible in the darkness, making it easier to talk freely. "My future, for one thing. Ranching has changed and I don't know how, or have the drive, to change with it. And the thought of growing old and stiff out here alone..." She didn't finish.

"What would your father have you do?"

"Stick it out to the bitter end, no doubt about it. Why do you hang onto your father's homestead, Tinker?"

"Can't say, now that you ask. Just seems the thing to do. I've had bad times there too, but I figure hard times turn sooner or later. And getting feeble minded is sure to be more fun on my own place where nobody can bother me than anywhere else I can think of."

"There's an emptiness in me, like I missed something somewhere along the way. Long rides on the prairie, sunsets, and campfires no longer fill the emptiness."

"Maybe you'll feel different when you get back from your trip." Tinker leaned on a porch post. "I heard you tell Newton about that, too. How long will you be gone?"

"About a month."

The night seemed especially still. Somewhere far away a Poorwill repeated his feeble call over and over. Across the barnyard Thomas and Pablo said their good nights to each other.

Nell stood. "I'll get your slicker." She returned a moment later. "You know, while I'm gone may be the best time for you and Pablo to work on the chimneys. I won't be in your way."

"Now, I thought you were a pretty fair hand myself, working on the windmill."

She still couldn't see his face clearly, only the white flash of his teeth when he smiled. She handed him the slicker. He tipped his hat.

*****

TINKER WAITED UNTIL he heard the soft thump of the door closing behind Nell before turning to leave. He walked around the house to the side yard gate, paused and glanced around. Convinced no one was looking, he tossed the slicker over to the other side. Then, instead of opening the gate to walk through, he performed a one-handed vault and landed solid on both feet on the other side. He picked up the slicker, hitched his britches and sauntered on to his camp where Jack greeted him with a yelp.

"Let me tell you something, dog. That lady can curl my whiskers. Not something I'm necessarily proud of, you understand."

Jack yawned.

"Has me behaving like some tin horn idiot." Tinker sat on his bedroll. Jack listened intently to every word.

"It's a mighty unsettling thought that a man as smart as me can get so riled up over a woman. Oh, she's fine, let me tell you, but just what in hell does a man like me think he..." Tinker strained to pull his boot off and tossed it out of sight. "Hell, you don't know about such things. I don't know why I ever try to talk to you."

*****

NELL WAS ON her feet and running long before she understood why. Turned out to be a reflex to the loud banging that echoed up the stairwell from the kitchen door. Someone was yelling, but in her sleep fog she couldn't determine who.

She flew down the stairs and glimpsed Thomas through a window. She grabbed Samuel's Winchester from the gun rack behind the door before flinging it open.

"Miss Miggins, it's Skin. Billy says you gotta come see."

"Skin?"

"He's a sight, I tell you. Billy says he don't know what to make of him." Thomas had started down the steps as he spoke. Nell followed. The sliver of moon was almost overhead which meant they'd been home from the Campbell's place only a few hours. Just long enough for her to reach a deep sleep.

In the bunkhouse Skin was sitting at a small table in the center of the room sobbing hysterically, his face wet and flushed. Billy sat next to him shaking his head hopelessly. "Son, you gonna have to tell us what's ailin' ya before we can help."

When Skin saw Nell step into the lantern glow, he threw his head back and let out a loud wail. His massive body quivered uncontrollably.

"Don't know what come over him, Missy," Billy said. "His blubbering woke me up about an hour ago. Keeps getting worse. All I can get out of him is some Bible talk about shaming hisself."

Nell took the chair Billy offered. "Something tells me that's not good for the rest of us."

Skin leaned forward to wail into his folded arms.

"Skin, get a hold of yourself and tell me what's wrong," Nell said.

He shook his head, mumbled something.

"I can't hear you Skin."

"My shame is God's revenge."

"What are you so ashamed of? Look at me, I can't hear you."

"I cain't look at you ever again."

"Has something happened? Have you hurt someone, tell me?"

Skin raised his head slowly. Looking from Billy, to Thomas and Goose, to Nell, he opened his mouth as if to say something but instead flung himself forward onto his arms bawling louder than before.

Nell closed her eyes, squeezed the bridge of her nose between her thumb and first finger then stood. "All right. Everybody take a walk. Out. Clear out, all of you. I want to talk to Skin alone."

Goose pulled on his boots. "Hell, I done told y'all he's loony."

"That's enough." Nell snapped back. When the bunkhouse was empty and quiet she tried again.

"Start slow, Skin. I've got all night, but start somewhere."

"I done a terrible thang, Miss Miggins."

"Worse than hitting Pablo?"

Skin nodded and wiped his face on his shirt sleeve. Nell went to the sideboard, poured water over a towel, handed it to him but remained just out of his view. "Go on."

"I cain't, I just cain't. It's awful bad." He shook his head. "Why cain't I get myself straight like most folks? You been mighty good to me, Miss Miggins. And little Juan and Lupe, they is just about the sweetest thangs this side of heaven. I got no call to harm 'em ever."

"Have you done something to hurt them?"

"It's too late."

"Let me decide that. Please." Nell placed her hand on the back of his chair steadying herself for what he had to say.

"When I first come to Wishing I's camping outside town, you know past the bridge, over the creek? And…" He paused to sob and wipe his red swollen eyes with the towel. "This bunch of Mexcans wandered by, called me *amigo*, and such as that." He glanced at Nell as she eased herself back into the chair next to him.

"Go on, Skin. You're doing fine."

"Well, I's kinda nervous at first, thinking they might be bandits and all. But they had a good smell, you know, like honey from cactus blossoms and that yellow tree grows 'tween here and the Rio Grande. They's nice to me. We played some cards and joked around. We even had us a snort of that *pulque* drink. Course, I didn't catch most of their Mex-talk, you know? Anyhow this one greaser, er ah, I mean fellar, told me all about how the rich ranchers in Mexico, *hidalgos* he called 'em, rule over the *peons* making 'em work for next to nothing. They ain't got a chanct to get ahead—" He stopped abruptly, glanced at her.

"What is it? Why have you stopped?"

"Like me, Miss Miggins. I'm a *peon*, ain't I?"

"No, Skin. You're a cowhand on my ranch."

"I was a *peon* before, though. That's why I done what I done."

"And…what did you do?"

Skin hiccuped and swallowed hard. "I give 'em some army guns so's they could fight the Rurales, them Mex-can government soldiers. They said when the poor *peons* win the revolution they'd give me land in Mexico for helping 'em out. Then, after I come here to your ranch…well me and them Mex-cans decided to meet where the draw cuts across to that empty house where Tinker took me to get the lumber."

"So it was you he saw in the rain that night?"

"What?"

"Never mind, what happened there?"

Skin sucked in a big breath then his face wadded into a red ball. Nell could do little more than wait. If she pushed him too hard, he might lapse into another hysterical spell.

"Skin?"

"By this time, I'm hearing 'bout all the bad stuff they done to ranchers like you, Miss Miggins, 'n them professors. I says to 'em that they hadn't oughta done that. I give 'em guns to fight the Rurales, not raid Texas ranchers and people minding their own business. Besides, I didn't have nothing to do with the army no more and couldn't get my hands on no more guns. They said fine, but their women and little babies was starving so I should help steal some cows to butcher iffen I still want a ranch of my own in Mexico."

He ducked his head, wrung the towel into a knot. "I done it, Miss Miggins. I brought 'em some of your beeves…for the little ones like Juan…over there in Mexico that they said was starving."

"But Skin," Nell said relieved. "You were right to try to help the innocent—"

"That ain't all."

Nell braced herself.

"The other night in the rain? Well sir, I told 'em I didn't believe they were feeding that rustled beef to no babies and women. Not from what I heard you and the others saying. I figured they was trading the beef for guns somewhere else. The leader, the one that talks good English says to me real uppity-like that I was sassing him, that I had to bring him a wagon load of ammunition." Skin's eyes grew larger as he spoke. His head moved side to side as if to deny the truth of his words. He looked at Nell. "I told 'em I didn't have no ammunition and wouldn't give it to them iffen I did. That's the truth, Miss Miggins. I swear. But that leader man, he said they would raid this here ranch iffen I didn't."

Nell slumped back into her chair as the gravity of Skin's words hit her. "When?"

"Could'a been he said it just to scare me. Oh, Lordy. There will be no end to my shame this time."

"Skin, listen to me. You're wrong. Your shame ends right here by telling me the truth, but I need help." She shook his massive shoulders. He looked confused as she dashed across the room and swung the door open. Billy and Thomas, who'd been listening at the keyhole, jumped back.

"I heard," Billy said.

"Gather all your guns and meet me at the house. I'll go wake Pablo."

"I done sent Goose."

Wheeling around to Skin, Nell asked again, "When do you think they'll be back?"

"Coming home from the dance, I noticed there wasn't but a little bit of moonlight. That's when they like to stir trouble and it's

two nights I haven't showed up at the other place like they said I
should."

"Help Billy load the guns."

"Yes, ma'am." Skin's face got pink and hopeful looking.
"I'll guard you and this here ranch with my soul, Miss Miggins. And
spend the rest of my life making this up to ya, I swear."

Nell held his gaze long enough to realize he had faced his
troubled past for what it was. And finally, in telling his awful truth,
set himself straight with the world in spite of it. Skin nodded as if
hearing her thoughts.

She grabbed the rifle and bolted out the door in a dead run
for the main house. Upon reaching the back stoop, she heard a shot
ring out from beyond the barn. The sound of it repeated over and
over in her head. She felt she was moving into a gray, cloudy space
between dream and reality.

Was this the price to be paid for staying with the ranch too
long? Or, the price for wanting to leave it? She should have given up
long ago, moved away like Hester. She had nothing to show for all
the work and hardship of being alone so much.

A choking weight pressed down on her as she tried to think
what to do. The cattle were as secure as they could be, given the fact
that there were few cowhands to keep them from scattering. And,
what of those who looked to her for direction and safety? In the
bunkhouse she'd behaved as if she knew what to do when actually,
she hadn't a notion. The ranch had never been attacked by bandits.
How was she to know what to do?

A memory vision flashed across her mind. She was a small
child in her mother's arms looking out one of the upstairs windows.
Samuel was below them on the porch steps with a rifle in his right
hand. It was dead winter. Sleet dripped off the wide brimmed hat of a
horseman who had led two others through the gate and right up to the
porch. The muffled talk between Samuel and the horseman stopped
when the horseman looked up at Nell and her mother standing in the
window. He'd grinned, showing rotted teeth and Nell felt her mother
tremble.

The stranger twisted in his saddle, said something to the others, and when he turned back, Samuel raised his rifle and fired point blank. He shot and wounded the other men before the first fell from his horse. Her mother's scream had filled all the rooms in the house and the sound repeated itself to Nell just now.

She ran through the kitchen to the hall where she grasped the newel post at the bottom of the stairway. Someone cried out from the direction of the barn, and for some ridiculous, absurd reason she realized she was bare footed. A gunshot echoed across the yard. Several more followed. At first Nell thought she heard the voices of dozens of people, then realized the noise actually came from chickens clucking in a frenzy. Horses' hooves thundered outside. She dashed up the stairs for her boots. Shouts were followed by the staccato pop of gunfire.

Before she made the upstairs landing, the front door burst open. A man, silhouetted by an amber light, stood in the doorway with his feet wide apart, a six shooter in each hand. He wore a huge sombrero with a band of thick silver conchos and belts of bullets strapped across his chest. In the seconds it took for his vision to adjust to the dark inside the house, Nell sprinted on up to the top of the stairs. Lupe and Juan flooded her thoughts. Were they safe? Had Goose had time to reach Pablo's house? She whirled around and raised the rifle.

"*Ay-e-e, bueno.*" The bandit sneered up at her. He raised his guns and fired all around the hall breaking mirrors, vases, and windows. He laughed showing yellow teeth.

"Stop!" Nell screamed, terror bubbling in her throat. She pressed the rifle to her shoulder.

The Mexican bandit, still snickering like a rabid rodent, started up the stairs, firing overhead as he went. Nell gulped air, tightened her grip and squeezed the trigger. The bullet grazed his shoulder. He stopped firing and looked, wild eyed, from his bleeding shoulder and then back at her before continuing up the stairs two at a time. She jerked back on the lever but it jammed. Horrified, she struggled to free it then gave up and dashed to her room. She locked the door, threw the rifle on the bed and frantically searched through the drawers of her dresser for the small pistol she had carried in her reticule years ago when she traveled to Fort Worth alone on horseback.

The bandit kicked at the door like a frenzied animal. Panic seized Nell. A booming voice called her name outside the open window. She smelled smoke. Horses were screaming. Her bedroom filled with a strange moving yellow light. She searched through drawers and boxes flinging them aside as she went, but was unable to find the pistol.

Again from outside, someone howled her name and the pounding on her door intensified. Nell gave up trying to find her pistol and reached for the rifle. As she struggled with the lever, the bandit managed to splinter the door above the knob. He reached in and felt around for the lock. She jabbed his hand with the rifle butt. He caterwauled like a mountain lion.

Nell ran to the window and realized the smoke and yellow glow came from the barn, which was engulfed in flames. Could she bring herself to jump? Nell glimpsed Pablo running across the open space between the corrals and the barn. Behind him horsemen were riding off into the dark night.

At that same moment, the bandit kicked the door open and lunged for her. Nell wheeled around and took a swing at him with the rifle. He knocked it to the floor with one hand, grabbed a fist of her hair with the other. A sickening grin curled under his thick, matted mustache. Nell kicked the mushy flesh of his groin. When he doubled over, she swung up with a balled fist, slammed the tip of his nose, then sprinted for the open door.

He managed to grab the hem of her nightgown as he dropped to his knees. She tripped to the floor with a thud. Air whooshed from her lungs. Gasping and clawing, she reached for the rifle that now was barely within her reach. She rolled over onto her back and used it to whack the bandit's head. She wiggled free of his loosened hold, stood and yanked back on the lever one last time. The used casing ejected and the next bullet slipped into place.

Nell pressed the rifle to her shoulder. The bandit pushed up from the floor and stood with the tip of the rifle barrel wavering inches from his chest. His eyes narrowed.

Nell understood he would either rape and kill her or force her to kill him. Either way, he controlled the situation and in that, considered himself triumphant.

He reached for her.

Nell thumbed the hammer. Sweet Jesus, let it fire, she prayed then squeezed the trigger.

The air in the room exploded. Something warm splashed her face and nightgown, the acrid smell of gun smoke burned her throat. The bandit froze, eyes wide, as he looked in disbelief at the great bubbling hole in his chest, and then back at her before falling backward.

The blaze from the barn illuminated the room with orange wavy light. Thick smoke boiled just outside the window.

"Nell!" A voice cried out below her window. A dog barked madly. Men were calling out to each other above the crackling blaze. Strange moving shadows everywhere.

Nell was seized by an unendurable need to scream but it caught in her throat, blocking her breath. She stared at the sight on the floor. A red, wet stain spilled around the man lying there next to her bed.

Then something was squeezing her shoulders, keeping her from wiping away the red liquid on her arms. A shadow hovered over her in the orange smoke. Scream, she thought. Scream. But the scream wouldn't come even though her mouth was open. The shadow spoke. Had daddy killed another man? No, she had killed a man. But then another was here holding her. Nell kicked and clawed but the man-shadow held her arms to her sides.

"Nell! Nell!"

The scream finally came tearing itself from her throat and she went limp with its release. What was to become of her? She had killed a man and had no energy left to fight unknown shadows.

The grip on her arms eased and a cloth, smelling of leather and wood and lye soap, came through the smoke toward her. It dabbed at her face and the fabric of her nightgowned arms.

"Tinker?"

"It's over. Pablo and the others are all okay."

He reached to wipe another splatter of blood from her arms, but she jerked back, shivering uncontrollably. He found a shawl draped across the end of her bed, handed it to her.

She pulled it tight around her shoulders and let him lead her toward the door. When she stopped to look back at the bandit, Tinker nudged her to keep moving. But her feet were rooted to the floor. In one swoop, he lifted her and carried her down the stairway.

***

SHERIFF WILKES CONFIRMED what Skin told Nell when he identified the dead man's boots as those belonging to Bob the Buffalo Soldier. The bandit was one of the Garza brothers, no doubt about it. His saddle had enough silver decoration on it to burden a pack of mules.

"All the telegrams I got about the brothers claim that wearing a lot of heavy silver is a passion for them. They were pretty tight, Nell. This dead man's brother might come back to avenge what happened here. Don't mean to scare ya. Just saying."

Thomas and Goose loaded the dead man's body on a horse for the sheriff to haul to Wishing.

No one else was hurt, though Tinker was fairly sure he had shot one of the bandits when he rode up from his camp. Skin had slumped pale as a ghost on the porch while the sheriff made his investigation. No one mentioned his bunkhouse confession.

Goose had awakened Pablo but they hadn't been able to make it back to the bunkhouse or main house before the bandits stormed the ranch. They fired guns from the windows of Pablo's quarters while Lupe and Juan hid in a trunk. Billy and Thomas had only one gun between them. Skin spent most the time squatting on the floor trying to free the hammer on a rusty pistol he found on a shelf next to some old rags. The bandits started a fire in the barn for a screen behind which they hoped to scatter livestock. The same smoke screen gave the cowhands in the bunkhouse the opportunity to pull the buckboard, wagon, and some of the equipment from the burning barn.

As soon as the sun bobbed up over the horizon, Thomas and Goose rode out to alert Newton Campbell. Newton sent two of his men back with them to help round up the scattered livestock.

Tinker moved his wagon up close to the house and openly grumbled about the state of the rifle Nell had used to kill the bandit.

"The miracle is that the thing didn't blow up in her face," he complained to Billy.

Everyone worked feverishly for the next several days to return things to normal. Newton's boys worked from sun up until sundown repairing the corrals. The cattle were still in fairly large bunches, easy to haze back to the holding pens. In all, Nell considered herself lucky that after final counts they lost only eight cows, two calves and one horse. She could hardly bemoan the loss of the barn for being so grateful no one was hurt.

Pablo suggested to Nell that he leave the livestock in Thomas' charge so he and Tinker could ride to town for lumber for a new barn. Nell agreed. Tinker ordered Jack to stay at the house, explaining to Skin that the dog would help alert them if there was trouble, but Nell felt another attack on the ranch was unlikely. If the bandits were still around, they knew by now that she had little they would want or need in the way of guns or ammunition. Still, the sheriff's warning made her uneasy.

A gloom settled on Nell as she watched Pablo and Tinker drive the scorched wagon down the road toward town. She had allowed everything to go wrong. She should have been more cautious where Skin was concerned. While she didn't believe he acted out of malice, she should have been alert enough to have had him partner with Thomas. In the old days her father always had new hands partner with older, trusted men. If she had followed the tradition, there might have been a clue as to Skin's coming and going. Yet in spite of everything she still believed he was more accurately judged by her heart than her mind. Her intuition told her that he was a good and gentle soul but confused and unsure about the line between right and wrong – and that's where the danger had been. In a conversation over biscuit dough, Nell learned that Lupe had come to the same conclusion. After the night of the raid, Skin slept on the front porch with a rifle ready at his side, stating again and again that he would spend the rest of his life defending the ranch. Nell half-heartedly insisted he return to the bunkhouse. But in truth she had grown accustomed to hearing his sweet hymn-singing drift up from the porch each night. Strange as it was, she sensed Skin was where he should be, a place he could fit into, to call home. A place where he could feel right with the world.

Nell regretted she'd ignored the need to have guns in good repair and on hand for the men. She should have had a lookout, both at the ranch gate and on the cattle – barn dance or no. She came very close to losing people she depended on and loved. Had that happened, she'd have been more guilty than Skin. At least, he had acted in good faith, thinking he was helping innocent, deserving people win a revolution. She, on the other hand, had failed to act at all.

Now, watching Tinker's thick broad back and Pablo's lean narrow shoulders sway with the wagon as it traveled away from the ranch, Nell felt limp with despondency. She should take charge, go along to help. But a troubling, unnamable affliction paralyzed her.

The two men, Pablo and Tinker, had become fast friends even before the events of the last days flung them into each other's company. They could not be more different physically and not more alike in temperament. Tinker had been a godsend. He stepped right in with the others taking directions from Pablo and at times offered suggestions.

Try as she might, Nell could not clearly remember the last moments of that terrible night. She did recall, however, as in a misty dream, that Tinker stood at the bottom of the stairs with her face tucked into the crook of his chin and neck. How odd that she could remember the feel of his thick arms around her with such clarity and yet little of anything else that was said or done after the attack.

Whenever she closed her eyes, she saw flashes of fire and smoke and heard a jumble of sounds, gunfire, men yelling. Lupe told Nell that terror had done that to her mind. That knowing she had killed a man had left her insensible.

For the first time in her life, Nell cowered, wanted to keep her face tucked under Tinker's chin. For the cowering and the want, she was profoundly humiliated and ashamed of herself.

***

TINKER AND PABLO drove directly to the lumber yard where Tinker selected lumber for the barn and Pablo bought replacement tools for those lost in the fire. Though he knew it was none of his business, Tinker worried about the expense. The people at Carrageen were a kindhearted bunch and he would have done anything to prevent the losses, both material and spiritual.

Pablo finished signing the necessary receipts and joined him in the lumber yard where their purchases were loaded.

Tinker looked around and down the street. "Pablo, do you know where I can send a telegram?"

"The depot," Pablo said without looking up from his list.

"Think I'll mosey over and take care of some business."

Pablo nodded.

After sending his telegram, Tinker returned to find Pablo loaded and waiting. In no time they were on the open road headed back to Carrageen. Tinker couldn't soak up enough of the view of the hills. He supposed he could stay a month on top of one of them watching days float by under wispy white clouds, and never get tired of it.

He leaned back on the seat and crossed his ankles. To the south, a red-tailed hawk soared on an invisible current of air. It looked as if it were toying with the wind, spiraling high then gliding down. "Does Nell still plan to go to San Antonio?"

"*Sí*. And then to the coast. I, for one, am glad. She needs it now more than ever."

Back at the ranch, Tinker seized the job of rebuilding the barn. The smell of new lumber and the odd rhythm of saw and hammer put to task were things he appreciated and admired.

Pablo, for the most part, concerned himself with the cattle. Tinker heard him tell Billy that the herd was to be resorted into three groups according to their ear notches as they had been before the raid. When Tinker asked Pablo what Nell planned to do with three groups of cattle, Pablo said he didn't know. It made sense, Tinker thought, that she would try to hold on to some brood stock and then sell the rest. But what of the third group?

He saw little of Nell during the following days. Like Pablo, she spent most of her time with the cattle or within the fenced yard around the house. She moved about with her eyes lowered. When she walked from the corrals to the house, her eyes scanned the ground just beyond the toes of her boots and when she came out again in the morning it was the same. He wanted to call her name from up on the ladder and have her hand him a hammer, just to see her look up, just once, so she would know things weren't really so bad.

Just now he heard a woman laugh. Though she was nowhere in sight, he remembered seeing Nell in the garden when he fetched nails from the supply box. Juan let out a squeal from the same direction.

"Oh, now stop! Get!" he heard Nell say.

He climbed down from his ladder, rounded the corner of the barn in time to see bean vines rustling in the garden. Suddenly Juan's head popped up above the vines. He ran down a bean row as fast as his little legs would carry him. Jack let out a high-pitched yelp from somewhere behind Juan. Juan squealed. Nell was still laughing.

"Jack!" Tinker yelled. Bean vines thrashed wildly.

Nell popped up above the vines, flushed from her giggles and brushed dirt from her clothes. Jack barked again and she jumped, startled.

"Jack!"

Juan squealed again and dove out of sight. When he reappeared at the garden's edge, he had a huge frog squeezed in his hands and was holding it out of Jack's reach.

"Get, dog!" Tinker yelled a third time. Jack tucked his tail and moved away. "Sorry if he bothered you." Tinker reached to re-tie bean vines Jack had torn from poles. But he wasn't really sorry, not if the dog made Nell smile.

"He gave me quite a start. I thought at first he had a snake cornered, the way he was behaving." She handed him a strip of cloth to use to tie the vines. "When I tried to scramble after my hoe, I got tangled in the vines and fell."

"I'll see he stays over by the barn."

"Oh, no. Actually, he's fine. I mean, no bother." She brushed a wisp of hair from her face. "Did Pablo tell you we'll start trailing the herd tomorrow?"

He nodded.

"Everyone is going, even Juan and Lupe. I'm not willing to take a chance on leaving them here alone.

"Are you afraid?"

"Of another raid? No, but I don't want to risk it. I-I don't think I ever properly thanked you for your help that night. I've been meaning to ask... I realize you may have other work besides what you're doing here, that you hadn't planned on building a barn. If you need to leave before it's all finished, I would understand."

"I'll see the job through, Nell."

Juan let out a piercing scream. The frog had gotten away from him and Jack was after it in short, playful hops.

"Here, dog! Stop." Tinker took off after the frog while Nell caught up to Juan and wiped his tears with the tail of his shirt. Tinker managed to capture the frog under his hat and then called out to Juan. "Come with me and I'll fix you up."

Nell followed them to Tinker's wagon.

"A fellar's got to be able to keep up with his livestock, now isn't that right, son?"

"*Sí*, yes." Juan said.

"Why, he almost never speaks" Nell was astonished.

"A man of few words, nothing wrong with that."

Tinker opened and closed several doors and drawers in the side of his wagon before finding the patch of leather he was looking for. Then he fashioned a small harness for the frog using tiny embroidery scissors and tweezers. Nell and Juan stood watching quietly as he tied string to the harness and to the end of the string, a stick.

"There you go, *amigo*." Tinker handed the stick to Juan. "Now don't let him go hungry. I bet you can find him some worms and bugs in the garden."

Juan took the stick and threw his free arm around Tinker's leg, giving it a tight hug. For a blink of time Tinker couldn't respond. His heart thumped a hard beat. "Well, now, you're mighty welcome." He patted Juan's back.

Nell took a step back. "I suppose you need to get back to work—" She backed into one of the barrel chairs and tipped it over. The contents scattered everywhere. "I can't believe I'm having such a hard time staying on my feet today."

She stopped short when she glimpsed a tooled leather framed photograph that had tumbled from the barrel chair. Tinker couldn't believe it landed face up.

Nell picked it up, studied the pretty woman with light hair and delicate features sitting on a small wicker bench, and next to her, a little boy about Juan's age. "What a lovely woman." When he didn't say anything she glanced up with a questioning look.

"My wife and boy."

"But you said you weren't married."

He took the photograph from her, dusted it with his sleeve, and put it, along with the other things back into the barrel chair. "My boy was one of the first to die when the yellow fever epidemic hit Galveston. He was five years old. She died a few days later."

"Oh, Tinker, I'm sorry."

"It was a long time ago, nearly fifteen years." He propped his foot on the barrel chair. "We all have private troubles, don't we, Nell?"

"Is that why you left Galveston?"

"I had no reason to stay."

Skin rode up and dismounted. "Pablo done sent me to see iffen ya need help with the barn."

Tinker hitched his britches. "As a matter of fact I do."

"I'll leave you to your work then," Nell said.

He watched until she reached the edge of the garden before turning back to Skin. "Help me stack that lumber over here."

Skin put his head down and went to work. Tinker was sorry for him. The more Skin learned about a better way of life, the more he would realize what an awful thing he'd done to lead the bandits to the ranch. "Pablo tells me you're from Alabama."

"That's right."

"Where'd you learn so many hymns?" Tinker hoisted a wide plank onto his shoulder.

"Well sir, I run away from home pretty young 'cause things was pretty bad there. East of Birmingham the weather turned bitter cold on me and I took sick. Some sheriff found me aside the road and took me to a doctor. Doctor says to the sheriff that he just as well take me to the preacher 'cause I wadn't goin' to make it and it'd give the preacher a little extra time to pray over me and all." Skin stopped.

Tinker motioned to another stack of lumber. "Go on."

"Why, I reckon I never told of it. Anyways, when I come to, I's laying in an honest to gosh bed. That was somp'in, you see, 'cause I'd been sleepin' on the frozen ground longer than I could say. Brother Jackson, that was the preacher's name, pinched his wife's cheek and said it was her doin' that I lived – her poultices and all – and she says no, it was his praying. That's kinda how they was.

Well sir, Brother Jackson gets me to stand up at meetin' time and says I's walking proof of the power of the Lord. On account of my white skin, I always look like I been at death's door so they got me to pass the plate when they told my story of being saved. Brother Jackson said I could live with 'em as long as I done my chores and passed the plate at prayer meetin' time." Skin dropped the last board in place and sat down. Tinker handed him a dipper of water.

"That still doesn't tell me where you learned to sing."

"Mrs. Jackson was choir leader. Could she ever bang that pianna. Made me go to all the practice times and she's always pushing food at me 'cause I's so skinny, believe it or not. I reckon they just wanted to keep me around to be part of the show. This ugly skin and my singing always pulled the crowds in, made people dig deep in their pockets. Anyways, that Mrs. Jackson taught me to sing hymns and a little opera on the side."

Skin got quiet for a minute, looked almost like he'd cry. "I thought I done found me a home there but..."

"What happened?" Tinker could have cut out his own tongue. The question just popped from his mouth.

"Mrs. Jackson sent me to take food acrost the railroad tracks to a poor family like she done every Wednesday, but this one time she followed me. Caught me peeking in a whorehouse window. She run me down the railroad tracks and out of town, a wavin' her Bible and whackin' me over the head with her umbrella."

Skin let a big sigh. "Spent the night under the stars without so much as a knife to kill and skin a critter to eat. I just sung my hymns to keep from thinking 'bout how hungry I was." He looked at Tinker as if he'd just thought of something. "I was a real old little boy, you know?"

Tinker nodded. He understood exactly.

"Next morn'n, I heard a train and started a runnin' to jump up on it. I eyeballed something to grab, missed on the first try but the second time I got a ladder rung. Only my leg hit a mile post and nearly got tore off. I flopped in that empty rail car like a dead fish, I tell ya, with my skinny ribs a heavin' up and down like gills. I swore then and there I'd never be hungry again...or cold neither."

"Didn't I hear you mention working in a saw mill?"

"Hell, Tinker. It's the same story all over again. I just ain't never been able to get myself right."

Tinker touched Skin's big shoulder. "I've got a feeling things will be different for you here at Carrageen."

Skin looked up at him. "I hope so. I surely do hope so. Least ways, I got my singing. Used to be I thought my keen sniffer would make me famous, but it sure failed me when it come to bandit trouble."

***

NELL HAD AN absurd urge to stay put and wallow. She must have been short on sensibilities when she planned her travels to coincide with trailing the herd to the railhead and putting her ranch up for sale. Even without the complications of a bandit raid, it would have been too much.

Skin drove the supply wagon, with Lupe and Juan as passengers. They left the ranch about a half hour before the herd to ride ahead of the dust and to have time to unload and make camp before dark.

Nell remained at Carrageen's gate with Pablo while Tinker and the other cowhands moved the cattle through. With Newton Campbell's men included, there were eight riders trailing the herd, enough to insure there would be little trouble.

When the last of the cattle moved out, Nell dismounted to close the gate. Early morning sun shine hit the ranch house at a peculiar angle. It looked gilded, durable, sustainable. If leaving Carrageen for a month is this painful, she wondered, how would she bring herself to leave forever?

Speckles bellowed after his herd. Nell couldn't see him, but she imagined he watched from some distant vantage point as his cows moved down the road. When it had come time to make the final cut of the herd, those that would stay and those that would go, she decided to leave the old bull behind. It seemed fitting that he should live out his days on Carrageen land, that his flesh should one day dust the violet hills, his bones left to bleach in the Texas sun. His bawling alternated between a roar and a painful wail, echoing far away in the hollows along the draw and bouncing off the rocky cliffs along the Guadalupe River.

"Time to go, *hermana*," Pablo said.

She closed the gate and swung up into the saddle.

At dusk Pablo, who was riding point, turned the herd to mill in a valley with a boxed canyon at one end. They knew the valley well, having used its natural configuration many times to hold a herd when trailing to the railhead. Nell caught the sweet scent of huisache blossoms. The scrubby low-growing trees grew thick along a stream formed by Huisache Springs. Any other time of year, Nell considered huisache a thorny nuisance, but in the spring the valley could be spotted from miles away because of a profusion of pale yellow blossoms that covered the trees.

Lupe and Skin had made camp and were dishing up beans and biscuits for the cowboys who were to take first night watch. Nell rode to the far end of a pool where water bubbled icy cold from the rocks. She dismounted and splashed her face and throat then sat back on her heels. A twig snapped behind her. She swung around with a start. Tinker was standing in slanted sunlight with a twig of blooming huisache in his hand.

He held the twig out to her. "Careful of the thorns." He rubbed his hand on his hip. "This sure is a pretty little valley."

She took the twig. "You think I'm wrong don't you, Tinker?"

"'Bout what?"

"Wanting to sell out."

He propped a foot on a big rock next to Nell. "Tell me it's none of my business if you want to, but seems to me this trip you're going on is a smoke screen. Something you can busy yourself with to avoid what's really bothering you."

She held the twig to her nose, used the motion to turn her face.

"Nell, sometimes a person can follow someone else's dream for so long they lose sight of their own."

She looked up into his face. How did he know she felt trapped, forced by some unwritten legend to continue operating the ranch as her father had?

Tinker wiped his face with his neckerchief. "What would you do different if you keep the ranch?"

"I–I don't have the heart for it anymore."

"If you don't sell out and could do anything, what would it be?"

Nell could see he wasn't going to let her get by without an answer. "Why...I'd..." He kept staring. "First thing I'd do is buy a couple of bulls."

"Yeah?"

"Cross bred bulls, maybe, with some Hereford blood like you did. Stocky cow but rugged enough to take this harsh country."

Tinker nodded.

"Then I'd look into seeding grasses in the river valley—" She stopped herself.

"Work fewer cattle, but healthier, heavier. Rotate the ranges." He finished for her.

Nell's heart sank. Maybe she should keep the ranch and try all those things. She couldn't make herself hold his gaze, so she took another sniff of the huisache twig before tossing it in the stream. "Will you take second watch with Skin?"

"Nell, I can't name what made me leave Galveston or what keeps me from going back to my homestead to live. But whatever it is stays with me wherever I go. And whatever you're trying to leave behind will go with you, too."

She closed her eyes and turned her back to him. She couldn't bear to watch his face or hear his words.

He took up the reins of his horse and headed over to the wagon where Goose and Skin sat arguing over the words to a cowboy song.

Late afternoon the next day, the herd reached the railhead holding pens outside Wishing. Nell had the herd sold and wages distributed in a matter of hours. She got as good a price as she could have hoped for, though it was still far below what her father had once been able to contract. She paid her due bills at the dry goods store and lumberyard and had some left to deposit at the bank. Her last and hardest task for the day, however, still lay ahead.

She walked the few blocks to the Sunday House where she joined Lupe and Juan who were waiting for Pablo. When he came in, Nell invited them to stay the night there with her, but Lupe explained that they would be staying with her newly married cousin whom she'd not seen for months.

After they left, Nell washed and changed clothes, then pulled a chair over to the window for extra light while hooking the buttons on her dress shoes. When she glanced up, she could see all the way down the side street, across Main Street, and down the next block to Grady Monroe's office. She'd made an appointment with him for that afternoon and hoped he hadn't forgotten.

Her thoughts were interrupted when Tinker and Grady came strolling down the sidewalk across the street from Grady's office. Sheriff Wilkes joined them and the three chatted. Grady gestured, slapped the back of one hand into the palm of the other while Tinker listened, back arched, arms folded loosely across his wide chest, nodding and thoughtful. She thought of his little boy in the photograph, the tilt of his head as if listening to something being whispered, like Tinker now, down the street.

No wonder he was such a gentle man. Sorrow had whittled down his edges, exposed soft places. She sighed, admitting to herself a sort of uncomfortable attraction for him. She liked being in his company, but his knowingness made her restless.

She waited until the men tipped their hats and Tinker had gone into the hotel before heading for Grady's office. It would get dark soon and she worried he would close up before she had a chance to talk with him.

"Nell girl," he said when she opened his office door. "I've been expecting you."

"I was worried you'd forget."

"Of course not. Forget, indeed. But I half hoped you would. You sure you still want to go through with this?"

"Yes."

Grady sat on the edge of his desk. "Someone interested in the ranch has already contacted me."

"What?"

Grady nodded.

"So soon. I'm shocked. Who is it?"

"The interested party wants to be anonymous for the time being. I'm thinking there are many details to be worked out, financing, that sort of thing. I just want you to be real sure before we move ahead."

"I see. Yes, by all means, move ahead." Nell heard her own voice, but couldn't believe her ears. She had assumed it would take a long time to find a buyer. "The house still needs work. The fire and bandit trouble set me back."

"The potential buyer knows about all that, but doesn't seem concerned. Still, it may be a good idea to sign a power of attorney for me in case they, or he, or whoever gets antsy before you get back from the Tres Palacios."

"I agree. But who could it be? Why anonymous?"

Grady shrugged. "I wrote to Austin explaining what your intentions were and asked for the legal papers showing there were no liens on the ranch. Could be someone there saw the request and is interested. Who knows?"

"Do you represent both of us?"

"No. You know better than that. Unethical as hell. I was contacted by a lawyer." Grady pushed off the desk and handed her a stack of papers. "Maybe by the time you get back all the details will have been worked out. Don't worry. Just go and have a good time. Tell that cousin of yours hello for me."

"What do I do with these?" Nell looked at the papers he handed her.

"Sign them, then have Pablo bring them to me to have his signature witnessed."

Nell was numb when she left Grady's office. A buyer? So soon?

Back inside the Sunday House her mind whirled like an uncertain wind in and out of memories. She couldn't sleep for all the voices talking in her head. Her father, grandmother, Hester, Grady, Pablo, all crowded her mind. And Tinker. He would probably be gone when she returned from her trip. Moved on to other towns and other windmills.

By dawn a damp wind blew down the street and pressed against the window where the day before Nell had watched Grady and Tinker. She was up and dressed when Pablo and Lupe knocked at the door. Lupe had a tin of biscuits and a canteen of coffee. As they ate, Nell was aware that Pablo watched her face with expectant glances as though this leave-taking was the Amen at the end of a hymn, or the closing of the front door at the end of a long day.

Lupe poured a second round of coffee. Nell handed Pablo the papers Grady had prepared for her, then pulled Juan onto her lap. Pablo waited for an explanation.

"It's a deed for two hundred acres along the northern portion of the ranch, bordered on one side by the river. The deed is made out to you and Lupe."

Pablo sat stone-faced. Lupe looked over his shoulder.

Nell reached across the table to flip the pages. "And this states that I have transferred ownership of twenty-five head of cattle to you. The twenty-five I had you ear-notch once. Those notched twice will be sold with Carrageen as brood stock." Lupe placed her hand on Pablo's shoulder. Nell rocked back and forth with Juan dozing on her lap.

"*Her-ma-na...*" Pablo looked down at the papers in disbelief. Lupe covered her mouth.

"Your birthright is with Carrageen as much as mine, Pablo."

He sprang from his chair, hugged her, and kissed both her cheeks before turning to Lupe. He swung her off her feet, twirled her around then quickly put her down. "But, are you sure this is your wish? There will be talk."

"Pablo, of all the decisions and changes I've had to face, this is the only one I've been sure about from the beginning. Besides, this town will get awfully dull without its old maid spinster around, so let them talk."

Nell reached for Lupe's hand. "You better start planning a house. I bet Billy and Skin, even Tinker will help while I'm gone."

"*Gracias. Muchísimas gracias,*" Lupe's eyes brimmed with tears.

"Take these papers to Grady as soon as you leave me at the depot. He will notarize them then send a surveyor out to mark the boundaries. Now I have only one concern left." Nell paused and looked down at Juan sleeping on her lap. "Since I have no idea when the ranch will sell or what I'll do or where I'll go, I didn't know how to provide for Billy."

Pablo glanced at Lupe. "He will have a home with us."

"*Sí,* of course," Lupe agreed.

Nell was flooded with relief her eyes brimmed with tears.

At the depot, while Lupe and Juan huddled against a gentle rain in the wagon with Skin, Pablo saw Nell to her seat on the train. She checked to be sure she had her grandmother's diary and the extra biscuits Lupe had packed for her. Outside the window she saw the conductor's mouth move saying "all aboard" but she couldn't hear him for a rumble of thunder. She turned to Pablo.

"I'll be home in one month."

"*Sí,* is good."

"Grady will help you with any business, legal or otherwise, should you need it." Pablo's sweet dark eyes held her gaze for a long moment. Her heart wrenched. He alone knew her as no one else in the world. He was her tie that binds. A smile trailed across her face.

Pablo thumped his hat brim. "*Adios.*" Then he turned and got off the train.

Nell settled in her seat next to a window and waved good-bye to the little group huddled in the rain. The train groaned then rolled inch-worm slow, its whistle blowing high and shrill. Jack was standing in the middle of the street, rain soaked, watching the train move away, barking relentlessly as dogs do to warn their masters. It was Nell's last image of Wishing before the train turned south into a thick grove of cottonwoods along the creek trestles. Then, in the blink of an eye, everything disappeared behind the cottonwoods, and she hadn't had time to look about for Tinker.

PART II

THE TRAIN SWAYED to its own clackity rhythm while a spring storm played out against the window where Nell sat. She felt cocooned in the damp passenger car, alone except for two men dozing under tented newspapers across the aisle and a few rows ahead of her. She imagined that from far away the train would appear as a long black thing, puffing and crawling, miniaturized by the vastness of Texas.

Memories ticked by as one image after another flashed into her mind like the moving pictures she had read about in a San Antonio newspaper, flickering shadows on a white surface in a darkened room.

A group of young fresh-faced soldiers entered the passenger car through the forward door. She assumed they were traveling to Fort Sam Houston in San Antonio. They settled into seats joking loudly and sputtering with laughter. Every now and then a few swaggered down the aisle to watch a game of cards in the rear of the car. Others sang songs she had never heard, while an especially homely soldier, thin as a willow switch and missing most of his front teeth, played a Jew's harp. Each time he finished a tune and lowered the harp, his toothless mouth glowed red from the vibrating metal.

The train stopped in a small town along the way and an elderly man and woman boarded. While the woman seated herself across the aisle, Nell watched her husband pause to talk with the soldiers. He patted a few on the back in a fatherly way and saluted those playing cards.

The woman leaned across the aisle toward Nell. "It's a man's endeavor, the business of war." She hadn't spoken in bitterness, though the notion was a terrible one. Rather, she'd said it as if they were all little children playing a pretend game without being aware of all the rules. Her husband eventually waddled down the aisle and settled, like a big rooster, shuffling feathers, wiggling and preening deep into his seat. As soon as he was still, he fell fast asleep and snored riotously all the way to San Antonio.

A steamy haze shrouded the waiting crowd when the train pulled into the San Antonio station. Nell was amazed to see the tangle of electric wiring that webbed the entire city.

Wilted and stiff, she looked forward to a few days of rest. She wanted to forget everything. Mountain lions, roundup troubles, wounded archeologists, bandit raids and broken down windmills. She hadn't written Hester about the raid on the ranch and worried that John would find out through his association with the Rangers. If that was the case Hester would never leave her alone about it.

Someone called out from her right. "Nell! Over here."

Tiptoeing, peering over the crowd, she glimpsed Marshall, Hester's oldest child and was shocked by how much he'd matured. Nothing of the little boy she had known remained on his face.

"Marshall, my goodness, you've grown so tall."

He leaned down to kiss her cheek. "Mother is waiting in the roadster."

They threaded through the crush of people and emerged at the street on the opposite side of the depot. Nell was dumbfounded by all the activity. She dared not take her eyes off Marshall's shoulder and risk losing him in the crowd. There were more people at the station than in all of Wishing. All of them moved in different directions, with separate purposes in what seemed total chaos.

"They are over there." Marshall motioned toward a big black automobile. Hester was sitting in the front seat like a queen on her throne. Her daughters were in the seat behind her. She stepped down from the automobile and gave Nell a quick hug.

Nell climbed into the back seat with the girls and took each of their hands into hers. Marshall supervised the porter securing her bags in the back of the automobile then hopped into the driver's seat. When he accelerated into the parting crowd Nell caught her breath. She would never admit to any of them that this was her first ride ever in an automobile.

Minutes later Marshall parked in front of their home a few miles from the bustle of San Antonio's business district. The girls bounced from the roadster, each pulling on one of her arms.

"Aunt Nell, come see my rabbits," Agnes pleaded.

Nan rolled her eyes. "Can you believe she gave up dolls then turned around and took up with a bunch of rabbits."

"Just think," Marshall said. "I don't have to listen to that kind of prattle after next week."

"Why is that?" Nell asked.

"He'll be going off to school." Hester answered for him. "John asked me to tell you he's sorry he couldn't meet you at the train station. He's at the recruiting office now. The Rangers have been asked to help lead a troop to the Rio Grande."

"Will John be going along?"

"Oh, heavens no."

Later that evening while waiting for John to come home, Nell and the girls worked on a jigsaw puzzle while Hester played the piano. In a private conversation with herself, Nell tried to assess what exactly made things under Hester's roof seem strained. But she decided to forget about it, get some rest and later on, when she reached the coast, try to sort out her own life.

Marshall clopped heavily down the stairs just before dark to announce he was leaving and wouldn't be home until late.

"Can't you wait until after dinner? It's Nell's first night with us." Hester sounded more pitiful than maternal.

Marshall kissed Nell's hand ceremoniously. "I'm sure she will excuse me."

"I'm not getting involved." Nell pulled her hand away and winked at Marshall though she wasn't sure she felt all that playful about being put in the middle.

He backed out of the room with a disquieting grin that seemed to ask: who can stop me? He left by the back door.

"I hope he comes home with his pockets loaded again." Nan pressed a puzzle piece into place.

"What are you talking about?" Nell asked.

"Why, he gambles, Cousin Nell." Nan's voice had a mocking edge to it.

"He does not," Agnes barked.

Hester pounded the piano keys. "Girls, stop." At the same time the front door boomed open and slammed shut, rattling all the windows.

John Woodvine paraded into the room with his arms wide spread. "Nell, good to see you." He squeezed Nell's hands and kissed her cheek.

Nell was startled by his appearance. The once thick shock of black hair was thin and gray, his eyes red and hazy. At one time she thought John was like a dust-throwing bull, charging through life without restraint. But now he looked almost seedy.

Hester led the way to the dining room. "John, I thought you were going to have a talk with Marshall? He's gone off again tonight."

"Leave the boy alone. It's perfectly normal for him to adventure at his age." John poured himself a large bourbon and cast a side glance at Hester.

He gulped his drink. "My dear, I will be leaving with the troops in the morning. I know you'll understand, and Marshall won't mind that I'm not here to see him off to school. Besides, you've handled these things on your own before."

Hester's fork froze in mid air. Her mouth, slightly open, formed a silent Oh. She put her fork down. "John, you've been away so much lately. Surely—"

He popped up from his chair to pour another bourbon. Nell glanced at the girls eating in silence, seemingly unaware of the sparks flying between their parents.

A loud clanging broke the strain. It startled Nell so much she tipped her water glass over. "What was that?"

"It's a telephone," Agnes said. "A wonderful thing to have. Daddy can call Mama or Mama can call the drug store and order things without having to go out."

A servant stepped in the doorway to tell John a colonel wanted to talk to him. When John left the room the girls excused themselves. Hester sat staring silently out the window. Nell moved around the table and squeezed her shoulder. John Woodvine had been difficult to tolerate in the past, but now Nell found his self-absorbed behavior sickening. He remained aloof - or tipsy - Nell wasn't sure which, the rest of the evening. She realized now that this was the trouble she had sensed in Hester during her visit to Carrageen.

Next morning with John gone, Marshall in a dead sleep, and the girls off to their piano lessons, Nell and Hester had their first opportunity to be alone.

"I had no idea things were so lopsided for you," Nell said.

"What do you mean?"

"I see how hurt you are, Hester. John's drinking—"

"It's nothing. All men want to be heroes, Nell. Don't be silly."

"What about Marshall? You yourself said that John should talk to him. So you can't deny there's something wrong. I heard him come in last night, or I should say this morning. He was drunk. Bumping-into-walls drunk."

"You've been stuck on that ranch too long with dirty, ignorant people—" Hester stopped herself. "What would you know about husbands anyway?"

Hester hadn't lost her skill for biting where it hurt most. But this time she was the one hurting, burdened under the weight of her own denial. Her eyes were glossy, mouth fixed in a false smile, as if she were carved of wood and sanded to a hard, smooth finish.

"You were always willing to say hurtful things to hush me up," Nell said. "But this time you and your children suffer for not facing the truth."

"And you would have me believe your life is all roses?"

"We're talking about you."

"Nell, for heaven's sake."

"All right. Have it your way."

In the following days Hester, Nell, and the girls rode the trolleys criss-crossing San Antonio sight seeing and shopping. Hester never again mentioned John or his absence or Marshall's nightly escapes.

One evening they stayed in town to have dinner at the Menger Hotel. Their table on a raised terrace overlooked San Antonio and the river. Electricity was still new in Wishing, but here the whole town sparkled with lights. Across the way, Nell could see the dilapidated Alamo in the center of town. Progress and posterity radiated out from it like spokes of a wheel. It was hard to digest all the changes that had taken place, not only with Hester and her family, but in San Antonio as well. And apparently in the whole state east of her own Carrageen Ranch.

The day before she was to leave San Antonio, Agnes and Nan planned a picnic at one of the deserted Spanish missions on the outskirts of town. They pleaded with Marshall to come along since he would be leaving for college soon. He finally agreed and drove them down a narrow dirt road curving and twisting its way southeast. He stopped in a grove of trees near an old mission that was little more than stacked stones outlining rooms.

Marshall lifted the basket of food out of the automobile while Hester spread a quilt on a grassy spot. They ate boiled eggs, sweet biscuits and opened a quart jar of peaches Nell had brought along from Fredericksburg.

When they'd finished eating Marshall stood and stretched his arms over his head. "Nell, have you learned to drive?"

"An automobile? Heavens no."

"Come on then. Any lady who can run a ranch the way you do can learn to drive a roadster."

"I like my buggies and wagons, thank you."

Agnes and Nan chimed in, pleading, jumping up and down, begging her to do it.

"We'll all go along." Hester pushed up from the ground. The children shrieked with excitement. It was the first time since she had arrived in San Antonio that Nell felt Hester and her children were capable of experiencing joy. And though the thought terrified her, she'd try to drive the machine just to see them stay that way a while longer.

She had no trouble with the steering but accelerating at the same time proved too much. She narrowly missed a tree. Marshall told her to brake to a complete stop and start all over. Finally she steered the car in a smooth, wide circle and relaxed a little. When she turned to the back seat to see if the girls were impressed with her progress, Marshall let out a howl and covered his face. The roadster bounced into a stream bed strewn with rocks. The sudden stop knocked Hester's hat askew and sent the whole group into side-splitting laughter.

"Give up?" Nell asked Marshall.

"Yes!" His eyes were full of tears of laughter.

***

THE BANQUET HALL in Chicago where Henry Burleson was about to give his presentation speech was packed. He scanned the crowd several times to be sure Anthony Delgar and his daughter hadn't decided to leave early. Mr. Delgar, or Tony, as he'd asked Henry to call him, was the single most important person in the hall as far as Henry was concerned. And his daughter, Loretta Delgar, the second most important.

"Gentlemen, gentlemen." Randolph Peirce, the regent president had approached the podium and was attempting to quiet the crowd. "And ladies, of course." The crowd settled, laughing at the feeble reference he made to the few women present. Archaeology,

Henry thought, was a man's science after all, but women made an evening so much more enjoyable.

Peirce continued. "First let me speak on behalf of everyone here when I say how glad we are to have Professors Lawrence Scott and Henry Burleson returned and recovered from the ravages of their field trip to the wilds of Texas to study pictographs."

The crowd applauded. Henry stood, nodding here and there, allowing his eyes to linger in the direction of the Delgar table. He held his wine glass up to Scottie and bowed slightly. Scottie, who made no attempt to stand, nodded. It worried Henry that Scottie was taking so long to fully recover from the gunshot wound. And if he didn't, would the regents support his expedition without Scottie at his side? All the more reason to woo Tony Delgar.

Tony was a prominent, wealthy banker in Chicago who collected antiquities and fine art. They'd met at a mutual friend's wedding the year before. Because of Tony's interest in ancient history and artifacts, their paths crossed often at special museum showings, allowing a casual acquaintance to develop. Tonight Henry hoped to influence Tony with his expertise and evidence regarding his Mayan project. With someone that influential backing him, others surely would follow.

Peirce made a few more announcements then introduced Henry as the program speaker. Henry approached the podium and took his time shaking Peirce's hand during the applause.

"Ladies... and of course, gentlemen." Henry shrugged playfully, looking back at Peirce. The hall roared with laughter. "I am not a blind man. I know who makes an evening like this sparkle." He peered directly at Loretta Delgar for a long moment.

"Let me begin by assuring you there is little doubt Professor Scott and I have made a major discovery. As is often the case in our field, the discovery, while enlightening, also raises a multitude of questions. So be warned that as soon as I have finished this presentation, I will solicit financial backing for an extended expedition to the Yucatán Peninsula."

Henry could tell he had the crowd in the palm of his hand. When he finished the presentation, the applause was resounding.

Peirce made some closing remarks while Henry threaded his way slowly through the crowd toward Scottie, shaking hands and accepting congratulations as he went.

"Well done!" Tony Delgar clamped a portly hand on Henry's shoulder. "Tell me, in your search for Mayan secrets, do you think you'll discover any tombs?" His thick gray mustache never moved when he spoke, but his bottom lip scooped up and down like a sugar spoon.

"Every archaeologist dreams of it." They moved toward the adjoining hall where an orchestra was playing a waltz.

"For example?" Tony asked.

"Mayan history is virtually unknown, yet their hieroglyphs are there, under jungle growth, waiting to give us the answers. This, as you know, is my pet interest, the transcription of glyphs. Just think what we could learn."

"Interesting." Tony looked around the ballroom, Henry presumed for Loretta.

"There is something I haven't mentioned to anyone." Henry lowered his voice in an effort to hold Tony's attention a little longer. "A *cenote* is located in the area I hope to explore."

"A what?"

"*Cenotes* are enormous sink holes, water wells, you could say. There's a possibility this particular *cenote* was used for religious ceremony. If so, Tony, I could find artifacts in or around it."

Loretta Delgar approached Tony. "There you are. I might have known I'd find you with Mr. Burleson." She turned to Henry. "He has tremendous respect for your work."

"Henry, you remember my daughter?" Tony put his arm around the ivory-skinned young woman.

"I have had the pleasure of meeting Loretta, yes."

"Any gold artifacts in these wells?" Tony asked.

"As I said, anything is possible." Henry knew he'd added just the right amount of intrigue to keep Tony interested. He turned to Loretta. "What I would like to know is whether or not Loretta will give me the pleasure of this dance?"

"I'm dying to dance."

From the dance floor, Henry glimpsed Scottie easing up to Tony for a chat. Good. A little more academic influence would help their cause.

"Does our business talk bore you?" Henry asked Loretta.

"Terribly. But this part of the evening makes up for it."

"Thanks to your being here."

She smiled coyly. When the music stopped, they rejoined Tony and Scottie.

Tony hooked his thumbs under his suspenders. "Tell me, Henry, how long before you leave for Mexico?"

"We can be ready to leave within two weeks of securing financial backing." He saw Scottie roll his eyes behind Tony's back.

"I see."

"Father, please," Loretta said. "I love this waltz."

Henry shot Scottie a side glance and whisked Loretta away to the dance floor.

Later that evening before leaving for home, Tony and Loretta invited Henry and Scottie to dinner the following night. Scottie gave an excuse, but Henry accepted. He was mildly surprised during the ride home that Scottie expressed doubts about his tactics.

"How do you expect to be ready for an expedition in a couple of weeks? It's preposterous."

"Our assistants are taking care of the details as we speak. All you need concern yourself with is getting the finances worked out."

"Sorry, but I don't know how I can help you sweep Loretta off her feet. I know what you are doing."

"Oh?"

"You are using that girl to get her father's financial support."

"If that were so, I don't think it would make any difference to her or her father for that matter."

"Henry, why are you in such a hurry? You've made a respectable name for yourself in your field, accomplished more that most—"

"I'm onto something and you know it. I'd be a fool to give anyone else a chance to make a major discovery based on information from *my* long hours of research."

When Henry drove up to the sprawling Delgar home the next evening, Loretta, dressed in an expensive looking blue silk dress, greeted him in the showy center hall.

Tony waited until dinner to turn the conversation to the Maya. "After you mentioned those *cenotes*, I did a little research on my own, strictly amateur, you understand. What are the chances there's a significant amount of gold in the region?"

"Some believe the Spanish hauled it all to Spain. Gold was, after all, one of the main reasons for the conquest."

"What's your conclusion then?"

"If there are antiquities of value, they're probably entombed." Henry paused, wanting to choose his words carefully. "The fig bark codices, which I hope still exist, will be invaluable for the information they reveal. Such as where to find tombs."

"Tell you what," Tony leaned forward, resting his elbows on the table. "I'll put up half the projected expense of an expedition if you can pull the rest out of the university and museum. All I ask is that I be allowed to view the results of the expedition – the artifacts – before any of it is made public."

"Neither the museum nor the university will sit still for that arrangement." Henry was surprised Tony was willing to voice his true intentions so openly.

"I'm sure you can work around that minor detail, Henry." Tony's mustache curled into a smile before he stood to lead the way back to the parlor. Loretta slapped her napkin on the table and crossed her arms with a disgusted sigh.

"Now, now, my dear." Tony put his arm around her stiff shoulders. "Hear me out. I think you'll like the rest of my plan."

His plan did indeed make his daughter happy. Tony explained to Henry that he owned sixty percent interest in a resort hotel on the Texas coast. He suggested the three of them travel to the Gulf of Mexico for the dual purpose of launching his investment and giving the archaeological expedition a proper send off.

"Wonderful!" Loretta whirled around to Henry. "There's a marvelous pavilion over the water where balls are held almost every night. It's huge, Henry. Come on. Let's take a walk and I'll tell you about Tres Palacios."

Tony held up his hand. "It's been a brutal day. I'll excuse myself and turn in, if you two don't mind."

Loretta led Henry to a small walled garden on the grounds surrounding the mansion. He pulled her into his arms. "Have you any idea how much I look forward to a holiday with you?" Loretta pressed against him and he had no trouble responding to her invitation.

***

TRES PALACIOS BAY reflected a blinding bright sky when Nell first saw it. The pier she'd read so much about stretched a quarter of a mile out over the water, and at the end, the enormous pavilion arched two stories high. A fancy gold and purple sign over the entrance read Tres Palacios Ballroom and Bathhouse.

Corseted women, wearing gauzy cotton dresses, protected their faces with lace parasols, while men in white linen suits and straw boaters milled about as if time and purpose didn't exist. She shaded her eyes with her hand and peered across the bay to the clean line of horizon. The salt breeze made her eyes sting.

Behind Nell was the much-touted Seasider Hotel. Its shady, geranium-bedecked gallery stretched three hundred feet across the front and looked inviting from where she stood in the sun's glare.

While registering at the front desk, she ordered a tray of cold food to be brought to her room and then followed the aged bellman up a narrow stairway to a second floor. There a narrow hall crossed the main hall and had a window at each end. Glancing through each, Nell realized the hotel couldn't be much more than thirty feet wide. The window facing south overlooked the bay and the window facing north overlooked the small town of Palacios.

The bellman deposited her trunk with a loud thud before taking her offered gratuity and then disappeared without a word. The room was small and simply furnished which suited her fine. She pulled a chair to the open window and watched the bay water pulse as it rushed forward and ebbed back like a living, seething thing with some exotic, secret life under its surface. She couldn't drag herself away from the rhythm of it. She was lulled like a child in a creaking rocker.

Nightfall found her still at the window watching as a parade of people meandered up and down the wide boardwalk to the pavilion. Soft music drifted on the tide-changing wind and made her long for things she couldn't name. She wept. Softly at first, then furiously. She felt she'd fooled herself into believing there had been some noble principle behind all the hand wringing she'd done to hold the ranch together during the years following her father's death. She didn't own the land any more than she owned heaven or hell. The ranch wasn't a thing she could put in her pocket or hold tight in her fist. In fact, the only owning done was *by* the land, for it now owned her father and mother, and the others before them.

She wept for her father and his disappointments. Railroads and barbed wire had squeezed his land from every direction. And for all his love of it, the land hadn't made him completely happy. Now, these stacked-up years later she doubted that her mother could have made him happy either.

Nell finally left the window to lie across the bed and used a pillow to muffle wails that refused to be stifled. Some of her tears were for Hester, who had hounded Nell all her life about the poor choices she'd made. Nell realized now that Hester was trapped by her own bad decisions and denial.

Nell's sobs were as unfamiliar to her as the white place she had come to. Her head throbbed and hammered like drums, reminding her of the old Comanche her father had invited to sleep in the barn one horrible winter night long ago. The Indian had pounded a flat drum monotonously all through the night as he called out to his dead ancestors, beseeching them to lead him homeward.

Just now, wind whooshed through the window and caught her loosened hair and blew it over her eyes. She must have dozed because when she brushed it away with the back of her hand, she saw Pablo. They were riding their ponies, he a little ahead of her. He called out laughing, "Faster, faster!" The prairie was water and grass splashed under their ponies' bellies. Her heartbeat matched the pounding of their horses' hooves as they clu-clumped along.

Nell could hear her own laughter. They rode free and wild across the water and she threw her arms up to catch the wind like her very own windmill, hair and blouse and skirts billowed with air. She was suspended and without worry. They were children again, and Nell reached out to Pablo, but before their hands touched he was gone and only his horse stood watching her with blank eyes.

When Nell woke from the tear-drugged dream, she moved like a staggering drunk to fetch the tray of food she'd ordered left in the hall outside her door.

By afternoon of the second day, sickened by her own self-indulgence, she washed and dressed then left her room to lounge on the gallery unnoticed with a book in front of her nose. She listened to the prattle and droning of doyennes as they talked endlessly about the difference between opera and lyric drama and Essie Wood's gaudy Easter hat. The men, heads tilted toward each other, talked about politics, investments and war. Nell lowered her book for a secret look at them. She thought of pigs in the pen back home, standing in a circle with snouts almost touching in the center like spokes of a wheel, all unking and oinking deep-bellied grunts.

Later she walked the beach, gathering seashells in her handkerchief for Juan. She strolled through some of the shops in the small town and bought a parasol for Lupe. In a leather goods store a block away, she purchased a mother-of-pearl bolo for Pablo then returned to the hotel by way of the beach which was all but deserted.

Nell sat in the shade of an oleander bush and took off her shoes and stockings to wiggle her toes in the warm sand. She got lost in the sleepy warmth of the day but then heard a low, muffled buzz like a far off motor car.

The sound grew louder. She rose and walked toward the water, looked up and down the beach. Except for gulls running to and fro at the water's edge, not a living thing was in sight. Turning back to fetch her packages and shoes, she caught sight of a wide, flat object in the sky. She froze, frightened to death, but was too curious to run. The thing grew larger and larger and louder and louder.

Her heart surged when she realized it was an airplane. She held her breath as it roared by with a great swoosh of air, sucking her hat from her head. From under the top wing, the pilot saluted and waved. Like a ridged bird, the airplane shot straight up and flew in a wide circle over the bay. Nell clamped her hands over her mouth when it swooped down again not twenty feet above the water. This time she clearly saw the pilot look directly at her. He wore a tight fitting skull cap, goggles and a cobalt blue scarf around his neck. He hailed her with another roguish salute.

Nell grabbed her shoes and packages and ran all the way back to the hotel where she joined a crowd that had gathered to watch the airplane fly loops high above the pavilion. She overheard someone say the pilot planned to land inland and return the next day to give rides in his machine.

"'Scuse me."

Nell turned to the woman addressing her.

"We was wondering if you would like to join us at a game of gin. Me and my sister here get mighty tired of each other's company, you see. And, well, we noticed you was alone."

Words jammed in Nell's throat. The woman wore a beautiful dress much like those in the latest ladies magazines and she would bet the hat was from Paris. But nothing about her appearance matched her speaking voice. A severe, dour looking woman with pinched lips stood slightly behind her. Both had mousy gray hair and deeply grooved, sun-browned skin.

"I-I'm afraid I'm not very good at card games," Nell said.

"It don't matter to us none. We might even be able to teach you some." The woman pulled a chair up to the nearest table and turned to her sister. "Ruby, fetch another chair yonder."

Ruby looked as if her face had been slammed in a kitchen door, a true hatchet face, with eyes so close together they looked askew. Nell bit her lip.

"My name's Maudeen Wooster, and yours?"

"Nell Miggins."

"Miss or Mrs?"

Nell hesitated, taken aback by Maudeen's brash manner.

"Well, it don't matter. I was just curious. Me, I'm a widow and Ruby here never married." Maudeen drew a deck of cards from a large bag and shuffled with flourish.

"Did you see the airplane?" Nell asked in an attempt to be friendly.

Ruby's pinched mouth stretched into a smile. "That was W.C., our sweet baby brother, flying it."

Since the sisters looked to be in their seventies, Nell wondered just how young the "baby" brother could be.

"Going to get hisself killed one of these days." Maudeen dealt the cards. "Not much he won't try to do at least once. Now take a look at them cards, honey."

"It's inconceivable to me that a machine can actually fly. Your brother must be very brave."

"No. Just an old fool," Maudeen said.

"Have you traveled far?" Nell asked.

"Nah. From just east of the Trinity River. My late husband, he had a little old dirt farm there when I married him forty years ago. Discovered oil late last year and got so excited he up and had hisself a heart collapse sure as hell. Left me rich as all get out. Me and Ruby here been traveling and doing all we can to have a good time ever since. Your turn."

Nell drew a card, studied it, discarded. "And, your brother?"

"Well, I financed his airplane to give him a way of keeping up with me and Ruby. You see, he can't seem to settle for doing things like most folks. Gets bored to death, he does."

Ruby rearranged her cards. "Are you going to the ball tonight?" When Nell looked puzzled, Ruby went on to explain that a ball was to be held that same night in the pavilion to launch a week of summertime activities.

"That's right," Maudeen said, "and tomorrow W.C.'s going to give any fool who wants it, a ride in his airplane. Then there's going to be a midnight boat ride out into the Gulf of Mexico."

After an hour of cards and prattle, Nell excused herself, explaining she wanted to write a few letters before dinner.

"Me and Ruby plan to eat a cold supper in our room, so we won't be seeing you in the dining room. But...would you like for us to stop by your room so's you can go to the ball with us? I mean W.C. will be there so it won't be like we ain't – I mean like we aren't escorted proper."

"I'm even less apt at balls than cards. It's kind of you to ask though."

"Well, honey, the way we see it, you ain't got but one chance at life. If you change your mind, holler."

That evening Nell was sorry the minute she stepped into the hallway to go to the dining hall. Groups of people rushed back and forth in elaborate evening dress creating a carnival-like atmosphere. She felt ill at ease and conspicuous being alone.

The dining room attendant seated her at a table where she could see most of the room and into the musician's alcove where a troupe played soft baroque tunes behind a veil of potted palms. On the other side of the alcove a familiar figure, a man, stepped out of the dining room into the outer hall. Nell tried to place him but couldn't get a good look at his face. With a swish of the menu she brushed the image from her mind and ordered her dinner.

After eating, she walked out onto the gallery. A quarter moon reflected off the quivering bay as a procession of hotel guests drifted down the pier toward the pavilion. Hoping to watch more comfortably from her upstairs window, Nell approached the double doors leading to the main lobby but a crowd pressed forward suddenly and engulfed her. People laughed and cheered someone who moved along in the center of the confusion. Nell struggled to free herself from the crush but gave up and allowed the crowd to carry her on its tide toward the pier. Gradually the mob thinned, and she worked herself over to the railing where she glimpsed the sisters walking unhurried behind the mob.

"Yoo-hoo! Nell."

"Hello, Maudeen, Ruby. I thought I'd be crushed to death. What is it all the excitement about anyway?"

"Why it's W.C. Everybody thinks he's some kind of hero," Maudeen said.

"Did you decide to go to the ball after all?" Ruby asked.

"No. I got swept along with the crowd."

"Well hell, come on along for a little while anyways, girl. Beats sittin' in a stuffy room." Maudeen hooked her arm in Nell's and the three women made their way down the pier. Until then Nell hadn't ventured out to the pavilion. The thought of being suspended over all that water frightened her. But in the cover of night and in the company of new friends, she was able to put her fears aside.

The domed ceiling of the ballroom was festooned with red, yellow and white streamers above a full orchestra playing "In The Good Old Summertime." Electric lights glistened from support beams here and there, casting a glittery glow over the crowd. A small wiry man wearing a blue neck scarf approached them.

"Looky here." He glanced from one sister to the other then took Nell's hand and bowed low to kiss it.

Maudeen rolled her eyes. "Oh, for Pete's sake, W.C., cut that out."

W. C. looked Nell in the eye. "I hope you don't mind if I tell you that you are the prettiest little lady in this room."

Nell smiled, unsure if he was serious or teasing. His green eyes sparkled. His speech had an Irish lilt to it and he was seventy years old if he was a day.

"W.C., hobble your lip. This is Nell Miggins. We met her today on the porch. Nell, this here's W.C., our brother."

"The pilot," Ruby added.

"I shall treasure this moment of meeting you, my lady." He bowed and nodded toward the dance floor. "Will you honor me with this dance?"

Maudeen patted Nell's arm. "He's harmless enough, honey."

W.C. gave Nell a flirtatious wink before leading her to the dance floor where he paid little attention to the music as he twirled her around and around. When the tune ended someone announced that fireworks were about to begin and the noisy throng of dancers drifted out to the pier. W.C. abruptly excused himself and disappeared into the crowd.

As Nell looked around for Maudeen, she again saw the familiar man, the one she had seen in the dining room earlier. He turned to offer his elbow to a beautiful young woman, and Nell got a full view of his face. She wheeled away to find an escape, but was too late. Henry Burleson had already seen her.

"Miss Miggins. Who would've imagined our paths would cross like this?"

"And so soon." Nell pretended pleasant surprise.

"Come to think if it, I do remember you mentioned a trip to the coast to that doctor, the one who took care of Scottie. But where are my manners? This is Loretta Delgar, whose father is a partner in this hotel."

Loretta's eyes scanned Nell from hair to shoes before she pressed her breasts against Henry's arm. The jade figurine Henry had been so concerned about at Carrageen dangled on a satin ribbon around Loretta's neck.

Nell nodded to the young woman then asked Henry, "How is Mr. Scott?"

"Recovered nicely, thanks to your kindness, but grumbling about not making this trip with me. You see, I'm on my way to Yucatán."

"A wonderful opportunity for you, I'm sure." Nell wondered how she could gracefully excuse herself. "And will you be going along, Loretta?"

"Goodness no. My father and I had planned to see Henry off, but father had to leave early to take care of some business problems in Chicago."

Henry rocked back on his heels. "I'm to leave for Galveston in two days and travel to the Yucatán from there by steamer. And you? Had any more unexpected guests lately?"

Nell opened her mouth but swallowed the impulse to mention the bandit raid on the ranch. The last thing she wanted at the moment was an involved conversation with Henry Burleson. "I got my herd trailed and sold without trouble. No more guests."

They drifted outside with the crowd. The night sky crackled and popped with fireworks, making conversation difficult. Nell wanted to run as fast as her legs would carry her. She felt robbed of her anonymity. As her old self-consciousness came rushing back, a rocket flared and cast blue light over the bay. From the corner of her eye she saw Henry watching her.

When the fireworks ended, Nell stepped back toward the pier. "Henry, the best of luck on your expedition. Now if you'll excuse me." She gave Loretta a quick nod then hurried back down the pier and raced up the stairs to her room. She was flushed and unnerved by the coincidence.

The next morning Nell found a note that had been slipped under her door. It was from Maudeen and Ruby asking her to join them for the boating excursion in the Gulf. She was to meet them at the pavilion at three in the afternoon if she wanted to go along.

While putting the note away, she heard W.C.'s airplane and from the window watched it glide down to land on the beach. A crowd had gathered by the time he climbed onto the wing where he bowed ceremoniously with his goggles strapped across his eyes.

Nell went down to the gallery where a long line had formed of those waiting to ride in the flying machine. Time after time W.C. took off from the sandy beach, but she never grew bored with the novelty of it. Nor did W.C. lose his grandiose guise. Upon each landing he stepped onto the wing, took a bow then assisted his passenger to the ground. He blew kisses to the ladies and clasped his fists together, shaking them over each shoulder. He reminded Nell of a giant bumblebee buzzing around a flower garden, sure and handsome in an antiquated sort of way. He seemed as amused with himself as the crowd.

When the sun grew uncomfortably hot, Nell retrieved her grandmother's diary and made her way through the lobby to sit in the gardens behind the hotel where palm trees and grape arbors shaded small tables arranged around a fountain. As she opened the diary, giggles trickled from an arbor across the way. Peering through leaves and limbs, she spied Henry and Loretta nuzzling each other. He kissed Loretta so passionately Nell flushed. He trailed kisses down the girl's neck and along her collar bone. She pushed him away with a giggle, but he kissed her again, moved his hand over her breast and down to her hip.

Nell dropped the diary with a loud thud, but managed to smother a gasp. Thank goodness Henry hadn't heard. He stood suddenly with a wicked smile and pulled Loretta behind him as he hurried toward the lobby.

After that Nell was unable to keep her mind on the diary. She slammed it shut and checked the watch pinned to her blouse. Nearly three o'clock. She rushed to the gallery hoping to find Maudeen and Ruby to join them on the excursion boat. Not an ideal way to spend the day. The thought of all that water still terrified her, but it had to be better than trying to chase unwanted thoughts from her head.

The sisters were nowhere in sight so she rushed up to her room, left the diary on the table and grabbed her parasol. Back outside, she hurried across the beach toward the pier where she ran into W.C.

He grabbed her arm. "How 'bout a ride in my flying machine, little lady?"

"No, no. I'm off to catch the excursion boat."

"It is not a good time to be on the water, my lady." W.C. looked puzzled. "Do I know you?"

"Nell Miggins. Remember, we met last night? I'm a friend of your sisters. I'm going to meet them now." He dropped his eyes and shook his head.

"Is something wrong, W.C.?"

"Oh no." He turned his face to the wind, removed his goggles. "I hear things, see things way up there in the sky."

The wind blew hard out of the south, whipped his blue scarf around. She turned to leave then stopped abruptly. "I've been wondering, what do the initials W.C. stand for?"

"Wild Cat." He flicked a salute off his forehead and slid his goggles back down over his eyes.

Nell surprised herself by quickly kissing his cheek before racing to the end of the pier where a group of hotel guests, including Maudeen and Rudy, waited in line to climb down into a rowboat bobbing in the rough water.

"My stars," Maudeen said. "We just about gave up on you, Nell honey. I'm so glad you could make it."

Ruby dabbed at the corners of her pinched mouth with a handkerchief. "W.C. said we shouldn't ride in a boat this evening."

"How many times do I have to explain it to you." Maudeen shook her head.

Ruby looked to be on the verge of tears. "She hasn't paid attention to what he has to say since a oil derrick collapsed on him. Knocked him cold, it did."

Maudeen turned to Nell. "The thing of it is we never know when he's in there and when he's not. In his head, I mean."

The rowboat made three trips out to the mouth of Tres Palacios Bay where the passengers boarded a double-masted schooner. Feeling the strength of the wind tugging her clothes made Nell regret her decision to go. The waves seemed much bigger out over the open water, and when she looked back toward the hotel, she was terrified to see how much water lay between her and it.

"Oh, Lord help me, Maudeen. Maybe I should have flown in W.C.'s flying machine instead." She grabbed Maudeen's arm to steady herself.

Maudeen led the way across the schooner's undulating deck to a bench along the railing where they watched sailors rush back and forth. With a loud pop sails caught the wind. The boat creaked and churned then lurched forward to skim across the water.

"Oo-oo W-e-e." Maudeen yelled over the wind noise.

Most of the passengers were holding onto hats or skirts. A young man and woman with flushed cheeks, who Nell thought must be newlyweds, sat adjacent them. Behind the couple, the horizon appeared unusually dark, and for the first time Nell realized how overcast and gray the sky had become.

But curiosity dashed her fears. Struggling to keep her balance, she made her way forward to lean into the force of the wind, let it blow away her inhibitions until she was near delirium.

A sailor called out and pointed down into the water to her right. There Nell saw huge fish leaping, racing the schooner. First one, then another would arch out of the water, as if taunting the boat with teasing smiles. When she turned back to the sailor, he yelled, "Dolphins." They were sleek and elegant the way they moved through the water. She had never seen anything more beautiful or graceful.

The horizon spread out ahead of her and was water, water, everywhere, and those magical creatures, the dolphins, moved under and in it, in a wet world that she had only read about. There was so much she didn't know, hadn't experienced. Yet oddly, watching the dolphins arch out of the water, she wondered if a world existed - in another dimension maybe - that knew of her, of her secrets and fears.

Darkness fell suddenly with a peculiar inky blackness she'd not experienced on land. The schooner churned wildly. Sailors lowered several sails, but the boat continued to heave and crash into huge waves. Nell held onto anything she could grasp to make her way back to where Maudeen sat.

"Where's Ruby?" Nell called out to Maudeen over the wind noise.

"Below. She can't stomach a little excitement."

"I could do with a little something to eat myself. I just realized I had no lunch."

"I heard them sailors say they can't serve the refreshments till they get us outta this wind. Some moonlight excursion this is!"

A spark of lightning jabbed the sky in the southeast. A second streak flashed horizontally, illuminating enormous black, roiling clouds and churning seas. Just then a sailor from high up one of the masts called to another who stood at the wheel. Nell, unable to understand over the wind noise, turned to Maudeen.

Maudeen looked worried. "Now don't go on none. They're going to try to outrun that little storm. On the water like this, it's a lot easier to do then on land, you see." Salt spray exploded over the bow of the schooner as it crashed into the storm's fury.

The newlyweds made their way below. A portly man – the captain, Nell guessed from his authoritative manner – huddled with a couple of sailors. All three kept shooting glances into the darkness. Wind and salt spray blew through the rigging and sails creating an eerie shrill noise. Finally a red-faced sailor with thick mutton-chop whiskers turned from the captain, cupped his hands around his mouth and called out. "Below deck, everyone!"

"What's happening?" Nell asked him.

"You'll be more comfortable below deck until we're out of this weather. Now be along with ya."

The passengers gathered below, hanging onto whatever they could to keep from being thrown around. Nell and Maudeen found Ruby in a far corner, white-lipped and shivering. "I told you we should've listened to W.C."

Nell wrapped her arms around what she assumed was a mast. The swiftness of the storm was terrifying. It seemed only moments ago they had been watching it from afar. The schooner heaved up at a sharp angle, twisted and crashed into an equally sharp angle downward. A little girl began to cry. A lone man crouched over a chamber pot to vomit.

When Nell turned back to where the sisters huddled, even Maudeen looked horrified. Had W.C. somehow known of the weather, perhaps from his flying so high in the sky, but was unable to explain or remember or reason?

Every now and then she heard the alarmed voices of men above deck. Her arms grew tired from the constant push and pull as she tried to hold onto the mast. She lost all sense of time. Water seeped in around the hatch and passengers pressed back to avoid getting wet. Just as she realized she was standing in several inches of water, the hatch blew open. Water sprayed in. Someone screamed. The mutton chop sailor struggled from above to close the hatch. Behind him, in a flash of lightning, Nell saw that one of the sails had been ripped to rags by the wind.

Some of the men below pressed forward to help close the hatch, but a wave washed over the schooner pouring water in on them. Panic took over then. Some passengers scrambled for the open hatch while others, like the newlyweds, sat stone still.

Nell was stunned, could not believe this was to be her end. The schooner heaved, rolled to one side. She felt the mast shudder in her arms as something crashed on the deck above her head. Another wave washed down the open hatch.

With water lapping at her knees Nell struggled toward the hatch only to be thrown down into the dirty water by the violent pitch and roll of the schooner. Coughing, gasping, she felt someone grab her elbow, pull her to her feet. It was Maudeen. She had Ruby's wrist in her other hand.

"Saints preserve us, Nell Miggins." Maudeen had to scream over the howling storm.

Nell reached for Ruby's other wrist, and together Maudeen and Nell pushed her up through the hatch. But before either of them could make their way clear, the boat pitched to one side. The motion threw them both back down into the watery hold. Again, Nell felt Maudeen pull her up then shove her toward the hatch. When she gained the top step, she turned to reach a hand down to Maudeen, but in a blinding flash of lightning she saw only Maudeen's loose gray hair swirling in the icy black water.

"Ma-a-au-deen!" Her scream was swallowed by the storm's fury. Something slammed the deck to her left. A white-hot sensation seared the left side of her face. Salt water burned her eyes and nostrils, pricked her skin. The deck tilted sideways, almost vertical like a child's toy, dumping everything overboard. Nell watched Ruby, limp as a soaked rag doll, slide into the swirling sea.

When the schooner swung around again it crashed into a colossal wave. The force of the blow pitched her out of the hatchway onto the deck. She pressed her burning face to the soaked deck and dug in with her fingernails.

For the wind... Why were those words coming to her mind? She should cry out, fight back, but...

For the wind passeth over...

She was so cold. Wasn't death supposed to be cold? But how could anyone living know?

...For the wind passeth over it, and it is gone...

***

"*CAPITÁN CAPITÁN!*"

Eduardo Gomez swung out of his bunk. Carlos, his deckhand, called out a second time. "*Capitán!*"

"*Ay-e-e.*" Eduardo groaned. Probably Carlos saw a shark and thought it was one of the sea monsters the *curandero* talked about at carnival. Humph, the *curandero*, nothing more than a shriveled old witch doctor anyway. Even Sister Tia Marie says so. *Ay-e-e*, hadn't it been hard enough to convince Carlos that as long as they were careful, the authorities would not suspect they were smuggling guns across the Gulf of Mexico from Campeche to Mexico? Then that stupid *curandero* and his gods... "What is it now, Carlos?" Eduardo called out, interrupting his own thoughts.

"A boat, I think. Come see, there."

Eduardo tried to look in the direction of Carlos' pointed finger but the sun's rays pierced his eyes like the sharp thorns of the *escoba* tree. "Is only *cachivaches*. Storm trash from the storm night before last. Now where is Paco with my coffee?"

From below the deck of the small fishing boat, Paco called out to his father. "I am coming."

"*Ándale*, before Carlos calls on his gods to save us." Eduardo scratched himself, looped his suspenders over his shoulders. He didn't feel any better than Carlos about smuggling guns and supplies to Mexico, even though it was for a good cause. That of fighting for the rights of *peons* who tilled the land until their backs grew bent like twigs. For hundreds of years, since the coming of the Spanish, men like himself had served the wealthy and not been allowed to own land. And, of course, fish the waters in someone else's boat for someone else's table. But he and Paco, for Paco had made him a grandfather already, had families to feed, and Mr. Santio, the *alcalde* of the village, paid them well, if not with coins, then with food and clothing and promises to watch after their families.

The storm had blown them nearly two hundred miles off the course he had set for the return trip to Celestún on the northwestern edge of the Yucatán peninsula. He'd managed to skirt the leading edge of the storm for a while, but it changed directions in the night, catching them off guard. After that they could do little more than try to stay afloat.

"Paco!" Carlos called from the wheel when Paco appeared with coffee.

"*Sí, amigo, sí*. There is another government ship after us just like yesterday and the day before. Is this so?" Paco teased.

"Ah, Paco, this time is different. Come, you will see."

Paco gave his father a side-glance then went forward to squint at the sea. His mouth dropped open.

"What did I tell you?" Carlos elbowed Paco's ribs.

Paco climbed the creaking mast, leaned into the wind. "*Dios. Dios mio*. Papa look! Carlos, turn the boat around, circle it, so I can get a better look." He slid down the mast and had his pants off by the time Eduardo grumbled his way forward.

Carlos and Eduardo watched Paco dive into the glassy water, swim to the flotsam and climb on. Eduardo soon realized that what at first looked like a heap of dirty rags was actually two people. Paco placed his hand on one, a man with big whiskers, then crossed himself and looked up at Eduardo where he stood on the deck of the boat.

"It is the way of all life sooner or later." Eduardo called down with a nod. Paco rolled the body into the water and watched solemnly as it slipped with slow, sickening ease into the clear depths.

"What of the other?" Eduardo called out. The face of the other person, a woman he would guess from the tattered clothes, was completely hidden under blood-matted hair. One arm lay at a peculiar angle to her body. "*Dios.*" Eduardo whispered.

Paco touched the woman's oddly stretched arm and a cry, like that of a cat mewing, sounded on the wind. He tried to move the matted hair from her face, but it was stuck in place like a jade death mask the villagers had found in the sarcophagus near the *cenote*. Fresh blood oozed onto his hands and the woman groaned, as if in great pain.

"The woman lives!" Paco screamed.

Eduardo crossed himself, but in his mind credit for a life spared went to the old Mayan deity, Itzamná.

Religion confused Eduardo. He wished he could be as sure of such things as Carlos, his deck hand, or Chiquita, his wife. Sister Tia Marie had taught all of them to pray to Jesus and Mother Mary and named all the saints and had ceremonies for life and death, and sacraments for sickness as well as celebration. But Xa Lum, the witch doctor-healer - *curandero* - had ceremonies too, for the gods of death, rain, the underworld and many more. Eduardo came to the conclusion years ago that the two religions were not all that different, and so he practiced a little of each.

Paco tied the end of a rope Carlos had tossed him to the death raft so they could pull it closer to the boat. Once it was in position, Eduardo lowered a fishing net and Paco wrapped it around the woman, taking as much care as possible with her damaged arm. Eduardo then hoisted her on board.

Though the smell of death was so close it repulsed him, Eduardo dripped fresh well water over the woman's face to loosen the mass of blood-caked hair. "This is why she still lives. It protected her from the sun and stopped the bleeding."

The woman made another mewing sound.

"Yes, lady. We will help you." Paco kneeled over the yellowing bruised body. There was no response.

Eduardo gently loosened the last of the matted hair from the woman's face and grimaced when he saw an open gash extending from her hairline in the center of her forehead down to her left cheek. It skirted her eye, barely missing the outside corner. Both eyes were swollen shut and her entire face was bruised black as an iron pot. Carlos shrank back, muttered to himself.

A groan rumbled in the woman's throat. She moved her head slightly. Eduardo repeated a prayer of salvation over and over to himself as he dripped water onto her lips. He doubted she would live until they made landfall.

***

CHIQUITA WAS OVERCOME with trepidation. News of the terrible storm had followed the jungle paths right up to the door of the hut she shared with her husband and seven children high on a limestone bluff overlooking a bright turquoise bay. From there she watched for her husband's sail and prayed to Itzamná, Lord of Life, to bring him home. Elena, their oldest daughter, plucked a chicken and watched after the younger children in the clearing around the hut.

Then suddenly there it was, Eduardo's sail billowing bright white on the horizon. Chiquita threw her head back, crying joyously to the thatched roof. She flung her tortillas aside to run down the path to the beach.

"Now, now, Mother," Eduardo said to his hysterical wife when he jumped into the shallows where he'd anchored his boat. "Look how you worry our children." Like Carlos, she paid too much attention to the words of the doomsayer *curandero*.

"Praise to Itzamná for he brings you home," she said.

"I bring myself home and my crew and fishes, too."

Carlos climbed down from the boat. "And, a Sea Woman from the land of the Dead as well. I'll not sail again, *Señor*. I have had my fill."

"But, Carlos, I got you home safe, did I not?"

Without replying, Carlos made his way down the beach with his share of fish in a basket balanced on his shoulder.

"What is this Sea Woman?" Chiquita's forehead wrinkled.

When Paco handed the net-shrouded woman over the side of the boat to Eduardo, Chiquita recoiled. "Carlos was wrong." She wailed, stared at the putrid, swollen face. "This is a horrid serpent tangled in the web of the Underworld."

"Shame to you, wife. This is a mortal being who suffers and we will help her if we can."

"How do you know this is not sent as a curse from Ah Puch, Lord of the Dead, for taking guns to Mexico?"

"And what would you have me do? Throw her back into the sea? What if you are wrong and this woman is sent from Itzamná? Or, from Jesus who said we must care for those who are weak? We will ask the *curandero* and then maybe Sister Tia Marie."

Eduardo started up the path with the Sea Woman hanging limp in his arms, giving everyone orders along the way. Elena and all the children were to bring fresh water from the *cenote* and fill the big urn in the hut. Paco was to find the *curandero* as fast as he could, even if he had to cover the entire maze of jungle paths from village to village and hut to hut in the region. For all Eduardo knew, Chiquita was right and this woman's appearance was a flesh and bone curse.

But, even though he couldn't rationalize his actions, he wasn't going to let her die without trying to save her. He paused out of breath at the door of the hut and turned to Chiquita. "By the goodness of Sister Tia Marie's God, or by the mercifulness of Itzamná, this woman has survived until now and I think we should see that she lives to tell our children of the storm that chewed her up and spit her out before the bow of my boat."

Eduardo laid the spiritless woman on a long low table in the hut and left her to his wife's care while he finished unloading his boat.

Chiquita and Elena cut away the woman's clothes. Her body was pale as goat milk except for her shoulder and arm that were bruised and swollen like her face. Bright red streaks marked the places where her clothes had torn away, allowing the sun to burn her skin. She was thin and, to Chiquita, seemed small.

Elena poured bowl after bowl of warm water over the woman's head to wash away the crusted blood. When she was able to run a tortoise shell comb smoothly though the long hair, she rubbed oil from the ground seeds of the *abogado* fruit into the woman's scalp and hair.

When long shadows reached across the only doorway to the hut, Chiquita covered Sea Woman with a length of cotton cloth then placed a lit candle at her head. She and Elena then joined Eduardo outside where villagers, who heard about the Sea Woman from Carlos, had come out of curiosity. They sat in small groups around the clearing and spoke in quiet speculation as if Sea Woman might overhear their foreboding thoughts about who she was and what powers arranged her appearance in their village. The *curandero* would come soon and tell them who among them was right.

Close to midnight, Xa Lum, the *curandero,* appeared on the edge of the fire's glow dressed in his white ceremonial sheath. A tapacamino bird called out plaintively, its cry echoing over and over before fading away somewhere deep in the jungle forest. Xa Lum scanned the darkness as if listening for more bird song then bowed slightly and proceeded to the hut. Eduardo and Chiquita followed.

Inside, Chiquita pulled back the cloth covering Sea Woman and explained to Xa Lum that only her arm and face were injured.

He nodded without a word. Eduardo and Chiquita, feeling dismissed, moved away to sit on low stools along the wall.

The healer pulled a jar of *balché* from a net basket he used to carry ceremonial paraphernalia. He held the jar high over his head for a moment before taking a deep swallow of the liquor. He sat the *balché* aside, reached back into his bag and withdrew a smooth glass ball that fit snug in the palm of his hand. He placed it between Sea Woman's breasts and began to chant a sacred prayer in the ancient Mayan language. Next, he withdrew a crucifix and with great dignity placed it next to the candle at Sea Woman's head. Every now and then, Xa Lum paused in his chant to sip the *balché*.

Finally Xa Lum spoke. "This Sea Woman is from a land across the water where her people sacrificed her to Chac, the rain god, so he would not send the storm to their village. Chac wishes her to live and become goddess of the *cenote*." When he moved to sit with them, Chiquita handed him a bowl of *zacá* and he drank the honey sweetened gruel in little sips. All the while his dark, cloudy eyes scanned the villagers sitting outside the hut.

"Why goddess of the well?" Eduardo asked.

"Chac wishes her to help him bring rain when we pray for it. Or, like the land far away, we may wish to sacrifice her to keep storms from our village. You must see that she lives or Chac will be violated and send a storm with thunder and yellow light."

"*Ay-e-e.*" Chiquita uttered a low moan, pressing her fists to her forehead.

"Can you help us save Sea Woman?" Eduardo asked.

"I will try. First, the women must make a paste with this." Xa Lum handed Chiquita a pouch of white powder from his bag. "Put it on the face and shoulder. You must also mix honey with the *balché* and give her as much as she will drink. I must find men who have been sanctioned or baptized by the Catholic priest to help me make the face and shoulder together again."

"The shoulder?" Eduardo was puzzled.

"The arm bone is away from the body bone and must be forced back in place." Xa Lum pushed up from the ground, hooked the tumpline of his net basket on his forehead and turned to leave.

"But Xa Lum, I beg you do not go. Stay here with us." Eduardo called after him.

His footsteps left a path in the damp dirt as he made his way under the thick forest canopy. He gave no reply.

***

CHIQUITA, HAVING COMPLETE faith in the old healer's assessment, paced in front of Eduardo, howling hysterically. One minute she waved her arms over his head and the next pressed her fists to her temples. "If Sea Woman dies our village will be destroyed by storms and everyone will blame us."

"Mother, you waste time. Do as the *curandero* told you." Eduardo flushed with impatience.

Chiquita and Elena propped Sea Woman's head and shoulders on a bundle of netting and prepared the poultice as Xa Lum had commanded them. Elena held the jar of *balché* to the woman's mouth but she choked and struggled, gasped for air and cried out words that were not clear to them.

When the children asked Chiquita why the woman cried, she told them demons from the Underworld were talking to her. They were fascinated by the pale body with the dark face that lay shrouded on the only piece of furniture in their home. Paco and his young wife came to sit and stare as well.

"Praise Itzamná, the Lord of Life, that you live." Chiquita whispered in the woman's ear.

The woman turned her head so she could see through the narrow swollen slit of her good eye. She saw Elena standing on the opposite side of the table. "Lupe?"

Elena dropped the bowl of poultice and ran for the door but stopped short when she saw Xa Lum, Paco and a man from the village blocking her way.

Xa Lum approached his patient. His brilliant white robe hung loosely from his bony shoulders. Tattoos, tiny dotted lines following the solemn furrows between his features, gave him great bearing.

"*Gracias* for returning, Xa Lum," Eduardo said.

"As I said I would." Xa Lum stepped closer to the Sea Woman and placed his hand on her breastbone. She strained to open her eyes, slightly rolling her head in an effort to see.

He ordered, "Give her more *balché*, all she will drink."

While Chiquita struggled with the woman and the jar of fermented drink, the men prepared for the ceremony. Xa Lum explained as he placed a ceremonial headdress of feathers and jaguar pelts on his head, that he needed three men to help with the ceremony, but only Paco and one other were brave enough to come into the hut.

"I have been baptized." Eduardo was hesitant. The last thing he wanted was to participate, but he'd had enough of the situation, wanted to be done with the ceremony as soon as possible.

Xa Lum instructed Chiquita to take Paco's wife and the children to the *cenote* of Ixchel to pray and wait there until Paco came for them.

As soon as Chiquita and the others were out of sight, Xa Lum had Eduardo line the walls of the hut with candles set at equal distances all around while he and Paco tied strips of cloth around Sea Woman's legs and ribs binding her to the table. Each time she mumbled or moved, one of the men forced her to drink from the jar. The *curandero* emptied his net bag of its contents onto two large palm-like leaves on the dirt floor. A small fish bone needle, cotton thread, another jar of *balché,* loaves of *tutiwah* bread, pouches of powders, and his glass sphere. A gentle rain splashed against the thatched roof as he dipped the cotton thread in the *balché*.

Xa Lum closed his eyes and smiled. "Chac is pleased."

He drew the thread through the fish bone needle and had Paco and the villager lay over Sea Woman to hold her still. Eduardo held her head. Beginning at her cheek, the *curandero* pierced the blackened skin with the bone needle and drew the thread through. A low cry of pain gurgled up from deep in the woman's chest each time Xa Lum pulled up on the bloody thread. Eduardo's courage faltered.

Xa Lum worked across the gash as he squeezed the skin together, closing the wound with tight, even stitches. When he finished, he knotted the thread and dabbed his work with a *balché* soaked cloth. He stepped back and nodded. Eduardo and the others slowly released their hold on Sea Woman.

"What must she think?" Eduardo asked in a low whisper. The other men moved away to drink deep gulps of *balché*, but he stayed at the woman's side. He leaned over the her and whispered. "It will be over soon, you will see."

"Billy?" She looked at him through the thin, watery slits of her eyes.

Eduardo touched the jar of *balché* to her lips. "It will help your pain, lady."

"Billy? Pablo?"

"We must finish," Xa Lum ordered as thunder echoed across the dark jungle. When he approached the table, Sea Woman, by turning her head just so, saw the dark tattooed face in the flickering candlelight and let out a banshee scream to match that of the jungle jaguar. Paco and the villager backed away. But Xa Lum admonished them. "Hold her as before! Chac will drown us all, for the rain is getting worse. I must use great force and she must not move."

The men glanced warily at each other. Sea Woman mumbled and began to shake.

Xa Lum nodded and again each man pressed the woman to the table with the weight of his body. Her mumbling grew louder. Slowly the *curandero* raised her arm, probed the bruises with his fingers.

Sea Woman struggled, called out, "No. My God please, no-o-o."

Xa Lum jammed her arm bone into her shoulder with so much force it jolted the table. Her raw, ragged cry pushed all the air from the hut. Eduardo's toes curled into the damp dirt floor against the sound of it. He turned away, sickened.

***

SHERIFF JOE WILKES was reading his favorite dime novel, *Shoot-out At Silbido Springs,* for the second time through when Petie Buckle from the telegraph office burst through the door. "You're not going to believe this, Sheriff Wilkes. Miss Nell Miggins is missing at sea!"

"What the hell you talking about?"

Petie shoved a telegram under Sheriff Wilkes' nose. After reading it he asked, "Any more telegrams this morning? One for Grady Monroe maybe?"

"That's the only one. Can you believe it? Miss Nell dead?"

Sheriff Wilkes grabbed his hat on his way out the door. "It don't say she's dead, Petie, just missing at sea." He headed straight for Grady's office where he wordlessly handed the telegram to the wheezing old lawyer.

Grady gave the sheriff a questioning look before reading the telegram. "This is grave news, Joe."

"That it is. I know how much you thought – think of Nell."

"I suppose I should send word to her cousin in San Antonio. After that, I'd appreciate it if you'd ride out to the ranch with me. Grave news, very grave news."

After sending a telegram to Hester Woodvine in San Antonio, Grady and Sheriff Wilkes climbed in the Maxwell and headed out of town in grim silence.

Pablo greeted them at the side of the house where he and Tinker were building scaffolding up the face of a chimney.

"*Buenos dias*, Sheriff, Mr. Monroe."

"Bway-no to you too, Pablo." Grady looked around the yard.

"More bandit trouble?" Pablo asked, apparently confused by the silent glances between the sheriff and lawyer. Tinker climbed down from the scaffolding. Lupe and Skin came out of the house.

"No, no. The sheriff here got a telegram from that hotel where Miss Nell is staying down at Tres Palacios, you see ..." Grady paused, not wanting to say what he had to say. Billy and two other cowboys walked up from the barn. Grady dug in his vest pocket for the telegram and read it out loud. When he looked up, all eyes were on him in staggering disbelief.

"It don't say Miss Nell is dead," Skin charged. Tinker stepped forward and took the slip of paper from Grady.

"That's exactly what I said." Sheriff Wilkes piped in, eager to end the gloom.

Grady shifted his weight from one foot to the other. "I suppose there will be searches at sea. Keep in mind that boats are sometimes blown far off course by those dastardly squalls. Why, I once heard tell of a fellow down near New Orleans. Got caught in one and ended up in Jamaica, forheavensakes." Grady looked around to see if anyone was paying attention. "It was three months before he got back home."

Billy looked at Pablo. "Maybe we should go looking for her. You know I never trust city dudes. Don't know piddly from a possum princess."

"Now hold on a minute." Grady's voice raised an octave. "I can do a little investigating via telegrams, find out what's being done and who's in charge down there on the coast before we all go off half-cocked."

"I ain't going off half-cocked, you shifty-eyed—" Billy flushed bright red before stopping himself.

Pablo put his hand on Billy's shoulder. "We will wait, give Mr. Monroe more time. Then if we are not sure that everything is being done to find out where Nell is or what has happened to her, I will go myself. Until then, we will keep on as before."

"A good plan," Grady said. "And, well, since I'm here anyway, I think all of you should know that a buyer has deposited earnest money for the ranch into Miss Nell's account."

Everyone stirred and spoke at once. Grady waved his hands. "Let me finish, let me finish. Nell gave me complete power of attorney before she left on her trip in the event someone wanted to buy the ranch in her absence. But now, in light of the news we've all just received, I intend to hold off signing any papers until such a time that I feel… Well, until we have a few more particulars."

"You think the fellar-buyer is going to go along with that?" Billy asked.

"I'm sure of it. Whoever it is wishes to have all of you stay on and continue to run the ranch anyway. So you see, Pablo is right, just continue as before."

Pablo's forehead wrinkled with concern. "What do you mean, whoever it is? You do not know?"

"No," Grady said. "I was contacted by an attorney in Fort Worth, said his client wished to remain anonymous."

Billy shook his head. "One of them city sidewinders back east, sure as hell."

"Billy?" Skin asked.

"What?"

"What's non-o-mous?"

"Secret. On the sly."

"There's one more thing." Grady shifted his weight again. "I don't know if Pablo here told the rest of you. Miss Nell got all her personal affairs in real good order before she left. I'm talking about her will and all." He looked down at the telegram Tinker had handed back to him. He folded and refolded the paper until it was crumpled and damp. "I know she would want me to tell all of you that whatever happens, you're not to worry." He turned on his heel and rushed to climb back in the Maxwell. Sheriff Wilkes pushed his hat down on his head and gave them all a nod before climbing in beside him.

Skin watched the automobile disappear down the road. "She ain't dead, I tell ya. I just know she ain't."

***

NELL STRUGGLED BETWEEN dark fuzzy dreams and hot jabs of pain. Each time she tried to give in to blackness, pain tugged her back to the light. Her lips and tongue felt thick. When she attempted to talk the words came out all wrong and worst of all, she couldn't see. Was she blind? Were her eyes even open? What had happened to her?

Now gentle hands touched her with something wet. Someone was washing her. She was naked. She tried to push the hands away but the pain in her shoulder and head made her weaken.

"Sh-h-h, pale one, be still. All will be good soon."

It was a woman's voice with a strange accent. Try as she may, Nell could not make her mouth form the questions storming her head. A drab netherworld swirled around her, pulled her down into a black abyss.

Someone was speaking again, a younger voice. Lupe? Who is Lupe? Something warm touched her lips. It was sweet and thick, almost frothy and she swallowed it in big gulps until her stomach ached. Then a liquid that smelled faintly like honey was forced into her mouth. She had to swallow to keep from choking.

Children's voices sounded in the distance. Or maybe they were close but so low they seemed far away. Nell felt disconnected. Something was keeping her from her own mind. A fog, an icy numbing fog, infected her mind. Long gray worms lived in the fog, feeding on her brain. A bird pecked at her eyes. It hurt. Everything hurt.

The younger voice poured liquid in her mouth again. She swallowed and let black swirls pull her deeper into the abyss.

From the Underworld she saw a dazzling yellow door. As she moved toward it, waves crashed over her as if she were a small rock on a beach being washed first this way and then that. Then everything was so brilliant she had to hide her eyes. Children's voices surrounded her. A small hand held hers and looking down, she saw a tiny face with black eyes. "Juan?" Was that her voice?

"Chac's bride is better, no?" A woman's voice.

She opened her mouth to speak again but was afraid she might slip back into the dark if she did. Were the faces she looked at real or of the Underworld?

Someone touched her lips with a jar. She pushed it away but the smell of it stayed with her. A familiar scent, sweet, yeasty. Finally she understood. It was the fermented drink that made her slip to the Underworld. Again the jar was pressed to her lips and again she pushed it away. She looked down at the hand that did the pushing. It was her own hand. At last she was back in her mind and was not blind after all.

When she looked up from her hand she saw a small chubby woman staring at her. "Eduardo! Come quick," the woman screamed.

A man appeared out of the brightness. "*Ay-e-e*, at last you are better, pale lady. My name is Eduardo Gomez. What is your name?" He spoke slow and deliberate.

Nell watched his lips move. He looked at the woman then back to her. "This is my wife, Chiquita. We have been taking care of you. Do you understand my words?"

When she nodded the movement made her dizzy. She reached for her itchy face but the woman, Chiquita, grabbed her hand and held it.

"Good," Eduardo said. "You see our English is not so good. The padre, he has taught us but sometimes we forget. What is your name?"

Was he talking to her or the woman in the Underworld? His face was dark and sweet like the little boy's.

"We have been calling you Sea Woman. We will call you that until you are better and we can talk, both of us. Is this good?"

She was slipping back into the quagmire.

"Chiquita will take you back inside now. Each day you will be better, you will see, and then we will talk." Eduardo patted her arm.

Chiquita took her hand and led her back into the darkness. There she was shown to a straw mat and told to lie down. Chiquita and a young woman sat patting something between their hands before a fire.

"Lupe?" Nell wondered at the name that came into her mind.

When the girl brought her the honey drink, Nell turned her head away, sure that finding answers to the questions swirling in her head depended on her ability to refuse the drink.

Soon, the familiar jabs of pain started back in her shoulder and head with throbbing agony. But she knew she had to stay away from the honey drink. She closed her eyes, listened to the women pat the flat, white cakes between the palms of their hands.

***

WHEN NELL OPENED her eyes, the same brilliant yellow light was spilling through the door. Sunshine. She moved to sit up but pain shot through her shoulder and arm. Someone had tied her arm to her chest and she was wearing a thin brightly-colored shift.

Cheerful voices, young and old drifted in from the sunshine. She managed to pull herself to a standing position and moved to the shadowy doorway. Eduardo and Chiquita were watching several children chase a squealing pig around a clearing in a forest or jungle.

"Sea Woman, Sea Woman." One of the youngest children had seen her in the shadows and tugged at Eduardo's shirt and pointed at her.

Eduardo helped her to the shade of tangled trees where she slid to the ground to sit and rest. "I hope our fun has not disturbed you."

Her eyes burned and teared in the blazing light. "What is this place? Why am I here?"

"This is my home, near the fishing village called Celestún."

"Is that near Padre Island?" She tried to think clearly. Padre Island was a barrier island that hugged the Texas coastline all the way to Mexico but she didn't remember hearing about a place called Celestún.

Eduardo looked at his wife, then back at her.

"What happened to my arm?"

"Eh-h-h." Eduardo looked at Chiquita again.

"The arm bone was away from the body bone," Chiquita said.

"What?"

"The *curandero*, eh, doctor," Chiquita continued, "he came and fixed your arm and face."

"My face...?" She reached up but Chiquita stopped her hand as before.

"It is not yet healed, Sea Woman. The *curandero* gave me medicine, which I have been keeping on it."

"Sea Woman?" Nell was exhausted but she had to find out what had happened. Chiquita and Eduardo exchanged yet another long nervous look.

"Nell slumped back against a tree trunk and spoke with as much courage as she could summon. "Eduardo, you better start at the very beginning."

When he finished his long, halting explanation, he wiped his sweaty face on his sleeve.

"I don't remember being in a storm or on a boat, but I know I'm not a goddess of any *cenote*."

"Then, lady, who are you and where did you come from?"

Nell felt sick. Pain hammered her head. "From...from Wishing. In Texas. Can you take me there?"

"Lady, this is Yucatán. Mexico."

Blood drained from her head. How could it be? She wanted to run. Run home, but which way was that? She struggled to stand. Chiquita held her, tried to calm her.

"But if that's so, what kind of fishing were you doing so far north in the Gulf of Mexico?"

Chiquita stood quickly and pulled on Nell's good arm to get her to do the same. "That is enough for today. "You are not well. Elena will bring you *balché* to drink."

"No! I want no more of that drink." Nell reached to rub her eyes. They were itchy and sore, especially the left one. Chiquita tried to stop Nell as before but she jerked away.

That night Eduardo put the two youngest children in a hammock together and insisted Nell take the one vacated. She stared into the darkness for a long time. She knew Eduardo was awake in his hammock. She'd heard him go outside to relieve himself only minutes ago.

"Eduardo?" she called in a low voice. "How long have I been here?"

"Many weeks."

"How many?"

"Four or five, maybe it is."

Her heart lurched.

"Eduardo?"

"*Si?*"

"I remember now. My name is Nell Miggins and tomorrow I want you to help me go home to Texas."

***

WHEN NELL MOVED to untangle herself from the hammock that morning, pain burned in her shoulder and shot flames up her neck. Chiquita, who'd been stirring a creamy mixture in an iron pot, was at her side in an instant. "You are better, yes?" She handed Nell a thin piece of bread, much like Lupe's tortillas.

Lupe? Pablo? Did they think she was dead? If so, no one would be looking for her. Her heart galloped ahead of itself, tightened her throat, paralyzed her lungs. She dropped the bowl, struggled to stand, but Chiquita fought her flaying arm and managed to ease her back to a mat. Eduardo heard the commotion and came running into the hut.

"Please take me back to Texas," she begged. "I'll pay you as soon as we arrive."

"It is not that easy."

"Why not? You have a boat!"

"I do not own the boat, lady. I cannot just leave like that."

"Who does then?"

"*Señor* Santio. He is *alcalde*, mayor of Celestún."

"Then take me to him."

Chiquita stepped in front of Eduardo. "You are too weak for such a long walk, Sea Woman."

"I am not Sea woman. My name is Nell! Call me Nell!"
Chiquita shrank back.

Eduardo held up his hands, palm out. "Lady, Nell, think about this. Eat. Rest. Chiquita will take you to the *cenote*. The water there is warm and will help you get strong. While you are getting better, I will see if I can find a burro for you to ride to the village and I will take you there. *Sí*, yes?"

Nell studied his face. The skin around his weary eyes was like hide. It would do little good to push him. His control over the matter seemed not much greater than her own. The lump in her throat grew unbearable. Her backbone turned to jelly.

When she didn't contradict Eduardo's suggestion, Chiquita looked him in the eye and nodded toward the door. Eduardo followed her outside where they exchanged heated arguments in a language Nell couldn't understand.

Later, Elena held Nell's good arm to help her down the long path to the *cenote*. Chiquita followed with a basket of soiled clothes balanced on her head. The children stayed behind with Eduardo, who had seemed subdued after his private conversation with Chiquita. The thought struck Nell that she had no way of knowing if what they'd been telling her was true.

The jungle grew more tangled as they moved away from the clearing around the hut. Mosquitoes buzzed her ears in the sultry, airless undergrowth. Just as she thought she could no longer walk, Chiquita called out to Elena to let her rest. The smell of decaying vegetation mixed with her own body odors repulsed Nell. The thin shift she wore was soggy with sweat and clung to her gritty skin.

When she quit shaking, they walked on a little farther and a bright clearing came into view. A high limestone shelf dropped down and sloped back into a cave-like opening. A shaft of sunlight beamed through a gap in the overhang and reflected off a shimmering pool of water. Elena eased Nell to the ground and without warning or modesty lifted her own loose dress over her head, stepped out of her undergarments, and waded into the pool.

Chiquita squatted at the water's edge to empty the basket of dirty clothes on the flat rocks. She said something to Elena that Nell couldn't understand, then laughed. Elena scowled at her mother, swam back to Nell and tugged on her dirty dress. Nell drew back.

"The water is very good from the underground and will make your arm better," Elena said. "Do not be ashamed. We have washed you many times."

Nell allowed Elena to help her out of the dress but held it in front of her as she waded into the pool. Odd waves of shimmering water washed against her skin almost as if there were two kinds of water: One cloudy and warm, the other cool and clear. She ducked below the water's surface, swished her head back and forth and rubbed her scalp with only one hand since her injured arm was still much too sore to move very much. When she came up for air and rubbed water from her face she felt a raised, tender ridge of skin on her forehead. Elena was watching her closely. Nell touched the sensitive skin again. It began at her forehead, moved downward to the corner of her eye and ended on her cheek in front of her ear.

"What happened to me?"

Elena shrugged. "No one knows."

"A mirror. Do you have a mirror?"

Elena shook her head no.

Nell moved to shallow water, stood and looked down at her body. Her white skin clung to ribs that stood out in high ridges above her abdomen. The area below her ribs caved inward down to the jutted-out points of her hip bones. When she looked up Elena, who had been watching, quickly looked away.

***

Several days later Eduardo made his way up the path from the beach with a basket of fish balanced on his shoulder. He beamed half-rotted teeth at his children. "Tonight we eat fishes, little ones!"

"Chac is pleased you saved Sea Woman. That is why we prosper," Chiquita said. She continued to refer to Nell as the goddess of the well or Chac's goddess or Sea Woman. Nell was sure Chiquita would do anything to block her way home.

Eduardo gave Chiquita no reply. Instead, he turned to Nell. "Tomorrow, Paco will come for us early with a burro. We will all go to the village for market."

Chiquita screamed like a cat. "How can you let her leave here after the *curandero* told you Chac sent her? Storms will come, you will see."

Nell steeled herself, determined to stay calm. "Chiquita, I'm not a goddess. I think the *curandero* made a mistake. Maybe I can talk with him and explain."

"He will shame you. Without my husband you would be dead."

"I know that and I am grateful."

"Then you must stay and bring rain for the corn. When the storms come, you will go to the *cenote* and pray to Chac for us."

Nell backed away toward the path to the *cenote*. "I will talk to the *curandero* and the *alcalde*, anyone who will listen." If she stayed and tried to argue her point, she feared she would make things worse.

On the way to the village the next day, Nell rode the burro Paco brought to Eduardo. Chiquita and Elena walked ahead of them with baskets of corn strapped to their backs. The younger children ran in front of them with a squealing piglet on a rope leash.

Eduardo who held the burro's halter, glanced up at Nell and spoke in a hushed voice. "It will be better for both of us if you find help in the village without me. No one must know. At the church, Sister Tia Marie. Be very careful who you talk to, lady. The government men from Mexico are sometimes about."

Nell had a dozen questions to ask Eduardo but they were nearing the village where the streets teemed with people toting baskets of corn, beans, tortillas, and chickens. Stalls were stacked with pottery and leather goods. She wouldn't have thought so many people lived in such a remote jungle world.

She spotted the church almost immediately, though the only difference between it and the other buildings was a low steeple with a cross on it. Villagers watched her with child-like curiosity, stopping Chiquita or Eduardo and speaking to them in the odd Spanish-Mayan dialect while gesturing with great fanfare.

While Eduardo led the others around the market area, Nell was able to slide off the burro and drape the saddle blanket over her head with little notice. She lagged farther and farther behind until she felt she wasn't recognized as part of Eduardo's family group then quickly doubled back and entered the church.

The chapel was small and sparse and smelled of candle wax, a confessional on her left and to the right a short hall made a blind turn. She heard footsteps approaching from the right.

A nun stepped around the corner and smiled with a look of mild surprise. "You must be the rain goddess I've heard so much about."

Nell had not known what she would say or do at this point. She certainly hadn't expected to bump into an Anglo nun with a clipped British accent. She was very pretty with sky blue eyes and ivory skin. "I'm Sister Tia Marie. I've been worried about you."

Nell opened her mouth but words froze in her throat. The nun took her elbow and led her down the hall to a tiny room where she motioned to a chair.

"I hope you understand that I couldn't visit you without arousing a great deal of trepidation from the old *curandero* and Chiquita. Not to speak of the danger it would have caused Eduardo Gomez."

"Is there a telegraph anywhere around here?"

"My goodness no, and very seldom does mail make it to foreign shores or I would have learned the whereabouts of your family and informed them that you were alive."

The nun looked at Nell's forehead and the left side of her face. Her eyes were tender and sympathetic. "What is your name?"

"Nell Miggins. How can I get home to Texas?"

"What did Eduardo tell you?"

"That he found me drifting on flotsam after a storm and that my shoulder was dislocated. I-I almost died, I think. And something happened to my face... I don't know what or how."

"Eduardo was not fishing when the storm blew him off course. He was running smuggled guns from here to a village near Matamoros, Mexico, just south of the Texas border. He has a brother living there. Eduardo and his brother lived here in Celestún back when the church had an orphanage."

The nun moved a chair close to Nell and sat with her hands folded in her lap. "Eduardo's brother was adopted by a wealthy Spanish family and taken away, treated like a slave. Both brothers will do anything to help overthrow a government that favors the wealthy. Authorities are already suspicious of Eduardo's activities and anxious to find evidence against him. If he discloses the details of your rescue – that you are from Texas – and he was so far north to have rescued you, he could be arrested."

"I would never do anything to bring him harm."

"You're in a very difficult position Nell, but not as dangerous as Eduardo. The villagers believe you are a deity. They won't harm you. But they will do anything to keep you here. Lock you up, or kill Eduardo should he try to help you escape."

Sister Tia Marie stood and moved to a trunk at the foot of a narrow cot. "You will have to trust me, Nell. I'll ask questions of the proper persons, find out what you need to know without raising suspicions. I'll keep you informed, probably through Eduardo."

She rummaged around inside the trunk and when she straightened, she held what looked like a photograph frame. The nun looked at it with a deep sigh. "I gave up such things as this when I took my vows. Don't know why I kept it all these years." Her voice trailed when she looked up at Nell. "This is a mirror. Perhaps you would like to see your scar while you are here with me. I have an idea it is not as bad as you think, and the sooner you see it, the sooner you'll get used to it."

Nell took the mirror to the window, raised it to eye level. A rush of air left her lungs as if she'd been punched in the stomach. An angry red line traced across her forehead through her eyebrow, just as she had expected, but wider on her forehead than on her cheek. The outside corner of her left eye drooped.

"Remember, Nell, all scars fade with time. Some day it will be as pale as the skin around it. A thin pale line."

Nell swallowed hard.

"And it appears you were very lucky not to lose the sight in your eye. It's not easy for me to admit, but Xa Lum does know his business when it comes to healing."

She knew Sister Tia Marie was right, but the woman in the mirror looked old and thin, eyes sunken with dark circles. She'd never been a beauty, but it was a grisly thing to have your face changed and not know how it happened.

"I'll never be the same, will I?" Nell lowered the mirror and turned to face the nun.

"Not many people look death in the eye the way you have and view life – or themselves – the same ever again."

Nell handed the mirror back to the nun.

Sister Tia Marie knelt in front of the trunk and ransacked the contents a second time. "We'd better hurry before Chiquita comes looking for you." She held up a white peasant blouse gathered with a ribbon at the neck to form a wide ruffle, then a brightly colored skirt made the same way with a draw string waist. "I'm afraid this is the best I can do."

Then Sister Tia Marie froze. "Wait... I just happened to think. There was a chap, an American, some scientist or other connected to the University in Mexico City. I've seen his assistant in the village. It's been a while but perhaps he will be able to help."

"It sounds too good to be true."

"I don't want to get your hopes up unnecessarily. He may have already left or he may not be in a position to help. I'll see what I can find out."

"Anything you can do to help." Nell felt on the verge of tears. She dared not hope too much.

The nun placed the clothes and mirror in the center of a shawl, gathered the corners and tied them into a tumpline and handed it to Nell. "We will leave through the front door as if you wandered by and I noticed you needed a little charity." On the way out of the room she handed Nell a thick block of soap.

***

A week later Paco appeared outside the jungle hut to tell Eduardo he thought they should try fishing a certain inlet to the south. Nell knew from their fidgety glances toward Chiquita that something more was on Paco's mind.

She had prepared herself for a long wait while Sister Tia Marie found a way for her to get back home. Meanwhile, maybe the nun had been right that in time she would grow accustomed to her scar and what had happened to her. All that had gone before seemed like an old dream. The dusty roundup before leaving Wishing, the raid on the ranch. Had she really killed a man? Tinker and the windmill. Skin's sad songs. Had it all been a dream or was she dreaming now?

Answers came in bits and pieces. While helping Elena with the wash at the *cenote*, an image of dolphins racing beside a boat flashed in her mind. And only last night she woke with a start, remembering Maudeen's hair swirling in the water. But the worst was recalling the feel of burning salt water in her nose and throat, the crushing force of the storm, the push and pull of the water on her limbs as if they were being torn from her body. The clacking sound of her own teeth as she drifted on the brink of a watery grave. She recalled the squeeze of death with chilling clarity. Now everything, the past and the future, had a new edge to it, as if viewed from another dimension.

Eduardo returned from the fishing trip alone looking tired and haggard with only a few small fish. Nell hadn't talked with him since market day. In fact, she avoided his eyes altogether. He did the same. Chiquita had grown frighteningly possessive and rarely let Nell out of sight.

Eduardo handed Chiquita the basket of fish with a grunt and squatted next to Nell who was shucking corn beside a fire outside the hut. He poked at the red coals until Chiquita disappeared inside the hut then without looking up said, "Tonight, as soon as everyone sleeps, go and meet Paco at the *cenote*. He will show you the way from there. Everyone will believe you have run away of your own doing." He put a few sticks on the fire. "Do you understand?"

"Yes, but how will I know my way from there?"

"Paco will explain." He stood and walked away.

The wait, first for nightfall, then for everyone to fall asleep, seemed eternal. The moonless night would help conceal her movements, but no moon also meant a darker path to the *cenote*. She imagined losing her way so many times her heart pounded with anticipation.

When the time was right, she slid from her hammock, grabbed her bag of soap and clothes, and moved soundlessly into the jungle. Strange grinding insect noises seemed magnified and close under the blanket of tangled growth. Her breathing became more and more shallow the deeper into the jungle she ran.

She paused to catch her breath and press the sharp pain in her side. By remembering the first time Elena led her to the *cenote* when she was nearly blind with swollen eyes – the feel of each tree trunk, the twist here, the double back over the fallen tree there – she was on her way again, relying on a sense other than sight to find her way.

Paco jumped to his feet when he heard her approach. "We hurry, hurry. Long way." He gestured to a path circling the *cenote*.

"Where are we going?"

"Sister says American is working in jungle near sacred grounds. You will be safe there. Safe from the soldiers and villagers. Is a long journey but with the burro from church, not as long."

He led the way around and up a narrow footpath above the limestone outcropping over the *cenote*. She crouched over the burro's neck to keep the low-growing limbs from knocking her off the animal's back. She was completely at Paco's mercy, had no idea how to move through the jungle maze, even if he'd been able to explain where and in what direction they were to travel.

A loud screech sliced through the muffled hum of jungle noise.

"Is tapacamino bird," Paco said when Nell gasped. "He cried out many, many times to help the *curandero* when you first come to us. The bird watches now. Is sad you leave."

Nell rode in silence for a long time after that. She understood the dangers Eduardo and his family faced because of the kindness they had shown her. It saddened her knowing she could never repay or thank Eduardo.

The somber, strange sounds, the shadowy sway of low limbs, insects chewing her skin, all made her see the jungle as a green living thing objecting to her intrusion into it. Just as the Gulf of Mexico seemed a living thing when she first saw it. Her shoulder ached from the constant hold she had to keep on the burro's neck, her bare feet and legs became bloody with scratches from the slaps of limbs and thorny twigs.

Something thick and cool bumped her forehead. The burro paused when she jerked back with a grunt. She squinted in the darkness to focus on the object. A snake as thick as her arm slivered from one tree limb to another. Nell dove for the ground screaming and clawing. The burro kicked and wheezed, and a roar filled all the spaces under the forest canopy as every conceivable bird, insect, and animal called out against her intruding cry.

Paco rushed to help her up. "Okay, okay." he said.

Nell backed away, nodded and took a deep breath.

"*Balché?*" He offered her the jar.

"No."

"*Un poco?*"

Nell shivered and rubbed her face. She took the jar, allowing herself only a tiny sip before climbing back up onto the burro's back. Soon a dim gray glow began to show through the trees. Dawn. They were on a low plateau, though it was hard to be sure because vegetation hid so much of the sky. Paco pointed ahead to a clearing with a small *cenote* in the center. They stopped and after drinking their fill of the cool water, he handed her the burro's blanket and told her to rest. In spite of her crawling, itchy skin, aches and pains, and troubled mind, Nell fell asleep immediately.

When Paco woke her, the sun was burning hot on her face. She had no idea how long they'd slept, whether they were walking east or west, north or south or if she even cared. After what seemed hours, they skirted a lagoon then changed directions. South? Or was it north? Paco stopped once to give her another sip of *balché* and some *tutiwah* bread, but before the circulation could return to her legs they were moving again.

Later, with the sun so low the forest was thrown into premature darkness, Paco motioned her to be quiet. The path had widened. Trees were freshly cut and undergrowth slashed. He stayed on the edge of the widened path.

After a mile or two, Paco led the burro back into the thick jungle, stopped and tied the burro to a limb and whispered that she should be very quiet and stay put. She clung to his arm, shaking her head. "No," she whispered. "Don't leave me."

He held his finger to his lips then gestured over her shoulder and parted a thatch of vine and undergrowth. About thirty yards away was a camp with several tents around a glowing fire. Lanterns hung from trees. Two men milled around the fire and to their left, in front of the largest tent, a man moved to a folding chair near a table. The American. Her heart tripped then thumped forward again. She started to call out, but Paco clamped his hand over her mouth. "May be not safe. I go alone to talk first."

"Do you mean he doesn't expect us?" Nell was incredulous.

"No time for that. Anyway, too dangerous. Who can Sister trust? Sister asked Paco." He tapped his chest. As witless as it might have been, Nell felt sorry for Paco. He was doing his best to help and the harder he tried, the greater the danger.

He turned back to the camp, whispered, "The government bribe villagers with *mordidas*, favors. May be soldiers there now in the tents."

Of course he was right. She twisted her fingers in the burro's mane to hold him still then watched as Paco crawled under the jungle growth and approached the clearing. He called out a greeting before showing himself. The American, as well as the men around the campfire, jumped to attention. Paco held his hands up, saying something to the American who motioned to the other men and they all relaxed.

Paco and the American talked with lowered heads for a long while. Once, the American's voice grew louder. He raised his arms waist high then let them fall to his sides. Paco shrugged, shook his head. When Paco gestured in her direction, the American turned. Nell's mouth fell open in unutterable disbelief. Of course. It made perfect sense. The American was Henry Burleson.

By the time she stumbled from the tangle of vines, Henry had moved to the edge of the clearing and he, too was dumbstruck. "Good Lord" was all he said.

Her lungs began a rhythm of breathing all their own. Her head felt like a spinning top.

"What in the...? Nell Miggins? How...?" Henry looked down to her bare, dirty feet and back up to her scarred face.

She felt her knees buckle. Paco rushed forward to take her arm. Henry took her other arm. She forced herself not to faint, to hold tight, stay in control.

Inside Henry's tent, Paco related the sequence of events that led her to his camp. Nell still couldn't speak, her heart pounded so hard she could feel her body jerk with each beat.

"I remember talk about a storm," Henry said. "In fact the steamer I was on glanced off the outer edges of it. That's been, what? Six, seven weeks ago?" He stared at her, studied her eye and forehead. "Incredible."

"I-I don't remember everything." She managed to say when she found her tongue. She knew this was to be the first of many scrutinizing encounters, curious stares that silently asked how it felt to have your face sliced open and not remember.

Henry moved to the flap door of the tent where he instructed one of the men to pitch a tent for her. Turning back to Paco he asked, "Do you need a hammock?"

"No." Paco stood and placed a hand on her shoulder. After a quick nod, the black jungle swallowed him whole. Nell strained to hold the image of his receding back. If she lived through this, she knew that remembering Paco would seem like a faded illusion. He and Eduardo had saved her life and she would never see either of them again. The irony jabbed at her. She clutched her elbows across her ribs and squeezed back the urge to cry.

Henry sat on a cot adjacent her. "What you must have endured. The possibility that we would meet again like this..."

"Can you send word to Wishing that I'm alive? A telegram, letter, anything?"

"Would you want me to do that knowing that the message could be encountered by the authorities? We'd probably be back in the United States before a letter has had time to reach its destination anyway."

"Then we can leave soon?"

"You must be starved and exhausted." Henry barked a few orders to a young man who had been walking by the tent, then turned back to her. "My dig is scheduled to end in a couple of weeks, before the rainy season. I realize you've had a terrible time of it, but I can't jeopardize the whole expedition by ending it before the scheduled time. You're safe here, and I trust we can make you more comfortable than you were in the village."

"Two weeks?"

"Give or take a few days. And if you feel up to it, you know, you may even find the dig interesting. As I remember from our conversations back in Texas, you have a mild interest in archaeology. And Andy, the university student who acts as my assistant and cook, will need that much time to fatten you up a little before you surprise the folks back home."

Nell gaped at him. Hadn't he understood? She hadn't simply taken a detour to end up here for a holiday. She'd nearly died, suffered weeks of itchy filth at the hands of a witch doctor and a hysterical woman. And Henry thought she might enjoy his dig? Had she misunderstood him?

Later, settling on a cot in her own tent, she felt as if her body had turned to stone. Her head throbbed and everything itched.

Henry's words, "a couple of weeks," repeated in her head. She recalled thinking the first time she met him that life had been wily with her, full of tricks to make her want to give up.

It was still working at her.

***

THE CAMP LOOKED deserted when Nell stuck her head out of the tent the next morning. Smoke rose from the campfire in a thin straight line into the sky directly over the clearing. Not the slightest breeze to stir the heavy humid air. A young man walked into the clearing and put a few knots of wood on the fire. "Morning, ma'am. I'm Andy, from last night, remember?"

She nodded, looked around.

"They're all gone to the dig. Mr. Burleson says I'm to watch after you. Would you like something to eat?"

"Yes." Nell stepped out of the tent. The smell of real food and coffee flooded her nostrils. Andy indicated a folding chair and after rattling a few dishes handed her a plate of food. She hunched over the plate, scooping food into her mouth in noisy slurps. When she caught sight of Andy's stare, she sat up straight, forced herself to eat slower.

"More?" he asked.

Nell shook her head no. "Where can I wash?"

"There's a *cenote* close by. Must have been something, that shipwreck. Hurt much?"

She assumed he meant her face since his eyes kept returning to the scar. She supposed she was glad Andy asked straight out without hedging. Maybe the second stare and question would be easier and that would make the third easier still, until she grew numb to the stares she would undoubtedly experience for the rest of her life.

"I was unconscious most of the time."

She followed him to a pool about fifty yards from camp. She and Paco must have walked right by it, but with thick undergrowth on one side and a low limestone rock wall circling the rest, it was all but hidden. The forest clearing put Nell in mind of a beautiful watercolor painting. Pale sunlight filtered through trees casting soft shadows on the vines and bushes growing in rich shades of emerald and jade. The pool shimmered bright aqua as water dripped from an overhanging rock.

"Now, ma'am, I got to stay close. But if you wade across the *cenote*, you'll see a cave entrance around that bunch of vines. Go on in there and you'll be in private. There's an opening overhead so you'll have plenty of light."

Nell waded across the shallow sandy-bottomed pool and into the cave where a wide ledge circled the waterline. The pool there looked about waist deep. She laid the tied scarf holding her clean clothes aside and pulled her dirty shift over her head. Then using the soap the nun had given her, luxuriated in a sudsy bath. If nothing else, after all that had happened, she'd never again fail to appreciate the privilege of a soapy bath in private.

Angry red insect bumps dotted her arms. Her legs were scraped and bruised, and the bottoms of her feet were beginning to show signs of infection. But none of it seemed as bad now that she was clean. She rubbed soap into her dirty shift, rinsed it clean then climbed out of the pool onto the ledge.

After she put on the clean clothes, she propped the mirror on a narrow ledge in the cave wall. She could see well enough to run her fingers through her hair and loosely braid it over one shoulder the way Elena had. As if having a curiosity all their own, her eyes moved to the scar. Her heart sank. It wasn't the disfigurement that weighted her spirits so much as the question of how she would face those back home in Texas. She loathed pity. It took the place of caring, and more than anything right now she needed to know someone cared that she was still alive and not drowned at sea.

"Ma'am, you all right in there?" Andy's voice echoed.

She returned the mirror to the bag and waded back through the shallow end of the pool, careful to keep the hem of her clean skirt out of the water.

***

HENRY HANDED A bucket of dirt and rock to the worker above the trench. He hadn't trusted the native workmen to perform the delicate task of removing soil from the actual glyphs. This morning his work concentrated on a low wall of hieroglyphs while the others removed topsoil from a trench next to the one he was in.

The appearance of Nell Miggins, like a battered apparition out of nowhere, completely flabbergasted him. She was in ghastly condition. That she had been near death, he had no doubt. Most perplexing of all was, despite her degrading condition, she managed to command the moment of their meeting with such fortitude. She hadn't whined or wavered. Henry asked himself now if he could have been as strong.

He was sorry if he seemed uncharitable by refusing to leave at once. The thought was absurd, really. His first loyalty was to the work of the excavation. If he seemed unkind, then so be it. He would try to make her as comfortable as possible, give her sanction, and provide transportation back to the United States.

When he returned to camp, he found Nell sitting on a mat outside her tent. She had one foot turned up to her side attempting to remove a thorn from her heel.

"You look better," he said.

"Because of the bath, you mean?"

He smiled. "And a night's sleep. Don't you have shoes?"

She shook her head.

He called Andy over and handed him a pouch of tobacco. "See if you can use this to barter sandals from the workers for Miss

Miggins." He turned back to her. "I hope you understand my need to finish here before heading back to the United States."

"I understand, but I don't like it."

Her reply surprised him. "Fair enough. Has Andy seen to your needs? Anything besides the shoes?"

"He's been very courteous. But I've wondered where Scottie is."

"Don't you remember, at the hotel in Tres Palacios I told you he was too fragile for this expedition?"

"I do, now that you remind me. More and more I'm aware of things I'd forgotten and some things I remember out of sequence."

Andy reappeared with a pair of crude, thin-soled sandals.

"I think I appreciate these as much as the food this morning. Thank you, Andy."

Henry held a hand out to her. "Join me at my tent. The heat becomes unbearable in the late day. I use this time to do my paper work, eat, anything to be out of the sun."

"Where is the dig you're working on?" Nell grimaced and caught her shoulder when she'd tried to push herself up from the mat.

"Very close actually. The jungle grows so thick here that its seems farther away than it is."

"I don't even know where I am."

"The ancient town of Chunchucmil, about halfway between the city of Mérida, or Tiho as it was called in the post classic period, and Jaina, a center of major religious significance between 1000 AD and 1550 AD."

"Chunchucmil?"

"Of course, it isn't on any map." He pointed to a chair in front of his tent. "Chunchucmil is buried under hundreds of years of jungle growth, as is most of Yucatán. That's why so little is known about the Maya." He paused as Andy approached with plates of roasted chicken and corn. "As a matter of fact, theirs is the only civilization known to have flourished in a jungle region."

"What happened to them?"

"That's the great mystery as I told you back at your ranch. No one knows for sure. Some believe disease brought to the peninsula during the conquest, or the depredations imposed by the Spanish caused the collapse of their world. Others say the Maya were weakened by agricultural failure brought on because of changing weather conditions."

"What do you think?" When he didn't answer, she asked, "Is something wrong?"

"No. I find your interest flattering." He studied her face, the green, slightly sunken eyes. When the scar fades, he thought, she will be just as compelling as before, maybe more so.

Henry pushed his plate aside. "When the sun goes down we'll walk to the site if you feel up to it. Then you can see for yourself the work involved in a dig."

Nell excused herself to rest until time for the sundown walk. But later, after calling her name a few times, Henry looked in her tent and found her in deep sleep with a film of perspiration glistening on her face and arms. Her breathing came in long, slow drafts as if she had been drugged. He left quietly and didn't see her again until the next day when he returned from the dig. She was lounging in front of his tent reading his reports.

She looked embarrassed. "I hope you don't mind. I got bored. I'm sorry I missed our walk yesterday."

"We can go later today if you're still interested."

"I am."

At sundown he led her over a plateau near camp and into a clearing where trenches had been dug in neat rows. He cautioned her not to slip as he guided her down into the deepest trench. "Here are the glyphs I'm working on now."

She touched the face of a monkey glyph, traced the outline of the skull below its hand. To the left of the monkey, she studied the profile of a Mayan god.

"How old are these carvings?"

"These are hieroglyphs. About nine hundred years, give or take a few."

"I feel like I'm peeking into someone's window."

"Actually, more like reading someone's diary."

Nell looked taken aback, puzzled for a moment. "What does this say?" She pointed to another monkey glyph.

"The god's head in the monkey's hand is facing up. That indicates the number six. The left-facing skull means the number ten. The monkey signifies day. So the block reads the sixteenth day."

"The sixteenth day of what?"

"I have to uncover the rest of the glyph blocks to find out. For every question you have, Nell, I have a dozen more. Do you know the Maya were great mathematicians and built huge temples to study the stars and solar system? They were fascinated with the concept of time. Past and future were the same to them. They were preoccupied with the idea of divine powers, and I believe they considered time a sacred power. As far as anyone knows, they accomplished all they did without metal tools, beasts of burden, or wheels.

He moved down three steps to a second level of the trench and lit a candle, then held it high so she could see the glyphs. "There were chiefs and priests who were knowledgeable in astronomy, mathematics, architecture, engineering and so on. They were the elite few who made the laws and ran the government, decided when and where to build the great temples of worship, when to plant crops."

Nell again reached to loosen dirt in a glyph.

Henry continued. "On the other hand, the multitudes, the peasants, supported the whole society with their labors in the fields, built the roads and magnificent temples of worship. I'm not sure how or why, but I believe this social structure had something to do with the disappearance of the Maya."

Nell stopped looking around. "It's fascinating." She swiped at a bead of perspiration rolling down from her temple. When she turned to climb up the steps, Henry noticed the thin cotton of her blouse clung to her damp back.

In the days that followed, Henry and Nell walked at sundown, usually to the site of the dig. Darkness progressed at a slower pace in the jungle of Yucatán. More so than anywhere Henry had been in his life. During the day the sky radiated ashen blue shafts of searing heat that turned white hot in the late afternoon. But by the time he and Nell took their evening walks, the sky had turned the color of pewter. Each day he could see changes in her health. Her eyes were not so sunken, and the terrible sores on her arms and legs were healing. She told him about the villager's misconception that she was a sea woman sent to them by a rain god and about the strange old man who doctored her.

"I can show you hieroglyphs depicting Chac," Henry said. "And, I bet the witch doctor had a tattooed face. Many Maya still practice the ancient ways."

What mystified him most was that he'd begun to find Nell captivating, as if she harbored a magnetic force that pulled him a little closer each day. Despite her troubles, she still possessed a certain winsomeness, different from any woman he'd ever been attracted to.

One morning, working in the trench, Henry called up to Andy to bring down his notebooks. He'd discovered a ceiling and floor in the area and now worked in a tunnel-like chamber fifteen feet below ground. The floor sloped downward at about a thirty degree angle.

Andy handed the notebooks to Henry. "Miss Miggins is up there wanting to know if she can help."

"Do you have anything she can do?"

"Not really. I have most of the workers clearing the mounds. Two are in the other trench and there's only room enough for them."

"Well, send her down then. I'll find something. You keep after that trench crew, make sure they don't damage anything. I think they're over a dwelling of some sort."

When Nell joined him, he explained the work was hot and dirty, not to mention cramped in the tunnel chamber. She shrugged without argument so he handed her a trowel and brush and gave her a few instructions. With her help, he was free to work on drawings and measurements.

But her presence distracted him. He couldn't concentrate, and yet he couldn't bring himself to send her away either. She worked on her knees with her head tilted so the arch of her neck received the full glow of his lantern. Her body glistened with a veil of perspiration like that first day when he'd looked in on her as she slept. When she drew her arm across her forehead just now, to wipe away beads of moisture, a brown smudge from the dust she'd stirred was left in its place.

That evening after she had returned from the *cenote*, she said. "I wonder about the person who carved all those stones. I mean, the man who placed that block in that precise spot a thousand years ago. Was he married, handsome, tall, worried? What was he thinking?"

Henry threw his head back and laughed heartily. "What a mind you have."

"Think about it. The glyphs make them immortal. You said they perceived past and future as the same—" Her sparkle abruptly died away. Her face grew serious.

"What is it, Nell?"

"Did the Maya think in terms of forever. Or, in terms of only the present?"

"I'm not sure I follow you."

"If one combines the past and future then present suggests only this moment exists." She stared at the ground, apparently weighing the concept.

He felt a need to change the subject. "Tell me, did you ever sell your ranch?"

Nell shook her head and told him about the bandit raid, the barn burning, and the delay in the repairs she'd planned. "I can't guess what's happening now. My lawyer had power of attorney and I gave him instructions to sell if a buyer showed interest before my return." She gazed into the growing darkness, shifted in her chair. "What about you, Henry? Where is your home and who did you leave behind?"

"The university and Scottie, respectively," he said.

"Sounds like a solitary life."

"It suits me, I suppose. Women find my dedication to work difficult to understand."

She smiled warily.

"Share your thoughts?"

"I'm thought of as a solitary person. My life has been uncustomary."

The next day, while working side by side in the tunnel, he removing detritus, Nell cleaning a glyph depicting a jaguar holding a gourd, Andy called down that Henry should come right away. Nell followed.

The men, who had been working in the adjacent trench stood around leaning on picks and shovels. When Henry looked in the trench, he saw the top half of a jar laying on its side gleaming red and brown in the sun.

"Good god, Andy." He jumped down into the trench. Andy joined him with a wood box, trowels and brushes. They meticulously cleared the jar of all detritus using tiny brushes and tweezers. Henry asked Nell to bring his notebooks so he could record the position of the jar in relation to the grid lines while Andy made sketches of the jar itself.

"It's a funeral vessel," Henry said. "This proves my theory that this area was more than just a farming village. I've thought all along that Chunchucmil was a religious center." He glanced up at Nell before gently lifting the jar to the box. Andy and Nell followed him back to camp where he placed it on a table.

Paintings on the eight-inch jar depicted two male dancers in jaguar pelt leggings. One held a serpent over his head while the other bowed to a sitting figure. A third figure wore jaguar mittens on his hands and had red smudges on his side just below his rib cage while a fourth figure held a red jar similar to the one they had found. At intervals between the figures were glyphs, most of which were faded and smudged.

"What do you think, Mr. Burleson?" Andy asked.

"The glyphs may be a death chant of some kind. I'll know more after I've had time to study it."

"And the red splotches on the dancers?" Nell asked.

"They portray blood. Look, here's another one on the sitting figure, faded, but I believe it depicts the same thing. A blood-letting ceremony maybe."

"Could this jar be the one they used to catch the blood offering in?"

"Hey, I bet she's right." Andy's voice was full of excitement.

"There's something else." Nell added. "I've been thinking about it, Henry, since you told me about the Mayan social structure."

Henry shifted his gaze from Nell to Andy and then back to her. "Go on."

"If the Spanish brought disease to Yucatán the chiefs and priests would have been the first to come into contact with them, and the first to get sick and die."

Henry's face felt like stone.

She continued. "With the priests and chiefs dying there would be no one around to tell the lower classes when to plant, how to irrigate or how to perform the religious ceremonies."

"I get it!" Andy said. "Probably starvation got them since they didn't know how to plan agricultural activity. So both theories, disease and crop failure, come into play."

"Exactly." Nell almost shouted. "And who knows, there could have been drought or flood, too."

Henry covered the funeral jar with a cloth. "There are a few problems with that theory."

"Oh?" Andy waited for an explanation.

"It's over simplistic for one thing. Any scholar would argue that peasant revolt and overpopulation played a part."

"But what Miss Miggins said could still—"

Henry held up a hand. "Andy, tomorrow, I want you to make plaster casts of all the hieroglyphs Miss Miggins has cleaned in the tunnel."

"But how—?"

"I'll worry about the particulars. Just get it done. Now I think we should let the excitement rest. This find means we have twice as much work to do in the time we have left. I need to think about redirecting our efforts from the tunnel to the trench."

The following day Henry grew more and more irritated with the Mexican workers. They kept slopping plaster on areas not sufficiently cleaned, which meant Nell had to work harder to stay ahead of them. And, to make matters worse, Andy told him the natives expected an early rainy season and wished to leave for their villages as soon as possible.

Henry had heard of digs being abandoned by native workers for little or no reason, leaving archaeologists completely stranded. The thought unnerved him so bad he couldn't concentrate on his transcriptions and in the end rolled up his sleeves and helped with the plaster casting. He had Andy rotate the workers so the dig could continue without a break through the usual siesta time. But as a result, one of the workers collapsed from the heat and rolled over into the area where Nell worked.

She returned from the shade tree where the others had carried the unconscious man. "Henry, it's been an impossible day. We're all too tired to accomplish much."

He removed his hat, ran his fingers through his sweaty hair. The muscles in his jaw twitched. "I decide when the work stops." He turned to leave but stopped short to glance back at her. He started to say something more, but shook his head and left.

That evening Nell ate in her tent. Around midnight Henry walked outside his tent hoping to find a stir in the air. He could see in the silvery moonlight that Andy had moved his hammock up to the plateau where the Mexicans camped, obviously looking for cooler air, too.

A *tapacamino* bird's unusually loud call echoed eerily. Stupid creature. Did it think it needed to warn the jungle of his presence? Damn nuisance, those birds.

Mosquitoes, attracted to the scent of human perspiration, buzzed his ears and neck. He paced, fidgeted. How could Nell sleep? He paused in front of her tent, slapped at an insect, then proceeded down the path to the *cenote*. A swim would cool him off and get rid of the insects.

The *cenote* glistened, phosphorescent under a high bright moon. Henry pulled his shirt off and tossed it, along with his trousers, aside. He waded to the center of the pool, rolled over on his back. Even with his ears in water, he could still hear the bird's relentless calling. The moon loomed over the *cenote* like a white castle. Mayan lords had been so preoccupied with the moon and stars, and the concept of time that they let the grandeur of their era disappear into baffling oblivion. The Maya, immortal beings from another millennium, Nell had said. Was she eccentric? Or perceptive?

He sat up then and waded to a large flat stone at the pool's edge. As he dried off with his shirt, he realized the bird had hushed and the jungle lay quiet as death all around him. Not a single leaf moved. He pulled his trousers onto one leg and thought he heard something in the water – soft dripping sounds – and froze. He strained to see into the cave but most of it was in blue moon shadow. Mexicans claimed jaguars frequently visited the *cenote* at night.

Something back toward the cave moved. Looters? Maybe looters got word somehow that he'd uncovered a ceremonial vase at the dig and had come looking for pieces of antiquity for the black market. He'd probably walked up on them getting a drink.

"Who's there!" he called. There was no answer but water at the mouth of the cave rippled. Henry found a loose stone to use in defense. "Show yourself." He called again.

A shadow rose up out of the water. In the lacy pattern of moonlight through vines, Henry saw Nell's white shoulders outlined in the gleaming water. He lowered his arm and let the stone fall to the ground with a thud.

"I couldn't sleep," she said.

"How long have you been back there?"

She didn't answer.

"Well, you'd better come on out. It's not all that safe."

She still didn't answer.

"Nell?"

"You go ahead, I'll be along in a while."

Henry leaned down to pick up his shirt and noticed her clothes on a rock farther back from the pool's edge. His skin shrank. How had he missed seeing them before? No doubt, she'd watched him the whole time. "I'll turn around."

"I'm all right. I'll be along."

He turned to face the path. "I'm waiting." He heard the break of water, felt it lap at his feet with the movement she made, heard water dripping from her body, the rustle of her clothes.

"All right," she said behind him. When he turned, he was looking down, directly into her eyes.

"Sea Woman, is that what they called you?" Her wet hair clung to her head and shoulders. The scar was barely visible.

He reached down, took the sandals she carried out of her hand, and sat on the flat rock. "You shouldn't have come here without telling anyone." He grabbed her ankle so suddenly she had to use his shoulder for balance. After drying her foot with his shirt, he slipped on a sandal.

She sat next to him, took the shirt, dried her other foot and put on the second sandal. Then she stood and held the shirt out to him.

He stood, too, and so close he could see silver drops of water on her eyelashes. When she didn't back away as he half expected, he placed his hands on her shoulders, moved them up her neck and cupped her face. He tilted her mouth up to his and kissed her cool tight lips then circled her mouth with his tongue until it warmed and softened. She sucked air, attempted to pull away, but he threaded his arms around her ribs and pressed against her. When he drew back, the jungle noises began again, as if on some primordial signal. He leaned to kiss her a second time, but she stepped back and started up the path toward camp.

***

SEVERAL DAYS LATER Nell watched as Henry prepared to send Andy and the workers to Mérida with crates of plaster casts piled high on the backs of burros. In Mérida, Andy would turn the casts over to the University of Mexico. Before returning to camp he was to arrange passage for the three of them back to Galveston.

Time held itself in check while Andy packed to leave. Heavy clouds moved overhead, damp and brooding. Henry's ridged posture set a tone of tension for everyone trying their level best to please him.

"No wages for the man who damages a cast." He rushed from burro to burro to check the load each carried. It seemed to Nell he twitched and picked over the smallest detail. He carried a notebook, referred to it often as he paced. If he stood still – even for a moment – without looking at the notebook, he'd use it to tap his leg repeatedly faster and faster, until he had to pace again.

Andy tied down a leather sheath of notes and reports. "It might do for Miss Miggins to come along with us. She could wait in Mérida for the four or five days it'll take me to return and finish up here."

"And who would take her place? One of these dolts, who can't read or write, let alone speak English? No, I need her here." Henry moved off down the line of burros.

When he was out of hearing distance, Nell said. "Thanks just the same, Andy."

"I've heard he gets like this. Mr. Burleson goads like he's got to ride roughshod over everything around him. Works himself into a frenzy."

She realized Andy and the workers wanted nothing more than to be gone. A foreboding, unnatural atmosphere hung in the distance waiting for Henry to be done with his tirades. A peculiar sense of anticipation wrenched Nell's stomach. She was fearful, yet eager. For what, she had no idea, but it was connected to Henry's mood, that much she knew. He seemed poised for someone to refute him. The deep hairline above his temples throbbed with big blue veins. He was like a kettle on barely glowing coals, its whistle blowing low, a promise of the explosion to come when the fire was stoked.

As Andy disappeared over the plateau on his way to Mérida, Henry shouted after him. "And try to find some decent clothes for Miss Miggins while you're in Mérida, and shoes!"

Sharp pangs of embarrassment smacked Nell.

Henry headed straight for the dig after they left. At noon, she carried water, a few bananas and tortillas to him in the tunnel where he worked.

"Is it raining?" was all he said.

She shook her head then began to brush and clean glyphs while he ate. The sound of low murmuring thunder rolled down the tunnel causing them both to hold still for an instant.

Since the night he'd kissed her, Nell sensed Henry's constant scrutiny, not so much with his eyes as with the movement of air between them. She was oddly tense, yet at the same time felt fluid, like warm oil. Her skin tingled. She even perceived the damp dirt under her bare feet as extraordinary, as if feeling it for the first time. Smells were stronger, sounds were clearer, something was ready to snap.

When Henry was close, as in the tunnel, the sensations were intensified. She thought she'd go mad wondering what made the air static. What was about to begin? And what ending would there be because of it?

If the rainy season was early, Henry had told her, the dig would have to be cut short. And he feared that by the time he returned the following year, looters would have despoiled any important glyphs remaining in the tunnel.

When she climbed out of the tunnel to empty her bucket, rain showered down in a gentle mist, but she said nothing to Henry about it. He finished eating and resumed working next to her. In the tight space their shoulders touched. Then reaching for his notebooks, Henry's arm brushed hers. They glanced at each other. She turned back to her work. But he reached a slender finger over to her wrist and traced a line to the soft skin inside her elbow.

She concentrated on the work in front of her. The glyph blocks ended in a vertical stack of four. She was cleaning the last of nine centuries' worth of dirt from a three-foot figure of a man. His head was turned to the right, eyes staring heavenward. His arms had deep vertical slashes on them like the tiny figurine Loretta wore around her neck back at Tres Palacios pavilion.

Nell used a small brush to remove dirt from the figure's open mouth, thinking his cry had been smothered until that moment. She touched the figure's lips and then its slashed arms. Henry touched Nell's face.

She moved aside, scooping several spades of dirt into her bucket before climbing up the ladder. Above ground, she emptied her bucket then turned, saw Henry at the opening to the tunnel. He looked up at the dark sky. That same moment, a clap of thunder slammed against the earth, followed by gray sheets of blowing rain.

Nell wheeled around and ran toward camp. By the time she got to her tent canopy, she was soaked and shivering, though not so much from being wet as from the earthy feel of the silent language that had moved between them. Henry had followed her and was standing across the way watching her. Her feet and legs moved through the veil of rain toward Henry. She had no control over them.

He moved toward her. They embraced and kissed until a fire between them turned the rain into a thick vapor with the two of them floating in its gray wetness.

Inside the tent they coiled around each other, arms and legs tangled, touching, stroking. They were driven by the sensual pulse of the jungle to quench a coarse carnal want. Nell marveled at the forces that drove her, shuddered with the sensations rocketing her body. Red seas swelled behind her closed eyes and wave after wave carried her to wonderments she hadn't imagined. She felt consumed then transformed into a slow-moving liquid.

That night, with the rain ended, they walked to the *cenote* and swam and washed and made love again on the rough rocky surface surrounding it. The moon towered over them, watching while the jungle caroled a night hymn.

Only later, half under him on his cot did Nell try to recall if he'd uttered a word since asking in the tunnel if it was raining. He'd not taken his eyes off her or stopped touching some part of her body, but he'd not uttered a single word.

When Andy and the workers returned, Henry moved across the clearing in long easy strides to greet them and listen with casual interest as Andy told of his trip to Mérida. Nell wondered if she too bore such obvious outward signs of the energy that had carried them, or at least her, to oblivion and back. In less than two days she'd been altered, changed. But she wasn't ashamed and that surprised her.

Henry made the decision to end the dig. They loosely filled in the tunnel with fallen trees, vines and dirt. Henry hoped to hide the site from looters until he could return the following year. In a gentle, misty rain they broke camp and rode burros up the backside of the rise above the *cenote*.

Nell turned to look back often, hoping to memorize the teeming, hostile grandeur of the jungle. The sky was the color of smoke. She would never forget the look of it, the smell of jungle rot, or mute Mayan gods petrified in a mysterious decaying land.

Peering into Sister Tia Marie's mirror before leaving Chunchucmil, Nell studied her scar and wondered how it would feel to be home again for she would return a different version of herself.

***

ON BOARD THE steamer headed for Texas, Nell joined Henry and Andy who were reviewing notes and drawings below deck. As she absentmindedly thumbed through a stack of papers, a particular drawing kept nudging her, pulling her eyes back to it time and again. The drawing was of a dog pounding on a gourd with its head thrown back howling.

Suddenly, she remembered Jack, Tinker's dog, barking in the middle of the street as the train pulled out of the station back in Wishing. Tinker had filled the empty spaces in the lives of everyone at the ranch, including hers. Why hadn't she realized it until now? Why had she felt the need to leave Carrageen? Pablo and Lupe, a baby coming soon. Billy, Skin and the others.

Home. The dusty streets of Wishing, the distinctive woody smell of horse flesh, mist rising off the Guadalupe of a morning, and most of all the wide open sky from horizon to horizon from her windmill.

"Is something wrong, Nell?" Henry asked as she rubbed her temples.

"I have a headache. I think I'll get some fresh air."

Above deck the eyes of the Mexican sailors followed Nell too familiarly to suit her, but could she blame them? There was no way to know what Henry told the captain the day they boarded. The captain had been concerned about the extra passenger, especially since she had no official papers indicating she'd ever sailed to Mexico in the first place. Henry leaned over and whispered in the captain's ear to which the captain laughed with a lewd glint and slapped Henry on the back.

Other than that, they had no trouble leaving the country. She had asked Henry to send a telegram to Scottie, who was to meet them in Galveston, and have him contact Grady Monroe and Hester with the news that she was alive and would be returning soon.

Nell moved to the bow where wind whipped her hair into tight tangles and tugged at the clothes Andy had brought back from Mérida. The shoes felt large and cumbersome and he'd not thought of any undergarments. But she was able to get by after picking up a few things in one of the larger villages they'd passed through on the way to the coast.

Dolphins broke the water's surface below her. They had been happy enough to escort her away from her home shores and now seemed just as happy to be bringing her back again.

It baffled Nell that so much could transpire between a man and woman in private, such raw physical intimacy, while they remained isolated and distant in the not so private times. She couldn't be near Henry without being jolted by the memory of those two days alone in the jungle. She wanted to reach out to him, brush his arm, but something unspoken from him told her she shouldn't.

She turned at the sound of approaching footsteps.

Henry walked up beside her. "I think you make our captain nervous standing so close to the heaving edge of his boat."

"The wind has such mighty power."

"You're not afraid?"

"What can the sea do to me now that it hasn't already tried?"

"I've been weighing the situation between us." He shuffled his feet casually, hands clasped behind his back. "We should marry.".

Her flinch stopped him for a moment, but he continued. "Surely you can see how compatible we are. Your interest in my work. My interest in you." He looked away with one corner of his mouth curling. "We could travel and work together. You said yourself we're both solitary, unconventional, similar in many ways."

She'd begun to shake her head, staring at him with fixed eyes. "Henry, I'm-I'm not some sniffling school girl. What happened between us just happened. I don't pretend to understand it fully, but I can assure you, you're not obligated to me in any way."

"Obligation has nothing to do with it, Nell. It just makes sense for both of us. Think about it. Can you give me one good reason we shouldn't?"

"It's ridiculous. We hardly know each other."

"On the contrary, we know more about each other than most entering into a contract of marriage."

She turned away, looked across the rolling water. She couldn't argue that point or put her mind quickly on a reason not to marry. "Surely you can see the problems I face, Henry. I've been lost at sea, probably presumed dead. I was on the brink of losing my ranch before all this happened. God only knows what I'll find when I get home. How can you ask me to make such a decision?"

"I'm confident you'll come to see things as I do."

***

LATE THAT NIGHT, before they were to dock in Galveston, Henry tapped on her cabin door and shoved quickly past her when she opened it.

"I've been wild, wanting to be alone with you," he said. "I can't sleep for thinking how impressed that puffed up university board is going to be when they see the funeral jar. You can't imagine how many hours of groveling it has taken to get recognition for my work."

She'd been sound asleep when he knocked, could barely make out the shape of him in the darkness.

He tangled his long fingers in her hair and kissed her. "Actually, this is why I can't sleep, Nell." He pulled her to him, kissed her so hard it hurt. She tried to pull away, slow him down, but he'd already raised her chemise above her breasts and his mouth was leaving wet trails across her body.

He pushed her to the narrow bed and, as if preparing to relieve himself, unbuttoned his trousers and pressed his full weight on top of her. "We were meant for each other." He breathed heavy against her ear then rolled to his side. He hadn't even bothered to undress.

In the dim light coming through the porthole from the deck above, she could see the shadowed pockmarks on his jaw line, the first distinguishing thing she'd ever noticed about him an eternity ago. They'd made him seem rugged, but it was an illusion. She knew that now.

"Henry, look at me, my face. Back in the jungle I fit right in with your mutilated gods and glyphs and ghosts. It won't be that way at home. I'll be a freak, a distraction."

"You're wrong." He got up and moved to the wash stand. "We'll marry as soon as you see to your affairs in Texas. Trust me, Nell."

"But what if my ranch doesn't sell?" She hadn't meant to sound as if she had accepted his proposal.

"It makes no difference to me what you do with your ranch. In fact, you may want to keep it. I'll have enough income to support it during the lean years. Now that I think of it, you may wish to keep it as a sort of summer home. I can study those Indian pictographs and return to the Rio Grande to retrieve that skeleton Scottie and I found. Now there's a piece of business left unfinished if there ever was one."

He seemed impervious to her worries, but what had she expected? He knelt beside the bed, kissed her lightly and was gone before she could think how to voice the questions and doubts rattling in her head. She had wanted to guard herself against Henry's impulsiveness but failed. There had never been any mention of the young woman he was with at the Seasider Hotel. Nor of her wealthy father who was supposed to have sponsored a portion of Henry's expedition.

The more she thought about it, the more certain she was that her choices were to marry Henry or continue to let life bump her around, that deciding to do something was better than doing nothing. Hadn't she learned that lesson after the attack on the ranch?

But she wasn't a fool. Henry hadn't said anything about love or tender feelings toward her. He'd come to her cabin like a bored child. But there had been no release for her. She hadn't turned to liquid and blended with the red waters behind her eyelids. He left her aching and vacant.

The boat creaked and rolled in the great waters off the coast of Texas, reminding Nell of events before the long blackness took her to the jungle land of the Maya. In the space between being awake and asleep, storm waters thrashed her this way and that, made her gasp and claw for air.

PART III

"IT'S A MORBID thing to be doing." Goose said to Skin, who struggled to hold a newspaper still in the breeze. They were sitting under a shade tree outside the bunkhouse, Goose teetering on the back legs of a chair that was old as the prairie, Skin clipping newspaper reports of the great storm in the Gulf of Mexico.

"Some of you sorry sisters ain't got no feel for the way of things, and you happen to be one of 'em. Only iffen I see her ghost will I believe Miss Nell is dead."

"Gah-all dern! If you ain't been outta my sight in weeks, I'd by-god swear you done given in to the temptations of the cup." Goose was indignant.

"You boys quit that spoutin' off, hear?" Billy yelled from inside the bunkhouse. "Fellar can't get a little siesta for all the squawking. Like a bunch of damn hens."

Skin and Goose watched as Tinker made his way around the corner of the main house and headed toward Pablo's quarters. He tapped the palm of his hand with a stack of envelopes as he went. Jack was a step behind.

"You suppose he's off to town agin?" Goose asked.

"It's a free country, ain't it?" Skin snipped carefully around a corner of text.

"What I cain't figure is who's he sending all them letters to."

"Don't I recall somebody saying he has a homestead somewheres? Maybe it's business to do with that place."

A few minutes later the screen door of Pablo's house swung open and Tinker crossed to the bunkhouse. "On my way to town. Anybody want to come along?"

"No," Skin said, "but I'd be mighty pleased iffen you'd buy me a newspaper."

"Ah, hell! There he goes agin." Goose let his chair tip forward.

"Hold on a minute." Billy called from inside the bunkhouse. "I'll grab my boots. I can't take this blamed bickering another minute. 'Sides, Jingles ain't been rode since..." Everyone looked away. "...Since Miss Nell left."

Billy and Tinker were half way to town before Billy broke the downhearted silence. "Wish I had half the faith Skin has that Nell could still be alive somewhere."

"If I thought it was possible, I'd go looking for her, Billy."

"Just don't seem right, this country without Missy. Why, since she was just a bitty thing she'd cut out 'crost them hills on horseback. Never give a thought to being a prissy girl. Though, I suppose in her way she was prissy enough."

"In her way, I suppose."

"And I still can't get a holt the notion she never married." Billy pushed his hat back, rubbed wetness from his eyes. "Too much woman for most men I guess."

"I'd say."

Billy reined in Jingles, rested his arm on the saddle horn. "You was sweet on her, wasn't you?"

"You might say that, Billy. Yes."

"Means you're as tore up as the rest of us, don't it?"

Tinker twitched, clenched his teeth so tight Billy could see muscles working in his face. He kneed his mount. Billy did likewise.

In town Tinker rode on to the post office while Billy picked up the latest newspaper for Skin. Later, Tinker caught up with Billy in front of the hotel, where he basked in the company of five old timers like himself, all chewing and whittling. Billy tried to introduce Tinker, but a fuss started up at the opposite end of the street near the depot. Everyone turned to see Petie Buckle hollering and running full out in the middle of the street waving a telegram over his head. He dashed out of sight into Grady Monroe's office.

"Somebody ought to shoot that boy," Billy said. "Cain't nobody get a telegram without his screaming of it clear to Tennessee."

A minute later Grady bolted from his office like a fat heifer out of a chute, jumped in his jalopy and blasted down the street. As he passed the hotel, he caught sight of Billy, slammed on his brakes, and yanked his stirring wheel so hard he traveled thirty feet in a sideways skid before coming to a stop in his own dust.

"She's alive!" Grady boomed. He jumped down from his vehicle and ran toward Billy in long strides. "Great guns, Billy don't you hear me!" He grabbed Billy's shirt, gave him a shake. "Nell Miggins is alive!"

***

NELL WALKED THE deck from bow to stern. Heavy fog the color of wisteria shrouded the horizon while a lone sea gull flapped over her head. She could hear air ruffle in its wings.

Andy walked up behind her. "Mr. Burleson sent me to fetch you, ma'am. Captain said there'll not be another chance to eat breakfast before we dock."

"Tell him I'm not hungry."

"I don't mean to be nosy, ma'am, but you've been standing here since daylight."

"Where are you from, Andy?"

"Ohio."

"Do you miss it?"

"I suppose. I miss seeing my family, but my studies keep me busy. That helps."

"I've missed Texas. My eyes are thirsty for the sight of it."

Andy transferred his weight from one foot to the other.

"Tell Mr. Burleson I'll be down in a little while."

Apprehension overwhelmed her. She needed to shore up, but she'd rather shrink and hide, sneak home quietly on horseback alone. In all probability though, Hester would be at the dock with Scottie, full of tedious questions and countless concerns.

A few hours later the fog lifted and the steamer slid into Galveston harbor. Nell was surprised by her own reaction when she saw Hester in the crowd. Her heart swelled for the simple blessedness of knowing that she was once again in the company of someone who knew her history. Had it not been for Henry's grip on her arm, she would have slipped to the ground on weakened knees. Her hat flew off when Hester, sobbing hysterically, threw her arms around her. As soon as she stepped back, Hester's eyes found the scar.

"Oh god, what hap—" Before Hester could finish someone in the crowd bumped Scottie from behind, pushing him between Hester and Nell.

"My dear, I never dreamed we would meet again under such difficult circumstances. Your cousin and I were beside ourselves wondering what had happened to you."

Henry dropped his hand on Scottie's shoulder. "Let's move out of this crowd. We can tell you all the details at the hotel while Andy sees to our baggage." He took Nell's elbow and tilted his chin toward the sidewalk. "I've got an announcement to make. Just you wait, Scottie."

In the hotel dining room over platters of food, Nell related to Scottie and Hester what she could remember of her experiences with Henry adding a synopsis each time she paused to breathe or eat.

"But have you no idea what happened to your face?" Hester asked.

Nell shook her head. The rich food was making her nauseous.

Henry ceremoniously ordered wine. "I think flotsam might have hit her in the face. She had trouble remembering things clearly at first so the blow must have been pretty bad."

When the wine had been served Henry raised his glass. "A toast to my soon-to-be bride." He leaned toward Scottie indicating they needed to tap their glasses. "Nell and I plan to marry as soon as she settles in."

Hester went white. "That's impos...I mean, shouldn't you..."

Nell was amused. "Hester, I've never seen you at a loss for words."

"To your future then." Scottie raised his glass. But when he leaned over to kiss Nell on the cheek, she noticed his smile didn't reach his eyes. It was an insulting, under-handed thing for Henry to do, make such an announcement with no discussion between them before hand. But at the moment she felt too sick to say anything.

Henry continued. "I plan to escort Nell back to Wishing and stay in her Sunday House while she decides what to do with her ranch. That way I'll have a quiet place to write my reports for the university while she gets her affairs in order. Meantime, Scottie, I thought I'd send the casts and funeral jar back to Chicago with you and Andy."

Hester turned to Nell. "Does this mean you'll keep the ranch?"

"I'm having second thoughts about selling it."

"I've encouraged her to keep it," Henry said.

Scottie set his wine glass down. "Then Andy and I are to leave first thing in the morning?"

"Yes, and our train to Wishing leaves in the late afternoon. That should give these two ladies time to find Nell some clothes. Can't have my bride walking around in these missionary contributions, can I?"

Scottie placed his napkin on the table. "In that case, my dears, I'll say my good-byes now. I need to find Andy." He clasped Nell's hand but avoided her direct gaze. "I'm sure we'll see more of each other in the near future."

Later that evening in the hotel room they shared, Nell dressed for bed, while Hester sat at the dressing table brushing her golden curls. "You're so thin." Hester studied Nell's reflection in the mirror over her shoulder.

"No. You're wrong. I've actually gained a considerable amount of weight."

"I can't believe you mean that. You must have looked like chicken bones."

Nell stretched across the big downy bed.

"Why don't you stay in San Antonio with me a while?"

"What you mean is give Henry time to change his mind, isn't it?"

"It's preposterous, Nell, really. You came so near death, alone in that horrible jungle. Aren't you afraid you're grasping at anything—?"

"All I know for sure is that this is the first time in months I've been in a real bed, my head is splitting, and I want to vomit. I'm bewildered having you and Henry tell me what I should do and how I should feel. I'm not a marionette."

Hester moistened a cloth and placed it on Nell's forehead before rolling her to her side. She loosened Nell's hair and brushed it with long gentle strokes.

Nell could barely to speak. "You and Henry can discuss concerns and make plans all you want. But I'm going home to Carrageen before I do anything else."

***

NELL WATCHED THE eastern sky outside the hotel window until clouds broke and bright beams of sunlight streaked the sky. She eased out of bed, dressed, and slipped quietly out of the door so as not to wake Hester. She made her way downstairs where she intended to send a telegram to Pablo. She'd been too ill the night before to think of it, let alone do it.

On the last spiral of the ornate stairway, she stopped short at the sound of harsh voices. From the landing she glimpsed Henry and

Scottie sitting adjacent one another in the high ceilinged lobby. Scottie's face was crimson as he leaned forward to jab a finger at Henry's chest. On impulse Nell stepped behind a large potted palm.

"And what about Antony Delgar? What are you going to tell him when he finds out what you're doing?" Scottie's lower jaw quivered with anger.

Henry waved a dismissing hand at his words. "Who'll need Delgar's money after I've made my Mayan discovery public? Universities and museums will be more than willing to support me and my work now."

"I no longer know who you are."

"Relax, Scottie. I've thought everything through. Marriage will add to my prestige. Respect, stability, that sort of thing."

Nell's stomach turned over. She shrank as far as she could behind the palm.

"You already have both. Why can't a normal amount of anything make you happy, Henry?" Scottie was standing now, almost yelling.

"I thought you'd approve of Nell. You've badgered me to settle down. Now listen to you."

"Don't try to twist this around. You know I think that lady is one of the finest. It's your using her for your own good end that bothers me." Scottie turned abruptly and Henry followed him out to the street. Nell watched them through the etched glass of the large hotel doors until they moved out of sight.

The only time Nell had felt as she did in that moment was after being thrown from her pony when she and Pablo were small children. She had landed flat on her back and for long moments couldn't breathe or move. Pablo knelt over her, screaming her name but she couldn't answer him. Only when he lifted her arms to drag her home, only then, was she able to pull air into her lungs.

Nell hurried on down the stairway and sent the telegram to Pablo in care of Grady. She had no doubt everyone along the way would read it, and word would eventually get to the ranch that she was on her last trek home, regardless of who she sent the telegram to.

But she wanted Pablo to know it was him and Carrageen Ranch she'd thought of first.

"PABLO RAMIREZ IN CARE OF GRADY MONROE: DO NOT BE AFRAID FOR ME. HAVE JOURNEYED FAR OFF COURSE. AM SCARRED AND MUCH CHANGED BUT WILL BE HOME DAY AFTER TOMORROW BY RAIL. HAVE JINGLES SADDLED."

On the train late that same day, Nell listened with half her mind to a conversation between Hester and Henry. She felt better but the drumming in her temples still made casual conversation difficult.

Henry and Hester sat next to each other, facing Nell so she could recline a little and rest her head against the window. She knew Hester was measuring Henry. Was he handsome? Intelligent? Prestigious?

Hester asked Henry, "Will political troubles plaguing Mexico affect your work?"

"In some ways I suppose it will complicate my plans, but I'm confident I can overcome the inconvenience."

Nell thought Henry said "confident" as if he'd invented the word. She watched his mouth. First one side then the other curled open as if letting off excess air. The muscles in his forehead flexed with the rhythm of his words, drawing his eyebrows high under lines of squeezed skin.

When Hester asked what led him to believe Chunchucmil would produce important artifacts, he said, "Oh it was very easy, really." His eyebrows moved up an inch as if adding, *if* you're as smart as I am.

Nell turned her gaze to the window, hoping to block the conversation from her mind. But it kept wandering back to Henry. Ambition dominated everything he did. His colossal ego craved control. Triumph over finding the funeral jar aroused his intellect and that in turn stirred his physical appetite. Like an ego-greed, she thought, and it controlled his genitals without involving his heart or conscience. A gross deficiency. It missed the point of things that passed between hearts.

On the other hand, Nell thought she was like a blind bird, yielding to the need for a sturdy, safe place to perch. She had looked into the hard eyes of death, had its bony finger tap her shoulder. For all she knew, writhing and grinding against Henry in a rotting jungle, she'd lost everything she'd honored. She'd learned from the mighty Maya how tenuous a moment or lifetime could be. She wanted certainty as much as anything else, and as many moments as she could consume in the time God granted her.

But how long could Henry, with his deficient heart and self-involved vision, give her certainty? He was not a bad person, only flawed like her.

The train arrived in San Antonio at midnight. Henry checked into the Menger Hotel while Nell rode home with Hester. The next morning she insisted over and over to Hester that she could face Wishing, scars and all, without her. Henry waited on the train platform while they said their good-byes and parted with promises of long letters detailing wedding plans. When Nell stepped up to Henry on the platform, she was glad to lean into his side and feel his arm around her shoulder. During the final stretch of the journey home, she concentrated on the train's clackity sway to still the butterflies in her stomach.

***

PABLO MOANED WHEN the wagon rounded the last bend in the road to Wishing. Half the population of Milcom County had gathered along Main Street to welcome Nell home. Even the Fireman's band milled around the depot, loosely poised to lead a parade.

Billy told him the mayor and minister planned to organize a celebration barbecue at the gazebo, while Junior Crawford and Sheriff Wilkes talked about signing up players for baseball teams. Junior wanted to call his team "The Lost" and the sheriff named his "The Found."

"Gussey's girdle! Would you look at that!" Billy said when he saw the crowd. "Well, reckon everybody will be glad to see Nell. We can't be selfish, now can we?"

"Glad or curious?" Pablo gave the reins a pop.

Goose moved out ahead of the wagon and called back over his shoulder. "Anytime a town announces free food and baseball, I 'spect a crowd."

This was true, Pablo knew, but still he wished they could greet Nell in private, then whisk her home as fast as possible. That is what she would want.

He pulled the wagon team to a halt near the depot and helped Lupe climb down. She was large with child now and moved about like a great turtle. Nell's disappearance had been hard on her. Eventually she quit going into the big house to dust and clean, and Pablo had been glad. He and Tinker finished building a new barn and repaired the house chimneys and windmill then turned their attention to building Lupe a house on land Nell deeded them before she left.

News of Nell's return gave Lupe an enormous burst of energy. All week long she barked orders to Billy and Skin, insisting on their help in cleaning and scrubbing the big house.

Pablo smiled to himself remembering how she had moved her cleaning fury from the main house to the cowhands. She lined them up for baths and spent an entire morning herding them through the rigors of boiling lye soap and laundry.

Pablo was proud of his pretty wife. She treated the ranch hands like loved children, or respected relations, depending on the situation, and they loved and respected her in return. He threaded his arm in Lupe's as they hurried down the center of the street toward the depot.

The air seemed thin because of so many people. When someone cried out that the train was rounding the bend, the band struck up a loud marching tune. Mayor Potts, Sheriff Wilkes, and Grady pushed through the crowd to stand next to him. Grady tried to yell something about speeches, but no one could hear over the band's pounding. Pablo finally gave up and waved him aside.

The closer the train got to the depot, the more painfully slow it moved.

"What if she is not in there?" Lupe yelled in his ear.

He put his arm around her hoping it gave her reassurance.

The train inched to a stop. The band's music died away a few instruments at a time. The sound was ugly and flat, like balloons losing air. When the last note faded, a silence crawled across the crowd. For one long minute nothing happened. Then Nell, gaunt and pale, stepped into the sunlight and scanned the crowd until her eyes found Pablo. She grasped the railing and moved down the steps.

Pablo took both of her hands and squeezed them to his chest. "We have much to talk about, *hermana.*"

Lupe touched Nell's scarred cheek, whispering in Spanish so quietly that Pablo knew Nell wasn't catching all of it. But as he had witnessed before, the two women somehow knew each other's minds. Nell touched Lupe's big belly. "And we have much to talk about, too."

"Nel-lie, Nel-lie." Nell looked up to see Juan riding Skin's shoulders. Then Billy stepped forward, his wrinkles contorted with worry. Nell pressed her face to the hollow of his bony shoulder and he patted her back as if she were a small child.

"You sure got one hell of a sad eye, Missy," he whispered in her ear. He stepped back holding her at arm's length. "But this here other eye looks happy enough to be home."

"Three cheers for our returned citizen, Miss Nell Miggins!" The mayor thundered. The crowd roared.

Pablo sighed with relief. The silence had been broken and the worst was over, thanks to Billy.

When Billy released Nell, her gaze went back to the platform where Henry Burleson stood leaning against the handrail, his legs crossed at the ankles.

"Mayor Potts, this is Henry Burleson," she said. "He gave me shelter in the jungles of Mexico and escorted me home."

"Three cheers for Henry Burleson!" The mayor called out and the crowd complied. After the cheering died down, Nell and

Henry were swept away to a decorated wagon that led a parade down Main Street. Nell looked back at Pablo and Lupe standing in front of the empty depot. Tinker had joined them. He was holding Jingles' reins in his hand.

Lupe waved limply. "She wants only to go home."

"You got any idea how she met up with that professor?" Tinker asked.

"None," Pablo said. "But we will know soon enough. At least Nell is home now."

***

ON THE OUTSKIRTS of town, under spreading oaks, Mayor Potts, Grady, and several reporters gathered with Nell and Henry while she explained as much of her story as she cared to share. "Now, I'll ask all of you to please give me a little room. I've been away a long time and would like to greet a few friends before going home."

"That's right, boys," Grady said. "My client has many legal and personal situations to tend to, so leave her be. The ladies over yonder laid out a fine spread of food. Help yourselves, and don't forget the baseball game starting up in a little while." He paused to look at Nell.

"Thank you," she said.

"But Miss Miggins, how do you feel about that scar?" a reporter from Austin asked.

"I don't think about it."

"What about you, Mr. Burleson," asked another reporter. "Can you elaborate on the story some?"

"Why, of course...that is?" Henry looked at Nell.

"Go ahead," she said. "I'm going to find Pablo."

Nell struggled through countless greetings while making her way around the grounds in search of her ranch crew. She was determined not to hide the scarred side of her face. If she met everyone face to face now, let them stare and whisper, appease their curiosity, then maybe her life would be easier.

Mimmie Campbell was one of those who stopped her with a loud cackle and heavy hug. "Honey, that windmiller fellar's been looking for you."

"Which way did he go?"

"Why, your whole bunch is over there past first base. Here he comes now. Yoa! Here she is, over here."

Nell thanked Mimmie then moved toward Tinker, meeting him on the pitcher's mound. They looked over each other's shoulders, off into the distance, then down at the ground. Tinker spoke first. "All of us over there feel mighty bad leaving you to the hounds, Nell. I was elected to pull them off if you've had enough."

"I've had enough."

He scooped his hat off, let a minute drip by. She looked away.

He looked back at the ground. "I'm awful sorry about your troubles. I expect you're about the bravest woman I'll ever know."

"Brave? To go off and nearly drown at sea?"

"Brave to survive it and face these people after all—"

"All the scars?"

"You're too smart for that, Nell." Looking directly into her eyes now, he offered his arm. "Come on over to the shade. Billy and Skin have been arguing for an hour about how you could've met up with that professor. You are the only one who can set them straight."

When she took his arm, the thickness of it, the feel of him, flashed a perplexing sharp memory in her mind. Not of an image or sound, but a kind of comfort or gladdening. She bit her lip against the feeling and for the first time since coming ashore in Galveston, Nell wanted to weep with relief.

Lupe offered her a plate of food but she turned it down. "You are so-o-o pale, but I will cook good food for you, *sí*?"

"Yes, Lupe, I'd like that. But right now I want to tell all of you what happened. This is the last time I intend to repeat it."

"I done told everybody you's alive, Miss Nell," Skin said. "I felt you alive in my bones."

"Be quiet," Thomas said. "Can't you see she's trying to explain?"

Nell bit the inside of her mouth trying to check her tears. "I appreciate that, Skin. There were times I wondered what would happen to me if everyone thought I was dead."

She explained everything she could remember in a more personal way than she had to the newspaper people, except of course, the details of her relationship with Henry.

"Lord must a been looking out for you to have that professor in Mexico same time as you," Skin said.

"Weren't you scared of that witch doctor?" Thomas asked.

"Yes. But I believe the drink he kept forcing down my throat dulled my senses enough that I...I wasn't aware most of the time."

Grady walked up to join them. "Baseball game's about to start."

Billy touched Grady's shoulder with the back of his hand. "You told Nell about that buyer yet?"

Grady studied Nell's face. "Are you up to a little business?"

She nodded.

"Well, it's like this. You got a buyer for your ranch. Been kinda standing by on account of I didn't too much want to use my power of attorney without a little more information on what actually happened to you, you see. Looks like that was a good way to go. Anyway, all you got to do to is sign the papers."

"Who's the buyer?"

"Same one I told you about the day before you left. Wants to be anonymous. Billy here figures it's some outfit outta—"

"—New York." Billy's upper lip curled.

Grady kept going. "He, or they, could be a bunch of investors, you know. Whoever it is wants everybody to stay on. Even you, Nell, to manage the place just like you always have."

"Managing what? Cattle? Sheep? Cotton?"

"Don't know. But the agreement says you'll receive instructions by mail monthly along with your pay. You, or whoever is manager, will be expected to send reports and such as that."

"Grady, that seems strange."

"Kinda thought so myself, but I've sniffed over the papers like a hound and it all looks clean. Some law firm outta Waco is handling things on the other end. I checked on 'em and they seem respectable enough. Think of it this way, Nell. You'll have a new job. Managing instead of owning and the rest of you'll get paid by a new kingpin. Simple as that."

Nell scanned the group before letting her eyes come to rest on her folded hands. "There's one complication."

"What is that?" Pablo asked.

"You changed your mind?" Skin chirped, his eyes big and round. She'd forgotten how his opal-colored face could pull at her heart. Before leaving Wishing she'd thought Skin had found his place in life and now here he was having to deal with the possibility of losing it because of a decision she'd make.

"Not exactly, Skin. But, there is one other thing I need to tell all of you." She looked at Grady. "Henry Burleson and I plan to marry."

Billy choked, Grady and Thomas began to talk over each other, Lupe shrilled with glee and grabbed Pablo. Tinker took a sudden interest in the toe of his boot.

"For the time being, Henry plans to stay in the Sunday House. This will give me time to decide what to do about the ranch. I —we haven't thought much beyond my coming home."

Pablo looked relieved. "This is wise."

She wanted more than anything to speak her heart to him in private but this was one subject she wouldn't expect him to be objective about.

"Well, tarnation! I can't believe it took a foreigner to appreciate your fine qualities," Grady said. "Congratulations, gal. And you take your sweet time with your decisions. I'll send word to that law firm in Waco. They can cool their heels a little longer, I suppose."

Henry walked up behind Grady. "Am I a foreigner?"

"No, no. Just a figure of speech. Congratulations." Grady pumped Henry's arm up and down and slapped him on the back, then announced that anyone interested in the ball game had better follow him or risk not getting a seat in the shade. Everyone nodded to Henry or limply shook his hand as they moved away.

Nell noticed Billy walking toward the baseball diamond with his hand on Tinker's shoulder. Both men had their heads down. It wasn't clear to her if Billy was leaning on Tinker, or offering a touch of support. But, for sure, the sight of them moving away slow and loose-jointed had the look of something gone all wrong.

Henry put his arm around Nell and pulled her to his side. "Isn't that Tinker Webb fellow the windmiller you left in charge of repairing the house and barn?"

"Yes, why?"

"He seemed reluctant to shake my hand. Is he jealous, do you suppose?"

"Your ego is shameless."

After the fourth inning Henry and Nell excused themselves, claiming fatigue from the long trip. Pablo said Lupe needed to go home as well so he drove the wagon and left the others to drift home on their own later. The ball teams had planned a dance after the game, which meant the cowhands would be late anyway.

Pablo pulled up to the Sunday house, unloaded Henry's bags, then waited in the wagon with Lupe while they said their good-byes.

Henry watched Pablo over Nell's shoulder. "When will we be alone?"

"Ride out to the ranch in a few days. By then I should be caught up on the situation there."

Henry pecked her on the cheek and Nell climbed in the wagon next to Lupe.

A few blocks from the Sunday House, Nell told Pablo she wanted to stop at the depot where Tinker left Jingles. There, she unceremoniously hitched up her skirt, slipped her petticoat off and handed it to Lupe. In one smooth movement she swung up into the saddle and galloped toward Carrageen in the long slant of the day's last light.

***

AT DAYBREAK PABLO stirred in the narrow bed he shared with Lupe. He rolled over, nuzzled the back of her neck. Her skin scent, so like warm bread and new summer grass, was something he could never get enough of. When she stirred, he wrapped his arms around her and cupped a warm breast in one hand and her swollen belly in the other. The baby rolled and kicked against Lupe's tight skin.

"Now see, you wake us both," Lupe said lazily.

"I will fix coffee."

"Did you have to wake me to tell me?"

Pablo nuzzled her collarbone then dressed and added twigs to the wood stove.

Lupe pulled up on her elbow. "Do you think it is strange that Henry did not see Nell home yesterday?"

"*Sí.*"

"And that he does not plan to come here today to help her settle in?"

"*Sí.*"

"Will you speak to her about it?"

"No."

Lupe flopped back on her pillow. "But you owe it to Nell to speak your mind. She needs to talk to someone who understands her."

"Since she told us she had not made up her mind about signing the papers for the ranch or a date for the wedding, I think it is best to hold my tongue. We do not know everything. Henry may be trying to give her time alone to get stronger and decide for herself. Now that would mean he is wise, no?"

"She is so thin." Lupe shook her head. "Pablo, she must—"

"Sh-h-h. She will be fine now with you to cluck over her." Pablo kissed Lupe's head and handed her a cup of coffee before taking the coffee pot across the yard to the main house. There he found Nell on the porch in dim morning light. She was barefoot in her nightgown with a shawl drawn tight around her shoulders. It seemed to him they had not missed a beat, that the music of their days had only paused for a while.

The evening before, when Nell dismounted to open the main gate, she tied Jingles to the wagon saying she wanted to walk the rest of the way. Lupe argued with her, told her she looked too tired and couldn't she walk another time. But Nell insisted, so Lupe watched from a window as Nell made her slow way across the pasture and into the live oak grove around the family cemetery. When she walked out of the trees again she stopped to stare at the house.

Pablo knew she would be surprised. The old house looked as it did when they were children. Tinker had repaired the chimneys so they no longer leaned at crazy angles, replaced the guttering so it no longer drooped, and solicited everyone's help in painting the house gleaming white. He'd made new shutters to replace the rotted ones and mounted them only a week before news of Nell's return.

"The house looks wonderful," Nell said as Pablo poured coffee.

"*Sí*. Tinker, he is a hard worker."

"And your place? Have you been able to get much done?"

Pablo grinned, thinking *his place* still sounded strange. Imagine how his father would have felt knowing his son owned land in Texas. "It is almost finished. We have a little work on the windows and porch."

"What about a well?"

"Sweet water."

"I suppose Lupe and I should get busy packing so she can settle in before the baby comes."

"She will not want to leave you just yet."

"That's nonsense. I proved I can take care of myself." Nell walked to the east end of the porch. "From now on you and Lupe have to think of your own family first. Owning your own place will make you independent, Pablo."

"I will always think of you as family."

She turned back to face him. "And I, you. But the time has come for us to make choices."

He nodded. In this way Nell was wise like Lupe. Would he ever know how the women in his life became so knowing? Perhaps Lupe had been right this morning and he should speak his mind. "Henry, he is different, no? How did you come to a decision about him?"

"Maybe it's his difference that appeals to me." She seemed unable to go on.

"To be married is very complicated. It is hard to make two lives go the way of one sometimes." He picked his words carefully. "Promise you will not hurry."

"I promise."

Jack ran up the porch steps from out of nowhere barking in sharp staccato yelps. When Nell laughed, he wheeled around in a tight circle.

"He's as glad to see you as everyone else." Tinker rode up on horseback. "Thought I'd ride out to check on the north windmill. We had a bad storm come through a few days ago and I need to check the sucker rod."

Nell tugged at her shaw. "Do you mind company?"

"It's still your ranch, isn't it?"

***

IN A PRIVATE conversation with himself while waiting for Nell to get dressed, Tinker let curse words flow freely. How in the hell had he gotten into this predicament anyway? He had been an hallucinating old fool to let it get fixed in his head that he would court Nell when she got home. He took a deep breath and blew out audibly, cheeks billowing.

How long can it take a woman to put on pants anyway? Tinker couldn't make up his mind if he hoped she'd keep the ranch or sell it. Either way, he wasn't ready to rearrange his plans just yet.

Eventually Nell reappeared and mounted the horse Pablo had saddled and waiting. She rode in a full gallop ahead of him without once looking back. At the draw she reined in and waited for him to catch up.

His head throbbed as if his brain was swollen. "What's your hurry?"

"Been away too long. I need to make up for lost rides."

"I wish you'd explain just one more time why you want to sell this place. You couldn't wait to go off on that trip of yours then you couldn't wait to get back here yesterday."

"Tinker...?"

"And now you're trying to make up for lost time so you can leave again with the professor."

She stared at him with big dinner plate eyes like he was a mooncalf or something. Well hell, he'd gone and done it. He dismounted, walked around his horse and kicked a rock. "Don't mind me," he said when he finished chewing his tongue. "I had too much whiskey at that shindig last night and not enough sleep." He wanted to add that she hadn't even been there to dance with either. "Damn it all, Nell. I'm sorry I spoke so hard."

She gave him a weak smile but in her eyes he could see she didn't understand. Tinker figured the best thing he could do was keep his mouth shut for a while.

"Then let's have a quick look at the windmill so you can get back to camp and catch up on your sleep."

He felt like a jackass.

At the windmill Nell sat with Jack in the sun on the high side of the tank while he stopped the wheel and climbed the derrick. The sucker rod still clanked pretty bad, and two blades had been blown away by the storm. He knew when he rawhided some of them in place that they were half rotted, but at the time he couldn't see waiting until someone made a trip into town for lumber to finish the job.

From the windmill tower he spied the blades twenty yards away. He climbed down, joined Nell and explained the situation.

"Some of those planks from your cousin's ranch weren't so good after all, but I think I can patch them one more time, and I'm going to have to pull the sucker rod to work on it. It's safe enough if you want to climb up."

"Let's find the blades and haul them up as we go." Sun light lit her face just so when she glanced up at him. At that angle, the sharp line of her jaw bone and the drooping skin around her bluish mouth reminded him of how much she'd been through.

He shook his head. "You go on up. Leave the work to me this time." He held her arm, thin as a twig it was, and gave her a hand up to the first rung and watched until she made it to the platform.

He found the blades, hauled them up the tower and maneuvered the first one in place. Nell handed him a nail. "There was never a breeze in the jungle." She gazed out to the south. "The land there is low and flat and the growth of trees and vines is so thick it traps moisture, keeps the sun from drying the earth. A slow steam all the time. Unbearable heat."

Tinker motioned to the oil can. She handed it to him.

"The Maya built huge towers kind of like the pyramids in Egypt to use as worship temples and to study the constellations. I think they must have enjoyed being high up like this between the wind and the clouds."

She caught him looking at her face. His gut twisted each time he looked at the scar, the sad eye. He said, "When I came home to Texas, after being away in the northeast, everything seemed clearer, brighter. Is it like that for you?"

"In some ways, yes. Being on the windmill is better than my memory of it. Of course, I've returned from a far different journey." She shook her head. "You know I keep going back to the feeling that I'll be betraying my father and grandfather if I leave."

Tinker finished with the oil can and sat next to her. "Your folks had no way of knowing what your troubles would be, Nell. It might be you should worry about betraying yourself."

***

IN SPITE OF Lupe's protestations, Nell organized a move from the foreman's quarters to the new house Pablo and Tinker had built. Tinker had concentrated his efforts on getting it finished so Lupe could settle in before the baby came. Though neither of them had said so, Nell knew Pablo and Lupe wanted the baby to be born in their own home if possible.

While Billy and Thomas drove a load of furniture to the new house, Nell asked Skin to follow her up to the attic. It was a ramshackle mess after Tinker moved things around to work on the roof and chimneys.

"What'cha looking for?" Skin asked. "Maybe I could hep ya find it."

"There's a small bed up here somewhere. Juan will need it when the baby comes."

"Thangs is sure a mess ain't it?"

She climbed over a dusty pile of clothes and caught a cobweb in her hair. Skin knocked over a coat rack.

"Set that aside," Nell said. "Lupe can use it." As always happened in the attic, Nell was soon adrift in memories and lost all track of time while sifting through a box of baby clothes. When she stood to unkink her knees a puff of dust made her sneeze.

"God bless you, Miss Nell."

She'd almost forgotten Skin while her mind focused on her task. His bulky body perched on a small footstool while he humped over an open book. He was tracing a finger under a line of words.

"I didn't know you could read." She picked up one of the books in the stack he'd found.

"Cain't much."

"My father bought these books from a traveling salesman when he decided to educate everyone living on the ranch." She fanned its pages. "*Children's At Home University*. I spent hours during long winter evenings with these. See, there's one for reading, one for arithmetic, one for art activities."

"Billy done taught me some arithmetic."

"Why don't you take these down to the bunkhouse. Some day Juan and the baby will need to learn to read and write."

"Reckon I could teach 'em?"

"I don't see why not. In the meantime, you can study them to improve your own reading, and have Billy help if you need it."

His grin showed yellow teeth that clashed horribly with the pink-white of his skin.

They found the bed and Skin brought it, along with the other things, down to the back stoop. Nell was dusting the headboard when the crew rode up from Pablo's place.

Billy pointed over her shoulder. "Who do you suppose that is riding in the gate?"

Nell shaded her eyes against the bright sunlight. "It's Henry."

He rode up to the house, dismounted, and stood looking at her dusty clothes. "The first thing I want you to do when we're married is hire a decent housekeeper." He brushed his arm where she'd touched him. She tucked a stray strand of hair into her braided bun and took off her apron.

"At least you're wearing a dress." Henry was the only one to chuckle at his critical humor. "A package arrived for you. Grady asked me to bring it out, along with some mail."

Billy cleared his throat. "I got a mess of stew going. And I'll have some biscuits ready by the time you have a look at your mail."

Henry and Nell drifted into the house while the others washed up in the tank house. Henry shuffled from room to room as if making an inspection of some sort. "I suggest that if you keep this place, you order new furniture right off the bat. And for heaven's sake, replace those heavy old drapes."

Nell ignored him, tore open the package. She was shocked when her grandmother's diary and the gifts she'd bought for Pablo and Lupe in Tres Palacios fell in her lap. A note from the hotel explained her trunk was being shipped by rail. By some trick of mind she'd forgotten about the things laid before her. She'd allowed herself to believe all that had happened from the time she left

Wishing on the train until she entered Henry's camp was an illusion, and if she refused to think about it, it would remain so.

Henry walked up behind her chair and kissed the nape of her neck. "Are you ready for the really good news?" He dropped to one knee in front of her. "I received a telegram from Scottie. I've been asked to give a symposium in New York ten days from now. Didn't I tell you the funeral jar was going to put my name right up there with the famous Mayanist, Alfred Maudslay?"

"Henry, that's wonderful. But I'm not sure I'm ready to leave here so soon. Lupe's baby will be coming any day now."

He kissed her hand, then kissed her mouth hard, holding the back of her neck so she couldn't pull away. He pulled back for a moment. "Then I'll go alone. We'll marry when I come back." His eyes were glassy and dark as he slid a hand up her skirt. "Let's go upstairs."

She grabbed his wrist. "Henry, not now."

"Why not?"

Just then Billy stepped out of the bunkhouse and banged on his skillet calling everyone to come and get it.

Halfway through the meal that Billy served outside under the oaks, Nell was ready to scream. No one had said a word so she attempted to break the silence. "Skin, did you tell Billy about the books we found?"

"Sure did. He said they's, I mean, he said they are a fine thing to have for learning to read and write."

"Henry taught me to read hieroglyphs when we were in Mexico."

"Hair what?" Goose asked.

"Hieroglyphs. It's writing in pictures."

"Well, not exactly, Nell," Henry said. "Pictures bring to mind a photograph or painting and that's not the case. A hieroglyph is a character in a system of writing. For example, a series of bars and dots represents numbers. The glyphs are carved in stone blocks so they aren't picture writing."

When Goose closed his mouth, Billy offered everyone more stew.

Henry continued. "As a matter of fact, I'll soon be giving a symposium on the subject in New York. You see, ah, what was your name again?"

Goose glanced over his shoulder then back at Henry. "Who me?"

"Of course, you. It is you I'm speaking to, isn't it?"

Goose looked at Nell.

"Henry, what do you think of the house? Everyone did a wonderful job, don't you think?"

"Thanks to Mr. Tinker," Lupe said.

Henry reached for a thick slice of bread. "By the way, where is he?"

"Turned in early." Skin swallowed a mouthful. "Said he'd need me to help him pull that bad sucker rod first thing tomorrow."

Talk turned to ranch events that took place while Nell was away and Henry soon looked bored.

When Pablo and Lupe left, Thomas and Goose gathered around Billy and started whispering. Billy shushed them long enough to explain to Nell that he had taken it upon himself to plan a surprise pounding for Pablo's new house. Thomas and Goose were going to ride out and invite all the neighbors.

"But hold up a minute boys, before you leave," Billy said. "You need to move one of them spare cots over to Pablo's empty quarters for Mr. Burleson."

Henry's fork stopped halfway to his mouth. He blinked, then took the bite.

While walking Nell to the house later, he asked, "How can you sit there and let that old man give orders for you? You are altogether too familiar with your employees, give them too much power."

"In this wide open country, Henry, you'll find there's no room for that frame of mind. Neighbors, family, friends or employers, employees – we're all related by way of the land. All of us are descended from pioneers who had no need for division of purpose. Mexican or Anglo. Blue blood or common man. Those who failed to understand that were the first to go under."

"Well, you may have to make a few adjustments when we travel other parts of the country."

"Besides, Billy wasn't trying to give orders in my place."

"Then what was he doing?"

"Protecting me from an embarrassing situation."

***

NEIGHBORS AND FRIENDS made a good show at the surprise pounding for Lupe and Pablo. Billy gave a speech about how old cowpunchers could be real particular about who they ride with and that he considered Pablo to be the best. He gave Lupe a two-gallon jar of jalapeño peppers, Pablo three silver dollars, and Juan a toy horse he'd carved out of mesquite.

Goose, Skin, and Thomas threw in together and gave Lupe a sack of canned goods – milk, beans, peaches and pickles. Someone gave a pound of salt and fifty pounds of barbed wire staples. Mimmie and Newton Campbell gave the couple a sack of flour and a pound of soap. Nell, a bag of sugar and a bag of coffee. Tinker walked up carrying a porch bench he'd made out of scrap lumber left over from the new barn. Like his barrel chairs, the seat raised up to give Pablo a nice boxed-in place underneath to store his tools.

While Goose played tunes on his harmonica, the crowd divided. Some played dominoes, others talked cattle prices and weather patterns. Nell watched Thomas elbow Tinker and point across the yard to where Henry and Newton had their heads together in conversation. Jack was sniffing Henry's leg. After a good whiff the dog shook his head and sneezed. Tinker and Thomas snickered like kids.

Later, Thomas and Louise Campbell walked the perimeter of the yard and corrals before settling on the porch steps. The next time Nell looked over that way, Newton had joined them and was shaking Thomas' hand. Newton turned to the quiet gathering of friends and called out. "Hey, everybody. I got a special announcement to make. Mr. Thomas Babb here has asked my daughter's hand in marriage and received my consent and blessing."

Everyone cheered and clapped.

Newton glanced at Mimmie. "And this won't be a surprise to most of you. Mimmie and I will move to east Texas pretty soon to join our relations there drilling for oil. Thomas and Louise will take over our cattle outfit."

Louise squinted at Thomas so hard it made Nell's eyes water. They were a match made in heaven, as perfectly suited for each other as Pablo and Lupe. In fact, Louise and Lupe had been sitting together most of the afternoon. They were the only young women in the group. Nell suspected they would have years of shared secrets between them, gardening, cooking and even baby-raising secrets.

***

HENRY STAYED AT the ranch for three days before leaving for his symposium in New York. During that time, he and Nell rode the range and picnicked and talked about the whys and why nots of keeping the ranch. Nell realized that his interest in the subject was limited, like his interest in her. Regret seemed ridiculous at her age. Why should anyone begrudge her being with a man if she was willing to settle for less than she'd hoped for?

One day out of the blue she asked, "Henry, why do you want to marry me?"

"That's a silly question."

"Why?"

"Because we're so much alike. I told you that."

"Is that the only reason?"

He moved to her side. "There's a mystery about you. I told you that before I left here with Scottie in the spring, remember? The mystery has only grown stronger the more I know you."

"Do you love me?" She knew if he said yes, she wouldn't believe him, but hoped at least that he wouldn't say no. Yet, what did she expect? Did she love him?

"Now you're being silly." Henry folded his arms over his chest.

Everything about him led her to believe that he lived on the edge of fantasy. She was his lost Maya, a foreign mystery, nothing more. He would soon grow tired of looking at her scarred face and impatient with ranch life.

***

FROM A WINDOW in the parlor Nell watched the cowhands outside whittling and one-upping each other's tales. The way she saw it, not much had changed since her father's day, the soft highs and lows of conversation, an occasional chuckle, a gesture here and there.

Henry had insisted after that last evening meal under the oaks, that the two of them eat indoors, "Like civilized people." They had moved from the cavernous dining room to the parlor where Henry now sat writing his speech.

Nell drifted out to the porch. She could hear Goose and Thomas tell the others about a canyon two day's ride west where mustangs grazed in large herds.

"I think we ought to round 'em up, break 'em over winter months," Thomas said. "Come spring we can sell 'em and divide the money. Then I could afford to up grade the fences at the Campbell place."

Pablo balanced on the back legs of a chair next to Billy. "*Sí*, and I will need to buy a bull for my heifers."

Goose laughed. "Hell, I guess I'd have to hang on to my share. I'm plum broke."

Nell leaned forward a little so she could watch the men as they talked. Billy paused in his whittling. "Hold all your chinning, boys. How you gonna to feed a bunch of penned-up mustangs over winter? Why not let 'em graze free until spring then take off after 'em before time to round up cattle."

Tinker stretched and approached the porch where Nell sat. "I'll be making a trip to Wishing come first light to pick up Mr.

Parker's block and tackle. I need it to pull that sucker rod. Do you need anything while I'm there?"

Henry stepped from the shadow of the doorway. "As a matter of fact, I need a ride to the depot."

"Fine then. Like I said, first light."

"I'll be ready."

Tinker wandered off to his camp and everyone else drifted inside except Skin who leaned in the doorway of the bunkhouse singing.

When Nell went back inside, Henry was putting his papers and books away. She sensed the same building tension in him as the day he sent Andy to Mérida with the plaster casts.

His movements were jerky, and he shuffled and reshuffled papers with unnecessary flourish. "You should make arrangements for the wedding while I'm away."

"I'd like a quiet occasion. Nothing elaborate."

"Makes no difference to me. I'm tired of being here with your watch dogs keeping an eye on my every move. I wish we'd stayed in town."

"Watch dogs?"

"That big buffoon who sleeps on your porch. Wouldn't let me get by him last night."

"Skin? What'd you tell him?"

"That I was after one of my books I'd left in the parlor. He told me I'd have to wait until morning or ask Billy." Henry turned down the lantern and drew her to him. He crushed her ribs until she couldn't breathe.

"Henry, this isn't—"

"I have needs, Nell. Surely you know that from being around men all your life."

She struggled free of his groping, turned the lantern back up. "I don't know anything about the needs you're talking about, but I do know about discretion."

He stepped back, red-faced, and let the screen door pop shut behind him when he stormed out.

The next morning Tinker was waiting when Nell looked out the window. Henry came out of the foreman's house, tossed his bag in back of the wagon then came into the house to tell her good-bye.

"I'll wire you, let you know when I'll be back. I plan to leave most of my books and correspondence at the Sunday House. When I return, I'll wait there until someone from the ranch can pick me up."

"Do you want me to forward your mail?"

"No, just put it in the Sunday House. That way I'll be near the telegraph and post office in case I need to send replies." He pulled her away from the open door and pinned her against the wall with his body then moved his hands over her breasts. "I'll finish this when I return."

***

"HOW MUCH LONGER do you intend to stay at the ranch?" Henry asked Tinker before they reached the river road.

"Until the work is finished."

"You don't like me much, do you?"

"Compared to what? A rattlesnake bite or, say, getting bucked off my horse in a field of prickly pear cactus?"

Henry ignored the insult. "I look for Nell to keep her ranch and as soon as she states that's the case, I want you to leave."

"Nell hired me, and until she tells me different, I take orders from her."

Later that day, Billy met Tinker at the barn to help unload the wagon. "Have a pleasant ride to town, did ya?"

"Just dandy. Got advance orders from the professor to leave as soon as Nell gives the what-for on keeping this ranch."

"Takes all kind, don't it? So you think she'll keep Carrageen?"

"He seems to think so and why not? Her reasons for leaving in the first place, best I can see, will be taken care of if she marries. She can travel with the professor and not have to worry about this place. Let you and Pablo run it."

"You got a plan?"

"Nothing beyond pulling the sucker rod and getting the windmill working proper."

Both men turned at the sound of horse's hooves. Skin was riding up in an all-out run from Pablo's place. He had started screaming by the time he reined in at the back stoop to the house. "Miss Nell! Miss Nell!"

Nell appeared behind the screen door.

"Lupe sent me to tell you the baby is a comin'."

Tinker and Billy jumped in the wagon they had unloaded and circled up to the stoop. When Nell reappeared, she had a big basket on her arm. She handed it up to Tinker before climbing into the back of the wagon.

Pablo was pacing outside with Juan when the wagon pulled up to the house.

"How long has she been at it?" Nell jumped down off the wagon and took the porch steps two at a time.

"An hour, maybe more."

At the doorway Nell turned back. Skin, whose gasping horse had given out under his load, rode up in a slow lope. "Take Juan for a walk," she told Pablo. "In fact, all of you take a walk. I'll fire a gun if I need you to go after Mimmie Campbell."

When Nell went inside the house, Tinker turned to Pablo. "Has she done this before?"

"Once, with Juan, she helped the doctor."

With Juan clutching his finger, Pablo led the way through a stand of post oaks down toward the river.

Skin sat on a log next to Billy. "I ain't never been near a birthing. Don't it hurt bad?"

"Course it does, but women got a way of taking it, seems like." Billy fished his whittling knife out of his pocket and started carving on a piece of dry wood he found at the river's edge.

Pablo picked up a smooth river rock, handed it to Juan. "A woman has such power to make a life, you know?"

All four men grew still and fell silent. Tinker sat on a clump of grass and chewed a dry reed. Then at dusk they wandered back toward the house. Pablo went inside and after a long while came back out.

Billy stood at attention. "Well?"

"Shouldn't be much longer. Why don't we build a fire out here? It's too hot inside to use the stove. Nell is mixing up some cornbread and has a pot of beans ready to heat."

It was full dark by the time everyone finished eating. Eventually, the men stretched out on the ground next to the fire and dozed off. When Lupe began to cry out some, Tinker took Juan on the horse Skin had ridden and headed for his camp. "I'll stay put there until someone lets me know to bring him home."

Hours passed before Pablo heard the baby cry. He jerked and accidentally kicked a log in the fire, shooting sparks into the black sky. Nell appeared in the doorway. "You better come help Lupe name your daughter."

"*Ay-e-e!*" Pablo yelled, relief flooded his face. Skin and Billy woke with a jerk and looked around confused.

"You look all wrung out," Billy said when Nell joined him beside the fire.

"Where's Juan?"

"Tinker took him to camp. I told him you'd let him know when the baby got here." Billy loosened his neckerchief. "Fact is, you can take the wagon. He'll need it come morning, unless you're too tired. I could have Skin do it."

"No, you and Skin need to stay here in case Pablo needs to send for help."

***

TINKER WAS SURPRISED to see Nell driving the wagon into camp instead of Skin or Billy. Juan had just fallen asleep on a bedroll with Jack. He gave Nell a hand down. "How's Lupe?"

"She's fine, a pretty little girl."

"Help yourself to coffee while I unhitch the team."

When he finished hobbling the animals and walked back into the lantern light, Nell was sitting next to Juan, stroking his head. "He'll seem older to me now with a baby around."

What could he say to a woman who was meant to have a house full of children but instead only helped bring them into the world?

"Mary." Nell tucked a blanket around Juan. Firelight danced in her tired eyes. "Pablo named his daughter Mary."

He poured coffee but she didn't want any.

"Tinker, are you happy?"

The question threw him. He shrugged, not sure what she was getting at.

"What makes you happy?"

"I guess I haven't thought about it enough to name things."

"Try."

"Why, simple things, like the stars rolling slow overhead, a sleepy little boy who doesn't know yet he's a big brother and..." He wanted to add having her in camp but didn't. "Such as that. I suppose I'm a pretty simple man."

"You said yellow fever, losing your wife and boy, was part of the reason you left Galveston."

He had forgotten he told her that. "I was never meant for city life and sure couldn't stomach it after what happened."

"You've never talked about it, have you?"

"What's to talk about, Nell? By the time I was Thomas's age I'd built up a good sized business, was a successful man compared to most. But I missed all this." He looked at the inky sky. "By the time I realized it, I'd married."

"What was her name?"

"Sarah. Met her the week I arrived in New York." Nell's look jangled him, made him forget what he was saying. He poured more coffee in his cup. "I quit New York and moved her and William, that was my boy's name, to my ranch. I'd had a foreman running the place while I was gone. But Sarah hated the heat and dust. This country was hard on her, so I went back into the architect business. Opened an office in Galveston thinking I'd be close enough to keep an eye on my place from there. That's when yellow fever hit the island."

He put another log on the fire. "I left Galveston after they died...but I have a hard time going back to my home place to stay."

He didn't say any more after that. They just sat listening to cicadas. Coyotes yelped way off somewhere, made Jack sit up and perk his ears. The campfire crackled, gave off an orange light.

Nell's eyes got thick-lidded. She laid her head on the bedroll next to Juan and curled her body around his. "Did you love Sarah?"

"Yes."

"It's a fitting thing you mill the wind, Tinker." She closed her eyes and slept.

***

NELL COULDN'T SAY why she hadn't walked on to the house the night Mary was born. The next morning Tinker was sitting just as he had the night before, except the coffee boiled fresh and hot. A large *rebozo* covered her, and Jack lay curled in the small of her back.

After coffee and biscuits, the three of them – Nell, Juan and Tinker – rode back to Pablo's house. Nell found Lupe sitting up with Mary at her breast. Juan had only the mildest curiosity for his sister, preferring instead to follow Pablo and Billy around as they went about their chores.

Nell sent Skin to Carrageen's smokehouse to fetch a ham and had Thomas stack plenty of wood close by before they left with Tinker to pull the sucker rod out of the well. It was a chore she knew they all dreaded and Goose was not modest with his complaints.

When Nell finished bathing Mary and had all the wash hanging out to dry, she stoked a good fire and began cooking large amounts of food to have on hand for a few days.

The next morning she and Billy took a basket of ham, sweet potatoes, boiled eggs, two pound cakes, and canned peaches to the windmill camp. When they rode up, Goose was leaning on a shovel grumbling. Billy yapped at him from the wagon seat. "I never heard tell of anybody drowning in his own sweat."

Skin and Tinker were maneuvering a pipe into the well while Thomas guided the horse that provided the power to lift it. Tinker had taken his shirt off and his fuzzy chest and arms were splattered with mud. Nell quickly looked away then back again.

"How's it goin'?" Billy asked.

"We ain't exactly havin' a tea party," Skin grunted.

Tinker muscled the pipe into place then sat back on his heels. "The leathers were worn all the way through. It's a wonder any water was getting to the top." He glanced at Nell with a quick nod before picking up his dirty shirt and threading his arms into it.

She climbed down from the wagon to unload the food and told Billy she didn't have time to dawdle.

With most of the men away, Lupe's household settled into a quiet routine. Evenings stretched, were lazy and mellow. Nell would think later that those days were her real healing time after the shipwreck and horrors of the jungle.

Helping a life come into the world and being with children had given her a lighthearted feel, put a bright slant on things. To her, every aspect of human nature was represented in those gathered around Lupe during the week of Mary's birth. Old men and children – the not so old making way for the not so young – the witless becoming wise and the wise accepting the inevitable. And all of it spinning without any of them having the power to change the natural course of things. Though where she fit into it all was still unclear. Nell sensed for the first time in a long, long while that she had enough stability to withstand just about anything the winds blew her way.

Lupe's dark eyes followed her throughout the day. Nell found it odd that she never mentioned Henry or their plans to marry, nor did anyone else for that matter.

"Lupe," Nell asked one lazy afternoon, "why doesn't anyone mention my selling the ranch?"

"We love you very much and wish you would not leave. But it is this same love that will not let us ask you to stay. You must make your own happiness. Is that not what you told Pablo? Make independent choices, you said."

"I know no one cares for Henry."

"It is not for us that you marry."

***

THOMAS BABB AND Louise Campbell were married in the little white church at the south end of Main Street during the season's first cold spell. The hands from Carrageen ranch wagered on how many times Thomas would fall flat on his face before he got to his "I do." They were sorely disappointed. The substance of Louise's love seemed to help Thomas keep his feet firmly planted. Skin sang, of course, and Louise and Thomas asked Pablo and Lupe to stand with them, an honor, Nell thought, that carried a cultural message to all of Wishing.

Thomas hounded Tinker to stay for the wedding even though the windmill repairs were finished. Billy backed Thomas, pleading almost, which seemed unusual to Nell at the time.

During the wedding ceremony Nell and Tinker were in charge of Juan and Mary, so they sat together near the rear of the church where they could leave quietly if the children caused a disturbance. Tinker, as it turned out, was a blessing with Juan, but she couldn't help feeling the boy brought back painful memories for him. While Skin sang, Nell noticed anew how wide and leathery Tinker's hands were. Just now one hand rested on Juan's shoulder as the boy sat on the edge of the pew with his neck craned to see Skin and his parents at the front of the church. Tinker's hand was as wide as Juan's whole back, yet she would bet his touch was as soft as a kitten's. He seemed such an ordinary man, really. She wondered if the space he kept between himself and the rush of life around him provided a perspective he preferred, or was it to protect an overly tender heart? She suspected a little of both.

A wedding party was held at the school house where, a lifetime ago, Nell and Hester had attended the Cattleman's Ball. Thomas kissed Nell's cheek and told her that she could count on him as a neighbor as much as she'd counted on him as a cowhand. That was, he added, if she decided to keep her place.

Billy ambled over when the music started, took Mary from her, then turned to Tinker standing nearby. "Take Miss Nell here for a spin around the dance floor and warm her up for me, will you?"

Tinker gave Billy a wary look then led her to the dance floor where he held her so loosely she had trouble following his lead.

"What's going on, Tinker?"

"What do you mean?"

"I can't quite put my finger on it, but Billy is up to something and you're dancing like you're dodging cow patties."

He chuckled, relaxed a little, but didn't answer her question.

When the music stopped, Tinker held the baby so Billy could take Nell for a twirl. But when Nell looked back at Tinker a moment later, he was holding Mary at arm's length. "We better go see if we can help him, Billy."

"I'm not sure how to handle this problem," Tinker said when they approached. Mary's dress was dripping wet.

Billy laughed and slapped his leg. "Hell, you just take off everything that's wet 'n put on dry. Seen women do it dozens of times." Tinker held the baby toward Billy.

"Just the same," Billy took Mary and handed her to Nell. "If there's a woman around..." He backed away and joined Goose, who was waving his missing-finger hand at the preacher to make a point and left the task to Nell.

"Anyways," Goose was saying, "them other boys had all been to town to one of them Dens of Iniquity you preachers is always talking about? They come back to camp drunk, spoutin' off like a bunch of ruffians. I's out rustling wood in the dark, see, and one of 'em thought I's a Injun and commenced to firing in the dark. Shot me clean through this here leg." Goose slapped his thigh and shook his head. "Trail boss sent that buckaroo packing without pay. Said he couldn't afford to have all his boys shot up. Hell, uh, heck, I been stove up ever since."

The preacher rocked back on his heels. "I've heard of a man homesteading on the Rio Grande near the Tornillo Creek juncture. He advertises that hot springs near the river there have curing powers."

"Yeah," Billy chimed in. "I heard of him. He built a bathhouse and the whole bit. Claims his waters cure everything from gout to boils and blindness."

"It's this dern north wind that gets me," Goose said.

Just then the fiddle player tapped Goose on the shoulder and motioned to the musician's corner. "Be right there." Goose gimped over to join them.

Nell saw the sheriff and Tinker talking and from the expressions on their faces it wasn't a small-talk conversation. Tinker motioned the sheriff in her direction. Sheriff Wilkes gave her a quick nod of greeting and got right to the point.

"Got a telegram about an hour ago. Appears the outlaw bandits that raided your place last spring are at it again."

Nell's stomach rolled.

"Rangers over near the border say the leader may be the one Tinker wounded, brother to the man you killed."

She sat down. "I remember. The Garza brothers."

"Right. Don't want to scare you, Nell, but you ought to know. He's a cutthroat, out for blood, ridin' around looking for a reason."

"And Tinker and I are reasons."

"Like I said, I'm not out to scare you, but thought you should know." Sheriff Wilkes pinched the crown of his hat and excused himself to tell the others.

***

THE COLD WEATHER blew itself out in no time and the days soon warmed back up. Tinker knew it'd take about three blasts of cold before winter took hold and stayed. He led a saddled horse out of the barn and noticed Nell in the hen house gathering eggs. He approached her and removed his hat. "Riding into town for my mail. Do you need any supplies while I'm at it?"

She stepped up to the chicken wire mesh that separated them. "I'd like to ride along. I have some business to take care of, if you don't mind waiting for me to finish here." She had on a slat bonnet and had to turn her face, good side up, to look him in the eye.

"With all of you busy helping Pablo, I've hated to ask anyone to go with me. Seems ridiculous. I've always ridden alone if I needed to."

"But after what the sheriff said, that'd be..."

"Oh, I know. That's why I've waited. Tinker, do you really think they are after you and me?"

Before he could answer, Goose came plodding up from Pablo's place. He stopped at the bunkhouse, and said something to Billy without dismounting. Billy shook his hand then pointed to the hen house. Goose walked his horse over and dismounted slowly. "I reckon I'll be on my way south, Miss Miggins. This here leg is givin' me fits since the weather's tried to turn. Goin' to give them hot springs on the Rio Grande a try."

"You're picking a poor time to leave Carrageen," Tinker said. "Time may come Miss Miggins here'll need an extra lookout or two."

Nell stared at Tinker for a beat then said to Goose, "Have you squared your wages with Pablo?"

Goose nodded. "I'm going to ride the chuck line back this a'way come early spring and hook up with the boys when they head out after them mustangs."

"You've done a good job for me, Goose. I appreciate it."

He painfully pulled up into the saddle with a groan, thumped the brim of his hat and walked his horse toward the main gate.

"Can't he see the chuck lines are gone?" Nell asked. She lowered the tilt of her head so Tinker could no longer see her eyes.

He knew she didn't expect an answer. "You'll be down to three hands when I leave."

"Thanks to you, the guns are in good shape, and as long as everyone is armed we'll be fine." She handed him the basket of eggs to hold while she scattered corn.

He wished to hell she wasn't wearing that bonnet. "I'll leave Jack here when I head to my place. He'll give you early warning if a stranger comes around."

"When will that be?"

"Tomorrow. Look, why don't you and Billy and Skin pack a few things and go stay with Pablo a while? Till the smoke blows over."

When she tiptoed to return the corn bucket to its hook, a dirt dauber angrily buzzed around her head. Tinker swatted at it with his hat, knocking her bonnet off in the process. "Sorry," he lied.

She righted it and turned for the house. "I'll be a few minutes."

While waiting for Nell, Tinker saddled Jingles and loaded a Colt .45 Billy kept stored in the bunkhouse. He holstered it then hung it on Nell's saddle horn. Jack watched, turning his head this way and that. Tinker knelt, gave the dog a good scratch and a few pats.

On the way to Wishing Nell seemed subdued. "I'm expecting a letter from Henry telling me when he'll be back. After I check on that I have to sign some papers for Grady then stop at the Sunday House to drop off Henry's mail. Why don't we plan to meet there to ride back to the ranch together."

"Sign some papers?"

"I'm going to sell the ranch."

Tinker felt hornswoggled. There he was sitting tall in his saddle thinking how nice it'd be if Nell kept her ranch, asked him to stay and help. He sure as hell didn't think she'd sell out. Nothing made sense to him these days. He ought to load his wagon and get the hell out of the county as fast as he could. This woman had plagued him since the day he walked in her door and laid eyes on her cloudy face.

He'd known then, though he wouldn't admit it to himself, that she was like a Texas river. Nell Miggins ran deep under her surface. She was the mighty coming together of everything upstream and he'd best put his tail between his legs and crawl away before the current of her pulled him under. And that damned old Billy could take his cupid tricks to hell.

"...if it's no trouble." Nell was saying.

"How's that?"

"To meet me at the Sunday House?"

"Fine."

They parted at the post office. Tinker watched her through the post office window as she crossed the street and walked a block down to Grady's office. He could try to stop her, but was it the right thing to do? No, he figured he'd interfered enough as it was. In fact, he might have made things a lot worse. He thought about stopping off at the saloon, but since he wasn't a serious drinker... Hell, he could mount up and ride like the devil, not stop till he got to Canada. But instead he walked to the livery stable.

An hour or so later, while talking with some locals, he spied Nell crossing Main Street on her way to the Sunday House. He unhitched their horses and rushed to catch up with her. From a block away, he could see that her pale face was drawn up, scar shining bright pink.

"You going to be all right?" he asked when he caught up to her.

She nodded, held herself arrow straight. "I need to leave this mail at the Sunday House then we can be on our way."

"So, when will Henry be back?"

Nell stopped, turned to face him with an impatient sigh.

"Okay," he said. "But I'm worried about you being at the ranch alone. You asked me back in the hen house about that band of outlaws coming back. Since I shot the man in charge and you killed his brother...and if his band continues traveling east, you can bet it's us he's after."

She resumed walking toward the Sunday House. "Henry's letter wasn't clear on the exact day."

When they neared the Sunday House, Nell stopped dead in her tracks. "What was that noise?" They heard a thump from inside the Sunday House.

"Mice?" Tinker wondered out loud. Another thump, some shuffling and a muffled giggle.

"Sounds more like a rat to me!" Nell dropped the mail and busted through the door.

***

TINKER'S FIRST RESPONSE to the woman screaming inside the Sunday House was to grab the gun he'd hung on Nell's saddle horn. But as soon as he did, Nell started a tugging match for it. Short of boxing her, the only thing he could do was let her have it.

Nell positioned herself just inside the door like a wall, feet apart, back rigid. Over her shoulder Tinker could see the screaming woman. She was naked as a baby. The only other time he recalled seeing breasts like that was back home when he was a kid. His mother had a favorite milk cow, a cross between a Jersey and Guernsey, named Blue. It was his job to milk Blue and sometimes, if he was late getting to the chore, old Blue had to walk splay-legged around her big blue-veined bag.

Nell raised the gun, cocked the hammer. Tinker leaned closer so his eyes would adjust to the shade inside. Not sure of what the danger was, he clutched Nell's belt ready to pull her back outside.

The woman kept screaming like a banshee, grabbing anything she could find to cover herself. Nell fired at the ceiling. Splinters rained down everywhere.

"You despicable worm!" Nell shouted.

"Now, I-I tried to tell you a man has needs." The man's voice came from the floor behind the bed. Tinker started for the source but Nell held out her arm to stop him.

She pulled the hammer back again. Henry Burleson slowly raised his head, peered over a pillow. Sweat beaded his white face.

Nell fired into the pillow and feathers spewed everywhere. The woman squealed, and dropped to her knees, begging Nell not to kill her. By some miracle of maneuvering she had managed to cover her elaborate chest, though her clothes were all tangled.

"Leave." Nell shook the gun at the woman. "Don't ever come here again."

Tinker stepped aside to let her pass. Damndest thing he ever saw, those blue tits.

Henry raised up on his knees. "Just put the gun down and I'll explain..."

"No, you white-livered son of a bitch. I'll do the explaining. Get up from there."

"I told you. A man has needs." Henry slowly stood. He used what was left of the pillow to cover his crotch. Feathers stuck here and there all over his pale, sweaty nakedness.

It looked to Tinker like Nell had everything under control. Like she said, as long as she had a gun she'd be all right. Actually, he felt kind of sorry for the professor. He hadn't any idea what he was up against.

"Tinker." Nell said without taking her eyes off Henry. "When does the next train leave Wishing?"

"Going east or west?"

"The next train away from here."

"Tomorrow morning."

"Sorry you have to wait that long, Henry," Nell said. "But I'm sure the sheriff can accommodate your sorry hide till then." With the tip of the gun she motioned Henry to the door. He grabbed for his pants.

"Forget it. Out."

"But—"

Nell fired over his shoulder, knocked a wall plaque to the floor. He ducked and lurched for the door. Tinker stepped aside, tipped his hat.

Nell's glance caught him. The look in her good eye was sinister.

Outside, Henry pleaded to Tinker. "Maybe you can tell her what it's like for a man to be denied—"

"No sir. I don't ever argue with a lady packing firearms."

"Jail is that way." Nell twitched her head.

"Good Lord, woman, let me have my clothes."

"Start walking."

Henry, still hugging the busted pillow to his crotch, started toward Main Street mumbling to himself the whole way. Nell followed his hairless body by ten paces. Tinker followed her with the horses. Jack was somewhere behind. He always was.

Little white feathers trailed Henry like floating snow. He reminded Tinker of a cattle egret. Long, slender, white body with a too-small pointed head teetering on the tip of a skinny neck. Yep, Tinker thought, that was the look of Professor Henry Burleson without benefit of all his finery.

Nell continued to grip the gun with both hands at arm's length. Tinker had a sudden notion that she'd like to fire it, maybe rearrange the professor's anatomy. Or, was that his own evil idea? The conniving crawfish deserved it.

"The unmitigated gall," Henry said when he reached the street corner. "The law can't touch me. I've done nothing illegal."

Nell kept her pace but Tinker thought he could see the tip of the gun wavering a little. A small crowd, having heard the shots, gathered along the street. Women gasped at the sight of a naked man and rushed away. Men snorted behind their hands. Henry looked like he might puke in the dizzy brightness of the street.

As the spectacle approached the jailhouse, Sheriff Wilkes rushed out, apparently having heard the commotion. "What kind of a fiasco do you have going now, Nell?"

"This man was using my Sunday House for a brothel."

"A what?"

"He was entertaining a hussy in my Sunday House."

Henry pitched his chin upward as if pointing at the sheriff.
"But you know...all of you..." He swept his free hand to the crowd.
"All of you know I had her permission to use her Sunday House."

Sheriff Wilkes' mouth twitched. "You best come on in and
let's see if we can settle this."

Tinker was almost sorry when the sheriff gave Henry a bunk
blanket to wrap around himself. But then maybe he'd catch the
mange from drunks who had used it. Now that would be justice.

Nell lowered the gun. "I gave Henry permission to conduct
his archaeological business in my Sunday House when he returned
from New York. He was to inform me when that would be. He did
not tell me in this letter when he'd return." She slapped a letter down
on the sheriff's desk. "I found him there just now with a harlot.
Hardly archaeological business."

"Well," Sheriff Wilkes said to Henry, "do you deny Miss
Miggins' accusation?"

"Of course!"

"Want me to go fetch the young woman?" Tinker asked.

"Did you witness the scene?"

"That I did. It was just as Nell said."

Sheriff Wilkes eased into his swivel chair. "Professor, looks
to me like you're belly up. Nell has two witnesses."

"I'll bring a lawsuit against this whole town if one of you
doesn't bring me my clothes at once."

"Do you want to charge him for trespassing?" Sheriff Wilkes
asked Nell.

"No, just see that he's on the next train out of town."

Henry leaned toward Nell. "After all I did for you. This will
come to blows, you ungrateful—"

Tinker stepped in front of him. "Way I see it, you're fenced
by your own doing...professor."

***

ALL THE WAY back to the ranch Nell looked flushed, her eyes red-rimmed. Tinker was glad he got to see the woodpussy professor get his comeuppance. Yet, he couldn't quite calculate where the day's events left everybody. Especially himself.

"I bet you could go back to Grady's office and have him tear up those papers." It was all he could think to say. He imagined she too, wondered where she stood. She had just sold her ranch and sent her future husband packing, all in one afternoon.

"No, like the cowboys say, it's time to move on." She set her jaw and kneed Jingles to a high lope. Tinker took it as a signal to back off, give her room and he did, though it was the hardest thing he'd ever done.

Back at the ranch, he reached for her reins so he could unsaddle Jingles, but she waved him away and did it herself.

Billy called from the far end of the barn. "Ho there. I's about to get worried about you two."

Tinker caught a look from Nell and was pretty sure he got her message.

"Ya'll look like you been eatin' burnt biscuits," Billy said when he got close.

Nell walked away.

Tinker turned Billy around and walked him toward the bunkhouse. "You won't believe it, old-timer. She just got through calaboosing the professor."

"No-o! I mean, Yessirree! That little gal must have her fight back after all." Billy considered a minute. "Bet she's feeling mighty poor about it though."

Skin was frying steaks when they went inside. Tinker explained what had happened and Billy choked with laughter.

Skin grew still. "Reckon I know how that professor felt. I met Miss Nell my own self in the middle of the street like that. Put me in my place too, right quick-like."

Then the humor of it was gone.

Tinker cut into the steak Skin served. "I guess, in a way, Nell's paying for the professor's humiliation."

"Signed them papers, did she?" Billy looked mournful.

Tinker hung around the bunkhouse a while longer, hoping Nell would show herself on the porch like most evenings, but when Skin started his sad singing, it was too much to bear. He moved on to his camp. Jack followed with his ears lowered and tail limp. It was hard figuring how the dog could match moods the way he did.

The sun looked as big as a wagon wheel dropping down out of a low bank of gray cloud. The cloud wasn't really gray, Tinker knew. He was just looking at the shadow side of it. Maybe the day was like that, gray and in shadow. And tomorrow, with the sun at a different angle, things would have better color.

He stoked a few glowing coals left from the night before, placed some twigs and a log over them, then spread a wagon sheet out in the open. This was one night he wanted to be close to the sky and Earth both. He threw a bedroll on the sheet and used it for a pillow, then he stretched out to watch the sun burn the evening sky first orange, then pink, then lavender.

Tomorrow? He supposed he'd pack the wagon and head for the home place like he planned. He could double back in a month or so to check on the windmill. But who did he think he was kidding? He was just scratching for any reason he could find to hang around.

He hated that he had complicated things. If he could just bring himself to talk to Nell about the ranch. But he couldn't do that, not yet. She wouldn't want to hear it. She was hurting bad and he'd have to wait until she finished reeling from the blow of things. Though by then it might be too late and she'd be long gone.

Maybe he should hang around in case that bandit comes back. Hell, here he was at it again. Any reason to stay. If he could just bring himself to tell Nell what...

Jack ruffed, tweaked his ears, even the flopped one. Tinker jumped to his feet, reached for his rifle. The dog took off, swirling his tail like windmill sails in a gale. That's when he saw Nell's silhouette against the twilight sky. She stopped to scratch Jack's ears before looking across the tall, autumn grass at him. Soap scents on the night breeze reached camp ahead of her. Her hair was damp from fresh washing and her skin glowed pink in the fading light. She stopped at the edge of the wagon sheet to gaze at the sunset.

The big orange ball had dropped out of the cloud bank and half of it sank below the horizon. Tinker fetched another bedroll and, as if she'd done it often, Nell sat, leaning her back to it without taking her eyes off the evening spectacle. He set the coffee pot on coals to warm.

Tinker had always felt it would be irreverent to speak while God was busy ending the day. But then he only had Jack, who never said anything anyway. It seemed Nell was of the same consideration. She hadn't uttered a sound.

As was the case every evening, the last light was the most remarkable, almost hypnotic before blue-black darkness swallowed the world and spewed heaven with a million stars. They watched it happen together, Tinker Webb and Nell Miggins.

A log on the fire spit a few sparks. Tinker poured coffee then fetched a deck of cards and a bottle of Kentucky whiskey he'd been saving for medicinal purposes. He figured they both needed medicine and whiskey was the best he could do, given the circumstances.

He splashed a shot in his coffee and held the bottle up to Nell with a questioning look. He was a little surprised when she held out her cup.

He was generous.

She took a swallow and cleared her throat.

He shuffled the deck, dealt a hand. "Five card stud." He handed her a handful of bolts and nuts from a rusty tin can. They each anted-up a nut.

"I'm not sorry, you know," Nell said.

It was killing him to be quiet. He bit the inside of his mouth.

She took another gulp of the liquored-up coffee. "Henry and I both got what we deserved." She discarded two cards. He dealt her two. "I knew when we boarded the train in Galveston that I didn't love him any more than he loved me. I wanted an easy escape and he offered it." She swallowed more coffee, coughed.

"Dealer discards one, takes one." Tinker took a long pull on his own liquored-up coffee.

"I heard him tell Scottie, his professor friend, that he thought I'd be good for his career, scar and all. In fact, my face would help bring him attention." She stared into the camp fire.

"Don't sell yourself short." Tinker spoke in a low voice, unable to check himself any longer. "He took advantage of your situation."

She drank.

"You can't tell me that had he come at you with the same proposition a month before you left or a month after you got back that your answer to him would've been the same."

When she fanned her cards, Tinker refilled her cup – without so much whiskey this time. She'd probably had enough. Her eyes were kind of bleary. He didn't know what else to do so he took a swig himself right from the bottle.

"Tinker, why haven't you ever remarried?"

"A-h-h, hell. At first it didn't seem right. My little bride and my boy wouldn't have died if I hadn't dragged them all the way to Texas. Then, by the time I recovered from the blow of losing them and figured those things happen outside of my piddly power, I was too set in my ways."

"Come on, there must have been a few ladies?" She blinked real slow.

"I'm not much with the league ladies, Nell." He swigged his coffee. "Though there was one filly over near the town of Comfort. Her daddy needed a well dug way out from his ranch house. Talked on and on about Isabella, his oldest daughter, the pies and breads and such the girl could bake. When the well was dug, this fellar insisted I go home with him, meet his family, have some supper." Tinker paused. Nell's eyes hadn't left his mouth but he couldn't tell if she was listening.

He kept talking anyway. "To tell you the truth, I think I romanced the name, Isabella. I mean, imagine Is-ah-bella. Well, Isabella turned out to be ugly as possum meat and three heads taller than me."

Nell smiled.

"This Isabella ended up telling her daddy I dishonored her so he tried to run me in with a ax handle." He shook his head. The movement made his head spin. "No-o, I'm afraid I'm just an old race horse put to pasture."

"Did you?" Nell discarded three cards.

"Did I what?" He dealt her three more.

"Dish-honor her?" She sounded like she had mush in her mouth.

"I did not, though she was willing, lem'me tell ya. All I could think was how I got suckered into the idea of a pretty little thing baking pies, yodeling pretty little tunes... jus' wait'n for me to sweep her off her feet. Hell, she outweighed her daddy's best heifer, I tell you. Dealer diss-cards four, draws f-four."

Nell shivered. Tinker dug around for the *rebozo* for her shoulders and wrapped a serape around his. They studied their cards, sipped whiskey.

"I saw a telephone on my trip," she said.

"Did ya' talk to it?"

"No. But I almost learned to drive an automobile. And I saw an airplane. W.C. was flying in it." She slumped with a big sigh.

"I saw some of those moving pictures in Fort Worth las' time I went through there. Did you see that on your travels?" His tongue felt too big for his mouth.

"No. But th-the water was so..." She shook her head then looked right into his eyes. "I got lost in it, Tinker. It was so wide and deep and quiet. The water burned my skin... Lost in the quiet of it. Then I heard children singing in the wind, a soft kinda lullaby of death-sleep and then I wasn't afraid."

He reached out to touch her cheek, but she tilted her chin away so he placed his hand on her shoulder instead and squeezed.

"I saw the man with me. I-I knew he was dead. Birds." She looked up at his face again like she hoped he'd make her stop talking. "Birds were pecking at him, his eyes. In a bolt of lightning, in one flash, Tinker, it was all gone. The schooner and all those people."

She hiccuped, swallowed some more whiskey, then told him about a couple of sisters, the fisherman who rescued her, and a tattooed witch doctor. Things Tinker thought she probably hadn't told anyone else. That she didn't know she nearly died until the day a girl took her to wash and she saw how skinny she was and felt the scar on her face. She told him about reading Henry's books and digging in the tunnel. Her eyes grew bigger the more she talked, but her speech more garbled.

"I... Henry... We..." She pressed her lips together and looked out into the darkness.

"More coffee?"

She held out her cup. This time he skipped the whiskey.

"I remember something in one of Henry's reports. A transcription, something from a Mayan prophet. 'All moons, all years.... all days, and all winds, take their course and then are gone.'" She shivered. "Something like that."

He clenched his teeth against the urge to do something that might spook her into locking the terrible tale back up in hidden memory before she finished telling it. She moved slowly, discarded a card. He dealt her one.

Nell, blinked so slow he thought she might topple over. "How long since you slept indoors?"

"Dealer diss-cards two, draws—" He forgot the question. "Speaking of telephones, what do you think about those Wild West Shows? People pretending 'n play acting about the kind of life we've lived?"

"Imagine that." Nell fanned her cards, laid them down on the wagon sheet. "Gin."

Tinker looked from her fanned out cards back to her bleary eyes. "Darlin', we're playin' poker." He glanced over at Jack. "I may have overdone the medicine a little. Mis-s-s Miggins is in her cups."

***

NELL WOKE WITH her face pressed against something solid and warm. She strained to make her eyes focus. It was Tinker's back. But how had they ended up sharing the same bedroll? It didn't matter. Everything, it seemed, had been leading her to this place and this time. She felt like a puzzle piece, lost for a long time in the dust under the sofa, and Tinker was the one to find her.

Jack, whose chin rested on her hip, straightened and yawned.

Tinker rolled over, puffy-eyed, blinked a few times, then squinted at her. He raised up on his elbow, looked around camp, at her, her hair, scar, mouth. With a pointed finger, he touched her cheek soft as a sparrow's breath. He moved her heavy braid off her neck and brushed the loose strands of hair from her face. Then he touched his thumb to her lips and something inside Nell's ribs fluttered.

Jack suddenly poked his nose in Tinker's face. They laughed uncomfortably and moved apart. Tinker handed her a chunk of bacon to slice while he stoked the fire and put water to boil. Nothing had happened between them, Nell was sure, but the time they had spent together had shifted things.

"Did you mean what you said last night about not being sorry?" Tinker asked.

"I meant I'm no worse off now with Henry gone than I was before."

"Strange how life can spin things around so quick."

"Yes, and I've learned the hard way we don't have much say-so about it either."

She looked up from the frying bacon. Her heart gave a great thump then fluttered like a bird caught in a snare. What had happened to the two of them? She recalled telling him about the Maya, and other things she hadn't let herself think about, but she shouldn't have taken his offer of whiskey. Her mind was still feeling its effects, her hands shaky. She cut day-old biscuits in half and put them in hot bacon grease to warm.

Tinker said, "According to Grady, when we thought you were... Well, not coming back, the new owner expected everyone to stay on at Carrageen. Will you?"

"I couldn't bear that. I'll go to the Sunday House, for a while at least, then maybe San Antonio." The angle of Tinker's profile dropped. "And you?" she asked.

"I'm heading to my home place as soon as I settle up some things with Pablo and find out if he still plans to set out for those mustangs next spring."

Nell dipped a leftover biscuit in bacon grease, threw it to Jack. "Did you tell Billy and Skin I sold the ranch?"

Tinker nodded. "And about the professor."

Nell remembered the first time they'd been on the windmill together and thinking Tinker was a gentle man full of harmonies, and she'd been right. Now, if only she could hear his tunes more clearly.

Tinker stood. "I 'spect Pablo is wondering what's holding me up."

He saddled his horse while she wiped out the skillet and swished a little water in the coffee pot. "I'll give you a ride to the house," he said.

"I'd like to walk."

"You need to be on your way pretty quick." Tinker pointed over her shoulder. She took a few steps out into the open. A blue-black cloud bank churned ominously low on the horizon. A blue norther, a blast of frigid wind and rain about an hour away.

Tinker swung up into the saddle. A gust of rain-scented wind puffed Nell's skirt. Time stopped. She felt the need to do something impulsive, to run, to shout. Tinker's horse pranced sideways, jittery because of the coming weather. Saddle leather creaked when Tinker shifted his weight. He glanced at the sky. She thought he was about to say something, but then he reined the horse toward Pablo's place and jabbed his heels hard into the animal's flanks.

Nell's heart vibrated like a dry leaf stuck in tall grass on a windy day. Her breath knotted in her throat and then Tinker pivoted his horse around so hard it reared up and danced sideways. He galloped back to her and was half out of the saddle when he jerked to a halt.

Nell ran to his open arms and for once the slow droning tick of time favored her. She locked her arms around his neck, let the closeness of him give blessed comfort. Tinker was in her blood. He'd soaked through her skin sometime in the night. She wanted to hold on to him forever with blind acceptance.

She pressed her face into his neck. He moved back a half step, held her face in his thick callused hands, and kissed her lightly at first then with more and more purposefulness until she thought she might swoon. When he drew back, she had to hold on to his shirt pocket to keep from buckling.

When he spoke, his voice sounded thick. "I forgot to tell you. Take Jack with you to the house."

She nodded like a mute and watched him leave a second time.

On the way to the ranch house, Nell had to keep glancing at the trees in the distance to make sure she wasn't tilted. Tinker had done that to her, completely rearranged her state of being.

At the side gate Jack let out a yelp, breaking her trail of thoughts. She remembered she needed to check the hen house for eggs. The clanking and whirring windmill above the tank house made her spirits plunge. She'd miss its familiar hum and the cool water it pumped. The expectancy and hopefulness she'd felt in Tinker's arms slipped away and an odd heaviness settled on her.

The hens were jittery. Was it the weather? She looked around at the empty corrals, the newly painted yet deserted-looking house, the vegetable garden gone to seed. She was completely alone, couldn't think of a single time, ever, in her life that had happened here at Carrageen. Someone had always been moving about for one reason or another. If not Lupe, a cowhand or Billy.

She leaned against the chicken mesh trying to absorb the sight, smell and sound of it all and was surprised when the sadness of leaving didn't fold her over. Maybe she was addled after drinking so much whiskey. She touched her mouth. Tinker.

Jack whimpered when she held the gate so he could follow her into the yard. Maybe he wanted to wait for Tinker. She let the gate swing shut. A blast of wind swept out of the north, churned the oaks in the family cemetery. The sky was now ominously black just beyond them. Jack backed up a few steps and barked high and sharp. Nell hurried on into the house.

Inside she had to light a lantern in the storm-dark kitchen. The house smelled stale and the same heavy, yawning silence she'd sensed in the hen yard seeped from the corners and closets in every room.

She started up the stairs with the lantern. The old house creaked in a gust of wind, then something, a shutter most likely, slammed the side of the house somewhere upstairs. Outside, Jack took up a staccato barking spell.

She wished she'd gone with Tinker after all.

***

PABLO POURED COFFEE for Skin, Billy, and Tinker. Lupe rocked Mary in the corner next to the stove while Juan played with the toy horse Billy had carved for him.

"Cain't ya stop her leaving?" Skin asked Tinker.

"Hell," Billy said, "I ain't never seen anything that could stop her once she's made up her mind."

Pablo pulled a chair up to the table. "Our fathers were friends. I am glad they are not here to see this happen."

Tinker set his cup down. "I'll leave the yard level and cutters you like so much. I can pick them up in the spring."

Pablo nodded.

"I'll be on my way then."

The group moved outside where the wind blew in rushing gusts and the first pellets of rain beaded in the dry dirt.

Billy studied the sky. "Sure you don't want to stay put till this storm blows over?"

Tinker shook his head. "Look, before I go need to tell..." He stopped, turned his ear to the wind, listening.

"What is it?" Pablo asked.

"I thought I heard Jack. I left him with Nell."

They listened, heard nothing.

"Anyway," Tinker put his hat on and pushed it down to keep from losing it in the wind. "I thought I could help Nell by—" This time Pablo held up his hand, motioning Tinker to be quiet.

"It's Jack, there." Skin pointed up the road at Jack running full out toward them. Three gun shots cracked in the far off, cloud-muffled air.

Tinker was the first to bolt for his horse. Pablo and Skin scrambled for their hats and guns before heading to the corral for their mounts.

"Billy," Pablo yelled, "stay with Lupe. She knows where the guns are."

Tinker's worst fears were realized when he approached the ranch house. Nell was hanging from her tied wrists from one of the oaks just outside the barn. Her feet dangled six inches off the ground. A dirty rag had been stuffed in her mouth.

She struggled red-faced, screaming through her nose, jerking her head toward the barn. He dismounted, reached for his knife to cut her down.

"*Ay-e-e.* Just as I thought."

Tinker whirled around and caught a blow in the face from a rifle butt. He dropped to his knees.

"You see, *Cicatriz Cara.*" The bandit growled at Nell. "He came just as I said he would, for his *Cicatriz Cara* – Scar Face." He looked at Tinker on the ground and laughed through gritted teeth. "Do not do anything foolish, my friend. There are many guns pointed at this whore's head."

Tinker stood, looked from the bandit to Nell. Her ribs heaved up and down under her tattered blouse. Terror paralyzed her face as she swung with each gust of the wailing wind. The cloud bank was directly over them now with icy rain blowing horizontal. If only he could warn Pablo, who would be riding up with Skin any minute.

"Ah, *gringo*, I thought you might want to see how murdering whores die. That is why I fire my gun. To invite you to watch."

"She didn't kill your brother, I did."

The bandit bashed Tinker's face again. Tinker recoiled, dropped to his knees a second time.

"You lie, *gringo*."

Behind the bandit, about twenty-five yards away, Tinker saw Pablo sneak over the corral railing, inching for the rear door of the barn, but a shot rang out before Tinker could call a warning. The shot diverted the bandit's attention, giving Tinker time to lunge and knock the rifle out of his hands. He swung a fist up into the Mexican's face, but the blow was blocked and they rolled to the ground.

A gun battle started up behind the barn. Rain blew in torrents. The sky was as black as first nightfall. Nell, drenched and shivering, struggled to free her hands.

The bandit wiggled free of Tinker's hold, pulled to his feet, and kicked Tinker in the back. Tinker rolled over, stood up and landed a sharp jab to the Mexican's chin.

Someone yelled from beyond the barn, horses scrambled, ran in wild circles in the corral. Shots popped off one after another in the howling wind. In a final all-out effort, Tinker socked the bandit in the tender spot between his upper lip and nose. Both men staggered bloody-faced before lunging at each other again.

Tinker hit the bandit above the belt, heard a whoosh of air when he doubled over, then swung up with a balled fist, but before the blow could land, the bandit grabbed Tinker's leg and jerked him off balance. Tinker rolled in the mud, tried to catch his breath. It gave the bandit an instant to grab for his rifle. Nell tried to kick at him but missed. The Mexican swung the rifle around and pointed it at Tinker's face.

Tinker froze.

Nell choked on a muffled scream.

A blast cracked the air and a hole popped open in the center of the bandit's forehead. His eyes crossed and blood trickled down his nose before he sank to the ground.

Tinker, gasping for air, turned and glimpsed Skin across the way with a smoking Colt in his hand. Skin wheeled around and hurried off around the corner of the barn. The gun battle had ended.

Tinker cut Nell free. She slumped to the ground, shivering so hard her teeth rattled. He pulled her to her feet and led her to the barn where they both dropped to their knees.

"I have to go see about the others." Tinker tried to loosen her hold on him.

She shook her head no. She was dazed. Her breath came and went in little grunts.

"Pablo and Skin. I need to go see if they're okay."

Her eyes focused on something behind him. "Pablo?"

Tinker turned and was struck heartsick by what he saw. Skin's huge frame filled the doorway. In his arms, Pablo was clinging blue-lipped to the last whispers of life. Rivers of rain-diluted blood dripped from his limp arms.

"No." Nell said, her voice flat and mechanical. Skin walked on into the barn and eased down onto one knee to carefully place Pablo on a mound of dry hay. Pablo's eyes rolled.

"*Hermana?*"

"Everything is going to be all right." Nell pulled his shirt away from the wound. Blood pumped from it freely.

"It is bad, I know," he whispered.

Tinker found a saddle blanket to tuck around Pablo's quaking body. Nell cradled his head, wiped at his face with her cold hand. "Hush now. I'll send Skin to town for the doctor."

Pablo turned to Skin. "Will you stay with my family, my Lupe?"

Skin nodded solemnly. "You can count on it, amigo." Skin sucked in his bottom lip and bit down hard.

"Nell?" Pablo closed his eyes. "I know and Lupe knows, you must follow your heart. We talked many times."

Nell shook her head. "Skin, ride to town. Get—"

"—*Hermana*, it was good, yes? Te-tell my children...what fun we had."

"Oh, Pablo." Nell kissed his cold temple. When she drew back, his eyes were like black glass, as if staring at his own spirit wavering above them.

Nell rocked back and forth, alternately wiping Pablo's gray face and then squeezing it to her bosom.

***

LUPE FOLLOWED THE hearse wagon to a rise of land straight out from her front door. "There we can keep watch over each other," she told Thomas when he came to help Skin and Tinker dig the grave.

She wore a black shawl drawn tight around her head. Juan moved along at her side with a wad of her skirt hem clutched in his fist. Skin, carrying Mary, followed Lupe and behind him a tight group of mourners trudged, heads bowed, under gray, solemn skies.

The crunch of hearse wheels on prairie grass gone to seed, the jingle of trace chains, and the thud of tramping feet sounded out a rhythmic dirge. Pablo's song, Nell thought. Grief was a terrible thing when it slammed into the lives of so many, leaving no one with strength enough to be leaned on.

Except Lupe.

As Tinker and Thomas lowered the coffin into the dark hole, Lupe tugged at Skin's sleeve. She reminded Nell of an iron fence post, small, black, and durable. Skin bent down to listen to what the tiny widow of iron had to say. He swallowed hard, tightened Mary's blanket against the cold, and nodded.

The priest prayed in Spanish with his arms held heavenward as if beseeching God to give back whole what they were discarding broken and too soon. Softly, Skin began to hum a tune. He sang the second verse barely above a whisper, his velvety voice vibrating with heavy sorrow. Nell couldn't bear to watch the big tears spill from his eyes as he sang the third verse. His singing carried out over the pastures, mournfully sad, the sound of it so pure, so clean that surely, Nell thought, even God knew what a hurtful thing it was to have Pablo gone from their lives.

Later Louise, the new-bride flush still on her face, helped Ernestine Wilkes and Sissy Spencer set up long tables of food for the mourners. Nell asked them to pass the word that the ranch house as well as the foreman's house was open to anyone who wished to stay the night. Some of Pablo's family had traveled more than a hundred miles for the funeral. But in the end, there was little lingering. The day was too cold for it, made more so by the godforsaken emptiness Pablo had left behind.

When the last of the mourners drifted off down the road, Nell and Lupe locked arms and walked back to the rise where fresh-turned earth blanketed Pablo's grave.

"Do you know what you would like to do?" Nell asked.

Lupe answered without hesitation. "I will continue as before."

Nell gazed back at the house, Pablo's new house, his own home place. He'd been so proud.

"And so should you," Lupe added. "It is what he would wish."

"I won't leave you alone."

"I have my children. Skin says he will help. And Billy needs a home as bad as my children need a grandfather. You know, everyone thought you were loco hiring Skin, but just look how fortunate we are to have him with us."

Nell watched Skin carry a table back into the house. His big lumpy body scrubbed, his hair tied with a strip of leather. He had not gone unclean for a moment after the day Lupe chased him with her broom and boiled his filthy clothes. His skin remained hopelessly opaque, even after a long summer of ranch work. Ugly as sin with the heart of a lamb, Nell thought for the hundredth time. "Do you know why I hired him?"

Lupe shook her head.

"Because of his singing. It's his heart that sings. I judged him by that."

Lupe knelt and pressed her hand to the cold damp earth as if checking to see if she could feel Pablo's warmth through it. When she began to weep, Nell knelt with her and held her tight so she could keen into the hollow of her shoulder.

***

WHEN NELL AND Lupe returned to the house, Tinker and Billy were trying to decide the best way to finish Lupe's porch, a chore Pablo had saved for winter months.

"Do not worry yourselves so." Lupe shifted Mary to her hip.

"You'll be needing a dry place to hang wash this winter," Billy said. "Skin don't have the know how yet, and I can't climb a ladder like I used to."

"And the men folks'll need a place to gather without getting in your hair," Skin added.

"That settles it then," Tinker announced. "Lupe, if it's all right with you, we'll spread our bedrolls here and get started first thing in the morning. I figure we can have the overhang finished and the porch floor framed in a day."

"Yeah, and me and Skin can handle the rest of the floor after that," Billy said.

"In that case," Nell said, "I think I'll go on home." She sent a questioning look in Lupe's direction.

"I will be fine," Lupe said.

Tinker walked Nell to her buggy. "Take Jack with you." He motioned to the dog who jumped into the buggy. He gave Nell a hand up but didn't let go after she settled in the seat.

"This kind of grief is new to us," she said. "When my father and Pablo's father died, it was natural in a way. Our fathers are supposed to die before us and we grieved. But Pablo?"

"How do we know how it's supposed to be, Nell?" He touched her cheek then released the buggy brake and stepped back.

Riding home, Nell thought of Tinker's wife, his little boy, how long he'd lived with the pain of losing them.

As for herself? She had no idea what to do, where to go.

She climbed the stairs in the damp, empty house wanting to scream at the sound of her lone footsteps. How did she end up the only one left behind to watch it all fade away one cow, one acre, one soul at a time?

In her bedroom, she unlaced her shoes. Pablo was dead. She looked out the window. Pablo? Dead?

How could she do anything ordinary when Pablo was dead?

She pulled a quilt from the bed and headed back downstairs to the sofa in the parlor. There she tumbled into a fitful, troubled sleep, dreaming for the second time of Pablo racing along with her on the beach at Tres Palacios Bay. And again, when she turned, only his horse followed her.

***

MORNING DAWNED BLINDING bright, an early winter day, when the air is crisp and cold against sun-warmed skin.

Skin rode into the barn at the ranch house looking for a particular level Tinker needed. When he saw the house was quiet, no smoke in the chimney, he knocked on the kitchen door. There was no answer so he went inside, calling out as he went. Nell was nowhere in sight. Back at Lupe's house he told the others he was worried.

"It is her way, to be alone to think her troubles through," Lupe said.

"Did you see Jack?" Tinker asked.

Skin shook his head no.

"As long as he is with her, she should be all right. But I'll check on her on my way to camp this evening."

"Will ya came back, like you said, for the mustangs in the spring?" Skin asked Tinker. "There ain't – I mean, isn't. There isn't no reason not to. Lupe here will still need the money and Thomas said he'd show me how to break horses. 'Spect even Goose'll be back."

Tinker tapped a board into place, dug a nail out of his pouch. "That depends."

"On what?"

"Gall dern," Billy snapped at Skin. "We've had enough of your questions."

"Easy, Billy," Tinker said. "On lots of things, Skin. But I'll do my best to see it works out so I can come back."

Lupe had been listening with a furrowed brow. "I think we should talk with Mr. Monroe. Carrageen's new owner will need to hire a foreman now that..."

"I took the liberty of doing that already," Tinker interrupted. "He said you're not to worry about anything. Get through the winter. Come spring, everyone can sit down and discuss the future. The new owner, says he would be much obliged if you all look in on the big house every now and then."

When work on the porch was finished, Lupe served the three men a hot dinner and poured a round of coffee. "Now I am worried also. Nell should have come here by now."

"I have a hunch I know where she's off to," Tinker said. "If I don't come back, you'll know I found her and she's all right." He pulled on his coat, positioned his hat. "I suppose this is good-bye then. Like I said, I'll do my best to come back in the spring."

"I reckon this bunch has had enough good-byes for a while." Billy shook Tinker's hand. "You just find that girlie and tell her a thing or two, if you catch my drift."

Tinker shook Skin's hand and kissed Lupe's cheek.

He rode up to the ranch house somehow knowing he, like Skin, wouldn't find Nell there. He broke into a full gallop, traveling northeast past his wagon camp. At Weaver's Draw, he slowed, noticing day-old horse tracks and dog prints on the muddy banks.

He spurred his mount up out of the draw. He had no idea what he was going to do or say to Nell. He just wanted to find her, be with her.

He continued northeast picking up more tracks between clumps of winter grass. He'd been right. She had headed straight for the windmill.

When he galloped up onto the tank dam, Jack whined pitifully and made a feeble attempt to turn one of his silly little circles. He looked like he hadn't eaten for days. The poor dog had suffered along with everyone else.

Something, a quilt or blanket, on the windmill platform flopped in a whispery breeze. If she was still up there, she would have seen him coming.

He climbed up and found her lying on the platform, half propped against a cross brace, white-faced, hair matted and tangled. She covered her face with her hands. He scooped her into his arms. She was deathly cold so he pulled the quilt over her shoulders.

"I've been watching the cloud shadows," she said after a time. Her voice was hoarse and raspy. He could feel her moist breath on his throat, hear the wind hum through the wheel above them.

"And for some reason," she continued, "they keep reminding me of what that Mayan prophet wrote. Do you remember? Did I tell you?"

" 'All moons, all years...' " That was all he could remember.

"...'all days, all winds, take their course and are gone.' " Nell finished for him.

Tinker drew her close. "We couldn't hold on to Pablo any more than we can hold on to those shadows." They wrapped their arms around each other and watched the day's light fade.

When the night wind whoosed down out of the north, Tinker nudged Nell and told her it was time to go home.

Back at the house, he built a fire in the kitchen stove while Nell peeled potatoes. She made boiled-water cornbread and fried the potatoes with slices of bacon. Tinker sat at the table watching her move around the warm kitchen. She handed him a plate of food then gave Jack a slice of bacon and chunk of cornbread.

"I've thought about your offer to leave Jack," she said. "Since I'll be moving to the Sunday House tomorrow maybe you should take him with you. He'll be happier following you."

"Come with me tomorrow, Nell."

She looked confused.

"I'll show you my homestead and cattle. The cotton fields."

"Tinker, I can't."

"Why not? It's not as if you have plans."

"I can't leave Lupe."

"But you say you have to leave the ranch." He hadn't intended to push or sound desperate.

"I've had recent experience in making impulsive decisions, remember?"

"I'm not asking you to do anything impulsive." He reached for her hand. "When I thought you had died at sea it crippled me. I was like a lame dog, Nell. That's when I knew how much was missing from my life, how much I loved you. Love you still." He pulled her to her feet and kissed her. Nell's deep-running current tugged at him, and more than anything in the world he wanted to flow with it.

But he drew back and tried to get a hold of himself. He had a pretty good idea of what happened between Nell and Henry in that jungle, could even understand it. But that was no reason to complicate this situation. He knew Nell's mind and it would bother her if he let things get carried away at this point.

"Marry me, Nell."

She touched his face.

"I don't promise an easy time of it or wealth or anything I don't have control over. But Nell, darling, I promise sure as night comes, I'll love you and give you comfort."

She pulled away.

"We can make Fredericksburg before dark tomorrow, find a preacher there. Before you answer I want you to know I did a real hasty thing." He stopped himself, couldn't finish what he needed to say. So instead he said, "I've loved you since that first day on your windmill. This isn't the time I would've picked, so soon after Pablo died. So take the night to think about it. I'll pass by here in the morning. If you're not waiting on the porch, I'll be on my way and not worry you anymore."

***

OF COURSE SHE wouldn't go away with him. Marry him? Her father had always said there was no shame in making a mistake once but he'd hear no excuses a second time. Besides, what had Tinker meant about doing something hasty?

Still Tinker told her he loved her. That was more than Henry could do.

She tossed all night remembering what Tinker had said about cloud shadows. Pablo loved Tinker. Each time she closed her eyes, she saw them leaning against the bunkhouse teasing with Thomas and Goose.

When the sun came up she wasn't sure she'd slept at all.

She pulled on her divided skirt but her fingers trembled too much to deal with the buttons on her blouse. She opened the window for fresh air to clear her head.

Had he left? It didn't matter. She couldn't let herself think about it. Tinker was a fine man, good man, but she had to start packing for the move to the Sunday House.

She pulled the steamer trunk from the hall and filled it with clothes from the wardrobe. When the trunk was full she searched for her mother's old carpetbag. She moved around absent-mindedly. She stopped once, realized she'd packed one glove and had no idea what happened to the mate. She looked at what was packed and couldn't remember having packed it.

Through the open window she heard the jingle of trace chains. She wouldn't look out. That would make it harder.

But then she heard Jack's sharp relentless barking and rushed to the window in spite of herself. From her high vantage, she watched Tinker's freight wagon creep up from the bluff, the sun gleaming bright in the crystal air around him. She pressed her hands to her mouth when he stopped in front of the house. Jack was standing on the seat next to Tinker watching the front door with his tail wagging expectantly. She took a step back into the shadows so they couldn't see her.

Tinker stood, studied the porch, looked across the way toward the barn. She turned away from the window and waited until the rumble of wagon wheels faded, then flopped face down onto her bed.

***

DOWNSTAIRS IN THE kitchen she started a fire in the stove and picked up Jack's dish. The muteness of the house yawled at her like the day of Pablo's funeral.

She poured coffee, sat at the table, stared at the chair where Tinker sat the night before.

She had no idea how long she'd been sitting there when she heard someone coming. She lunged for the door. But it was Skin riding up with Lupe and Billy in a cart.

"We's worried about you," Billy said. "Tinker said he'd come tell us if he couldn't find you, but we thought we'd come check anyway."

Nell waved her hand indicating they should come into the kitchen. "I've started packing for the Sunday House. I suppose I'll have to make several trips before I have everything I need."

"And Tinker, where is he?" Lupe asked.

"Gone. About an hour ago."

Lupe sighed, shifting Mary to her left arm. "I am surprised. He did not really want to leave I think."

Billy slapped his leg. "Women! Of course he didn't want to leave."

"What are you talking about, Billy?"

"Why, I thought maybe he'd have a talk with you. Ask you to go with him." Billy studied her with one eye squinted as if he were sighting down a gun barrel. "He did, didn't he?"

Nell poured coffee.

"Damn it, girlie! Tinker just as well been talking Chinese to a pack mule."

"I am not a girl." Nell banged the pot down on the stove. Mary began to cry.

"Tell you what," Billy said, "sit down here and let's calm ourselves. I've known you since you's in diapers like little Mary there. You'll always be a girl to me. And, I'm going to tell you straight out 'cause I'm an old man and earned the right to speak my mind."

Nell sat down.

"It's your own strength that'll be your undoing, Nell. Let go that iron grip you have. Don't be so afraid of a little chance."

"Billy is right," Lupe said. "It is good to be strong, but to be wise is better. How do you feel about Tinker?"

"Now he's gone, awful, just awful. But I didn't know until I heard his wagon pass through the gate this morning."

"Did not know what?"

"That I love him."

Lupe handed Mary to Billy. "Skin, saddle Jingles." She grabbed Nell's arm and pulled her upstairs.

"It's too late," Nell argued when they reached her bedroom.

"You are still breathing. Is this not so?"

"Lupe?"

Lupe stopped rearranging the clothes in the carpetbag.

"What will I say to him?"

"You will know when the time comes."

Skin had Jingles saddled and waiting when Nell and Lupe rushed downstairs, struggling with the carpetbag between them.

Billy met them at the front door holding little Mary like a veteran nanny. "Women! You ain't goin' to need all that much."

Nell kissed his cheek. "Do you think I can catch up with him?"

"Take the river road to Silbido Springs and cut through the Brady place. You may even beat him to the cut north."

She kissed him again. "Thanks, Billy."

She hugged Juan and brushed at the plume on the crown of his head. For one glorious moment, Pablo seemed near at hand. Not a vision exactly, but if she'd been able to see what she felt, Pablo would have been grinning big enough to show the gap in his teeth. When Nell turned to Lupe words calcified in her throat.

The little iron widow smiled. *"Vay con Dios, hermana.* Until spring."

Skin tied the carpetbag behind the cantle. "You be careful, Miss Nell. We'll all get along just fine so don't you worry."

Jingles pranced sideways then danced in a circle anxious to tear out into the cool prairie air. Nell took one last look her Carrageen outfit. Billy, Skin, Lupe, Juan, and Mary, and with a wave, dug her heels into Jingles' flanks.

***

"HUSH YOURSELF DOG." Jack had been whining and fidgeting for the last mile or so. He climbed up onto the bedrolls stacked in the wagon box, barked a couple of times.

Jack swished his tail across the back of Tinker's head. When he yanked his hat off and turned to swat Jack, he saw a rider coming hell-bent up the road behind him. He grabbed for his rifle and waited.

By god, it was Nell. The hair on his arms stood up like cactus spines. What could have happened now? How much more could the folks at Carrageen take and how much more could he endure, loving her the way he did?

Nell pulled Jingles to a halt beside the wagon, swung out of the saddle and nearly stumbled to the ground.

"What's wrong, Nell?"

She braced herself on the wagon wheel. He couldn't figure the look on her face.

"I-I. Tinker, I—"

Tinker jumped down from the wagon, grabbed her shoulders. She stopped huffing and drew a few slow, deep breaths. "I want to be your wife."

"But this morning?"

"I was afraid. Love is so powerful, Tinker. I tried to fight it."

He tied Jingles to a bucket hook and stood with his weight over one hip, staring at the ground.

"Tinker, I didn't know until you were gone how much I want to be with you, love you."

He grabbed her arm, motioned to the back of the wagon where he fetched a leather envelope from a wood box. He handed it to her. "Do you remember when I said I'd done something hasty, without thinking?"

"Yes, and I wondered—"

"Open it."

Nell untied the thick waxed string and withdrew papers folded inside a heavy blue cover. She glanced at Tinker then read.

"I don't understand. This is a deed? To Carrageen?"

"I deeded it back to you."

"You did what?"

"Months ago I had my lawyer contact Grady thinking you'd stay if you didn't have to worry about your debts."

"Then it was you all along?" She reeled and took a step backward.

"I hoped you'd change your mind about selling out when you came home. Then when Grady told us you were lost, I figured I would go ahead and buy it anyway, let Pablo and the others stay on. When you came back with the professor... God, Nell, I just wanted to make things easier for you, that's all. But I didn't want you to know it was me and feel trapped or obligated. After you said you and Henry planned to marry, I didn't know what to do."

She took another look at the deed. Flipped through the pages with her eyes darting back and forth. After a while she tossed the stack of papers up into the air. When they hit the ground she squared herself in front of him.

"Let me be sure I understand. If we marry, you'll be marrying the money you paid for the ranch. Is that it? Is that what you're trying to do? You want the money and the ranch?"

"No. That's why I'm telling you now and why I deeded it back to you, to prove my intentions. Remember the day you ran Henry off? I tried to get you to go back and have Grady tear up the papers. I knew then you'd always wonder what my motives were, that you'd have trouble trusting me if you found out."

Nell leaned against the wagon and pressed her temples. Tinker walked off a few paces, squatted on his heels and plucked a blade of grass. "I was trying to tell Pablo and the others the day the bandits came back. Before that, several times, I started to tell you but so much was happening." He stood, pulled his hat off. "Nell, I'm a wealthy man in terms of worldly things. Sarah and I set up a trust for our boy when she inherited her father's estate. On William's eighteenth birthday, it all fell into my accounts. That, along with insurance, Galveston real estate, my ranch..." He leveled his gaze on her. "It isn't for your ranch or money that I've stayed around."

She looked dumbstruck. "I don't know whether to laugh or cry. When you came to Carrageen, I was so busy looking back, holding on to the past, I didn't see what was right under my nose."

"And I was wearing my misery like a shield so nothing could touch me again."

"What now?"

"Nothing's changed the way I feel." He leaned against the wagon next to her.

Nell shrugged. "Then I have one only more question."

"Let's hear it."

"What's your real name? The name on the deed said Mr. C. Webb. What's the C for?"

Tinker shot her a pained look and looped his big thick arm around her shoulders.

***

JACK TRIED TO squeeze between Tinker and Nell on the wagon seat. Tinker swatted at him. "Get." Jack gave up after a while and crawled back onto the bedrolls.

At a clear water pool on the south bank of the Pedernales River, Tinker washed and changed into a clean city shirt while Nell picked wild buckwheat and broomweed for her wedding flowers. In Fredericksburg, they located the courthouse and applied for a marriage certificate, then had to wait an uncomfortable length of time while a clerk summoned the justice of the peace. Tinker squirmed on the hard bench with his hat in his lap. Nell sat next to him and tried to keep her wildflower bouquet from quaking in her perspiring hands.

A door at the end of the hall opened and a little man with a backbone shaped like a shepherd's hook appeared. "Let me see here now, you folks want to marry, is that it?"

"That's right." Tinker adjusted his string tie.

"What? You better speak up. I'm very nearly deaf, you see."

"Yes sir," Tinker shouted. "We want to marry."

"Well, I reckon I can take care of that."

Nell and Tinker exchanged glances while following the justice to his chambers. There the crooked little man unceremoniously read from a worn black book and when he got to the part asking Nell if she took Tinker for her husband, she answered, "I do."

"What was that?"

"I said, I do." She yelled the words.

"What have you to say to that, son? Though I suppose you look a trifle old to be called son, let alone marrying, if you ask me."

Tinker yelled, "I do."

"Fine then, you're hitched. Kiss your bride and gimme two dollars. The wife's waiting supper."

Tinker handed him the two dollars. "Where can we find a hotel?"

"Tinker, no." Nell interrupted. "I-I think we should camp at that little pool by the river."

The Justice squinted at her. "What's that? You say you got a bad liver?"

Tinker grabbed Nell's elbow and scrambled for the door.

They were still laughing when they rolled up to the spot where Nell had picked her flowers. Tinker went to fetch water while Nell unpacked her hairbrush and the mirror Sister Tia Marie had given her. She hung her dressing robe on a wagon hook, then smiled when she saw her grandmother's diary in the bottom of the carpetbag. She set it on a barrel chair.

Across the meadow Tinker stood stone still while gazing across the river. The grassy bank opposite him shimmered bronze in the setting sunlight and there a flicker of movement caught Nell's eye. It was a doe. The animal observed Tinker with an indignant air as if he'd intruded. Tinker eased his free arm up slowly and tipped his hat at the beautiful animal. The doe blinked at him a few times then pranced regally into a thicket of willows.

As the doe disappeared from sight, a gust of wind swooped down, ruffling the pages of the diary on the chair behind Nell.

She moved to put it away but the upturned page snagged her attention.

March 11, 1868

My sons think I'm an old fool sitting next to their father's gravestone all afternoon. They are young yet and unknowing.

The sky looks like buttermilk. Winter's drab brown still covers Carrageen's hills. I'm reminded of a Psalm: 'As for man, his days are as the grass; as a flower of the field, so he flourisheth. For the wind passeth over it, and it is gone; and its place thereof shall know it no more.'

" 'For the wind passeth over it'," Nell repeated out loud. It was the entry she'd read in the grape arbor at the hotel before running to catch up with Maudeen and Ruby. Those were the words that came to her when she clung to the deck of the schooner.

"You look like you've seen a ghost." Tinker put the water bucket down.

She sat on the barrel chair shaking her head. A soft darkness had fallen around them.

"A Psalm in my grandmother's diary is incredibly like the Mayan passage I told you about. It's unnerving."

Nell thought about the time she left her hand prints on the high rocks at Carrageen, but said nothing to Tinker. She guessed it wouldn't matter to anyone in her lifetime. Still, she couldn't help but wonder what some drifting soul might think upon discovering the hand prints decades into the future...maybe that whoever had made them didn't want to be forgotten?

Tinker knelt on one knee and began to unlace her shoes. "Not surprising, when you stop to think that those old boys, the Psalmist and the Mayan, spent a lot of time studying the same stars. It makes sense that they'd come to the same understanding."

He set her shoes aside, let his gaze arch across the night sky. "The same stars," he said, unbuttoning her blouse. He kissed her throat and traced the line of her collarbones with his thumbs. She kissed his fingers then turned his hands over and kissed his palms.

He gathered her into his arms and carried her to the wagon sheet where he loomed over her in the dark like a wide watery mirage. She lost herself in the feel of him and let the power of his tenderness engulf her.

He kissed her soft skin, breathing deep until she filled his emptiness. He no longer felt lame nor she flawed. They touched and loved and laughed, moved across the night like spirits. He watched stars reflect in her shadowy eyes. She listened to the pulsing murmur of his fine heart. Then they loved again.

Like a vapor, their soft talk and laughter filled the river valley while the night sky sighed its windy breath over them.

ACKNOWLEDGMENTS

I am deeply grateful to Sally Jo Baker, Nancy Bell, Susan Luton and Linda Clayton for holding me together through the bad years and for encouraging me to persevere. Extra special thanks to Susan Luton for her unwavering patience with my endless midnight emails seeking advice about grammar, English-Spanish translations, story line and character development. A note of gratitude also goes out to the members of Women Writing the West for sharing all they know about writing nuts-to-bolts. Thank you, Heidi Thomas, for your expertise. Thank you, Alice Trego for excellent feedback and Susan Balmos Trial, my spirit sister, for naming Nell's town "Wishing."

I am indebted to my sister Renee Casey Rabke for offering to be a final reader, and to Cathy and George Berger, sister and brother-in-law, for allowing me to seek writing refuge at their beautiful Berger Ranch near Weimar Texas. **The Dividing Season** cover photo was taken from their front porch ... nothing short of paradise for a writer.

Texas native, Karen Casey Fitzjerrell has written features, personal narratives, and travel articles for several top Texas newspapers and magazines. She lives in San Antonio, Texas but calls the entire state "home."

Watch for her next novel, **Forgiving Effie Beck**, scheduled to be published summer 2012. The story deals with small town complacency, abuse and infidelity and what happens when all the "good people" look the other way.

Karen invites readers to contact her at:
kcfitzjerrell@gmail.com

Or, visit her website:
www.karencaseyfitzjerrell.com